To my precious and sweet wife, your encouragement + helpful critism is much appreciated

ZETEL,
Biography of a Soul

SAM GOLDENBERG

 FriesenPress

Suite 300 - 990 Fort St
Victoria, BC, V8V 3K2
Canada

www.friesenpress.com

Copyright © 2017 by Sam Goldenberg
First Edition — 2017

All rights reserved.

No part of this publication may be reproduced in any form, or by any means, electronic or mechanical, including photocopying, recording, or any information browsing, storage, or retrieval system, without permission in writing from FriesenPress.

ISBN
978-1-5255-1172-1 (Hardcover)
978-1-5255-1173-8 (Paperback)
978-1-5255-1174-5 (eBook)

1. FICTION, HUMOROUS

Distributed to the trade by The Ingram Book Company

Dedicated to the extended Goldenberg family
whose members appear, in one form or another, in this book

Table of Contents

Part One — Early Years	**7**
CHAPTER 1 — Zetel and the Arc of Souls	9
CHAPTER 2 — Zetel is born	20
CHAPTER 3 — Zetel's first day	27
CHAPTER 4 — Zetel arrives in Canada	34
CHAPTER 5 — Zetel in Montreal	45
CHAPTER 6 — Zetel is circumcised	56
CHAPTER 7 — Zetel at the doctor	66
CHAPTER 8 — Zetel and the Oedipus complex	76
CHAPTER 9 — Zetel and the god of war	83
CHAPTER 10 — Zetel has a close call	90
CHAPTER 11 — Zetel in school	102
CHAPTER 12 — Zetel and the boarder	116
CHAPTER 13 — Zetel wins a friend	129
CHAPTER 14 — Zetel, the Bar Mitzvah boy	141
Part Two — Middle Years	**149**
CHAPTER 1 — Zetel has a near disaster	151
CHAPTER 2 — Zetel meets his bride	168
CHAPTER 3 — Zetel and Sarah are engaged	182
CHAPTER 4 — Unto Zetel a wedding and a child	196
CHAPTER 5 — Zetel in Toronto	215
CHAPTER 6 — Zetel at 50	231
CHAPTER 7 — Zetel meets an old friend	248
CHAPTER 8 — Zetel and a death in the family	267

Part Three — Later Years	**273**
CHAPTER 1 — Zetel faces more challenges	275
CHAPTER 2 — Zetel in transition	296
CHAPTER 3 — Zetel on vacation	308
CHAPTER 4 — Zetel at the Millennium	327
CHAPTER 5 — Zetel faces another plot	337
CHAPTER 6 — Zetel and the Divine Conclave	352
CHAPTER 7 — Zetel on Trial	367
CHAPTER 8 — The judgement of Zetel	389
Acknowledgements	**393**

PART ONE
EARLY YEARS

CHAPTER 1 —
Zetel and the Arc of Souls

Several million years after the world was created, the Earth was encompassed by an enormous Arc of tiny fluffy white clouds. Each cloud was no more than a yard long, a half-yard wide and two inches thick. They lay in a broad swath around the Earth in a single layer, high enough in the sky to avoid the volcanic upheavals and boiling frenzy of the lands and oceans beneath them. Had there been observers on the early Earth, the clouds would not have been visible to them nor did they block the strengthening beams of the young sun.

For the gods and goddesses of that time, the clouds were simple stepping stones and formed convenient pathways around the new world. They flitted and danced across the Arc, leapt high in the thin air, somersaulted, bounced up and down, and often grasped each other and rolled over and over on the soft blanket of clouds in lust filled ecstasy.

For millions more years, the gods and goddesses continued their blissful ways, often punctuating their carefree existence with forays into amorous adventures which led to jealous clashes among them as well as many children.

One day, a Roman god, Mercury the Messenger, asked irritably, "Why are the clouds here?"

With his winged sandals and helmet, Mercury didn't need the clouds and, in fact, they got in his way. To deliver his messages, he had to follow the curve of the Arc rather than cut right through.

He addressed his question first to Jupiter, chief of the Roman gods, next to Zeus, head of the Greeks, then to Wotan, the top Teutonic, to Indra who led the Vedics, and to all the other celestials that lived on the Arc. No one knew. There were lots of theories.

"They are meant to keep us from falling onto the Earth until it cools," was a common notion.

Ra, the sun god of what would later become Egypt, disclaimed the importance of the clouds: "They do not interfere with the passage of my vital rays and therefore they are irrelevant."

Finally, a strongly held view was loudly proclaimed: "Whoever put the clouds here should answer the question."

"I put the clouds here," said a stern, male voice that emanated from a massive cumulus cloud of vertical development. "I created the world. I alone. I am The-One-True-God."

This caused an angry protest from all the godheads. Since the Creation, they had become aware that this particular god was trying to manifest his dominance and would like nothing better than to push them aside.

Hera, enamoured of Zeus, eager to protect his status but not taking any chances, called out sweetly, "If, indeed, you are The-One-True-God, then you must be able to answer the question. Why are the clouds here?"

"The clouds are the souls that will inhabit the bodies of the mortals yet to come," answered the Voice.

This statement surprised everyone. What was a mortal and was there to be more creation? Since it did not make sense, the gods and goddesses shrugged their shoulders, laughed uproariously and continued to skip happily over the clouds. Even Mercury forgot about the clouds as an impediment to his messenger function and revelled in his ability to fly well above the others and to mount high enough in the heavens to circle the moon.

Each cloud in the Arc was linked closely one to the other and waited patiently for its Orders. One cloud appeared restless. Waves undulated along its short body. It widened its width, shortened its length, and bulked up its thickness in a vain attempt to dislodge itself. This woke up its neighbours all around whose complaints reached The-One-True-God.

"Why do you squirm?" He asked.

"Great One, how much longer must I lie here?" said Zetel (that is, the soul who would someday be Zetel). "I am action oriented and find this inaction totally boring."

"Nevertheless, you will await My call. It will not be long — perhaps a few hours."

Zetel groaned in dismay. A few hours of celestial time could mean billions of Earth years.

"Great One, instead of just lying here, may I travel the universe you have so beautifully created? I would love to explore its many stars and planets, comets and meteors. Of course, I would return quickly when You call?" Zetel asked respectfully.

In reply, the huge cloud occupied by The-One-True-God grew even larger as its cloudy mass bubbled and bulged higher into the heavens and blocked out the sun. It blackened, roared its thunderous disapproval, belched forth myriads of lightning bolts that lit up the dark sky and caused all the gods and goddesses to cower in dread and fear. Slowly the thunder cloud moved on, its blackness fading to a gray and then white, but still growling and sputtering out the occasional bolt.

"You may take it," said Zeus contemptuously, standing over Zetel, "that the answer is 'no.'"

"Be kind to the little cloud, Zeus my love," Hera said and put an arm around him, affectionately pulling him close. "The poor cloud must lie in tedious immobility waiting for some event in an unknowable time. Time is endless for us too but we can gambol freely around the heavens and indulge in other pastimes." The last was said suggestively.

The touch of Hera's body had an immediate effect on Zeus.

"I would possess you," he said, his voice thick with desire. He threw off his cloak, undid the gold circlet around Hera's waist and cast her garment aside.

Zetel, his curiosity piqued, watched them intently. Both Zeus and Hera were tall, their features and bodies felicitously proportioned. They embraced tightly, ran their hands over each other, and fell on Zetel. Astonished, he saw the member between Zeus' legs slowly extend and become large and saw him plunge it into the body of Hera.

"Did you see that?" Zetel exclaimed and nudged his neighbours but they ignored him and continued in their catatonic state.

A soul with no connection to a physical body, Zetel could feel none of the lust and passion that the two lovers experienced. But he decided that their actions could be important at some later time and recorded in memory their sighs and groans and frantic convulsive embraces and kisses. The two lay a long while seemingly spent, then Zeus mounted Hera again and repeated the actions that so captured Zetel's attention. Once more, the two lovers lay quiescently in each other's arms, slept, and then dressed and walked away slowly, arm-in-arm.

"When I have a mortal body, I will try that," Zetel said.

"But you cannot foretell whether the body you inhabit will be capable," a young woman objected.

The woman was slim with a narrow waist and small hips. Her face, like Hera's, was beautifully proportioned, with dark brown eyes, a thin aquiline nose, a high forehead and blond hair tied in a golden clasp at the nape of her neck. She wore a short tunic and blouse, held a bow and had a quiver of arrows hanging by a leather thong on her back.

"Who are you?" demanded Zetel.

"I am Diana the Huntress," she said proudly, lifting her head. "I am the virgin goddess of the hunt."

"Well, goddess Diana," Zetel said, somewhat smugly, "surely The-One-True-God who allows what seems like pleasure to gods and goddesses would allow such pleasures to mortals. Have you not experienced what Hera has?"

"I am a virgin. I have sworn never to lie with a man. There are others like me who have committed themselves to celibacy."

This caused Zetel a moment of profound reflection. The joining together of Zeus and Hera was not universal among the gods and goddesses. Were the relationships of mortal men and women to be equally complex? Nevertheless, what Zetel had witnessed was compelling and he would attempt a union the moment he had a chance.

"You will not be a virgin for long," a hoarse rasping voice called out.

Towering over Diana was a giant figure, rippling with thick muscle barely concealed by his body armour and heavy mail boots. A helmet with nose piece revealed only a black bearded round face. He carried a massive shield in his left hand and a double edged iron sword in his right.

Diana shrieked and quickly loosed an arrow that was blocked by the shield.

"Shoot all your arrows, Diana, you cannot win against Mars, god of war. Come, my lovely one, let my one arrow vanquish you."

Mars advanced on her, stepping on Zetel who forced the middle of his cloud body to dip, momentarily causing Mars to lose his balance which allowed Diana to flee.

"Ha," laughed Zetel, "some god of war you are. You can't even capture a goddess."

"Laugh at me, do you," raged Mars, his face flushed with anger. "The god of war brooks no interference."

He clashed his sword against his shield, emitting a clang that swept around the entire Arc of Souls and caused all the gods and goddesses to pause and look fearfully about. Only The-One-True-God, immersed in His cloud and contemplating the creation of the First Man, paid no attention.

"There will be one soul less," Mars shouted and brought his sword down lengthwise on Zetel.

Exerting all his willpower, Zetel pushed himself to one side. Mars fell through the gap, vainly tried to grab hold of a cloud, and plunged to the earth below. Zetel watched him land on a mountain they were passing over.

Thus did Zetel, owing to the Law of Unintended Consequences, unwittingly bring war to the world.

Assured her oppressor was gone, Diana returned to Zetel to thank him for saving her.

"Not all threats to my vow of virginity are eliminated," she explained, "but Mars was the most aggressive. As for the others, my hunting dogs warn me in time."

Diana came often to visit him and they passed many an eon in pleasant conversation. He admired the clean cut of her profile as though her features had been chiselled out of marble: the alabaster cheek, the high ridged nose, the thin lips. At his insistence, she removed the clasp that held her hair and allowed the golden ringlets to cascade over her shoulders. At the sight, Zetel felt a glow pervade his cloud body, a sense of well being and a regret that he could not touch her. She leaned forward and allowed her hair to fall on him. He reached out with tendrils of cloud wraiths to fondle her tresses and curls.

Diana sighed. "It is fortunate you are but a cloud soul. Were you a god, I fear I might compromise my vow."

"Will it be different when I occupy a mortal body?" he asked. "Will we no longer meet and talk as we do now?"

She shook her head. "No, my dear friend, I too will descend to the Earth and eventually become a mortal as will all the others. This has been foretold to me by Gabriel, an angel of The-One-True-God."

This was new to Zetel. "What is an angel?"

"An angel is a celestial being like gods and goddesses but serves only The-One-True-God. Gabriel is part of the huge army of angels that is being marshalled to drive out all other celestial beings so that The-One-True-God can establish His hegemony over the heavens and the universe. If He succeeds, it will mean the twilight of the gods."

Zetel was disturbed. Apart from Mars who was gone, all the others, especially Diana, seemed like good spirits, interesting to watch and to talk with. Without them, he would have nothing to spark his interest but the constantly burgeoning cloud inhabited by The-One-True-God.

"I must ask the angel why this is happening and whether you can be spared," he said.

At her next visit, Diana brought with her a being dressed all in black. Black trousers and boots peeped out from a long black coat. His face was clothed in a coal black beard and a black hat crowned his head, its brim sloping low over his dark eyes.

"Gabriel declined to join us," explained Diana. "He has just been promoted to Archangel and must attend to his many new responsibilities. However, the angel with me agreed to come. He is part of the army that is being assembled but is not happy with his role. He is prepared to defy The-One-True-God."

"Why are you dressed in this manner?" asked Zetel. "No one else is."

"I do not want to look like anyone else," said the angel.

"What is your name?" Zetel asked.

"Lucifer," replied the angel. "The-One-True-God is a jealous god and seeks sole power. He demands complete loyalty from his angels. Not only must we follow His Orders with total obedience but we must also report back to him and keep him updated on what is happening. He will soon introduce mortals into the world below and will not tolerate these mortals worshipping any god but Him. We, the angels, must oversee these mortals and ensure their obedience and loyalty to Him. If not, we must find ways to encourage penitence or arrange for their death."

"But how can mortals die?" Zetel asked. "We don't die"

"Unlike us, mortals will not live forever," Lucifer replied. "After a certain period of time which will vary with each mortal, they will cease to live."

"If they are going to die anyway, why should they be loyal?" Zetel said.

"Because the threat of punishment or an early death will bring most into line."

"How will you kill the disloyal ones, the ones who truly refuse to repent?"

"We do not have the power to kill directly," Lucifer acknowledged. "We must arrange things in such a way that death occurs."

"It seems you have an important role," Zetel said. "Why do you wish to defy The-One-True-God."

"I do not agree with His thirst for supremacy. I cannot tolerate His intent to totally control me, to turn me into a slave. I would not banish the gods and goddesses nor would I create mortals. I will not serve Him and there are many like-minded angels who follow me."

"But if no mortals are created, I will lie here forever," Zetel protested.

"I will make you into a god," Lucifer said soothingly. "Just promise me your support."

Their conversation was interrupted by cacophonous rolls of thunder that reverberated throughout the heavens. Too late, they realized the massive cumulus cloud of vertical development was almost upon them. Diana sprang away precipitously and tripped over her hunting dogs. Lucifer, at first transfixed, tried to follow her. The lightning bolt and shock wave that followed blew him through Zetel and into the void. Zetel's cloud restored itself but bits of Lucifer's clothing mingled within it and turned its formerly pristine white into patches of smudgy gray.

The-One-True-God moved on but continued in anger, His thunder increasing. Soon Zetel saw scores of other angels spewed into the void, dispatched with Lucifer deep into the world. After millennia, when things had quieted down, Diana returned.

"Oh, my dear friend," she said sympathetically, "I did not expect to find you. You have indeed suffered. Parts of you have turned gray."

Zetel looked at her. "You, too, have suffered, goddess. Your hair is singed, some of your golden curls gone."

"My tresses will grow back," Diana assured him. "But Lucifer and his followers are not as fortunate. Archangel Gabriel tells me they are banished below the world to a dreadful place called Hell and will be joined in the future by all those who defy The-One-True-God. Archangel Gabriel describes Hell as eternal suffering and punishment."

Shortly afterwards, no more than a jubilee of millennia, Zetel noticed first one cloud and then another fall out of the Arc of Souls and descend rapidly towards the land below.

"What is happening?" he called out. "Where are those clouds going?"

"Do you still not sleep? You are indeed irksome," said the stern Voice of The-One-True-God. His cloud rumbled with thunder as it moved closer to Zetel.

He braced himself for a bolt of lightning, wondering whether he would be sent to Hell like Lucifer. Instead the Voice softened, became almost rhapsodic: "I have launched the creation of mortals. The First Man and the First Woman, infused with the souls you saw descending, now walk the Earth in the Garden of Paradise.

Soon there will be many more and they will beget others. You will see an avalanche of souls fall to the Earth."

As time went on, the prediction of The-One-True-God was confirmed. Zetel watched as more clouds left the Arc and sped toward the land. The clouds on either side of him departed. After a brief interval, one ascended and took its place beside Zetel.

"Why are you back?" Zetel demanded for he had relished the space left by the departing soul.

"My body ceased to exist," said the returned soul. "I must wait for another."

This was an exciting revelation to Zetel. Unlike the celestial beings, mortals did not live forever. When their bodies no longer functioned, their souls returned to the Arc for reassignment. A plethora of existences awaited him, an endless variety of lives to offset the monotony of the Arc.

Ages passed. He watched large numbers of clouds depart and then return to the tight grid of the Arc. He waited his turn with growing impatience.

Diana was a constant visitor. Her hair had grown again. She would dutifully allow the curls to fall on Zetel whose wraithlike tendrils would flow around them and reach up and surround her face in a misty haze.

"This is my last visit," she said to him mournfully one day. "Very shortly, we must depart for the world below. Only The-One-True-God and His angels will inhabit the sphere of the heavens. We gods and goddesses will be worshipped for a time and when that ceases, we will become mortals. Farewell my dearest friend."

"Wait," said Zetel. "Do not go. Take me with you."

"It is impossible. How can I?"

"Your hunting knife," Zetel whispered desperately. "Cut me loose."

"I dare not," she pleaded but still drew the hunting knife from its sheath.

"Try," he begged. She looked around. The massive cumulus cloud of vertical development was far off and no angels in sight. She slashed between Zetel and the adjoining clouds and seemed to succeed for Zetel felt himself coming loose.

"Again," he said. "I will soon be free."

"What do you there?" shouted an angry Voice still far away. "Begone goddess."

A blast of wind blew Diana away but ripped open the last links holding Zetel to the Arc and flung him towards the Earth.

"That soul is escaping. It is yet too rebellious to be allowed free. I want it back," ordered The-One-True-God.

"Do not fear, Most Holy," said Archangel Gabriel. "I have assigned it to a mortal unlikely to live long. It will return soon."

Thus did Zetel leave the Arc of Souls.

CHAPTER 2 —
Zetel is born

"Vai, Yoisef, I'm really not feeling well," Ettie moaned and grasped her bloated belly, her face contorted with pain. "I think it's coming out."

Joseph looked at her in dismay. "But, Ettie, you still have two months to go. In a day, we'll be in Canada. They must have hospitals and doctors. Shloima says there are good doctors."

Ettie covered her face with her hands, fell back on the narrow bed, and shrieked, "I'm telling you, it's coming. I told you we should stay put until afterwards."

Her obvious pain and discomfort aroused feelings of guilt in Joseph. They had discussed at great length whether they should wait until after the birth. But Joseph persuaded her that the situation in their little town of Zetel was becoming tense.

"You've listened to him on the radio, Ettie," he insisted. "The man is a stark raving maniac but the Germans think he's their saviour. He blames us for everything. For generations we've lived here in peace and quiet. Now even our oldest, friendliest neighbours treat us like we have leprosy. I've been told by some to get out — it's going to get worse for the Jews. People no longer come to the store. In the last week in the shop, I sold one scarf and one blouse. I have a chance to sell the store to one of our suppliers at a decent price. Let's do it, Ettie. I already have the passports and the other papers. Let's not wait."

"So what if we wait another two months," Ettie objected.

"Who knows what will be in two months? Who knows whether we'll be able to sell the store in two months? The burgomeister of Zetel, who likes us, told me Berlin is coming out soon with terrible laws for Jews. Faigel wants to come with us and she also has all her papers. She can be helpful to you on the journey. Let's go while we can."

Faigel, a close friend, lived a few blocks away. Plump, with a ready smile on her engaging face, she was an accomplished seamstress who assisted Joseph in running his dress shop.

In the end, Ettie agreed. They sold or gave away everything, packed two suitcases, and left. Even with Faigel's help, it was an arduous journey for Ettie. A still friendly neighbour brought them by horse and buggy to the port of Wilhelmshaven 12 miles away. They boarded a small freighter that housed Joseph and Ettie in the medical aid cabin and Faigel in a bunk in an auxiliary cabin for the journey to Southampton. There they had to wait a week, staying in a small, grubby but inexpensive inn, until they could finally board a passenger ship bound for Canada. Along with hundreds of other immigrants, many of them Jews, they were crowded below decks into tiny cabins or packed dormitories. Joseph and Ettie were lucky. They managed to get a private cabin but Faigel had to share with two other women.

Ettie's screams penetrated the thin walls of the small cabin. There was a banging at the door and Faigel's anxious voice called out: "Ettie, Yoisef, are you alright?"

Now panicking, Joseph opened the door and grabbed Faigel by the shoulders. "Faigel, something's wrong. She thinks the baby's coming."

Shaking, her body contorted in pain, Ettie cried: "For God's sake, do something. My water just broke. It's coming."

Faigel struggled free of Joseph. "There must be a doctor on board. I'll get him." She walked rapidly down the corridor, swaying from side to side, partly because of her weight, partly because of the slight rolling of the ship as it steamed through the North Atlantic.

The surgery was located forward on the upper deck, close to the First Class section. The doctor frowned. A young man, handsome in his dark blue uniform, white starched shirt and collar, black tie and epaulettes on his shoulders, he did not relish a visit to the steerage passengers' crowded cabins below the water line. The smell of unwashed bodies, remnants of food, vomit and fouled toilets was not to his liking.

He turned to the medical intern. "Mr. Jackson, see what the problem is and whether I am needed. Take Nurse Murphy with you. She's also a mid-wife."

The cabin was too small and Joseph was ushered outside while the intern and the mid-wife examined the patient.

"We'll have to get her up to the surgery," Mr. Jackson said.

"It's too late," said the mid-wife. "She's giving birth. Get me lots of towels and at least one bowl of hot water.

Mr. Jackson grabbed Joseph by an arm. "Come on, we need your help."

Zetel was free and falling fast. He whirled several times around the globe, marvelling at how large it was and how much land and water covered its surface. He exulted in his freedom and his escape from the confines of the Arc. His only regret was he did not know what had happened to Diana and whether they would ever meet again. He pushed this concern aside as he watched, with growing alarm, an ocean rising rapidly towards him. An angel had explained that the waters of Earth teemed with fish which served as food for mortals. He did not want to be the soul of a fish.

Abruptly, his headlong flight flattened out. He flew a few yards above the water, occasionally feeling the ocean's cold breath when taller waves splashed over him. Then, coming towards him, he saw a massive structure moving through the water, cleaving the waves. He swung in a wide curve and flashed through the side of the structure into a maze of walls and spaces and people.

His flight came to a sudden stop. He found himself in an airless, dark, watery enclosure, confined on all sides by a warm pulsating slimy container. He was forced into a tiny being in a crouching position, its knees close to its chin, its arms wrapped around its legs. The stench, the heat, the tightness of the space was not what he had expected or would tolerate. He wanted out.

He wriggled his body and thrashed about with his arms and legs, trying to tear open the sack that imprisoned him. He detected a stretchiness below him and pushed hard with his feet. He felt the sack rip and the water around him trickle away. He turned his body over and pushed towards the tear. A narrow tunnel greeted his head. Great tremors convulsed the tunnel and propelled him forward. He heard screams and a calm but authoritative female voice calling out: "Push now, push hard, hard, hard. It's coming. Its head is appearing, one more push, one more, one good push, give it everything you have — it's out!"

He emerged in a slush of blood and mucous into the hands of a woman. He was rubbed all over with a cloth and towelled. He felt a sharp pain and a voice announced, "The umbilical cord is cut."

The mid-wife held the baby up and said to Ettie, "It's a boy, madam."

Outside the cabin, passengers gathered in the corridor slapped Joseph on the back, shouting "Mazeltov (*congratulations*)." But Joseph was worried. The ordeal was over for Ettie but the boy was two months premature. Would it survive?

His fears were confirmed a moment later when he heard the mid-wife exclaim: "He's not breathing. The umbilical cord was wrapped around his neck. He's turning blue."

She held the baby upside down by his feet and slapped him sharply across the buttocks.

"He's still not breathing," she reported. "He did not respond at all. I'm afraid he's gone."

Where have I gone, thought Zetel. I'm still here. Then he felt a tug and realized he was edging out of the body. In sheer terror, he screamed, "I'm returning to the Arc."

His scream awakened the hopes of the mid-wife. She gently massaged his chest. "I'm trying to get his lungs working."

Zetel fought the force pulling him from the body. He pleaded for the lungs to work. Air began to filter into his body.

"His lungs are inflating," the mid-wife said.

The intern pressed his stethoscope to the baby's chest. "The heartbeat is intermittent at best. Dammit, we'll lose him yet."

The pull on Zetel was becoming irresistible. With one last effort, he shouted, "Dammit!" repeating the intern but not at all certain what the word meant. "Dammit heart, beat, beat, beat. Don't send me back to the Arc."

"His heartbeat is getting stronger," said the intern. "He just might make it after all."

The minutes ticked by. Ettie, totally exhausted, was crying softly. Joseph, out in the corridor, was praying. The crowd of well wishers was silent.

Finally the intern announced that the boy's heart was beating well and he was breathing normally. The group in the corridor applauded noisily and several men held onto a nearly fainting Joseph.

"Is the father here?" the intern asked, stepping out into the corridor. Someone pushed Joseph forward. "We must bring mother and son up to the surgery," said the intern to Joseph. "I understand this is a premature birth and the child may require further care."

At this moment, the doctor arrived wearing a procedure mask. "I was told the baby is dead," he said.

"He was, sir," said the mid-wife proudly, "but he has miraculously returned to life."

"Doctor, Nurse Murphy should be mentioned in your report for her skill in birthing a premature baby and returning him to life," the intern said.

The doctor nodded. With his stethoscope he listened intently to the baby's heartbeat. He examined his body carefully, peered into his nose, ears and throat, and took his temperature with an anal thermometer.

"This child cannot be premature," the doctor said after noting all the vital statistics. "He is healthy and complete in every respect. His heart is strong, his lungs are working normally, his skin is clear, and all bodily apertures are unobstructed. His parents must have miscalculated the date of conception. I have great experience with premature babies and this one is not premature."

The doctor turned on his heel and left the cabin.

Mr. Jackson smiled at Nurse Murphy and shrugged his shoulders, "Well, let's secure the afterbirth, get the bedding changed, and the mother comfortable. We'll check every now and then just to be sure and we'll do a thorough examination before disembarkation tomorrow."

They allowed a happily tearful Joseph into the cabin. He kissed Ettie, looked at the baby, hugged the intern and kissed Nurse Murphy's hand.

"Danke, danke, danke," he said in German, then remembering the little English he had, repeated, "T'ank you, t'ank you, t'ank you." And for good measure, added in Yiddish, "A laib oif dein kop." (*A blessing on your head.*)

They shooed him out of the cabin, and made motions to go for a walk.

"You know, Mr. Jackson," the mid-wife said, "I don't believe I saved the baby. I think the little one decided to live."

Back on the Arc, Archangel Gabriel concluded that the runaway soul had somehow survived and would not return soon. He looked around guiltily but noted with relief the cloud housing The-One-True-God was nowhere in sight. Perhaps He will forget about it for a time, thought Archangel Gabriel.

Thus did Zetel find and keep his mortal body.

CHAPTER 3 —
Zetel's first day

Zetel was annoyed. He had escaped one prison for another. He was now swathed in a towel and couldn't move. A mortal was poking him all over. The body he inhabited was grumpy and mewling and quite small. Even his cloud body had been larger.

A woman held him and showed him to another woman who was lying on a raised platform who smiled at him and touched his face. He noticed tears streaming down her face and the woman holding him was tearful too. A man came in, looked at him, touched him. He, too, had tears in his eyes. The only other time Zetel had seen tears was when Diana said farewell to him. Was his arrival on earth as a mortal a sad event? He should be the one crying. Here he was, sequestered in this tiny body. Why was a large body like these other mortals denied him? Was he punished by The-One-True-God for escaping from the Arc?

"Fool!" growled a voice. "All mortals start life as small babies. In time you will grow like me."

"Who are you?" Zetel asked. The voice seemed to come from the woman holding him.

"I am the soul of the nurse who delivered you. She and I do great things — birthing babies, treating the sick and hurt. It is often unpleasant work but very rewarding."

"Oh dear," said the nurse. "My stomach is making noises. It's way past my lunch break."

"We must be quiet now," whispered the nurse's soul. "You will be alright. Just do what your mother and father tell you. They look like nice people."

There was much activity in the small cabin. Zetel was laid carefully on a small table out of the way. With the help of a female steward, Nurse Murphy ensured the soiled linen on the bed was removed and replaced with clean sheets and blanket. Ettie was sponge washed and when dry was put back in the bed and Zetel placed in her arms. By this time, Zetel's body was complaining loudly.

Ettie kissed and stroked the boys cheeks, presented a breast to him and gently pushed the nipple into his mouth. Pressed against the breast, Zetel remembered the pleasure Zeus had expressed as he kissed and fondled Hera's breasts. As he sucked on the breast, Zetel suddenly understood what had so attracted Zeus. A warm sweet liquid squirted into his mouth and descended down his throat. Within seconds, a calm contentment spread over him and quickly swept away the disappointment and annoyance of his new existence. He sucked away, his eyelids fluttered, the view of the breast arching above him and the serene, smiling face of the woman above it slowly faded and he fell into peaceful slumbering oblivion.

Frequently during the rest of the day and through the night, he awoke and applied himself to the breast. Each time he congratulated himself that he, unlike the other souls around him, had watched carefully the actions of Zeus and Hera. Without that knowledge, he would have missed the pleasure of the breast and its secret well of a wondrous elixir.

During the day, Nurse Murphy and Mr. Jackson returned to examine the mother and newborn. Another man in the cabin also held him from time to time, kissed him, and smiled tearfully at him. Zetel was annoyed that the man's cheeks grew less smooth as the day wore on but the patch of hair under his nose tickled him. Zetel opened his mouth wide and gurgled.

"Ettie, he's smiling at me. My boy is smiling at me," Joseph said.

"Our boy, Yoisef," Ettie reminded him firmly. "Isn't he beautiful?" — and added hurriedly — "Kin ain ahora." (*without any hex*) "We must thank the Almighty for giving us such a boy and two months early at that."

"You are so right, Ettie," Joseph agreed, nodding his head vehemently. "The Almighty has favoured us. There is no other way to describe it. Despite our leaving home so quickly and quietly, He found us on this ship in the middle of the ocean, although — don't take this as any criticism — better He should have found us when we got to Montreal."

"Oi, Yoisef," Ettie said, rolling her eyes, "here we are blest and you're complaining again. When I took my time getting pregnant, you blamed Satan. The Evil Eye, you said, is getting even because you married such a good looking woman. When I got pregnant, you complained to the Almighty that it was not the right moment for us to have a baby in Germany. So here we are, far from Germany, a miracle that God even found us and you're still complaining."

Joseph looked affectionately at his wife, leaned over and kissed her. "Everything is planned by God, my sweet Ettie, even my complaining and you putting up with me," he said laughing. "God never makes mistakes. Everything is planned, especially our baby boy."

"Are you so certain?" Zetel asked. "I'm here because I was accidentally blown from the Arc of Souls."

"Did you hear that, Ettie?" Joseph exclaimed. "Have you ever heard such a belch?"

Neither Joseph nor Ettie slept very well that night. The baby demanded feeding every two hours.

"He must have come with a clock," Joseph mumbled.

In the morning, Nurse Murphy arrived with an armful of diapers donated by the ship. She and Ettie washed and changed the baby and wrapped him in clean towels. She motioned to them to dress and pack and stepped out into the corridor.

"So what's happening?" asked Faigel.

"Both the mother and the baby are doing very well. I'm taking them to the Surgery for final examinations. Also, the doctor must issue a birth certificate."

"Maybe I go with you," Faigel said. "They speak English only a little. I can help."

In the Surgery, the doctor gave Ettie and the boy a thorough examination and pronounced them fit for disembarkation.

"Amazing," said the doctor to the intern and the nurse, "She's still a bit weak but otherwise fully recovered. I challenge any doctor to tell me the baby isn't full term yet the husband showed me a paper he received from their general physician which indicates the boy is premature. Maybe these Germans are supermen like their Fuhrer insists."

The intern laughed. "Doctor, these are Jews. I don't think the Fuhrer includes them in the superman category."

"They're not poor people," Nurse Murphy added. "I wonder why they travelled third class. The lady is well dressed. Those buttons on her indigo striped blouse are silver and the blouse is silk. The skirt she's wearing is in the latest mode. And the husband, too, is well dressed in his tailored worsted suit. He's skinny yet it fits him snugly. I like his thin face and that he's clean-shaven except for the moustache. A very good looking man."

"His wife is also very pretty," the intern said. "Those dark eyes, black hair, pale round face and red lips — for her, I might even change religions."

"Mr. Jackson, Nurse Murphy, may I remind you this is a professional medical Surgery and we do not engage in the personal attributes of our patients," the doctor expostulated indignantly. "Each patient will be treated equitably based on need and not preference. I will now meet with the parents to draw up the birth certificate."

Mr. Jackson and Nurse Murphy made appropriate noises of apology but surreptitiously looked at each other and smiled. They both knew the doctor was giving undue attention to a wealthy, young, attractive woman who seemed to be suffering nothing worse than a little seasickness.

The doctor returned to his desk in his small inner office and spread the blank birth certificate out. Nurse Murphy seated Joseph and Ettie and the sleeping baby and ushered in Faigel.

"Doctor, this lady is a friend of the parents who speak little English. She has offered to translate."

The doctor gave a curt nod to Faigel.

"Family name?" the doctor asked.

"Shuster," Faigel said.

The doctor consulted a voluminous hinged file. "Are you sure? According to the passenger list, Shuster is a single woman travelling alone."

"That is correct, Herr Doctor."

"You mean, that man travelling with the mother is not her husband?

"Oh, he is her husband, Herr Doctor," Faigel said. "I was at their wedding five years ago."

"Then why is Shuster listed as a single woman travelling alone?"

"That's what I am, Herr Doctor," Faigel said sadly. "I am not lucky enough yet to find a good man." She gave what she thought was a suggestive look by slightly pursing her lips and inclining her head.

The doctor stared at her incredulously. "Miss Shuster," he said speaking calmly and firmly, "We seem to have a misunderstanding. I do not want your name, I want the family name of the parents. Do not worry about the spelling. I will consult the passenger list. What is their family name?"

The doctor could barely control his annoyance. He heard his seasick patient ask for him at the reception counter. He thought

Mr. Jackson's reply that the doctor was engaged at the moment and that he would be happy to assist her came too quickly.

"Ländau," said Faigel.

"Is that 'Lendau' or 'Landau?' Is it an 'a' or an 'e?'"

"It is an 'a,' Herr Doctor, but the 'a' has two little dots over it and is pronounced 'e'," explained Faigel.

The doctor shook his head, somewhat bewildered. "I will spell it as it is in the passenger list. 'Joseph Leonard Landau and Esther Ida Landau.' (pronounced Landaw) The date of birth is September 16, 1935. Now, the boy's name, please."

Faigel turned to Joseph and Ettie. "What are you calling your beautiful boy?" she asked in German.

Joseph and Ettie looked at each other in consternation.

"Yoisef," Ettie said, "in all the excitement, we never thought of a name."

"A name?" Joseph repeated, staring helplessly at the ceiling. "Who can we name him after? My parents are still alive, thank God, and so are yours. I have only one brother, Shloima, and he's waiting for us in Montreal, and your brothers and sisters are all alive. Even our grandparents still live. What about cousins?"

The doctor heard his seasick patient talking vivaciously with Mr. Jackson and the latter's gushing replies. He had to complete the birth certificate quickly.

"His name. His name," he barked.

"Herr Doctor, they are trying to decide on a name," Faigel said, trying to soothe the doctor's obvious impatience.

"Are you telling me that they've had the baby for 24 hours and haven't decided on a name," the doctor exploded. "I need a name now."

He walked around his desk and stood over Joseph and Ettie.

"Just give him a name," Faigel pleaded.

"Ettie, what shall we call him?" Joseph said.

"The doctor is getting angry. Give him any name," Faigel urged.

"Vai, Yoisef, I knew we should have stayed in Zetel until he was born," Ettie moaned.

"That's it," Joseph exclaimed. "That's his name. Zetel."

"Zetel?" asked Ettie.

"Zetel?" asked Faigel.

"Zetel?" asked Zetel.

"Zetel," said Joseph.

"Zetel," said the doctor and inscribed the name on the certificate.

"Yoisef," Ettie said, "Zetel is where we lived. Our tradition is to name our boy after a beloved relative who has passed on. It is not our tradition to name a child after a town."

"We were very happy in Zetel. The town is now dead to us," Joseph said defensively. "Besides we can name him properly at the bris *(ceremony of circumcision)*. Right now, he's Zetel Ländau."

The doctor signed the Birth Certificate, folded it and gave it to Joseph who slipped it into his coat inner pocket. The doctor left his office and went quickly to regain his seasick patient from the clutches of Mr. Jackson.

CHAPTER 4 —
Zetel arrives in Canada

Jammed with hundreds of other passengers along the upper deck, Joseph and Ettie watched the approaching shore of Nova Scotia and the city of Halifax. Bright clouds competed with blue patches of sky. The sun was still warm despite the autumnal September afternoon.

"Look, Zetel, that's our new country," Ettie said excitedly and held the boy up.

Zetel was apprehensive. They were too near the railing and he could hear the splash of water.

"Step back," he ordered but all that came out was an incoherent gurgle.

"He likes our new home, " laughed Joseph.

The ship made its way slowly past McNabs Island and the Pt. Pleasant light and entered the harbour. Its engines slowed, the ship crept toward Georges Island and then stopped altogether. Tugs came out, grappled the ships lines, and slowly pulled it towards its berth at Pier 21.

They now had a good view of Halifax. A patchwork of green parks and low buildings swept along the shore and up a long incline, punctuated by church steeples and protected by a walled citadel that rose high up in the centre. A single gun from the citadel boomed out a greeting to the arriving vessel. Further into the harbour, Joseph could make out several naval ships and a military base. Smaller boats of all descriptions plied the waters and gave way to a ferry heading to the shore opposite the city. There was a bustle to the city as people, horses and buggies, and the occasional car and truck moved along its many streets.

The doctor insisted that a steward push Ettie in a wheelchair into the pier warehouse.

"Tell your friends," he said to Faigel, "the mother is still weak and the Line does not want any accidents disembarking."

Zetel sat on Ettie's lap and looked curiously at all the people shuffling along, struggling with their belongings and herding their children. He was enthralled. Here he was riding in a wheeled conveyance while everyone else was walking. Surely, this was a sign of distinction favouring his mortal body. He snickered — if only The-One-True-God could see him now.

But The-One-True-God peering down from his massive cumulus cloud of vertical development was startled and not amused.

"Gabriel," He shouted and growled thunder. The hapless Archangel came running. He knew from the sound of the Voice he was in trouble.

"You told Me the escaped soul would soon return," the cold, steely Voice said. "Yet he inhabits the new mortal Zetel Ländau.."

Gabriel prostrated himself and held his hands over his head. "He was too strong, Most Holy, too insistent on living. I beg your forgiveness," pleaded Gabriel and braced himself.

The bolt of lightning flung Gabriel head over heels around the Arc but did not annihilate him.

"I am just and merciful," said The-One-True-God. "Nevertheless, I demand transparency and accountability."

Joseph and Faigel, carrying and dragging their suitcases and bags, followed the steward who pushed Ettie and the baby across the gangway from the ship to the pier building, along a lengthy gallery and down a ramp into the cavernous Customs and Immigration Inspection shed. They joined long lines of passengers jostling into the dozen queues set up to handle the crowd. When they reached the head of their line and were called forward, the steward gently assisted Ettie from the wheelchair, wished them all well and returned to the ship.

Joseph and Ettie, accompanied by Faigel, warily approached the Immigration Officer. The latter was an intimidating figure. He was well over six feet tall. His uniform buttons barely contained a huge paunch. A handlebar moustache stood out prominently from his florid face, overtopped by a bulbous nose and suspicious eyes. He did not smile nor did he look welcoming.

Joseph knew that Canada did not welcome Jews and they could be easily rejected admission to the country. Trying to lighten the moment and perhaps curry favour with the Officer, Joseph mustered a few words from his meagre English vocabulary: "Hallo, we happy Canada come."

"Passports, Visas, papers," was the Immigration Officer's reply to Joseph's friendly overture.

Joseph, completely cowed, handed him a large manila envelope.

"Am I to mail this, sir, or is there something inside that you wish me to see?"

"Yoisef," Faigel said quietly, "Give him what's inside the envelope." At the same time she handed her own papers to the Officer.

Joseph, his hands shaking, removed the contents of the envelope and gave them to the Officer.

The Officer's suspicious eyes narrowed even further. "You seem very nervous, sir. I hope your papers are in order."

"They are, sir," Faigel assured him. "These are honest people."

The Officer glared at Faigel. "I will be the one to determine that, madam. And who are you? Are you all together? Your name is different from theirs."

"I am a friend of the family. I help translate for them."

"Madam," said the Officer imperiously, "if translation is required, the Canadian Immigration and Customs Service will provide a translator. Please return to the queue."

Haltingly, worriedly, Faigel retreated.

"Are you rejected?" Joseph asked.

"No, he won't see us together. Just calm down, Yoisef. You'll be fine."

The Officer studied the documents carefully. "Everything seems in order. Your passports are from your country of origin, your entry visa is from the Canadian consular service in Berlin, your ticket is prepaid, you have the required $250.00, you are a significant family member of a landed immigrant, and you have a letter of employment in Montreal. You must be an important person or a rich one, because you also have the Special Permit from Ottawa. There is only one problem, Mr. Landau."

"Ländau, Mein Herr," Joseph said, trying to be helpful.

"Don't 'mein herr' me," barked the Officer. "It says here Landau and that's what it is. But there is a major problem. You are three and the documents say two."

Joseph looked puzzled. The Officer pointed to the papers and held up two fingers. He pointed to Joseph, Ettie and the baby and held up three fingers.

Faigel shouted from the queue: "The baby was born yesterday."

"Madam," the Officer said grandly, lifting his head, "I was not born yesterday. This baby is more than one day old. Kindly refrain from interrupting."

"You are Jews," the Officer said. "Let us see if this baby is Jewish." He motioned to Ettie to undress Zetel.

Quickly glancing at the naked baby, he observed, "Just as I thought. The baby is not circumcised and therefore it is not Jewish and not yours. Are you trying to smuggle in a child that is not yours? What is the provenance of this baby?"

"Sir," cried Faigel, "Jewish boys are not circumcised until eight days after birth."

Those in the queue who understood English voiced agreement.

Zetel felt refreshed naked, free of the imprisoning towels and diapers. But he was annoyed. Who was this man to impede his progress and cause the nice woman with the tasty breasts to break out into sobs? He sought a weapon and found one. The cold of the Inspection shed permeated Zetel's body and tripped a threshold nerve in his bladder. The stream of urine arched into the air and dribbled down the buttoned jacket of the Officer.

Even desperate refugees, waiting patiently in long lines, about to face obdurate immigration officials wielding implacable bureaucratic rules, eager for acceptance and dreading rejection, knowing they must show signs of submission and respect, cannot always control their reaction to a risible situation. Shrieks of laughter erupted on all sides. The Officer shrank back. Joseph grabbed a towel and dabbed at the Officer's uniform while Ettie quickly wrapped up Zetel.

Between gasps of laughter, Faigel shouted: "Yoisef, the paper the doctor gave you. Show it to him."

The Officer's florid face, flushed with anger, had become a deep purple. He snatched up the REJECT stamp, mashed it into the ink pad and raised it to imprint the Admittance Form. He paused and read the birth certificate which Joseph had retrieved from his coat pocket. While the birth certificate explained the discrepancy, as an Immigration Officer, he had sole discretion to reject this family anyway and, given the humiliation he had suffered at their hands, he was tempted to do so. He looked down at the baby.

Zetel was still laughing at the Officer's discomfiture but all he emitted was a gurgle and a smile. The sight awakened a happy memory, a nostalgia on the part of the Officer. He thought of his own five children in their infancy and the joy they had brought him. He put away the REJECT stamp.

"If you had shown me the birth certificate right away, we would not have had this unwelcome circumstance," the Officer said.

A bewildered Joseph looked at him uncomprehendingly. The Officer shrugged, stamped The Admittance Form ACCEPT and waved them on.

"What am I letting into this country?" was his parting shot.

He dealt quickly with Faigel as though to avoid any further embarrassment. He stamped her Admittance Form ACCEPT without further questions, and said to her, "You better stay close to them. They need you."

At the Customs Inspection Counter, a bored official yawned in their faces. The Officer, his uniform too large for his short stocky frame, his cap not quite straight on his dishevelled hair, motioned for the suitcases to be placed on the counter and opened before him. He rifled quickly through the suitcases, barely examining the contents and was about to wave them on when he spotted a large felt portfolio decorated with strange writing in Joseph's suitcase.

"Open it," he ordered Joseph, pointing to the portfolio.

Joseph dutifully removed the object within the portfolio and held up a thickly folded length of cotton fabric. The Customs Officer unfolded the item and spread it over the suitcases. It was a large square of material, at least two yards by two yards, with black and white stripes and fringed at each corner.

"Whose flag is this?" demanded the Officer. "You Germans will not bring your flags into this country. My father was killed just before the end of the Great War. It's bad enough I have to let Germans in but I won't let your flags in."

He was about to throw it into a large waste bin beside him.

"Sir," Faigel said, "it is not a flag. It is for prayer."

"For what?"

"For prayer, sir. Mr. Ländau uses it on Saturday in the synagogue."

The Officer, skeptical, ordered, "Show me how he uses it."

"Yoisef, show the man how you use the tallis (*prayer shawl*)," Faigel said.

"Where? Here?" Joseph objected. "It's sacred."

"Yoisef," Ettie commanded, "put on the tallis or we'll all end up back in Zetel."

Hearing his name called, Zetel awoke and realized another man was blocking his progress.

"Woman," he said to Ettie, "make me naked again so I can water him." But all that came out was a noisy belch which caused the Officer to step back and nearly fall into the waste bin.

Joseph draped himself in the prayer shawl. He pulled part of it over his head and surplus folds over his shoulders so that his arms were free and allowed the rest to fall down his back to his ankles.

"That's how he wears it in the synagogue," Faigel said.

"I've seen a picture of a rabbi dressed like that. So that's how it's worn. Let me try it."

He took the shawl from a reluctant Joseph, wrapped himself in it, covered his cap with its ample folds, and walked to an adjoining counter.

"Look, fellows, I'm a rabbi," he called out to his colleagues.

There were some chuckles and cynical rejoinders. "Maybe you'll do a better job." "I hear it pays better." "Pity, you'll have to be circumcised and it's already too short."

The Custom's Officer threw the shawl back into the suitcase, stamped the Admittance Form CLEARED and sent them on.

They followed the line of immigrants and Canadian citizens returning from abroad to a door marked EXIT – TRAINS. Before they could leave the Inspection shed, an Officer ensured their papers were all properly stamped.

"You are allowed entry into Canada," the Officer announced. "Just remember, if you lose your job, get sick, can't pay your debts, or commit even a minor felony, you will be immediately deported to your country of origin. This is no idle warning. Every year we deport thousands."

Joseph, elated at having passed the two hurdles of immigration and customs and not understanding the import of the Officer's speech, shook the official's hand and said, "T'ank you, t'ank you, t'ank you. We happy Canada come."

"A wiseacre, eh?" said the Officer snatching away his hand. "You think I'm fooling? We can save a lot of time and fuss by putting you back on the ship."

"Sir," Faigel appealed to the Officer, "please forgive my friend. He speaks not English. I make sure he understands everything you say."

The Officer grunted and waved a dismissive hand in the direction of the exit.

Joseph realized he had done something wrong and turned to apologize but Faigel sternly pushed him from behind and Ettie, with a free hand, pulled him forward.

Outside the Inspection shed was the train yard. A train with a dozen passenger cars, a baggage car, headed by two steam engines snuffling quietly, awaited the connecting ocean travellers. The late afternoon sun, low on the horizon, was no match for the chilling breezy wind from the Atlantic.

"Oi, my poor boy," Ettie said, hugging Zetel close, "you will freeze."

"Don't worry, sweet woman," Zetel reassured her. "I lived for many years in cold conditions."

He pulled in a lungful of air, gasped, gurgled and felt his mouth twist into a smile.

"Yoisef," Ettie said, "nothing bothers our Zetel. He's such a happy baby."

Helped by a porter, they boarded the train and found their reserved seats, two wooden benches with padded fabric upholstery facing each other. Ettie, totally exhausted, collapsed onto a window seat, Joseph sat next to her, Faigel across from him and Zetel was placed carefully on the fourth seat.

The din in the coach was shattering. Passengers rapidly filled the space, clattered their bags onto the overhead racks, called out instructions and advice to family members, tried to calm crying, protesting children hauled onto seats and crowded together.

Despite the noise, Ettie fell asleep, Faigel held her hands to her head as though to ward off the chaos in the coach, and Joseph watched as the crowd slowly organized into relatively quiet blocks of orderly families and friends. He closed his eyes.

Zetel was not tired. He had rather enjoyed the adventure through the large building and revelled in the new sights of people, their actions, their voices, some whining and pleading, others calm and commanding, others speaking in hushed tones or loudly to those around them. However, there was a more demanding reason for his lack of fatigue. It was several hours since his last breast feeding and the inordinate pleasure it gave him.

"Sweet woman," he called out, "it is time again."

His plaintive screeching and blubbering caused Ettie to open one eye, blink, and close it again. The crying went on, growing ever louder. Joseph looked nervously about, worried about upsetting the other passengers. Faigel picked up the baby and rocked him gently in her arms. Zetel reached up and tried to grasp the bosom hanging above him. His pudgy hands stroked the underside of an ample breast.

"Nain, mein klaine Zeesuh," (*no, my sweet little one*) Faigel said, sighing regretfully. "Mine are dry. Soon your mother will wake up."

Zetel was not inclined to wait nor was his body. His screams penetrated the wall of unconsciousness surrounding Ettie and startled her awake. She snatched Zetel from Faigel and began to undo the buttons on her blouse.

Joseph was aware that the passengers on all sides were looking on with growing interest. A Trainman in his Canadian National Railways Passenger Service uniform walking through the coach stopped beside Joseph just as the unbuttoning blouse revealed the first fleshy outline of its hidden treasure.

"Madam," said the Trainman, "may I remind you this is a public place."

"Ettie, wait," Joseph said. "we need to cover you."

He jumped up to his suitcase on the rack, snapped open the spring locks, and pulled out the prayer shawl. He draped the shawl over Ettie and the baby just as the breast and its nipple came into view. The baby suckled away happily, offering the occasional contented coo.

Meanwhile, back at the Arc of Souls, Archangel Gabriel was in a quandary. The-One-True-God had made it clear: the soul of Zetel Ländau must be recalled quickly, but Gabriel had no idea how to accomplish such a feat. First, he consulted with Archangel Michael.

"As he who performs on behalf of the Almighty acts of power and justice, what would you recommend?"

Michael was tall with rippling muscles, curly blond hair surrounding a handsome clean-shaven face. He wore a mail cuirass over a short white skirt and carried a bronze sword.

"To my knowledge, Gabriel, the baby at this stage of infancy has committed no evil deeds, nor have the parents sinned in any meaningful way to be punished so gravely. Therefore, I can find no reason to take action at this time since my mandate is to carry out acts of justice."

Raphael also demurred from being involved. "I am the Almighty's healing force," he said to Gabriel. "Neither the parents, the child or the friend suffers from any physical or spiritual illness where the removal of the child would be of benefit. Therefore, I'm out."

Metatron laughed when he was asked for his advice. Well above normal height, wearing a voluminous black robe which contrasted with his silvery flowing hair and thin white bearded face, the angel carried a parchment scroll tucked under an arm, a clay inkpot in his left hand and a goose quill in his right. "Gabriel, I am a scrivener, a clerk. I record men's deeds and maintain the Books of Life and Death. I would not know how to recall souls. Besides, I do not see the boy's name in the Book of Death any time soon. Give up your quest."

In desperation, Gabriel called upon Samael. No one liked Samael. He was physically unattractive: thin to the point of emaciation, naked except for a loincloth, bald head, eyeless, perpetually slobbering at the mouth whence came a foul stench. In addition to his physical imperfection, his responsibility caused everyone to look away or to avoid him entirely.

"As the Angel of Death, Gabriel, I can arrange for the soul to return. However, you must understand that I do not carry out assassination but make arrangements for death to occur. For example, the target is on a train. I can arrange for a derailment, a head on crash with another train, a riot on the coach, etc., etc."

"But that would kill others besides the baby," objected Gabriel.

"There is often collateral damage in my work," observed Samael solemnly.

In the end, Gabriel took it upon himself to visit Zetel and try to persuade him. When he arrived at the coach, he found the baby wrapped in the prayer shawl, asleep on his mother's breast. An aura of sanctity suffused the shawl, the sleeping mother and baby. Gabriel backed away. You are saved for a little while longer, brave soul, thought Gabriel and returned to the Arc.

Thus did Zetel in his second day don the prayer shawl of his father and preserve his mortality.

CHAPTER 5 —
Zetel in Montreal

"Yoisef, I'm in seventh heaven," said Shloima, grasping his younger brother in his arms and lavishing his face with teary kisses.

Strange, thought Zetel, I don't remember more than one heaven, unless you count the space below the Arc of Souls, the Arc itself, and the space above the Arc. Even so, that makes only three. This man can't count.

Ten years older than Joseph, the same height but a little rounder, Shloima was clean shaven with a small clipped moustache. A black felt hat covered most of his greying hair. His black suit, grey vest, white shirt, starched collar, blue cravat and patent leather shoes completed the picture of a prosperous businessman. In these mid-depression years, the glances levelled at him by passersby were not always admiring.

Bessie, his wife, was as tall as her husband, slim, with a pinched pale face framed by silky brown hair. She wore a long blue dress with mauve stripes, a string of pearls around her neck, and high heeled shoes in the latest fashion. She carried a small black hand tooled leather purse.

They were easy to pick out on the railway platform. They stood like two crags in the tidal wave of passengers that erupted from the train as it came to a halt in Montreal's downtown station.

Bessie was equally effusive in her greeting of Joseph and Ettie. They embraced Faigel warmly whom they remembered from Joseph and Ettie's wedding.

"Thank God you got through," said Shloima. "We were so worried you would be rejected and sent back. This country does not like immigrants, especially Jews."

Shloima and Bessie were in raptures over the baby.

"We thought you had months to go," Bessie said. "What happened?"

"I needed a body," Zetel said.

"I think the baby said something," Bessie said.

"No, he just gurgles and smiles," Ettie laughed. "Look, he's happy to see you."

Bessie took Zetel from Ettie, cradled him and then pressed her cheek against his and pecked him on the cheek.

"What a wonderful smell," said Zetel. "I must get to know the fragrances of life." He continued confidentially to Bessie. "The only women I have smelled recently are the sweet woman and her friend. They smell like Diana after the hunt and Hera after her prolonged activity with Zeus. The sweet woman says she smells sweaty and stale. What do you think?"

"Ettie," exclaimed Bessie, "I think he's talking to me. He's saying something."

Shloima laughed. "Bessie, you put on too much perfume and the fumes have gone to your head. Come, let's go. My car is parked just outside the station. There's room for all of us and the trunk will take the suitcases."

Shloima eased his way through the mid-afternoon traffic of cars, trucks, streetcars, and the occasional horse drawn wagon, turned up St. Lawrence Boulevard and proceeded north away from the downtown.

"This is the factory I own and where you are employed — that is, if you can stand me as a boss," Shloima said and stopped in front of a three storey building. "I rent the top two floors. We're at the corner of Rachel and St. Lawrence — remember this corner. It's easy to get to. A streetcar goes all the way along St. Lawrence. I use it myself. I rarely take the car unless I have deliveries or meetings."

Joseph read the sign that stretched along the top of the building just under the roof — S. Landaw & Company Ltd.

"Shloima, why did you change our name?" he asked.

"I got tired of constantly correcting people and trying to explain what an 'umlaut' is and 'au' is pronounced 'ow.' So now the name is Landaw. Believe me, it's much easier to spell your name the way people see it. By the way, my first name is Sheldon at the factory and in business. The less Jewish you sound, the better. There's lots of anti-Semitism in Quebec. There's even a Nazi group here led by a mamzer (*bastard*) by the name of Arcand. The Church doesn't help either. So just watch out."

"So why did we come here?" Faigel demanded.

"Yes, Shloima, you painted such a great picture of Canada," Joseph added.

"Is that why we were so rudely treated by the immigration and customs?" Ettie said.

"It's a better place than Germany for us," Shloima insisted. "At least the laws here are not against us and most of the people leave us alone. Some are quite friendly. We also have three Jewish members of Parliament in Ottawa. How do you think you were able to get the Special Permit? Take it from me, you're better off here."

They continued up St. Lawrence Boulevard. At Fairmount Avenue, Shloima turned left and stopped at the first street. He pointed to a building across the street.

"We're at the corner of Fairmount and Clark. We own that building."

It was a two storey building in yellow brick that stretched from the corner to a laneway that cut the small block in half. A balcony jutted out of the second storey, overlooking the corner and partly shading the entrance to a small grocery store. An entrance door near the laneway gave access to the building.

"We live upstairs. Faigel, you can have the lower flat for the time being. It's small but comfortable. Yoisef and Ettie, I found you a place not far from here on Casgrain Street. It's the best I could do. There's a real shortage right now. Because of the depression, no one's building and even if you do, there's a question whether you'll get your rent money."

Shloima did a u-turn and parked near the entrance door. "We knew you would arrive without furniture or household things so we furnished both places. Bessie insisted she knows what you like so if you have complaints" — laughing, he pointed to Bessie — "there's where you go."

"The only things I didn't get were for the baby, thinking there was lots of time," Bessie said. "Ettie when you feel up to it, we'll go shopping."

"Thank you, both of you, for all you've done," said Ettie. "You're more than generous. But all I want now is a bath and bed."

The baby began to whimper. "And all Zetel wants is to drain my milk supply."

"Shloima, why don't you get Faigel settled and then take Yoisef and Ettie to their new home," Bessie directed. "Colette — she's our day maid — can help. In the meantime, I'll walk up to the school to get the children."

"The Fairmount School is only a few blocks from here," Shloima explained, as he helped Faigel out of the car and carried her suitcase. "Right opposite the school is the shul (*synagogue*) we go to, the Bnai Jacob, which everybody calls the Fairmount Shul."

Shloima had rented for Joseph and Ettie the bottom flat of a two storey building on Casgrain Street between Maguire and Fairmount. Two large double rooms plus a bathroom made up their residence. The two rooms at the back of the house were the kitchen and dining room; the two rooms at the front were their bedroom and living room. Joseph did a quick inspection. The flat needed a coat of paint but was otherwise clean and in good condition. The kitchen had a large sink, lots of cupboards, a gas stove and an icebox. There was a table with four chairs in the dining room, a double bed and dresser in the bedroom and a sofa and two easy chairs in the living room.

"I know it's not what you had in Germany," Shloima apologized, "but just accept it for now."

Joseph embraced his brother. "It is marvellous what you have done for us. It no longer matters what we had in Germany."

Ettie nursed Zetel and then climbed blissfully into the bath that Joseph had prepared for her. Joseph filled the kitchen sink with warm soapy water, bathed Zetel and replaced his soiled diaper with one of the few fresh ones left. He helped Ettie out of the bath.

"Are you hungry?" he asked her affectionately. "What would you like?"

"Bed," she replied. Normally, that was their signal for lovemaking, but she fell instantly asleep as soon as she lay down.

An hour later, Shloima and Bessie arrived with their two children, Chaim, an eight year old boy, short and stocky with a shock of brown hair and a pleasant round face, and a five year old girl, Rivka, thin like her mother with straight light hair and gleaming mischievous eyes. This was the first Joseph had ever seen his nephew and niece although his brother had sent pictures.

After hugs and kisses, he told them fondly, "We've brought you a cousin and I hope you will all get on well together."

He showed them the baby who was lying on the kitchen table, cooing and smiling.

"This is Zetel," Joseph said proudly. "He's only three days old."

Zetel reacted in disdain. "Three days? You mean three billion years old. Well, a long time, anyway."

"He says he's much older, Uncle Yoisef," Rivka said.

"Who says?" asked Bessie.

"Zetel says," Rivka replied.

"Zetel can't talk yet," Joseph said. "See, all he does is make funny noises."

"Uncle Yoisef is right, my little Rivka, the noises he makes sound like talking. Even I was fooled," Bessie said, patting Rivka's head.

"How's Ettie?" Shloima asked. "I'm amazed she was able to get around so soon after giving birth."

"She's completely done in and fast asleep," Joseph said. "Zetel was an exhausting experience. So unexpected."

"What do you mean she's exhausted?" cried Zetel. "Look at what I had to do to get here."

"You did nothing," Rivka said angrily. "All you did was come out of Auntie Ettie's stomach."

"Who are you talking to, Rivka?" Shloima asked, a frown creasing his forehead.

"To Zetel."

"That's enough, Rivka. Zetel doesn't speak yet and he can't understand you. No more play-acting. Rivka wants to be an actress," Bessie explained to Joseph.

"If you want to be an actress," Zetel said. "I may be able to help. During my time on the Arc of Souls, I met and often talked with the nine Muses representing all the Arts. As soon as I can locate them, I will introduce you. They are very nice women and will be eager to assist you."

Rivka was about to thank him but saw the look of annoyance on her mother's face and discreetly nodded and backed away.

Shloima shook his head. "Kids these days. They are walking imaginations. It must be the radio and all those soap operas. Bessie, we have to put some limits."

"Shloima, our children don't listen to soap operas. They're in school. Maybe it's all those bubbe meissehs (*fairy tales*) you tell them about the Golem."

"The Golem is not a bubbe meisseh," declared Chaim. "He actually existed."

"See what I mean, Yoisef," Bessie said, shrugging her shoulders. "Soon they won't be able to tell what's real."

"Bessie, Shloima and I were raised on these bubbe meissehs including the Golem," Joseph said. "Some of our most revered rabbis claim they witnessed him in action or saw his remains after he was closed down. Whether true or not, it was nice to have an artificially made figure fighting for us against anti-Semites and pogroms. It didn't change anything but at least made us feel better. Besides, who knows what special talents children have. Maybe Rivka does hear something from Zetel we can't hear. Zetel is a miracle baby — the nurse on the ship said so. Maybe God gave him special knowledge."

Shloima looked at his younger brother. "Yoisef, I think you need a good night's sleep too. We won't talk work until Monday. Tomorrow, shop for what you need. There's a kosher butcher shop called Stolberg Brothers on St. Viateur Street as well as a bakery and grocery stores. We'll keep checking in on you. In case you've forgotten, this weekend is Rosh Hashona (*Jewish New Year*). Come join us for dinner Friday night and then we'll all go to the Fairmount shul."

After the long morning prayers on Saturday and a quick lunch at Shloima and Bessie's, both families and Faigel walked up to Park Avenue for the traditional High Holiday annual promenade along the avenue. Zetel was in a baby carriage borrowed from a friend of Bessie's. He was dressed in a red long sleeved jersey, blue cotton pants, white stockings and a woolen bonnet for his head.

Shloima frequently met people whom he knew and introduced Joseph and Ettie and the baby. All admired and gushed over the baby and marvelled at the miracle of his birth. "Premature and just six days old? He looks at least three months," was the common expression. Zetel listened to the story with growing irritation but resolved not to react. If they wanted to give The-One-True-God all the credit, so be it.

Ettie became exhausted after an hour and held onto Bessie who pushed the carriage and brought them to Chez Emilie, a small cafe on the west side of the street. They sat at a table and sipped their coffee. Shloima, Joseph, Faigel and Chaim continued on. Rivka joined the two women and gently rocked Zetel asleep.

"Do you smoke, Ettie," Bessie asked, taking a silver cigarette holder and a pack of cigarettes from her purse.

"Do you mind if I do?" she said when Ettie shook her head.

She inserted a cigarette into the holder, snapped a match into flame, took a long deep drag, and puffed out a cloud of smoke. She inhaled again and added to the smoke hanging over the table.

Ettie coughed and startled Zetel awake. All he saw was a large cloud of burgeoning smoke as Bessie exhaled again.

"It's The-One-True-God coming to get me," he screamed.

His piercing cry shattered the relative quiet of the cafe and the low buzz of conversation stopped. Several patrons stood and all looked at the screaming baby now held and cradled by the attractive woman with the pale face and black hair adorned with a fashionable hat.

"Zetel," Rivka said consolingly, "don't be afraid. It's just mummy smoking."

Bessie put her cigarette out. "What are you talking about, Rivka?"

"Mummy, he thinks God is coming to get him."

Bessie rolled her eyes. Before she could reprove Rivka, a man at the next table came over. He spoke in broken English, "I help maybe?"

He was tall, very muscular with brawny arms that threatened to burst his shirtsleeves, a round swarthy face with narrowed black eyes, a black generous moustache, a battered nose and a mass of black unruly hair.

"I have car. Go hospital?" he continued.

"He's just colicky," Bessie said. "He'll be fine in a moment. You're not from here?"

The man shrugged his shoulders. "Who from here? Only Indians. I Greek."

Zetel looked at the man and grew apprehensive. He could not remember where but he had seen him before. Although the man was friendly, Zetel detected menace. "I do not know what a hospital is but I know I should not go with him. He is evil." He stopped screaming, gurgled happily and twisted his face into a smile. Best to stay calm, he thought.

"There," Bessie said. "He has recovered and is quite happy. Thank you for your kind offer, Mr. ..."

"Hegimoon," he said, "Parme Hegimoon from Athens."

"Thank you Mr. Hegimoon. I think we will take the baby home now."

As they left the cafe, Rivka said quietly to Bessie, "That is a bad man, mummy."

"My sweet little girl, how can you say that? He offered to help us. He looks different because he's from another country. Why do you think he's bad?"

"Zetel said so."

Both Bessie and Ettie laughed and continued on their way home. After awhile, Parme Hegimoon left the cafe and slowly sauntered along well behind them.

"You have done what?" thundered The-One-True-God. The massive cumulus cloud of vertical development was a boiling frenzy of thick darkening mist, reddened with internal lightning that threatened to burst out, and roiled by loud shrieks of screaming wind that signalled the intense anger of The-One-True-God.

Archangel Gabriel crouched at the edge of the cloud, surprised by the reaction, believing his news would elicit gratitude, and prepared himself for eternal punishment. Oh well, he thought, I had a few good billions of years. When I was appointed Archangel, I was told it would be a challenging job but I took it nonetheless. So now I go below. I must check out the parole system.

"Most Holy One," he pleaded, "in order to fulfill your command to bring the soul of Zetel Ländau back to the Arc, I needed to enlist help. Our angels are too caring to carry out the deed or don't see it as part of their function, and Samael is too busy at the moment in other parts of the world. Therefore, I called upon someone who has no scruples, who has put in place all the seeds required for the next war that will soon grip the entire world, and so has time to spare. I told him it had to be a surgical strike — only Zetel and no one else. He agreed. He also has a personal score to settle with the soul of Zetel. He is happy to carry out this assignment for his own sake."

"The fact of the matter is you hired Mars, the god of war — a pagan god!— to carry out the Command of The-One-True-God. Is this not a monumental error in sound judgement? What were you thinking? Do you believe I need the help of false gods? Withdraw him immediately. Now! Or risk the consequences."

By the time they reached the corner of Clark and Fairmount, Ettie was too tired to go further.

"Come up to our place, Ettie. You can nurse Zetel and have a nap," Bessie said.

She helped Ettie up the stairs. "Rivka, tuck the baby carriage under the staircase and close the street door," Bessie ordered.

Rivka closed the door. She noticed standing at the corner was the man from the cafe. As she watched, a mist like fog swept around him and when it cleared he was gone. She ran up the stairs but decided not to tell her mother. She waited until Zetel was nursed and was placed in the middle of her bed and the two women had left the room.

"That man at the cafe," Rivka said, "he followed us here but a fog came over him and took him away. You don't have to worry about him anymore."

"Thank you," said Zetel and fell asleep.

CHAPTER 6 —
Zetel is circumcised

On the Monday immediately after the Rosh Hashona weekend, there was high excitement in the Ländau household on Casgrain Street. Just before noon, a dozen people crowded into their living room. A beaming Joseph greeted each guest with a handshake for the men and a kiss on the cheek for the women and accepted their "mazeltovs" (*congratulations*) with a smile that ignited his thin, usually pale face.

"The Rabbi will be here very shortly," he announced.

"This is indeed a lucky day for the boy," said Issie Goldenstein, a brother-in-law of Ettie's grandfather and the most senior member of the family in Canada. He had immigrated to Canada in the early 1900's and had helped bring Shloima and Joseph to the country. He was a large avuncular figure with drooping chins and eyelids, a bloated waistline, and baggy clothing. He and his wife Dobresh owned and still managed a second hand clothing and special items store cum pawnshop.

"To have your bris (*circumcision*) during the High Holidays is good for the boy. Who's the mohel (*the person performing the circumcision*)?"

"Rabbi Koltonsky," said Joseph. "Highly recommended."

"Yoisef," Issie objected, shaking his wattles vigorously, "Rabbi Koltonsky is older than I am, and I was born the same day as

Methuselah. He needs a driver now to get to his customers because he can't see."

Joseph blanched and looked at Shloima.

"Uncle Issie, Koltonsky can't see long but he can see short. Stop worrying Yoisef," Shloima said.

"Yoisef, don't pay any attention to Issie," Dobresh added, wagging a finger at her husband. "Nobody's ever good enough."

Dobresh was shorter and thinner than her husband with a pleasantly round figure, a sweet face framed by unruly grey white hair, and a mellifluous voice.

Issie sighed. "Dobresh, a mohel needs more skill and experience than a surgeon. A boy has only one pickle which he needs all his life. One mistake and he's done for good. By the way, talking about pickles, there's a delicious smell coming out of the kitchen."

At this moment, Ettie appeared with Zetel cradled in her arms. Shloima introduced her to all the guests.

Hershey Levitt, an athletic looking man in his 30's, nattily dressed in a beige suit with a red waistcoat and light brown cravat bookended by very starched collars, did not hide his admiration.

"If I'd known there were such pretty girls in Europe, I might have immigrated back," he said.

Sylvia, his wife, attractive, provocatively dressed in a tight fitting skirt that fell just below her knees, and a blouse slightly too small for the ample cargo it contained, shook her head. "Ettie, ignore him. He thinks he's Clark Gable."

"I saw a film with Clark Gable last year," Ettie said shyly. "He's very handsome."

"Me or Clark Gable?" Hershey asked.

"Not you, Hershey," Jack Greenberg jumped in laughing. "It's true you look like a movie star. More like Stan Laurel, or maybe Mickey Mouse."

A short fleshy man with a balding head, Jack was a close friend of Shloima and Bessie. A department store manager at Eaton's on

St. Catherine Street, he was dressed for work in a black striped suit, matching vest, solid blue tie, and spats on his black shoes. Faigel showed immediate interest in him when she discovered he was a widower.

The front door opened wide hitting the vestibule wall and a gnome-like man came bustling in. No more than five feet tall, wearing a black homburg and black coat, he looked like a walking mushroom. He carried a prayer shawl in his left hand and a small black bag in his right.

"Welcome, Rabbi Koltonsky," Shloima said while Jack helped the Rabbi off with his coat and hat. A skull cap graced the Rabbi's wispy haired head. He put on thick glasses and stroked his white beard into order.

"Mazeltov, mazeltov, mazeltov. I congratulate you on your son," the Rabbi said and vigorously shook Shloima's hand.

"I'm not the father, Rabbi," said Shloima, pointing to Joseph. "It's my brother's son."

"So you're not happy with the boy?" the Rabbi asked.

"Of course, Rabbi, we're all happy with him."

"So why you don't accept my mazeltov?"

Shloima looked to Bessie for help but she had turned to the wall and from the shaking of her shoulders, he knew she was laughing uncontrollably.

Meanwhile, the Rabbi shook hands with Joseph, nodded at Ettie and wished everybody a "mazeltov" in a high pitched elderly voice.

"I must hurry," he said. "I have two more to do by 1:00."

He put on his prayer shawl after making the usual blessing and draped the surplus folds over his shoulders so that his hands and wrists were free. Both Joseph and Shloima put on their prayer shawls as well.

"First, who are the kvatter and kvatterin (*godfather and godmother*)?" the Rabbi asked.

Jack Greenberg and Faigel stepped forward.

"And now the sandek (*person who holds the child during the ritual*)."

"I will be the sandek," said Shloima.

The Rabbi laid out his instruments on a side table. He opened a bottle of red wine and poured some into a silver goblet. He inclined his head to Faigel. Faigel took Zetel from Ettie and handed him to Jack who carried him carefully over to Shloima.

"Sit down on the sofa," the Rabbi instructed Shloima. "Put this pillow covered with a towel on your lap and place the baby so his legs are towards me. You must keep him from moving."

Bessie had settled in one of the easy chairs but the rabbi directed her to get up.

"This chair must remain unoccupied during the entire ceremony. This is the chair that Eliyahu Hanovi (*Elijah the Prophet*) will use to watch us perform the rite. Eliyahu is present at every bris (*circumcision*)."

The rabbi made the customary blessing for the ceremony of circumcision, dipped some gauze into the wine and inserted it into the baby's mouth.

"I know he's below the drinking age," said the Rabbi smiling broadly, "but this will act as an anaesthetic. I will now perform the bris."

Archangel Gabriel hurried along Casgrain Street towards the Ländau home. He had to stop the ceremony. Once the boy was circumcised and therefore confirmed as part of the Covenant of Abraham with The-One-True-God, it would be more difficult to pull his soul back to the Arc.

While Gabriel couldn't stop the ceremony, he could delay it. No one had told the Rabbi that the boy was premature and needed a decision from a doctor that he was healthy enough for circumcision.

Even after receiving such assurance, the Rabbi would have to wait an additional seven days. This would give Gabriel more time to come up with a solution to the problem of Zetel.

He was almost at the house when a decrepit looking man in black ragged clothing accosted him.

"Hey, buddy, got a match? I need a smoke badly." He pulled a half-smoked cigarette butt from a pocket.

"Sir, I'm in a terrible hurry. I have no time to stop." Gabriel said and tried to get around him.

"Buddy, just give me a match and you can go as fast as you want."

Gabriel tried to push him aside. "I don't have a match."

"Alright, just give me a nickel and I can get a box of matches," said the man and put a restraining hand on Gabriel's arm.

"I have no money."

The man looked at him pityingly: "Gabriel, next time you set out on a mission, do some research, determine what you will need in costume and effects, and outfit yourself properly."

Startled, Gabriel looked closely at the man's face, the black beard, the squinting black eyes half hidden by the brimmed black hat. "Satan!"

"The very one," the Devil nodded. "Who dressed you? You must have consulted Zeus or Hera. Your tunic, blouse, and sandals tied to the knees with linen straps aren't quite in vogue at this time."

"Never mind my dress. Why do you stop me?"

"Because the circumcision must go ahead. Because I can't allow the boy's soul to go back to the Arc yet. Look at me. Why am I so ragged? The shreds of clothing missing from me were mixed into his soul when the Head of Heaven blew me through him. I will secure them from him but I need time. Besides, he, like me, has rebelled against your boss's authority. That makes him a kindred spirit whom I must protect."

He blocked Gabriel from walking around him and they grappled.

"Messieurs, s'il vous plait, allow us to pass."

Bessie's daytime maid, Colette, had picked up Rivka and Chaim at school for the lunch break and was leading them to the ceremony.

The two angels respectfully stepped aside. Satan bowed: "We beg your pardon, madam. Such beautiful children — they're like angels."

"Are you clowns?" asked Rivka. "You're dressed very funny. Aren't they, Mademoiselle Colette?"

"You're from a circus, aren't you?" demanded Chaim. "Mademoiselle Colette, can we go to their circus?"

"You don't want to go to our circus," laughed Satan. "At least, not yet."

"Come along, children," the wary maid said. "We mustn't be late." She shepherded the children quickly past Gabriel and Satan.

The two angels watched as the maid and the children walked up the few stairs to the house where the ceremony was taking place. They argued no further, sped to the brightly lit window and launched themselves through the wall into the living room.

Gabriel fell into Elijah's seat and Satan stood close to the Rabbi. No one seemed to notice them except Rivka who with Collette and Chaim had just entered the room.

"How did you get here so fast?" Rivka asked.

"I took a taxi from Eaton's," Jack Greenberg replied. "I wasn't that fast. Traffic was heavy."

"I don't mean you. I mean him," Rivka said pointing to Elijah's chair.

"Rivka, that's enough," Bessie said.

The angels ignored her and focussed on the Rabbi. The Rabbi was poised over Zetel's penis, instruments ready to begin the procedure.

"Rabbi, the baby is premature," Gabriel said.

The Rabbi paused and looked up. "A thought just struck me. I haven't had time to check the records. Is the baby healthy and full term?"

"The baby is very healthy according to the doctor," Joseph was quick to assure him.

"And full term?"

Shloima discreetly nodded as a signal to Joseph but he didn't notice.

"No, two months premature."

The Rabbi was indignant. "Then the circumcision cannot take place without a doctor's full consent. You are wasting my time."

Before he could withdraw, Satan seized the rabbi's hand and pushed the scalpel into the foreskin making a long superficial cut which produced a thin red line.

"What have you done?" cried Gabriel. "You are indeed a devil."

"Not 'a' devil — 'the' Devil," Satan said, unperturbed.

"I'm terribly sorry," the Rabbi said. "My hand involuntarily jumped. Premature or not, I will have to finish now."

The quarrel between the two angels woke up Zetel. "What are you doing here?" he bellowed, his anger exacerbated by a sharp pain in the lower part of his body. His scream elicited an immediate response from Ettie. She charged through the assembled guests, bounced off Faigel, thrust Jack Greenberg sideways into Elijah the Prophets chair knocking it over, and sending Gabriel sprawling through the wall.

"Serves you right," Rivka called out to the disappearing angel.

"Rivka, that's no way to talk to Mr. Greenberg," admonished Bessie.

Satan, fearing Ettie would stop the Rabbi from proceeding, wrapped an arm around her and slowed her down sufficiently so the Rabbi could finish the procedure.

The Rabbi was bandaging the wound and Zetel was still crying, but Ettie found a new target of concern. Shloima's face, tanned after many summer outings, had changed colour and was somewhere between apple and hunter green. She watched as his eyes rolled up into his head leaving only the whites showing.

"Bessie!" Ettie called out.

Bessie ran over and slapped Shloima across the face. "He can't stand the sight of blood. I told him don't be a sandek, your nose will be right in it but he said it's his duty, there's no zaidah (*grandfather*) here."

Satan still had his arm around Ettie. "Leave my sweet woman alone," Zetel said angrily.

"Don't worry, I'm going," Satan said, freeing Ettie with some reluctance. "When you're older, look me up." He leapt through the wall.

"There, mama," the Rabbi said and handed the baby to Bessie.

"I'm not the mother," she objected and gave the baby to Ettie who gently rocked him in her arms.

"Auntie Ettie," Rivka said, patting Zetel's head, "Zetel is not angry with you but with the two clowns."

Bessie took her daughter aside and said quietly, "Rivka, the Rabbi is not a clown and who's the other one? Mr. Greenberg was knocked over by Auntie Ettie and you can't talk about your father that way. Anyone can get sick when they least want to."

Rivka realized she had strayed into difficult territory again, said, "Not daddy," and walked away.

The Rabbi asked for silence. He lifted the silver goblet and made the blessing over wine and beseeched the Almighty to give the baby good health. Then he followed with the naming prayer.

"Creator, may it be Your will to accept this circumcision as though I had brought the boy before Your glorious throne. In Your abundant mercy, through Your holy angels, give a pure and holy heart to..." Here the Rabbi looked expectantly at Joseph.

"Zalman Yaakov Zetel," Joseph said proudly.

"Zetel?" asked Ettie. "We never agreed to include that name."

"Zetel?" asked Bessie. "I thought that was just temporary."

"Zetel?" asked Faigel. "Not again."

"Zetel?" asked Shloima weakly, not quite recovered. "Never mind. Let's get this over with. I won't last much longer."

"Zetel?" asked the Rabbi. "In all my years as a rabbi and mohel, never have I heard this name."

"Zetel?" asked Zetel. "Why not? I like the name. Everyone calls me that."

"Zetel," insisted Joseph. "It's in memory of a home and place once dear to us. Besides, Zetel likes it — look at that smile."

Zetel was grinning broadly and moving his arms up and down.

"Then Zetel it is," said Ettie.

"Fine," said the Rabbi. "Zalman Yaakov Zetel, the son of..."

"Yoisef Lipah," Joseph said.

"...who was just now circumcised in Your honour and in accordance with the Covenant of Abraham. May his heart be open to comprehend Your holy law, that he may learn and teach and keep and fulfill Your laws."

Everyone applauded and there were handshakes and kisses all around. Ettie, with Zetel in her arms, was embraced and kissed by Joseph and hugged by Faigel. Shloima, staggering slightly, paid the mohel's fee and the Rabbi quickly departed.

Bessie proclaimed in a loud voice: "Our hostess and beautiful mother of Zalman Yaakov Zetel invites you all to lunch. The food is set out on the dining room table. Please help yourself. And I can tell you, she has something very special for you gourmets."

"I always wondered what they did with the foreskin," quipped Jack Greenberg.

Bessie and Ettie looked horrified but Faigel giggled and slapped Jack playfully on the shoulder.

"Madam," Jack said, bowing and extending an arm, "may I escort you to the feast?" Faigel blushed, eagerly grasped his arm, and they walked majestically with heads held high to the dining room. Hershey Levitt gave his wife Sylvia a significant and knowing look as they followed them.

"Dobresh," said Issie, "make me a plate. I'm going to wait here. Let me hold Zetel, Ettie, so you can look after your guests."

Issie placed the baby on his knees because his mature waistline took up most of his lap.

"Dammit," said Zetel, "I'm not a happy soul."

"What are you unhappy about?" asked Rivka sympathetically.

"Me? I'm not unhappy," said Issie. "A little hungry, maybe."

"No, not you, Mr. Goldenstein. Zetel. He's complaining. He says he's in pain and is using bad language."

Issie stared at Rivka and a worried look spread over his face.

"Sweetheart, go get something to eat. You have to go back to school soon."

Dobresh brought Issie a dinner plate piled high. "Issie, you should see that table. All your favourites are there. Chopped liver with schmaltz (*chicken fat*), verenikes, potato knishes, chopped herring, sweet lokshin kugel, challah, rye bread, pumpernickel, and the special dish is the most tender peppercorn crusted brisket in a tomato sauce the like you've never eaten. And there's also wine, tea, and mandelbrot cookies. We have imported a great cook."

"As good as you?" asked Issie.

"Better than me."

She brought her own plate and sat down near her husband after placing Zetel on an easy chair.

After awhile, Colette appeared with the two children in tow to return to school.

"Bye, bye, Zetel," Rivka said. "Daddy says the pain will soon go away. It was done to him and to all the men here and also to Chaim and no one remembers the pain."

"The body forgets but the soul remembers," said Zetel grumpily.

CHAPTER 7 —
Zetel at the doctor

"You failed again."

Gabriel, terrified, trembling violently, lay prostrate before the blackening massive cumulus cloud of vertical development. He offered no defence but waited, eyes shut, for the horrific blast of fiery heat that would send him headlong flaming into the infernal depths.

"Outwitted by Lucifer."

Gabriel pushed his face into the cloud soul he was lying on and covered his head with his hands. After several years and nothing happened, he turned his head sideways and opened one eye. The cloud in which The-One-True-God resided continued to belch lightning bolts and angry rumbles of thunder but had greyed and was turning white at the edges. Was this a good sign?

"If Lucifer had not embarked on his ego trip, I would have made him Archangel. You won the job by default."

The Voice was still condemnatory but had softened. Gabriel breathed a sibilant sigh of relief.

"You are not off the hook yet," the Voice darkened again. "I want a plan, a strategy to achieve what I have commanded, or at least, if nothing else, an indication that the return of the soul they call Zetel is imminent."

Gabriel, still prostrate, lifted his head. "Most Holy One, Creator, it is true that unforeseen circumstances have interfered with my mission, for which I humbly crave forgiveness and exult in being allowed to continue serving You despite my failures, and to honour You as a Master of peerless..."

"Stop fulminating, Angel. Get on with it," the Voice, frustrated, impatient, shouted angrily. A lightning bolt snapped over Gabriel's body, singeing his hair and causing thin chimneys of smoke to erupt on his cloak. He rolled over and over and put out the flames.

Gabriel rose to his knees, his hands in the supplicating position of prayer: "Hear me, Most Holy, it is true the soul called Zetel has survived thus far. However, there is growing evidence that the premature birth of the body it inhabits is not without physical consequences. He is frequently seen by a doctor of medicine. No doubt, it will not be long now."

"How often have I heard that. Keep me posted," said the Voice, as the cloud moved off.

Bessie and Ettie stood in front of Doctor Zabinsky's office on Park Avenue between Fairmount and Laurier. It was a remarkably warm day in January with an occasional shower from the grey clouds that scudded across the sun. Zetel was in his stroller absorbed by the constant traffic of streetcars, trucks, autos, and horse pulled wagons. A horse trotted by, its nose in its feedbag.

"Look at the horse, mama," he said. "It eats while it works. Does papa eat while he works?"

Ettie gazed at him lovingly and smiled, "Papa is not a horse, Zetel. He eats when he comes for dinner and supper."

She turned to Bessie, "I'm almost afraid to go in. He must think I'm an overbearing parent, always looking for the least sign of sickness."

"No, Ettie," Bessie said, "if you're worried about something, then you're right to look into it. From my experience with Zabinsky, he's a very conscientious children's doctor. Besides, that's how he makes his living. Why should he care how often you come with Zetel?"

The Doctor was also very reassuring, "Nice to see you again, Mrs. Landaw. I hope it's nothing serious this time." He quickly consulted Zetel's file. "Your boy has certainly had his share of medical difficulties. First, there was that severe reaction to the smallpox vaccination. For awhile, we thought the vaccine had produced the disease in him. Fortunately, after a couple of weeks, he was back to normal. Then, you had great difficulty weaning him off breast feeding. He refused to drink from a bottle and quickly lost weight. Well, he got over that. But then, a new problem arose. He developed a continual throat infection which made it difficult for him to even drink and he lost more weight. The removal of tonsils and adenoids made him better and he has more than regained his weight. What seems to be the problem now?"

The Doctor sat back, pushed his glasses up on to his well combed dark hair, and gave Ettie an encouraging smile. The truth is, he told himself, it's a delight to look at her but he had to remain professional and mask his intense admiration of the black haired white faced beautiful woman before him.

"Go ahead, Ettie," Bessie said. "Tell the doctor what is bothering you."

"Doctor," Ettie began hesitantly, "my little boy drinks enormous amounts of water — bottle after bottle when he was younger and now many glasses each day. There must be something wrong."

"Does he go to the bathroom very often? In other words, does he relieve himself of the liquid?" the Doctor asked.

"Yes, he goes quite often. His diapers are always wet and now we are trying to train him to use his potty, he fills it up."

"Polydipsia and polyuria," said the doctor. He pulled his glasses back onto his nose and added to the notes in Zetel's file. "These could be symptoms of an underlying condition. I will examine him and take blood and urine samples. Kindly undress him and place him on the examination table."

Zetel stepped out of the stroller.

"My, my, he's tall for a three year old," the doctor said. "He's a cute little fellow with his head of curly blond hair. I see mischief in those blue eyes. Are you a good boy?"

"He certainly is, Doctor," Ettie said. "And very clever. Already, he can read his English baby books and he knows the Hebrew alphabet. Aren't you a smart one?" Ettie said affectionately to Zetel who nodded vigorously in agreement.

Bessie and Ettie put Zetel on the examination table. The doctor listened attentively to his breathing and heart function, looked into his ears and nose and down his throat. He took a couple of droplets of blood from a finger and positioned Zetel on the floor over a small ceramic pot.

"Now, young man, just pee into the pot," he directed.

"Doctor, the pot is not large enough," Ettie warned.

"Not to worry, Mrs. Landaw, it will hold more than his bladder," the doctor said confidently.

A stream of urine arched through the air into the pot which began to fill rapidly. When the level of urine was close to the top, the doctor said, "That's fine, young man, stop now."

But Zetel could not stop. The urine slopped over the top and ran in several rivulets across the shiny hardwood floor of the doctor's office. Bessie and Ettie stepped out of the way and watched in horror as a rivulet came up against one of the doctor's shoes and washed around it. Another rivulet found its way to the door and spread under it into the waiting room. Finally, Zetel had finished.

The doctor picked Zetel up and put him back on the table. He poured a small amount from the pot into a urine sample container and labelled it. He turned to Ettie and Bessie both blushing in embarrassment and said rather curtly: "I have to make a house call now. Please ask the receptionist for a bucket and mop. Come see me in a week when I will have the results of the tests."

They returned in a week and profusely apologised to the doctor for the desecration to his office. He brushed their apologies aside.

"Happens all the time with children," he assured them. "As for Zetel's results, and the reason for his excessive liquid input, I've ruled out diabetes — his blood sugar and insulin levels are normal. There are several other possibilities. One, check his diet and make sure it is not too salty or sweet. Two, his excessive drinking may be a psychological reaction to being weaned. Three, he may have less kidney function as a result of his premature birth. There are some indications in the urine sample but these are so slight as to be negligible. We should continue to follow him over the years but right now I don't see any cause for alarm. Of more concern, I noted his adenoids and tonsils are growing back, not unheard of but unusual nevertheless. He may require a second tonsillectomy at some time in the future. Also I detected a slight abnormality in the heartbeat but again so slight as to be scarcely audible. Just something we should follow up."

He noted the worried look on the faces of the two women. "Ladies, let me stress — there is no need for alarm. These are things to watch out for in the future. Right now he's a healthy baby boy."

"So that's your plan?"

The Voice from inside the massive cumulous cloud of vertical development was skeptical, even dismissive.

Gabriel nervously clasped his hands in front of him. "Yes, Most Holy, he is saddled with several diseases, one of which will no doubt be fatal."

"When?"

"That is hard to predict, Most Holy," Gabriel said wringing his hands.

"Might he live a normal lifetime despite his illnesses?"

"I believe that is not possible, Most Holy. His illnesses will worsen as he grows and will prove fatal."

The Voice sighed. "I detect a lack of conviction. There is an endpoint, Gabriel. In five billion years, the sun of this planet Earth will cease and all will die. I hope I don't have to wait that long for the soul Zetel to return to the Arc. I want more assurance. Stay close to him."

Gabriel bowed his head but was relieved to see the massive cloud drift away. Regretfully, to stay close to Zetel, he would have to spend more time on Earth. He rather enjoyed his status as Archangel and the wide expanses of heaven above the Arc of Souls. His days were relaxed since he delegated most of the assigning and reassigning of souls to a coterie of devoted angels. Mind you, activity in this regard had increased once again with the accession of men such as Stalin and Hitler which required finding many more places to store the souls. Still, his angel helpers seemed up to the task with little supervision from him. He wished desperately to remain in heaven but realised he had better plan some time on Earth if only to placate The-One-True-God.

"The strangest thing happened today," exclaimed Jack Greenberg as Joseph opened the door to him at their Casgrain home. A blast of frigid February air accompanied by a shower of snowflakes blew in with him. Joseph hurriedly closed the door and helped his guest take off his coat and hat. Jack kicked off his galoshes. "Let me tell you all about it, not that you'll believe me."

"Come in first and get warmed up," Joseph said. "Faigel's been waiting patiently and is already worried you were stuck in a snowdrift and wouldn't be found until spring."

"What took you so long?" demanded Faigel as she embraced Jack, the diamond on her wedding finger sparkling brightly in the ceiling light.

"That's what I want to tell you about," said Jack. "Today I had the most extraordinary experience of my life."

"That's what you said on our wedding night," Faigel said laughing. "For this man, everything is extraordinary."

"Let's all have a schnapps first," said Joseph. "Or a glass of wine if you prefer. We always celebrate on Friday night and the dinner won't spoil, will it, Ettie."

"No," Ettie said, greeting Jack with a kiss on the cheek, "I have it on a low fire."

"What is wrong with all of you? The most unusual — the most unexplainable — the most unimaginable thing happens to me and all you want to talk about is drink and food. You want to know why I'm late. I had to talk to the police and try to explain what happened. Of course, they didn't believe me, they think I'm crazy, even the store manager looks at me strangely and says he'll make a report to Mr. Eaton in Toronto."

"Now, don't get excited, geliebter (*sweetheart*)," Faigel said gently, "you know it's not good for you. Have a drink and tell us all about it."

"Alright, I will describe the incident as calmly as I can. When I get through, promise me you won't tell everybody that an asylum is my next stop. In fact, promise me none of this will be told to anyone, not even Shloima and Bessie."

They all nodded. "Can I tell my friend Fivey?" asked Zetel, who had been sitting quietly on a hassock in the living room reading a book of fairy tales.

"Don't tell Fivey," Joseph said. "He's not your friend. He's a little bully."

"Zetel, if you're my friend, you won't tell anyone," said Jack. He drained his schnapps in one gulp, closed his eyes as the whiskey trickled down his throat, and took a deep breath.

"This afternoon I'm standing at one of the big windows in my men's clothing department, looking out at the blizzard and hoping it will stop soon. Of course, there are no customers — who goes out on a day like this? There's only one salesman on the floor, the others are taking an extended lunch. I look around. There's no one in sight. I turn back to the window. A voice behind me says, 'Sir.' I just about have a fit and turn around so quickly the man jumps back.

" 'Oh, I didn't mean to startle you,' the man says.

"Startled, you bet I was startled. He came out of nowhere. And I get more startled as I look at him. He's tall, slim but not skinny, long hair to his shoulders, clean shaven, a friendly face, but it's his clothing that gets me. A cloak covers his body, tied with a gold belt around his waist and sandals on his feet. In the middle of February!

" 'How can I help you,' I manage to say.

" 'I plan to spend some time in Montreal and I need clothing appropriate to a gentleman,' he says. His voice is very soft, so soft I have to lean forward to hear him. 'Apart from what I'm wearing, which is not suitable here, I have no other clothing.'

"Of course I'm suspicious. My next question is: 'Sir, do you intend to pay with cash or by cheque? If by cheque, sir, I'm sure you will understand that we will have to hold the clothing here until the cheque clears.'

"He gives me a disturbed look: 'I must have the clothes today. I will pay immediately in pieces of gold.' He takes out from a pocket in his robe a linen bag which he opens and spills out on a table. There are twenty gold coins. I pick one up and I guess it's about 5 ounces. If the coins are real, he has over $3000 on the table.

"I call over my salesman. 'If you don't mind, sir, my colleague will look after you while I take these coins to our jewellery department for evaluation. I will be back in a jiffy.' He doesn't seem to mind. I explain to the salesman what the customer wants and I head off with the bag of coins.

"Our top jeweller is a gold expert. He carefully goes through the coins, weighs them, and whatever else jewellers do and announces after a good half hour that the coins are real and worth $3500. As unusual as his method of payment is, at least I know the customer can pay. So I return to the floor and help my salesman.

"After a good hour, the customer is resplendent in our best imported line of suits, Savile Row no less, and everything else he needs, including underwear, shirts, collars, cuff links, ties, stockings, shoes, a winter coat, hat, a scarf, gloves. He asks for a second suit but instead of blue, this one should be in brown. That means he needs brown shoes and everything else to match except the winter coat which is black. So we bring him all these articles and he returns to the change room to try them on.

"From where I sit the change room is in full sight. My salesman is nearby talking on the telephone. There is no way the customer can exit without going by us. After about twenty minutes, I knock on the door and ask him if everything is to his liking. The salesman is beside me in case something has to be changed. There's no answer. I knock again. Still no answer. I begin to fear he's died or collapsed and quickly open the door. The change room is empty!

"We both stand there with our mouths open and barge into the room, checking behind the door and under the change bench. He's not there. We are completely dumfounded. Where'd he go? How did he get out without us seeing him? Is he some kind of Houdini?

"'Well,' I say to the salesman, 'at least we have more than enough to pay for the clothes.'"

"That's our next shock. The bag with the gold coins is gone! We've been taken by a master thief. I call the store manager and the store detective who calls the police. Of course, at first nobody believes us. No one saw the man anywhere in the store or leaving it. The only thing that saves us is the jeweller who remembers examining the gold coins and notes the fabric of the bag they came in is a cloth made up of finely spun gold and linen, something he's never seen before. In addition, when the man was trying on his new clothes, we took his robe and waist belt and put them in a paper bag near the cash register. We still have that. The jeweller looks at these. The robe is also finely spun gold thread and linen. The belt is made up of long strings of pure gold held together by a solid gold clasp. The jeweller says their value is more than the merchandise that disappeared with the man. So no crime has been committed and I'm in the clear. The police look around, take down a description of the man, and leave. The store detective calls in a local detective agency to scour the store to ensure the man is no longer on the premises. So that's the story."

There was dead silence. Faigel hugged and kissed Jack: "No wonder you're all upset. What an experience!"

"Jack ," Joseph said, "truly a frightening experience. I'm surprised the thief left his cloak and belt behind since he seems so clever."

"I wondered about that too, Yoisef. Either he didn't see it or felt the rustling of the paper bag would alert us. As far as how he got out without our seeing him, I think we were hypnotised somehow. It's the only answer I can come up with."

"Come, Jack, let's sit down for dinner," Ettie said, smiling. "Let's make the food disappear."

CHAPTER 8 —
Zetel and the Oedipus complex

Dr. Zabinsky ushered Ettie and Zetel into his office and said in a welcoming way, "How nice to see you and the boy again, Mrs. Landaw. Just let me review his file first before we talk."

He concentrated on his reading and then looked up. "What brings you here on this beautiful spring day? Mind you, April is always an unpredictable weather month. They're even predicting a snowfall tomorrow. Not to worry though — these weather people often get it wrong. Do you find our winters difficult?"

Ettie looked at him in surprise. He was unusually talkative, almost affable, contrary to his characteristic quick professional manner of getting to the issue, examining the child, making a decision, and getting them out again.

"We had snow in Germany," she replied, "but nothing like in Montreal. Also the winters are much colder here. But we manage quite nicely except during the blizzards. Zetel seems to enjoy the winter. He plays in the snow and throws snowballs at my husband. The other day when the snow was right, they made a snowman. Our flat is quite warm, some days too warm, and I must open a window. I still find it hard to believe when I hang out the wash that it freezes solid and still dries. But, Doctor, I am talking too much and taking up your time."

"Not at all, Mrs. Landaw. I'm always interested in the views of newcomers to Canada. I was born in this country, on a farm just north of Montreal. My parents still own and run it. Winters weren't too bad for us since there was no farming in the fields and all the milk cows were safely lodged in the barn. School for me was just down the road in a one room school house. The first floor was for the regular school. The upper floor was the cheder (*school for Jewish studies*) and a rabbi would come three days a week at 3:30 to teach."

"Why did you not stay on the farm?" Ettie asked. "Does your father not need help?"

"My father told me when I graduated from elementary school, that I would live with my aunt and uncle in Montreal, that I would go to high school and then university, and become a professional, any professional. I chose medicine."

"You must have had a difficult time," Ettie said sympathetically. "Away from home."

"Yes, it was difficult but my father made the right decision. I love my work. And talking about work, what is troubling our Zetel? I've weighed him, and measured his height. He is well ahead of other children his age. Probably in the 90th percentile. He'll only be four in September but he's already more like a five year old."

Ettie hesitated. "Come, come, Mrs. Landaw," Zabinsky said encouragingly, "whatever it is, it will be taken seriously." He pushed his glasses up on to his head. He had a fleeting thought that he looked better this way.

"He sometimes says strange things."

"Strange things?" the doctor repeated, pulled his glasses back on, and sat forward. "What sort of things?"

Ettie looked down and there was an embarrassed silence.

"Mrs. Landaw, nothing a child says can shock me. I've been dealing with children for 10 years, and my files are full of their cute and not-so-cute things they come up with."

Ettie nodded, and cleared her throat. "The first incident was about a year ago. Rivka — that's the other Mrs. Landaw's daughter — spends a lot of time with Zetel. You really like each other, don't you Zetel?" She paused while Zetel nodded gleefully. "They were playing in the living room while I was in the kitchen preparing supper. My husband arrived and, as usual when Rivka was visiting, walked her home. It's not far away. That night, after Zetel was fast asleep in his crib in the dining room, and we were in the living room, my husband told me about the strange conversation he'd had with Rivka. She said that Zetel was afraid some people were trying to kill him. We treated it rather lightly. Kids get all kinds of ideas. Maybe it was something he heard on the radio or from one of his friends on the street. Also, we talk often about what is going on in Europe, Kristallnacht in November, the concentration camps, the ghettoes. It's all pretty terrible, as you know, and our families over there are all frightened. So we may have influenced him. Anyway, the next day, the child did not seem at all concerned and we forgot about it."

"You said that was the first incident. There were others?"

"Just last week," Ettie said. "We were visiting Bessie — that's the other Mrs. Landaw, Rivka's mother — and she asked Zetel, jokingly, for she was tickling him at the moment, whether he was still afraid. Zetel became very agitated and started screaming and crying. It took us a long while to calm him down, he was so frightened. What can we do, Doctor?"

"How do you feel now, Zetel, on such a sunshiny day?" the doctor asked.

"I am still afraid," Zetel said. "This man wants to make me dead. He says so."

Fearfully, Ettie patted Zetel's head. "No one wants to make you dead, Zeesuh."

The doctor in a casual voice asked: "And who is this man, Zetel? Do you know his name?"

"Gabriel," said Zetel.

"Do you see Gabriel often?" the doctor asked.

"No, once at my bris (*circumcision*) and yesterday."

"You saw him at your bris? Very few remember their bris."

Zetel was about to point out the soul remembers everything, but detecting a note of disbelief in the doctor's voice said nothing.

"What about yesterday?"

"He had on a disguise. He dressed like my papa but I knew it was Gabriel. He said I was such a pretty boy to mama. I told mama to chase him away."

"It was very embarrassing," Ettie said. "He was a very well dressed, good natured man who stopped to look at Zetel while we were walking back from shopping. Zetel screamed as soon as he saw him. The man apologised, bowed, and left us."

"Tell me Zetel," the doctor said, "what would you like to see happen to this man if you see him again? Should your mommy call the police?"

"Yes, and the policeman must shoot with his gun and dead him."

The doctor paused, a frown on his face. "That seems rather drastic, Zetel. Shouldn't the policeman ask him questions first? Perhaps he just reminds you of Gabriel. Then the wrong man would be killed. And if he looks like your daddy, you might make a terrible mistake."

"Even if he disguises himself as my papa, I would know, and the police must still shoot him."

"Zetel, what an awful thing to say," Ettie admonished him. "We have to be certain first that the man means you harm."

"Is Gabriel a name you heard on the radio, Zetel?" the doctor asked. "Or from one of your friends when you were playing?"

"No, I heard it when I was still in heaven."

"I see," said the doctor. "Has your daddy or mommy read you stories from the bible?"

"My papa does. When I go to bed. I like the stories."

"Now, Zetel, why don't you play in the reception room while I talk to your mother."

Zetel dutifully and quite happily went to the play area outside the doctor's office.

"Mrs. Landaw, I'm not a psychologist but I have studied Freud and others as part of my medical training." The doctor paused. "In fact, at one time, I became so interested that I considered making psychology my life's work." He paused again. "Nevertheless, I'm not an expert but I can claim to be an informed amateur. However, if Zetel's fears persist, or if you wish, I can arrange a visit to a real professional."

"Not right now, Doctor," Ettie said. "I don't want people to think my Zetel is crazy. Please tell me what you think."

The doctor nodded, happy to continue to have the beautiful troubled face before him.

"There are several explanations I can offer. Clearly these are uncertain times in the world, particularly for Jews. We are all burdened with our fears regarding events in Europe. We cannot hide our uncertainty, our worry, our very apprehensiveness from our children. Even if they don't fully understand, they can feel, they are attuned to us. I'm sure you and your husband, in talking about Kristallnacht, have discussed the murders of Jews during that time and the wholesale persecution and upheavals that occur daily now."

"You're quite right, Doctor," Ettie said. "We are worried sick about what is going on over there. We haven't heard from our grandparents for a while now. For the moment, our parents are safe — mine are in Poland and my husband's moved to Lithuania. But we have heard nothing from the rest of the family except for a letter we received from my sister that she and her family are in Budapest. We talk about nothing else. We even say how nice it would be if someone shot Hitler."

"It would not surprise me, then," the doctor said, "if Zetel expresses your fears in his own way, a function known as 'transference.' Perhaps he heard the name Gabriel in one of the bible stories, and since you've mentioned shooting, he has adopted the idea. So that's one possibility."

"Can there be another possibility, Doctor? Your explanation seems to fit my son's behaviour."

"Well, Mrs. Landaw, there is another approach I could take, a more profound approach, reflecting a darker aspect of the human personality. It's a complex that was identified and described by Freud and supported by some of his cases. Freud believed that in the deepest depths of every boy's psyche is a desire to kill his father and form a union with his mother..."

Ettie jumped up, aghast: "Doctor, how can you say such a thing? It's impossible."

"Now, now, Mrs. Landaw," the doctor said soothingly. "I realise such a proposition can startle and cause anxiety. Please let me finish."

Ettie slowly sank back into her chair and regarded the doctor with narrowed skeptical eyes.

"Mrs. Landaw, I don't blame you if the idea strikes you as ludicrous. When Freud first broached it, he was greeted with a hail of criticism. Since then, most practitioners accept that there is some validity to his theory. He called it the Oedipus Complex. The concept comes from a Greek myth where Oedipus, lost to his parents as a baby and unknown to them, returns to his country, unwittingly kills his father, comforts the grieving widow and marries her."

"Fine," Ettie said. "I know the story but it's a myth, a very tragic one. How does it apply to Zetel. How can you even think it applies to him."

"Let's look at a couple of indicators which could lead to such an interpretation," the doctor said. "And please remember, Mrs. Landaw, I say this is only a possibility. Twice Zetel spoke of the man as dressed like his daddy and was very eager to see him killed by a policeman. Even when I pointed out that if the man looked like his daddy, shooting him could be a terrible mistake. In other words, I was suggesting it might be his daddy. Nevertheless, Zetel insisted he would know and the policeman should still shoot him."

"But he said he would know if it wasn't his daddy," Ettie objected.

"Quite right, Mrs. Landaw. As I said, these are only indicators. There is never a fully rational or logical sequence of events. It is only a possibility at this stage. Furthermore, it is nothing to worry about unless his speech becomes more violent and more insistent."

"Doctor, if this is only a possibility, then I would appreciate it if my husband never hears about it."

The doctor nodded, abashed by the coldness of her voice. He recognized he had lost the warmth of her regard for him.

"Of course, Mrs. Landaw. But there is another possibility and one that should be taken more seriously. It's unusual, but there are men who prey on pretty boys. If the well dressed man should appear again, try to find out something about him — his name, where he lives, where he works. If he has ill intent towards Zetel, the child may have detected it and reacted. This I think you should discuss with your husband."

"But Doctor, the man was very kind, immediately apologised when Zetel made a fuss, and left. He seems like a real gentleman."

"He probably is, Mrs. Landaw. All I'm suggesting is to be cautious."

Ettie nodded and rose to leave. Then she giggled: "I suppose, Doctor, there is another possibility. Zetel did meet Gabriel in heaven and Gabriel wants him back."

They both laughed and the doctor felt gratified that some of the warmth had returned.

CHAPTER 9 —
Zetel and the god of war

"Shloima, please come home," Bessie pleaded when her husband, summoned by the receptionist, answered the telephone. "And bring Yoisef with you. Ettie is here almost beside herself. Come home right away."

"Bessie, what's wrong? We're right in the middle of filling a big uniform order. In a few hours we'll be home anyway," Shloima said. "What's with Ettie? Is Zetel alright?"

"Shloima, haven't you heard? Hitler, the Nazis, they've invaded Poland. Ettie's parents moved there to escape Germany. My parents and all my cousins are in Poland. We need our husbands here — now."

A half hour later the two men, pale, grimfaced, arrived. Joseph immediately embraced Ettie and tried to calm her. News broadcasts regarding the invasion dominated the airwaves. They listened in growing fear and horror as reports of troops, tanks, artillery and air bombardments made it clear this was no mere raid in an attempt to reunite Silesia with Germany.

"Can't anyone stop that mamzer?" Shloima said. "Where's our God? Where's the Polish God if ours is too busy?"

"Yoisef, what will happen to mama and poppa?" Ettie moaned, her face even whiter than usual. "They will be put in concentration camps. That's what happened in Austria and the Sudetenland."

"Let's not all panic," Bessie said, trying to keep her voice even. "The British have a treaty with Poland and they've given Germany an ultimatum. The British will stop them."

Joseph shook his head despairingly. "Will they be able to? They've allowed Hitler to build up an enormous army. Even their prime minister was fooled and tried to appease him."

"Well, there's no doubt in my mind," Shloima said. "Hitler will ignore the ultimatum and Britain will declare war on Germany. Probably France will too. And they're not ready."

"But Shloima, surely we're not going to have another Great War," Yoisef said.

"Yoisef, who knows what that lunatic is going to do or has in mind. No, it's war, that I'm sure of. It's Friday and too late to do anything but after shabbos (*the Sabbath*) tomorrow, I'll get in touch with the Canadian Jewish Congress. I know Bronfman and Caiserman. Let's see if they can do anything for us."

Rivka joined them. The adults had tried to shield their anxiety over the events in Europe from the three children and had encouraged them to play in another room. However, their concern and the constant radio reports had filtered through.

"What is it, Rivka?" Bessie asked. "Are you getting hungry? We'll soon eat."

"Mommy, Zetel is very sad and crying," Rivka said. "He says war is all his fault."

Joseph immediately went to fetch Zetel and returned carrying him in his arms and followed by Chaim. "What is it, Zetel?" Joseph asked solicitously, kissing away the tears coursing down the boy's cheeks. "How can war be your fault?"

"Papa's right, Zetelleh," Ettie said. "If there's to be a war, it's the fault of that bad man Hitler."

Between sobs, Zetel sputtered out, "Because of me, Mars fell to the world."

"No, Zetel," Shloima said. "Mars is still up in the sky far away."

Zetel looked puzzled. "Uncle Shloima, I saw him myself fall onto the world. He tried to make me dead and tripped and fell."

"Zeesuh, who tried to make you dead? Gabriel?" Ettie asked.

"No, not Gabriel. Mars. He's a very bad god," Zetel insisted.

They stared at him, perplexed.

"He means Mars, god of war," Rivka explained.

"Yoisef, what have you been reading to this boy?" Ettie demanded angrily.

"Ettie, all I read to him are stories from the Torah (*bible*). There's no mention of Mars in the Torah. Zetel, listen to me. There's no such thing as Mars, god of war. He's just a myth, a fairy tale. Maybe you had a bad dream."

"Uncle Yoisef, we saw pictures of Mars last Sunday when you took us to the library," Rivka said. "They were in a book."

"Yoisef, what library did you go to?" Bessie asked.

"The Jewish library at the YMHA," Yoisef said, shaking his head in disbelief. "I thought they only had Jewish subjects."

"That means Mars was Jewish. His original name was probably Marsky," Shloima said. "Zetel, did the pictures frighten you?"

Zetel shook his head. "No, he's much badder looking than the pictures."

"There was also a picture of Diana who is Zetel's best friend apart from me and Chaim."

"Diana is Zetel's girlfriend," Chaim mocked. "When he grows up he will marry her. If he can find her."

"Who is Diana, Zetel? Is she someone we know?" Ettie asked, trying to sound casual.

Zetel recognized the wall of disbelief that separated him from the adults and fell silent.

"Her full name is Diana the Huntress," Rivka added. "She is very pretty. Zetel says she is even nicer than the pictures."

"Zetel, let me tell you something," Shloima said. "Even if Mars fell to the Earth, he has nothing to do with this war. There is only one god of war at the moment and his name is Hitler. You're not to blame for anything."

"Uncle Shloima is right, Zetelleh," Ettie said. "Maybe you should stop looking at those books. And you're such a pretty boy, when you grow up, Dianas will come calling."

"Let's go eat," Bessie said. "Come, children, you can help."

The two women and the children left the two men still sitting before the blaring radio. Shloima turned it down. "Yoisef, your boy sure has an imagination."

"It's a worry to us. It's not the first time he comes out with these strange ideas. We've even discussed them with Doctor Zabinsky. He says it's just childhood fantasy. But your Rivka seems to believe him."

"Yoisef, my Rivka is also a child, even if she's five years older than Zetel. Chaim just laughs at the two of them. Just dreams, Yoisef. Remember how you used to see the Golem when you were their age. Don't worry about it. Your Zetel and my Rivka — they'll soon, all too soon, grow out of it."

Yoisef sighed. "Well, we could use a Golem now, fantasy or not."

The Canadian Jewish Congress occupied a small office in the Baron de Hirsch Institute on Bleury Street in downtown Montreal. Shloima climbed the stone staircase in front of the building and pushed through the double doors at the top. Hananiah Caiserman, the General-Secretary of the CJC was waiting for him and ushered him into his office.

"Mr. Bronfman telephoned me you would be coming. It's a pleasure to see you again."

They shook hands. Caiserman's desk was strewn with papers and files and was set against a wall under a large window that provided day light and muffled the sound from the busy street. A table lamp lit up his desk and an overhead lamp in the ceiling illumined the rest of the room. Two metal filing cabinets and two chairs for visitors filled most of the remaining space. Shloima sat in one of the chairs at the end of the desk.

He liked Caiserman. He had seen him during the rallies and the fundraisers and as a colleague on one of the many committees sponsored by the CJC. Caiserman was soft-spoken, with dark eyes looking sympathetically through round spectacles perched on a round face. His suit was rumpled but his cravat was carefully tied and pushed up the starched points of his shirt collar.

"I understand your concern for your family still in Europe," Caiserman said after Shloima had despondently explained the reason for the visit. "It is a concern I hear very often now from our people. War is terrible for everyone, but it will not be a long war. Of this, you may rest assured. Britain and France have declared war on Germany and there is already news that the Royal Air Force has attacked the German Navy. Hitler will soon be stopped."

Shloima shook his head. "Mr. Caiserman, I pray that he will be stopped but it won't be quickly. Hopefully, Britain and France will keep Hitler busy enough so he takes his mind off our people. Is there any way to get our families into Canada, at least our parents and grandparents?"

Caiserman looked at him sadly. "Very difficult. There is such opposition to immigrants at this time. The Depression still has many out of work and this forms the basis for the opposition. Mind you, no one says it out loud but by immigrants, they really mean Jews. It's not just in Quebec that anti-Semitism is strong. The rest of Canada is quieter but just as strong."

"I know times are difficult for us even in Canada," Shloima said. "But Bronfman has lots of influence and is admired by the business community. Can't he put a word in the right place? Surely the CJC can do more than just hold rallies?"

Caiserman sighed. "It's even difficult to get permission to hold a rally. I'm sure you're aware that at our rallies, we never plead specifically for help for the Jews of Germany but talk of the atrocities committed against all the people in Germany and in the path of the German army. That's Bronfman's policy. He calls it the 'shashtill' approach— keep quiet, don't make trouble, don't make it appear as a Jewish cause. We have to get the goyim (*non-Jews*) to support us and the only way to do that is to appeal on behalf of all people, even though, up until now, it is mostly our people who are persecuted."

Both men were silent for a moment.

"Well, Mr. Caiserman, I'm sure Mr. Bronfman, and you and the CJC know what you're doing," Shloima said at length. "But is there nothing can be done for our families? Right now, our Polish family is in Warsaw. The German side of the family has moved to Lithuania."

"I have their names," Caiserman said. "For the moment, Lithuania is reasonably safe. For your Polish family, we have contacts in the Red Cross and we can get a message to your family via our agents. The message will be that they should flee east, keep ahead of the advancing Germans and, if necessary, cross into Russia."

"Russia?" Shloima exclaimed, jumping to his feet. "That's like going from one frying pan into another."

"Possibly," Caiserman said. "But so far, Jews are faring better in Russia than in Germany. Besides, the Germans and the Russians have a non-aggression pact so the Nazi's won't invade Russia. That's my best advice and we have counselled others the same way."

Shloima thought it through but could come up with no better idea. "You're sure, there's no way to get them here?"

Caiserman shook his head. "Mr. Landaw, it's not even worth trying."

"So be it," Shloima said resignedly and shook Caiserman's hand. "Go ahead."

Shloima left the building and walked slowly up Bleury Street deep in thought, his hands clasped behind. He bent slightly on the long hill leading to Sherbrooke Street. Maybe Zetel is right, he thought. Maybe there is a Mars who is god of war. Maybe he's taken over Hitler. How else could a madman persuade so many people to follow him. He shook his head. No, we can't take any blame away from Hitler. If you repeat a lie often enough and forcefully enough, people can be fooled, particularly if you have a private army of thugs to soften up the opposition. No, we better leave Mars where he belongs, in the fancy of my imaginative nephew.

CHAPTER 10 —
Zetel has a close call

The gloom in the Landaw families deepened as the early days of September slowly passed by. News reports revealed there was significant resistance by the Polish army but German forces were closing in on Warsaw.

"I hope those agents Caiserman talked about were able to move quickly," Shloima said doubtfully.

The two families met even more frequently than before, listening carefully to the radio broadcasts, gleaning what they could from the newspapers, looking for any kernel of news that might provide some optimism. On Sunday, the tenth of September, Jack and Faigel Greenberg, Hershey and Sylvia Levitt joined them for tea and cake at Shloima's and Bessie's. They sat around the large dining table while the children had their milk and cookies in the kitchen. It was late afternoon, the sun low in the sky, the weather mild except for a light cold wind that flirted with the leaves on the trees still untouched by the autumn.

"This Wednesday evening we will have a lot to pray for," Bessie said glumly, "when Rosh Hashona (*Jewish New Year*) begins. I find it difficult to wish people 'gut yomtov' (*good holiday*) without choking up."

There was a sudden banging and shouting at the street door. Shloima ran to the balcony.

"The street is full of people. I can't tell whether it's a riot or a rally or what's going on."

"Let me find out," Jack said. They heard him open the front door and allow in a flood of excited voices. He returned after a few minutes. "We're at war. Canada has declared war on Germany. At least, that's what the crowd is saying."

Shloima snapped on the radio. They listened intently as station after station confirmed the news. "Well, we shouldn't be surprised," Shloima said. "The Prime Minister in his speech last week made it clear he would ask Parliament to approve so this is just the official outcome."

"Hitler will really be worried now," Hershey added sarcastically.

"Don't sell us short, Hershey," Jack said. "We did well in the Great War — Passchendael, for example."

"Besides, every man counts," Faigel insisted. "What would be really nice is if the US declares war on Germany. That would make Hitler take notice."

"It would be nice," Joseph agreed, "but it won't happen. They have declared their neutrality."

"I read FDR's speech in the paper. It sounds to me like he would really like to go against Hitler but can't get the support," Shloima said.

"Maybe he isn't trying hard enough," Sylvia said. "The US wasn't exactly welcoming Jews either during the last few years when they were trying to immigrate."

"Ettie, you're awfully quiet," Bessie said. "Have you given up all hope?"

"Hope? No. What I feel right now is shame — shame for being so stupid. That madman has said for years he would go after the Jews as soon as he could. And we didn't believe. We thought we were so part of German society, why would anyone want to harm us? So we all stayed, even after he came to power. We, personally, only managed to get out in time thanks to you, Shloima. We should have followed Einstein in '33. He, after all, is a genius. And we should have insisted our families come too."

"Ettie, geliebter, it was easy for Einstein. He had a job wherever he wanted and he had no trouble immigrating wherever the job was," Joseph said. "But we were happy in our little town, making a nice living, a comfortable house, lots of friendly neighbours. Sure we were uneasy when Hitler became Kanzler (*Chancellor*) but it took awhile before we realized how bad it was going to be. Besides, we thought we were doing right by getting our parents and grandparents to leave Germany."

"Ettie," Faigel said, "this is no time to start blaming ourselves. We did nothing wrong. I refuse to feel guilty. There is still a God in heaven and why He's allowing this to happen, I don't know. But the High Holydays are here in a few days and I shall pray that He puts an end to Hitler and the Nazis."

"Amen," said Shloima solemnly.

The Jewish New Year is not a celebratory event like its calendar counterpart but a period of grave reflection and introspection. It was even more so in the dark days of September, 1939 and was accompanied by despair and a sense of helplessness as the worshippers filed into the Fairmount synagogue.

"Now is not the time to forget our faith in the Almighty, in our sacred Torah, and in our people," the rabbi said in his sermon. Draped in his prayer shawl, his head covered with a black Homburg, a long white beard hiding most of his face, he stared out at the listless faces, aware that some had already received news of tragedies that affected them personally. "Now is the time to devote ourselves to prayer, to penitence for our sins, to show the Almighty that our loyalty to Him is not diminished by the burden placed on us. And we do this, not only for our own people but for the sake of all those who cherish what we cherish — the right to live in peace, the right to pursue our livelihoods, the right to raise our families in our traditions, the right to just and fair government.

"A few days ago, Canada joined the war against the Nazis. I do not naively believe that Canada has done so because of the injustices meted out to the Jews. The Prime Minister's anti-Semitism is well known. Rather, Canada, like Britain and France, has awakened to the fact that the monster and his corrupt ideology pose a threat to all. We must show our fellow citizens that we Jews will participate in the struggle. Therefore, I encourage all young men to consider signing up and everyone to find ways to help in this war."

"Yoisef, don't get any crazy ideas. You're already too old — you're thirty-five," Shloima said after the service and they were walking down Fairmount to his home for lunch. "Ettie needs you. I need you. We have too many uniform orders for the army and for the nurses for me to handle alone. You're a first class designer, and since you took over the cutting table, productivity is up and waste is down. The workers like you. The place hums. You can do more for the war effort by staying where you are."

After lunch, they walked up to Park Avenue and joined the crowds ambling along both sides of the street. All were in their holiday best: the men in dark suits, the women — at least those who could afford it — in the latest fashions, hats perched on the side of the head, hemlines now between ankles and knees, leather purses in brown, beige and black hanging from a shoulder or clutched under an arm, high heeled buckled shoes. While the good wishes that passed from group to group were well meant, a sadness permeated the gatherings.

The two Landaw families, after parading up and down for a couple of hours, slipped into Chez Emilie. The parents sat at one table with their coffee and cakes while the children were at the table next to them savouring ice cream slathered in chocolate sauce. The restaurant was busy, and hazy with the smoke of cigars and cigarettes.

Ettie was deep in conversation when she felt Zetel tugging at an arm.

"What is it, Zeesuh?" she asked, holding him affectionately against her.

"Gabriel who wants to dead me is in the corner," Zetel said, pointing further into the restaurant. "And I know the man with him. They are not nice men. We must run away."

Before Ettie could react, they were interrupted by the arrival of Jack and Faigel. In the greetings and good wishes that followed, Zetel, although acknowledged, hugged and kissed, found his concerns ignored. Impatiently, he tried to pull Joseph aside who was listening intently to Jack and the latest war news.

"Uncle Yoisef," Rivka said interrupting him, "Zetel really needs to talk to you."

Distracted, Joseph said, "Zetel, What is it?"

But Zetel was no longer there and Joseph went back to his discussion with Jack. Rivka saw Zetel leave the café and ran after him, followed by a curious Chaim.

Two men, sitting in a back corner of the restaurant, also saw Zetel leave. They quickly rose and left the table. A waitress stopped them and held up the bill: "Messieurs, l'addition, s'il vous plait."

The tall brawny man with the round face, broken nose and shock of unruly black hair, rummaged fruitlessly in his pockets. "Gabriel, no money." The other man, a little shorter than his companion, and dressed in an expensive blue suit, looked to the front door and said, "If we don't hurry, we will lose him." In desperation, he gave the startled waitress a gold coin, said, "Keep the difference," and both men pushed past the crowded tables, and edged discreetly around the Landaws and Greenbergs standing in the way.

"Hello," Bessie said, "I remember you. You're the nice Greek gentleman who came to our assistance when the baby was screaming. Mr...."

"Hegimoon, Parme Hegimoon. Sorry. No can talk now. Late. Must go," he said and turned towards the door.

"You!" exclaimed Jack as he caught sight of the other man. "You're the man who disappeared on me at the store. You created quite a problem for me. Tell me, what happened to you?"

Gabriel spoke quickly as he watched Hegimoon push through the front door and stand just outside. "I am sorry if I caused a disturbance. You were asleep. Both of you. I couldn't wait and left. If there are any amounts owing..." he said and made towards the door.

"No amounts owing," Jack called after him. "Come back anytime. Happy to serve you but wake me up next time."

"Yoisef," Ettie said, "that's the man who frightened Zetel but you see how nice and gentlemanly he looks."

"He looks gentlemanly because he's wearing the clothes I sold him," Jack said. "There's something funny there. I don't trust him."

"Where are the kids?" Shloima asked.

In blind terror, Zetel struggled to get the front door open and raced from the café. He paused momentarily and then plunged into the slowly promenading crowds of people. He weaved his way along, constantly looking back at the restaurant which he caught sight of through breaks in the crowd. In front of him and off to one side near the kerb, he saw the dark blue uniform of a patrolling policeman and ran over to him.

"Eh, petit guy, ou vas tu?" the policeman asked, holding Zetel by an arm, and bending down on one knee.

"There's a man coming to dead me," Zetel cried, tears streaming down his cheeks. "You must shoot him."

The policeman looked up but could see no immediate menace. "This can be very serious," the policeman said placatingly. "Where is the man?"

"He's in the restaurant over there," Zetel said pointing towards Chez Emilie.

"Let's go talk to him," said the policeman. "Where are your parents?"

"They're in there too."

At this moment, Chaim and Rivka caught up with Zetel.

"These are my cousins," Zetel explained.

"Zetel believes a man in the restaurant wants to kill him," Rivka said to the policeman.

"Don't believe a word," said Chaim. "They make up crazy things."

"Peutêtre," the policeman said. "But for the sake of my little friend here, I must investigate."

Through a break in the flow of people, Zetel saw Hegimoon and Gabriel standing in front of the café and looking around.

"There he is," Zetel shouted. "Shoot him!"

Gabriel spotted the children advancing with the policeman. He grasped Hegimoon's arm and propelled him into the crowd and both walked quickly away. Joseph came out of the restaurant, saw the children, and ran towards them.

Zetel, turned to face the policeman, kept on shouting, "Shoot him."

Joseph grabbed Zetel who screamed, "Don't let him take me. Shoot him."

The policeman put a restraining hand on Joseph. Ettie, following closely behind, heard her son urging the policeman to kill Joseph. Dread flowed through her as she remembered Dr. Zabinsky's words. "Zetel, no, it's your father."

Zetel realized it was his father holding him and said hurriedly to the policeman, "Don't shoot him. He's my papa."

"Who are you? What is going on here?" the policeman asked, clearly annoyed.

Joseph shook his head. "I don't know, Sir. I'm his father. Our boy suddenly left the restaurant."

"He told me a man wants to kill him and I should shoot him. Something or someone definitely frightened him."

"Zetelleh," Ettie said, wiping away his tears, "Who did you want the policeman to shoot? Surely not your papa."

His voice still breaking, Zetel said, "No, not papa. The man in the restaurant who wants to take me back to heaven. His name is Gabriel. I saw him come out of the restaurant. That's the man I want the policeman to shoot."

Joseph picked up Zetel and cradled him in his arms. "But Zetelleh, the only people who came out before us were Mr. Hegimoon and the nice gentleman with him whom Uncle Jack knows. You can't mean either of them."

"Uncle Yoisef and Auntie Ettie, those are exactly the two men Zetel is afraid of," Rivka said. "He saw them sitting in the back of the restaurant and when you wouldn't listen, he ran away. Then they came out from the restaurant and looked towards us and went the other way."

"So you see, Zetelleh," Joseph said, "they weren't after you at all."

"Maybe the policeman scared them off," Chaim said. "This sounds like a story from the Hardy Boys."

The Greenbergs and the Landaws pushed through the knot of curious onlookers that had gathered around. "What's going on?" Shloima asked.

The policeman pulled a notebook from a back pocket, flipped the cover back to reveal a blank page, and took copious notes. He wrote down a detailed description of the two men.

"I will make my report and I will also keep an eye open during the rest of my patrol. The boy was very frightened. He either felt they intended harm or his child's imagination ran away with him.

We will try to find the two but I urge you to be vigilant and if you see them, notify the police right away."

Ettie thanked the policeman for protecting her son and keeping him from running further. Any annoyance the policeman still harboured melted away as he stared into the large dark eyes of the beautiful white face framed by its cascading black hair.

"Madame, we will do our best to find and question these men," he assured her. "If you have any questions, please call the Police and ask for me, Jean François Lapointe. If I'm not there, anyone will be happy to help you. As for you, mon petit ami, you're parents will protect you so stay close to them." He inclined his head to Ettie, nodded to the others and left.

"I tell you there's something funny about the one Zetel calls Gabriel," Jack said. "That guy's up to no good. Yoisef, Ettie, don't let him get near Zetel. He might be the kind that likes little boys and Zetel is a pretty little fellow."

"Lots of people like children," Chaim said. "What's wrong with that?"

"We'll talk about it another time," Shloima said. "Bessie, I think you have to tell them the facts of life."

"I have to?" Bessie objected. "You've fathered two children. I never felt you were ignorant of the facts of life."

"What are the facts of life?" Rivka asked.

"It's about how babies are born," Chaim replied with an air of authority. "It's got nothing to do with the men Zetel thinks are after him."

"I know how babies are born," Rivka said. "We came out of mummy's stomach. Zetel says as soon as a baby is ready to come out, a soul is stuffed into it and that's why it's alive. Gabriel wants to take Zetel's soul back and Zetel doesn't want."

Shloima rolled his eyes. "This is all very interesting," he said, "but it's soon time for the evening service so let's start walking towards the shul (*synagogue*)."

"If you don't mind, Shloima," Joseph said. "I'd like to get Ettie and Zetel home while it's still daylight and stay with them. I'm rather nervous about what happened."

"Sure, Yoisef, see you tomorrow."

Police Officer Lapointe sauntered slowly along Park Avenue, paying close attention to the faces he encountered. He indulged in the thought of finding the two men and requesting the beautiful woman to identify them. Just to see her again would be sufficient reward. As he neared the corner of Park Avenue and St. Viateur Street, his wish seemed to come true. There, waiting for the light to change, were two men who matched the description. Lapointe had caught a glimpse of one of them at the restaurant — the brawny fellow with the shock of black hair.

He approached carefully and stood just behind them. The light changed and he followed them across the street. They continued walking and passed Jeanne Mance Street when the two turned to face him.

"Why you follow us?" asked the brawny one.

Gabriel put a restraining hand on his companion. "Sir, we are both new to this country. Have we done something wrong?"

"An incident took place in Chez Emilie, and I am investigating it," Lapointe said.

"We were in Chez Emilie a little while ago," said Gabriel. "However, we saw no incident."

"The incident involves a boy and his family, and a suspicion that you mean the boy harm." The policeman rocked back on his heels and stared hard at the men. The brawny one narrowed his eyes and flushed with anger. The other showed no sign of emotion.

"Sir, this cannot be. We were simply having a cup of coffee in the restaurant, discussing some important business. We were not even aware of anyone else. Surely there must be some mistake," said Gabriel.

"Possibly, but nevertheless I require your names, addresses and identification," the policeman insisted in the firm authoritative voice he had been taught to employ. "Otherwise, I will have to ask you to accompany me to the Police Station."

Hegimoon's fist landed squarely on the policeman's jaw, knocking him back, down and out.

"Why did you do that?" Gabriel demanded.

"You can go back to heaven. I stuck here," Hegimoon said, slapping aside a man who tried to stop him. He and Gabriel both fled down Jeanne Mance Street.

"You're too impulsive," Gabriel berated him. "We could easily have talked our way out of it. Nobody will believe the boy. Now we've attacked an officer of the law and resisted arrest. We are in real trouble."

"The god of war does not take orders from a mortal," Hegimoon said grandly.

"You're no longer the god of war. You're a mortal yourself," Gabriel said.

At the Fairmount Street end of Jeanne Mance, he saw a police car turn the corner and come towards them. " They can't be after us yet. They've been called to the corner. Stop running. Walk slowly. Pretend we're deep in conversation," he said to Hegimoon.

The god of war did not heed Gabriel's warning. The police car swept past them. The sudden screech of its brakes warned them they had not escaped notice.

"Quickly, in here," Gabriel said and leapt down a small flight of stairs to a basement apartment. He gestured, the door opened, and they fled into the apartment, closing the locked door behind them. There was no one in the apartment. They raced out the back door into a laneway.

"What now?" asked Hegimoon.

"I am taking you back to Greece," Gabriel said. "You can help your countrymen fight the Italians. I won't be needing you again."

Despite an intensive search of the area by dozens of police, the two fugitives could not be found.

Lapointe did realize his dream of seeing the beautiful woman again. Joseph and Ettie visited him in hospital where he was recovering from a broken jaw and a concussion.

Gabriel noted with some relief as he approached the Arc of Souls that the massive cumulus cloud of vertical development that greeted him was not black as he had feared but grey, and while it bubbled, burgeoned and surged unpredictably, it emitted few lightning bolts and the rolls of thunder were muted. Clearly, he was not going to be severely punished.

"You failed your mission completely," accused the angry Voice from within the cloud. "Not only is the soul you were supposed to bring back still occupying his host body, you and that idiot Mars are now the subject of a police search, and your descriptions are on every news broadcast and in all the newspapers."

" I beg Your forgiveness, Most Holy and Sacred One," Gabriel said, prostrating himself. " The soul is very resourceful and has ingratiated himself with his family who unwittingly protect him. If it is Your wish, I will return immediately."

"Fool! You cannot go back for a long time. You will be discovered and arrested. Besides, I cannot give the matter any more attention right now. The human race is in danger of annihilating itself and we must devote all our efforts to protecting My Creation. Try at least to do that right."

CHAPTER 11 —
Zetel in school

Months went by and no word was received from their families in Europe. The gloom in the Landaw households deepened and solidified into a permanent artifact of their consciousness. As such, it could be set aside, not ignored, but felt more as a gnawing pain that was usually tolerable enough to allow ordinary life to continue.

While the news from Europe during 1940 indicated successive failures on the part of the Allies to stem Nazi success, the war was having a beneficial effect on the Landaw factory. It operated full out, its order book overflowing with orders for uniforms for the Canadian Army and Air Force and for nurses of the Red Cross. Shloima constantly had to recruit new employees, mostly women, as many of the men joined the armed forces or sought employment in better paying military equipment industries.

Joseph had become an indispensable member of the production group. He managed the design and cutting operations and was responsible for Faigel's team of seamstresses and off-site sewing activities. Productivity and quality were high and completion dates were met. It allowed Shloima to search for more business and to secure financing for the business.

He was generous with his brother. Joseph's income increased to the point where he could afford a larger flat. They moved to the ground floor of a two storey building on St. Urbain Street just south of Bernard Street. Their new home boasted two bedrooms, a large kitchen and dining room and a double living room as well as a decent sized bathroom and an entrance hallway with a clothes closet. The flat was clean and recently painted.

Moishe Rappaport, the owner of the building, was a tall muscular man with a round clean shaven face, topped with greying black thick hair, a slightly hooked nose and a wide mouth with large lips. He lived upstairs with his wife Zelda and their twelve-year old daughter Beatrice.

On May 1st, moving day, Zelda greeted them as they arrived. A pleasantly plump woman, she gushed as she hugged and kissed Ettie and vigorously shook Joseph's hand.

"We're so happy to have you and really hope you'll enjoy our house. If you have any problems, we're just upstairs."

Zetel had been watching the movers unload their furniture and now came up to his mother and held her hand.

"What a beautiful boy!" Zelda exclaimed, lifted Zetel up and crushed him against her.

"That's our son Zetel," said Joseph proudly. "He's four and a half years old."

"Only four? I thought he was at least five or six. You're going to be a tall, handsome man," Zelda said as she put him down. "You will have lots of girlfriends."

"When I grow up," Zetel said, "I will marry Diana. She's my best friend. But first I will have to find her. I don't know where she lives now."

Zelda looked at Ettie questioningly. "Zetel saw Diana's picture in a book," Ettie explained. "Diana the Huntress, a Roman goddess. He likes the picture and imagines she is real."

Zetel was about to insist she *is* real but realized he would not be believed and merely nodded.

Shloima and family joined them at the end of the afternoon and helped them unpack and move furniture around. Ettie prepared a quick supper of smoked meat on rye bread, pickles and coleslaw, washed down with whiskey and wine for the adults and soft drinks for the children.

The Rappaports came down and introduced Beatrice, a somewhat less plump but equally pleasant version of her mother. She immediately took charge of the children, telling them all about the neighbourhood and the friends Zetel was likely to have.

Towards the end of the evening, Moishe said, "Yoisef, there's one thing I must show you. Even though it's springtime, we will still get cold days and maybe even snow."

Joseph followed him to a door off the hallway and descended a circular wooden staircase into a large dug out earthen floor basement. At the far end of the room was a coal furnace from which radiated hot water pipes to connect with the heating radiators on the floors above.

"All you have to do, mostly during the winter, is order a ton of coal from the coal yard at the corner. Then, before you go to work, when you come home, and before bed, shovel the fire box in the furnace full. This keeps the building warm day and night. Hot water for washing is supplied by the boilers which run on gas. I'll pay for the coal, you do the shovelling."

Zetel had accompanied Joseph on the tour. The few overhead lights in the basement lit up the way to the furnace but threw shadows into the rooms deeper recesses and the mounds of earth heaped against the foundation walls. Suddenly fearful, Zetel clutched his father's hand tightly.

"I saw a shadow move," Zetel said, his voice trembling.

"As we move along, the shadows seem to move," Moishe explained. "Here's my flashlight. Shine it anywhere you want and you'll see there's no one here but us."

"Papa, you shine it," Zetel said. He stood behind Joseph and peered around him as the flashlight delved into all the corners.

"See, Zetelleh, there's no one there," Joseph reassured him.

"You don't have to worry," Moishe said. "The only other way anyone can get in is through that door." He pointed to a door opposite the furnace. "Make sure that door is always locked. You open it only to take out the ashes from the furnace, and garbage."

"Gabriel doesn't need doors," Zetel said. "He can go through walls."

"Gabriel?" Moishe asked.

"Gabriel is a man the police are looking for who tried to harm Zetel," Joseph explained. "But, Zetelleh, we haven't seen him since that day at the restaurant. Besides, he doesn't know we've moved and where you live now."

Zetel was silent. He knew Gabriel could find him but these grownups would not believe him.

"Don't you worry, Zetel," Moishe said. "If you see him, just tell me and I'll run him over with my truck."

Moishe Rappaport owned and operated a secondary materials business. He collected and sold residential and commercial castoff items. He specialized in refurbishing old mattresses and in cutting up and washing textile fabrics of any kind to be sold as 'wipers' to the automobile garages all over the city. As the war progressed, he also collected scrap metal which he sold to large scrap yards. He liked to think that the metal ended up in the war effort against Hitler.

A truck was his main operating vehicle which he supplemented occasionally with rental equipment. He employed three men and a woman — one helped him on the truck, two worked in his warehouse on Van Horne Street not far from St. Urbain Street and the woman ran his cubby hole of an office in one corner of the warehouse. Moishe was entrepreneurial by nature and a capitalist by conviction.

Zelda, on the other hand, was enraptured by the changes in Russia brought about by the Bolsheviks and then the Communist Party.

"Before we left Russia, it was a terrible place to live if you weren't an aristocrat or at least a landowner. If you weren't rich, life was miserable. That's why we came to Canada. Now Russia has taken all that money away from the upper classes and given it to all the people. Everyone is equal. Everyone is a tovaritch now. Lenin was great but Stalin is even greater."

Ettie was having tea with Zelda in the upper flat. After talking about the children and gossip in the neighbourhood, Zelda had launched into her passionate defense of Russian communism.

"Look at his picture," Zelda said ecstatically and pointed to a large photograph of Stalin hanging above the dining table where they were sitting. "Is that not the face of love for the common people?"

"But, Zelda," Ettie objected, "what about the thousands jailed or killed during the Great Purge? What about signing a pact with Hitler? What about the invasion of Poland? What about the…"

"Ettie, that's all propaganda from the capitalist countries," Zelda interrupted, flailing her arms. "Some people either didn't understand or stood in the way of his vision for the new Russia. They schemed against him. It needed stiff resolve on his part to keep Russia from falling back to where it was before 1917. And why should he oppose Germany? A capitalist country at war with other capitalist countries. No, once these capitalist countries destroy each other, communism will take over."

Ettie allowed the barrage to pass over her, sipped her tea reflectively for a moment, and then said, "Zelda, Canada is one of the capitalist countries fighting Germany. Do you want to see Canada destroyed? A Jew can at least survive here."

"Canada has made a choice," Zelda responded obstinately.

"Zelda, your husband works hard at his business and provides you with a nice living. If you were still in Russia, he would be in Siberia. If communism came to Canada, he would be among the first to be arrested and dispossessed. Be careful what you wish for."

Zelda was silent. Ettie had identified the one flaw in her Russian Communism fervour. She loved her husband and was proud of his achievements. He had told her many times he would never accept communism and referred to Stalin as "that butcher." He was contemptuous of the Jewish support for Fred Rose, labour activist and candidate for the Communist Party of Canada. Ettie was right. In a communist Canada, her husband would not fare well nor would his family. Perhaps communism wasn't right for Canada but it was definitely right for Russia.

They dropped the subject and talked of the pleasures of the balmy summer weather and beaches that were open to the public.

Zetel liked his new home. He had a room all to himself just off the dining room. A window gave him a view of the back yard, a cemented space partly hemmed in by the garage housing Mr. Rappaport's truck, a staircase that led to the upper flat, and a narrow corridor which ended at the gate to the laneway.

He still feared the return of Gabriel and vigilantly sought for signs of the Archangel. When after several months, none was forthcoming, he began to relax and to enjoy his new friends in the neighbourhood.

"There is no sign of Gabriel," he told Rivka and Chaim on one of their visits.

"Maybe he doesn't know where you live now that you've moved," suggested Rivka.

"It's not that way at all," Chaim insisted. "These were two bad men who wanted to kidnap Zetel for ransom. The police scared them off. They won't come back."

Zetel was not so sure. "Gabriel will come back. He told me once I must return to the clouds soon. And I remember now the man with him. He is Mars, god of war, who hates me because I stopped him from hurting Diana."

"Zetel, you should write fairytales," Chaim said, laughing.

"Zetel," Rivka said, "don't tell Chaim anything. He doesn't understand. He just makes fun of you. When you go to school in September, don't tell anyone about Gabriel. They will only laugh at you."

Zetel was two weeks short of his fifth birthday when he started school on the day following Labour Day. Both Ettie and Joseph walked with him that first day, along Bernard Street past the large Catholic Cathedral, its bells ringing out urging the devout to prayer, and up the long block of Esplanade Street to the school.

Edward VII Elementary School was Protestant open to all denominations in the Quebec system that split education between Protestant and Catholic religions. Both Joseph and Ettie were quite secular in their thinking. Rather than send Zetel to one of the Jewish parochial schools, they chose a public school education for him. For his Jewish education, they arranged for him to study with a rabbi in a cheder (*small private tutorial school*) three times a week, an hour each time, where he would learn the Hebrew alphabet and to read the Torah (*the first five books of the Old Testament*).

Zetel was awed as he and his parents stood in front of Edward V11 Elementary School, a large, rectangular, four storey building with a school playground at either end.

"This is bigger than the boat where I was born," he said, his tone hushed.

Joseph looked at him quizzically. "How do you know anything about that ship?"

He was about to explain that when still a small cloud, he had a full view of the ship as he flew inside it. He sensed the wave of disbelief that would emanate from his parents and instead said, "The picture you showed me in your camera book. It doesn't look as big as this school."

He saw both parents visibly relax. "The boat may not look big in the picture," Ettie said, tousling his hair, "but it was much larger than this school. Don't forget, part of it was underwater and doesn't show up in the picture. You were born in the part below water."

Zetel settled easily into the Kindergarten class led by Mrs. Candlish, an older woman with many years teaching experience. She regaled them with stories of her brave husband who had died in battle near the end of the Great War. Very devout in her religious beliefs, she frequently told them that just as her husband had given his life for Canada, Jesus had sacrificed his on their behalf.

"You must love and pray to Jesus," she urged her five-year olds. "Be good and don't do bad things if you want to join Jesus in heaven someday. Remember, heaven is a place of joy, peace and contentment."

"Where we don't have to go to school?" asked one of Zetel's less ambitious classmates.

"Peter, you must raise your hand if you wish to speak," Mrs. Candlish said sternly. "If you're especially good, you might even be lucky enough to study with Jesus."

Zetel raised his hand.

"Yes, Zetel," Mrs. Candlish smiled approvingly. She rather liked this quiet, well brought up boy who listened avidly to everything she said, was quick to follow her directions, and participated eagerly with the other children in class projects. The only thing that puzzled her was his intense interest in Roman and Greek mythology whenever they visited the library.

"Mrs. Candlish, heaven is not a good place. When your body no longer works, you become a cloud again and go to the Arc of the clouds. There you have to wait, sometimes a long time, until you go to your next body. All you do is sleep. It's boring."

The benign expression on Mrs. Candlish's face as Zetel began to speak turned to horror as he finished.

"Zetel," she admonished him, "what you're describing is reincarnation. That is a pagan belief. Christians — and Jews as well, for that matter — do not believe in reincarnation. When we pass on, we go either to heaven if we've been good and accepted Jesus or to the place below where we are punished. I don't know where your fanciful idea comes from but I don't want to hear it anymore." She made a mental note to call his parents.

There was tension in the classroom during the rest of the day. Mrs. Candlish made it clear she was displeased with Zetel, and her displeasure pervaded the class. His classmates didn't quite understand what had so shocked the teacher but blamed him for the withdrawal of her warmth. After school, Beatrice came looking for him to take him home and noticed he was standing apart from the other boys.

"Did you have a fight, Zetel?" she asked. Zetel, sullenly, did not answer.

Zetel was silent on the way home and refused to talk with Beatrice. As part of her child minding task, she escorted him to the cheder which was at the corner of St. Viateur and St. Urbain Streets, a block from where they lived. Beatrice was allowed to stay on the premises and do her homework while waiting for Zetel.

The rabbi, white haired, bearded and spectacled, was slight in build and slighter in patience. He carried a 12-inch wooden ruler which he used to point to the place in the book or to slap across the knuckles if the pupil did not respond quickly or correctly. Today the rabbi was intent on reviewing the first chapter of Beraishis (*Genesis*).

Zetel knew The-One-True-God had created the World and found the chapter interesting because it described how He had actually done it. In Jewish, he repeated to the rabbi each step in the process until he came to the creation of man in God's image. Zetel knew he should say nothing but he still rankled from Mrs. Candlish's anger. I know what I saw and what happened to me, he thought, so why can't I talk about it.

"Rabbi," he asked, "how can we know what God looks like? We never saw His face or his body. All we saw was a very large cloud and His voice coming out of the cloud and sometimes lots of thunder and lightning when He was angry."

The rabbi's face flushed. He scowled at his pupil, pushed his hat back on his head, and was about to strike him with the ruler but decided to control himself. "Child, do you disagree with our sacred Torah? Do you not know the Torah is the word of the Almighty? What do you mean all you saw was a cloud? Where did you see this cloud? Was this a dream?"

Zetel shrank back in his chair, wary of the ruler poised in mid-air, but pressed on. "When I was still a soul, before I was me, I saw the cloud and heard the Voice of The-One-True-God coming from it. Sometimes, He was angry with me or others and the cloud would turn black and make a terrible thunder storm. We were all afraid. But we could never look inside the cloud nor did He come out."

The ruler still hovered. "Is this a dream you had last night or something someone told you? Or a picture you saw in a bible with pictures?"

"No, Rabbi, I was there a long long time, many, many, many years, waiting for The-One-True-God to send me to the world."

The rabbi dropped the ruler, pulled his hat forward on his head, stood up and paced the room, muttering to himself, as he plodded through an intense debate with himself:

1. The boy speaks with great confidence, he believes he is telling the truth.
2. On the other hand, he could be crazy — crazy people believe they are truthful. But he shows no sign of being crazy.

3. Then again, he's smart, maybe even a genius. He's picked up the alphabet and can already read. Slowly, of course, and makes mistakes, but that is only to be expected. Yet, how can he know about souls. We haven't even reached that area of study.
4. On the other hand, we believe our bodies contain a soul, only we don't remember the time when we were a soul.
5. How can he possibly remember that blessed state? Why would the Almighty grant him this memory? Even our gaonim (*renowned ancient sages*) never commented on their time as a soul.
6. On the other hand, there is one soul that may remember. The Kabbalah tells us....no, this is not possible. He is only a little boy with a vivid imagination.

"Have you ever heard of the Kabbalah?" he said, standing over Zetel who shrank even further back in his chair.

"No, Rabbi."

"Those of us who are versed in the Kabbalah believe that the soul of the Meshiach (*Messiah*) exists since the beginning of time and travels from man to man as the Almighty determines to support his people in times of great trouble or change. The soul of the Meshiach may have rested in Abraham, in Moses, in David, in many others, perhaps now in ..." He caught himself. No use giving this boy ideas beyond his ability to comprehend. Besides, how silly he would feel if the boy went home and told his parents 'the rabbi thinks I'm the Meshiach.' No, better to teach him as best I can, and look for signs of his holy status.

The rabbi picked Zetel up, hugged and kissed him, put him back down, put away the ruler in a desk drawer, and said, "Let's continue your lesson. Please make sure you understand everything I teach you. Do not hesitate to stop me if I'm going too quickly for you."

On the way home that evening, Zetel told Beatrice the rabbi was now very nice to him but Mrs. Candlish had said he was bad.

"Now, why would she think you are bad, Zetel? If I become a teacher, I would love to have a whole class of boys like you."

"I told her heaven is not a good place. It's boring there," Zetel explained. "She became angry and the other children blamed me for getting her mad and wouldn't talk to me."

"Was she talking about Jesus?"

Zetel nodded. Beatrice, remembering her own days with Mrs. Candlish, said, "Zetel, just agree with everything she says and you'll have a good time in Kindergarten. As for the rabbi, if he's nice to you, that's wonderful."

Joseph worked late that night and when he returned home, Zetel was already asleep. After a quick supper, he and Ettie sat close together on the sofa in the living room, holding hands and listening to a concert playing softly on the radio.

"Yoisef, I received a couple of strange telephone calls this evening — before you came home," Ettie said, frowning. "They concerned Zetel."

Joseph was on the point of dozing off but looked at her enquiringly.

"The first was from Mrs. Candlish, you know, the very nice Kindergarten teacher, Zetel's teacher."

Not quite fully alert yet, Joseph nodded.

"I could tell she was upset with our boy, not angry, but stern on the telephone."

Fully awake now, Joseph sat up straight. "What's he done that would get her upset? At the Parents Teachers meeting with her just a couple of weeks ago, she was loud in her praise of him." A sudden thought struck him. "Did he talk about Gabriel or Diana?"

"Oh, no," Ettie said smiling mischievously. "It seems our son is a strong believer in reincarnation, a doctrine Mrs Candlish said that's contrary to Christian and to Jewish belief. She wonders where such heresy comes from."

"I've never heard him use the word," Joseph said. "I barely know what it means."

"He didn't use the word 'reincarnation,'" Ettie said. "He merely explained that before he was born, he was a cloud waiting for a body and when his body dies he will go back to being a cloud in heaven waiting for the next body. I've often wondered where souls went between jobs."

"Ettie, this is not funny," Joseph said. "Why would a well-trained experienced teacher take the imagination of a five-year old seriously?"

"Because she's very religious and is concerned for the soul of our little boy. I told her we would talk with Zetel."

Shaking his head, Joseph leaned back on the sofa and put an affectionate arm around Ettie.

"Would you like to hear about the second call?" she asked.

"I'm almost afraid," Joseph said.

"This one was from the Rabbi at the cheder. He was lavish in his praise of Zetel. 'Such a fine boy. A genius. A boy who with the right teaching may very well become a Tsadek (*saintly person*).' I thanked him for saying such nice things about Zetel. Then he begged me to allow him to continue Zetel's learning on a one-to-one basis and he would cut the usual fee in half. I said I would talk to my husband. Yoisef, that would bring his fee to what we're paying now for class instruction, so I really think we should agree."

"I don't mind agreeing," Joseph said. "It is strange, though. I wonder what made him suddenly so generous."

"I asked him that," Ettie said. "His reply was curious. 'The boy's soul remembers.' He would not explain further but seemed very excited."

Joseph shrugged. "Not bad for a day's work for our boy. He has a soul that flies from body to body and remembers. The teacher thinks he's a heretic, the rabbi sees Tsadek written all over him. We always considered him our miracle baby. Perhaps he's more of a miracle than we think."

Almost in unison, they arose and went to Zetel's room and looked in. He was sound asleep, lying on a side, clutching his favourite stuffed teddy bear, the blankets partly thrown off.

"Even miracles need sleep," said Joseph.

CHAPTER 12 —
Zetel and the boarder

December of 1941 was a bitterly cold month and the weather showed no sign of letting up as New Year approached. By the end of the month, a foot of ice and snow lay on the ground, impeding wheeled traffic and pedestrians and causing horses pulling sleds to slip and slide. The main streets, including St. Urbain Street, were plowed, the snow pushed up in banks along the sidewalks.

Heads bent against the wind, faces covered with scarves or partially protected by the upturned collars on their winter coats, Joseph and Ettie's New Year's Eve guests passed happily into the hallway of their home, sighing with relief as the warmth hit them. Shloima and family were first to arrive and Rivka and Chaim were designated, along with Zetel, to take the guests' coats and place them on Zetel's bed.

The house was decorated with streamers and colourful twisted crepe paper and balloons hung everywhere. An urn of hot mulled wine on the dining table greeted each guest who gratefully filled a mug and slowly sipped the steaming liquid.

"Thank you, Yoisef and Ettie," said Sylvia Levitt, cupping her hands around the mug, "because of this hot wine, I might even survive. Hershey, tell me again. Why do we live in this country?"

"Because we like it here," Hershey answered as he shook Joseph's hand and kissed Ettie on each cheek. "Besides, it's hot in summer, so on average we're ok."

"You're hand is cold, Hershey," Jack Greenberg said, pumping Hershey's hand. "It's time you bought yourself a pair of gloves, and I know just the place."

"Let me guess," Hershey said and kissed Faigel. "I bet the best place to shop for gloves is the Men's Department at Eaton's."

"Hershey, you're a mind reader," said Jack.

"Sell him something for his face, too," Faigel said. "His lips are cold."

"In my experience, at the right moment, his lips are not cold," Sylvia said.

"Yoisef and Ettie, what kind of people do you invite?" demanded Hershey. "This is a New Year's Eve party, I'm hardly in the door and the Greenbergs want to sell me things."

"If that's bad," said Issie Goldenstein, as he pushed his bulky body into the dining room and made for the mulled wine, "I'm glad I left my catalogue at home."

"Issie, say hello first," ordered Dobresh from the doorway.

Ettie laughed, "It's alright, Dobresh, I'd rather he warms up first."

Dobresh hugged and kissed Ettie. "Your Zetel is so handsome and such a good boy. I like his knickerbockers and stockings and he's wearing a shirt and tie. He's just a vision. And your children are also growing up, Bessie. Rivka is really a young lady now in her skirt and blouse and Chaim a real gentleman in his suit with a shirt and bowtie. Such lovely children. You are so blessed."

The Rappaports arrived at that moment and Joseph introduced them to the other guests. Moishe was dressed informally in brown slacks and a turtle neck sweater that Zelda had knitted. Zelda had put on her best outfit for the occasion, a black silk skirt with a long sleeved white cotton blouse and a burgundy wool jacket. Beatrice wore a flowered print dress that fell just below her knees. Her long brown hair was tied in a ponytail which emphasized the dimpled roundness of her face and large blue eyes.

Hershey said, "You must be Eskimos. How else do you go out without coats?"

Chuckling, Joseph explained they lived just upstairs. "Moishe is our landlord."

"Oh, oh, Yoisef" Sylvia said. "Now we'll have to behave. We don't want the Rappaports to discover what kind of family you have."

"I already know what kind of family he has," Moishe said. "He's a wonderful tenant and I do business on a regular basis with Shloima. If you're all like them, you're a nice family."

"I can support what my husband says," Zelda added, as she and Ettie exchanged hugs.

"Well, since we're all here," Joseph called out, "fill your glasses — there's the mulled wine or other wine or whiskey on the table —and let's toast 1942 and all those on the front line in the fight against the Nazis."

There was a clatter and tinkling of glasses as the party helped themselves. Bessie poured soft drinks for the children including Beatrice. They raised their glasses and gave a resounding "L'chaim" (*cheers, literally: to life*).

Issie had downed his glass of wine in one gulp and quickly refilled it. "I think we better do some more toasting. So far, the war isn't going that well for the Allies and the whole world is in it now. We thought the Great War was big enough but it's starting to look like a family squabble compared to what's happening now. Where's the Aibershter (*Almighty*)?"

"Issie, it's easy to get depressed," Shloima said, "but right now, I'm feeling optimistic. Sure, Britain is having a tough time what with the bombardments and some of their defeats on land and sea. Sure, the Germans seem to be winning and have scooped up most of Europe. But now the Americans have joined the fight. Now there's a real force the Nazis will have to face. You'll see, things will soon start turning around."

"But the US is fighting the Japanese as well," Ettie objected. "The Americans will be spread everywhere."

"That's right," Sylvia said. "All my US cousins have had to register for the draft and expect to go to the Pacific, not Europe. The US may be large with a large army, air force and navy but because of the war in the Pacific, Hitler will see only a small part of American might."

Sylvia had been born in the United States and had emigrated to Canada when she met Hershey at a wedding in New York.

Hershey stared at her in admiration. "Sylvia, I never knew you're an expert on military matters. Shloima, I don't want to sound like a wet blanket, but Sylvia's right. The Allies are shut out of Europe since the Dunkirk evacuation. So what can the Americans do? Join the fight in Africa, I suppose. So we capture Africa, so what?"

"Never mind the Americans," Zelda said. "The Nazis made a big mistake when they attacked Russia. Stalin will finish them. Look, already, he's beaten them off at Moscow. Soon he'll kick them out of the Soviet Union altogether. That's the power of communism."

"Well, apart from Moscow, the Germans are all over Russia," Hershey said. "So if you think communism has power, the Russians better start rushin'."

"You young people have no idea," Zelda said, offended by the remark and the lightness of tone. "Stalin was taken by surprise by the German invasion. It's difficult to be prepared for a war you didn't expect. You'll see the German army run once the Russians get going."

"Zelda," Shloima said, "the Russians are helped right now by winter weather which is even worse than here in Montreal. The German army may have to stall for a few months but when spring and summer come, they'll make up for it. Mind you, the country is so large, the German army couldn't possibly occupy all of it. The hope I see for the Allies is that fighting the Soviets will keep the Germans busy and take away some of their army from Europe."

"Let's stop planning the war," Ettie said, smiling graciously and looking ravishingly beautiful in a black evening dress that clung provocatively to her. "Leave that to the generals. For a few hours, let's forget about all the terrible things happening in Europe and just enjoy ourselves. There's a card table set up in the living room and the kitchen table can serve as another if you don't mind the heat and smells coming from the oven."

"Ok, Hershey, Faigel and I will take on you and Sylvia in a no holds barred game of Gin Rummy. Just a warning though — I won the championship at my club."

"Sylvia and I accept the challenge but we didn't bring any money," Hershey said.

"Jack will take promissory notes," Faigel cut in. "But don't worry, Hershey. The championship that Jack won was for Pool."

The four filled their glasses and debated which table to take.

"There's no way I can concentrate when Ettie is cooking," Faigel said. "Let's go to the living room."

"But, Faigel," Sylvia objected. "if we're in the kitchen, we get first pick as the food comes out."

"It's fine for you, Sylvia. Nothing seems to affect that figure of yours, but those of us with more mature features take pains to avoid temptation. I vote for the room furthest from the kitchen." Faigel grabbed Jack and pulled him towards the living room.

"In a purely democratic vote," Hershey intoned solemnly, "the 'Aye' has won." He and Sylvia followed them.

"I'm not a card player," Zelda said, "so the rest of you go ahead and I'll help Ettie."

"Moishe, I know you're a card player," Shloima said. "But I'm not going to play Poker with you. Not after that last game. Why don't you join the rest of us for Gin Rummy."

"And here I thought I was going to make some money tonight," Moishe chuckled and followed the others into the kitchen.

"What would you children like to do?" Ettie asked.

The four, absorbed in a heated conversation, were sitting on the floor in the hallway. The talking paused as Ettie approached. Zetel looked angry, Rivka indignant, Beatrice uncertain and Chaim smug.

"Auntie Ettie," said Rivka, "Chaim is making fun of Zetel, calling him a cloud, and laughing about Gabriel."

"Now, that's not very nice, Chaim," Ettie said. "Especially not at a New Year's Eve party. Zetel, why don't all of you go into your room and you can play records on that gramophone we just bought. Show Chaim how to wind it up. And not too loud."

Beatrice hung back for a moment. "Is it true, Mrs. Landaw? Zetel believes he was once a cloud and that Gabriel wants to kill him?"

"Beatrice, Zetel is a very clever boy with a wild imagination. We just ignore his idea that he was once a cloud, but there is a Gabriel who wants to harm him. We don't know why. But we haven't seen this Gabriel again since the Police went after him. Chaim shouldn't make fun of Zetel. Perhaps you could remind him if he starts again."

As the evening wore on, the sound of laughter and banter from the living room and the kitchen, and the music coming out of Zetel's room accompanied by Beatrice and Chaim singing told Ettie the party was successful. With Zelda's help, she took out of the oven and served platters of hot hors d'oeuvre and cold noshes (*snacks*).

"There's no formal meal tonight," Ettie announced. "So feel free to eat as much as you want of the appetisers. Everything's on the dining table so just help yourselves."

There were dishes of spinach filled bourekas, kreplach stuffed with ground beef, potato knishes, chicken liver pâté mixed with rendered chicken fat and fried onions, a plate of smoked salmon with capers and onions, a large platter of smoked meat, bite size squares of carrot and potato kugel, a large bowl of coleslaw, a large bowl of herring tidbits in vinegar and wine, and baskets of sliced challah, black bread and bagels, followed by date and nut mandelbrot with tea or coffee.

"Without a formal dinner, I don't know whether I'll last till midnight," said Issie as he lined up with the others at the dining table to fill his plate.

"If on top of all this, there was a formal dinner, we'd all need ambulances to get home," Sylvia said.

"Issie," Dobresh cautioned, "remember, you're on a diet. Only one slice of bread."

"So can I help it if Yoisef cuts them so thick," he said, taking two slices of challah and holding them tightly together.

"Herring and coleslaw are my addiction," said Faigel.

"My addiction is food," said Jack. "Especially everything on this table.

"Ettie, give up your mad career as a housewife and go into catering," Hershey advised her. "Your Uncle Issie can help you with the funds."

"Where's your money?" Issie asked.

"I'm a little short right now," Hershey said trying to look woe-begone.

"We'll all help her," Jack said. "The only condition, apart from the usurious interest we'll charge, is to be able to eat the product as often as we want."

"From what I see now," Joseph said, "with that condition, there'll be no profit in the business. Besides, Ettie will soon be busier since we're getting a boarder, a German man."

"Have you heard anything more, Yoisef?" Moishe asked.

"Yoisef, don't tell me Shloima isn't paying you enough that you have to take in boarders," Hershey said.

Shloima shook his head. "Hershey, in case you've forgotten, there's a war going on and Jewish refugees are now being admitted to Canada. The Jewish Agency is scouring the neighbourhoods looking for places to put them."

"We told the Agency we have place for one," Joseph said. "We can set up the backroom as a bedroom. I was using it to design and size patterns but I can move that to the basement. I hope if the Agency contacts you, you'll find a way to help. I remember how we felt when we sailed for Canada, how relieved we were when we were admitted. We couldn't turn down the Agency's request."

"It's what I would expect of you two," Faigel said. "Have you met him yet?"

"No," Ettie said. "The Agency told us something about him. He's a banker from Frankfurt, about 50 years old with no family. Since he's German speaking, there should be no problem with language in our house and, according to the Agency, he also speaks English. The day after Kristallnacht, he decided it was time to leave, so he escaped, first, to France, and when the French capitulated, to Spain. So far, the Spaniards are not turning over their Jews to the Nazis but the Agency is not taking any chances, and trying to move refugees to Canada or the US."

The telephone rang at that moment and Joseph went to the kitchen to answer it. Ettie could hear the conversation was in German but with the laughter and bantering of the guests was unable to understand what Joseph was saying. A few minutes later he returned.

"Speak of the devil, that was the boarder," Joseph said. "He realizes it's New Year's Eve but would like to meet us and our family and friends, to make sure there will be mutual satisfaction in the arrangement."

"But we're not ready for him," Ettie protested. "The backroom is not even set up."

"He knows that and will not stay but will return to his dormitory until the scheduled day, February 1st. Ettie, I told him it was alright to pay a visit. I hope you others don't mind."

"How did he know we're all here?" Jack asked.

"He smelt the food," Hershey said. "Besides, I look forward to meeting a banker."

"Hershey, he's a banker without a bank," Sylvia said. "That won't do us much good."

"Is there enough food?" Issie asked. "This is too good to share."

Ettie laughed, "Don't worry, Uncle Issie. I know you have a good appetite. There's lots to eat. Yoisef, how's he getting here? The dormitory is downtown."

"He said he'll take a taxi but I warned him on New Year's Eve it will be difficult to find one. Let's just go on with the party. When he gets here, he gets here."

They filled their plates and glasses again and returned to their places to eat and drink. Hardly had they settled when the doorbell rang.

"He must have hailed an airplane," Hershey said.

Ettie and Joseph welcomed the man who stood in the doorway. Joseph helped him take off his fur trimmed overcoat and black Homburg hat. All the guests gathered in the living room to greet him.

A man of average height, he was impeccably dressed in a black pinstriped suit with a grey vest, a white starched shirt with raised collar and black bowtie. A somewhat long face sported a trim black beard, topped with carefully combed greying hair. Dark eyes looked out through Prince Nez glasses perched on an unassuming nose. To the assembly of family and friends, he presented an attractive, almost courtly appearance, evoking a time in the swiftly receding past when he could mingle freely with those in the upper echelons of society.

He bowed to Ettie and Joseph and to the guests and then announced: "Meine Damen und Herren, Ich wunsche ihnen einen herzliches Neues Jahr und alles gute in zvei und vierzig."

"If you don't understand what he's saying," Joseph explained, "he's wishing you all a happy New Year and everything good in '42."

"I can speak English but no Jewish or Hebrew," the man said in a remarkably unaccented voice. "My name is Ludwig Konrad Fuhr — at least, that is my German name. I am now called Louis C. Fuhr, the name I am told is better for Canada. One must not be German here."

Joseph introduced each guest.

"There are too many names to remember," said Sylvia, solicitously. "We will remind you."

"You are very kind, Frau Levitt, but as a banker, I had to remember the names of hundreds of clients," he said, bowing courteously to Sylvia.

"Are you actually Jewish?" Issie asked.

"My mother was, my father was not, Herr Goldenstein. To the Nazis, it is all the same."

"Herr Fuhr," Shloima asked, "given your background, will you be able to return to your profession?"

"Regrettably, it does not look possible, Herr Landaw," he replied with a disconsolate shake of his head. "I have made inquiries but even Herr Bronfman, despite his best efforts, could not assure me of a place. Beginning the day after tomorrow, I will begin employment with Phillips Styling for Gentlemen."

"Selling suits?" Bessie exclaimed.

"No, I'm sure he will be in their back office on the accounts," Faigel said.

Fuhr smiled. "Thank you for your confidence in me, Frau Greenberg, but it will be as Frau Landaw says. I will be selling suits and articles of clothing for gentlemen. The Jewish Agency helped me get this position."

"But this must be difficult for you," Jack said. "It's quite a drop from being a banker. In fact, many banking executives are clients of Phillips. You will be serving people who were once your peers."

"Thank you for your concern, Herr Greenberg," Fuhr said. "However, it has been a while since I had to leave my bank, and in the meantime, in France and in Spain, I held even more menial positions in order to eke out my savings. No, I am looking forward to beginning my employment and, having met my hosts, Yoisef and Ettie Landaw, and their family and friends, to moving here and getting to know you better."

"Herr Fuhr, as a banker, I suppose you do not accept communism," Zelda said.

"Zelda, leave it alone," Moishe muttered, annoyed.

"It is not a problem for me to answer your wife, Herr Rappaport," Fuhr said smiling, showing remarkably white and even teeth. "You are quite right, Frau Rappaport, I believe communism is not an effective economic doctrine, especially as it is practised in Russia under Stalin. However, I do have respect for some of its social policies."

"Come, let's stop badgering Herr Fuhr with questions," Ettie said. "Can we offer you something to eat and drink? Hopefully, we can improve upon the dormitory food."

"Hopefully?" Dobresh chimed in. "Mr. Fuhr, you need not worry. Ettie is a great cook."

"Frau Goldenstein, I have not the slightest worry," he said as Joseph and Ettie accompanied him to the dining table.

"This man is pretty amazing," Hershey observed. "He remembered everybody's name. He's dressed better than our revered Prime Minister. And he doesn't seem to mind that he's going to be a floor salesman in a haberdashery shop. You know, Jack, I might even go there for gloves."

"Vai iss mir (woe is me)," Jack said, pretending to tear out his hair. "Another disloyal client. Just a piece of advice, Hershey — my prices are lower."

"This food is indeed excellent," Fuhr said and lifted his glass in a toast to Ettie. "My compliments to my gracious hostess."

At that moment, the four children came out of Zetel's room.

"So many children?" Fuhr said, worriedly. "I was told there is only one."

"There *is* only one, Herr Fuhr," Joseph said and pulled Zetel forward. "The taller young lady is Beatrice Rappaport who lives upstairs, Chaim and Rivka Landaw are my brother's children and live, of course, with their parents, and this is our Zetel, who is now six years old. Children, this is Mr. Fuhr who will be living with us soon."

The children greeted him politely and began peppering him with questions which he answered, smiling affably. Zetel held back shyly and then asked, "Have you been to this country before?"

"No, I arrived only two months ago. It is a nice country but very cold," Fuhr said.

Zetel nodded but the frown on his face deepened. "Do you know Gabriel or Mars?" he asked.

Fuhr looked perplexed and Joseph intervened. "Zetel, Mr. Fuhr does not look at all like Gabriel or Hegimoon, he is a refugee from Germany like us, and he has only recently arrived. Remember, we explained to you that he needs a place to stay, and he came tonight to meet us."

Joseph turned to Fuhr. "Our son had a bad experience about a year ago. Two men tried to kidnap him, assaulted a police officer who accosted them, and escaped. Zetel is worried they will come back."

Fuhr shook his head and looked sympathetically at Zetel. "What a terrible thing to happen. I can assure you, young man, not only will I not harm you but I hope we can become good friends."

He reached out and gently took Zetel's hand. The warmth of his hand and manner suffused Zetel with a glow of peace and amity. He smiled but decided to hold judgement until they became better acquainted.

"There, mein Zeesuh (*my sweetie*), you have a new friend," Ettie said, beaming happily at both Fuhr and Zetel. "Now, please let the poor man enjoy his meal."

After he had eaten, Fuhr suggested that he should return to his dormitory having inflicted himself for too long on their celebrations.

"The New Year is in the half-hour," Joseph said. "Please wait until then so we can all bring it in together."

As midnight approached, Joseph put on the radio for the final countdown. Their glasses full and raised, they shouted their welcome to 1942, with hugs and kisses all around. Through the crowd of men and women, Fuhr caught Zetel watching him, his eyes squinting worriedly.

This is a clever, astute, suspicious boy, Fuhr thought. I shall have to work hard to gain his trust.

CHAPTER 13 —
Zetel wins a friend

Fuhr arrived at the Landaw household mid-morning on February 1st in the midst of a heavy snowfall. He pushed through the snow drifts that had accumulated on the margin of the street, and carried two heavy outsized valises up the few steps to the door. Before he could press the buzzer, Joseph opened the door, effusively greeted him, seized one of the bags, and, staggering under its weight, ushered him inside.

"Herr Fuhr," Joseph said, after he had helped the boarder shake off the snow from his homburg and coat and hang them up in the hall closet, "I envy your strength. I could barely carry your one bag and you seemed to have no trouble with two."

"I was better balanced with two," Fuhr said smiling. "Good morning, Frau Landaw," he said as Ettie came from the kitchen to greet him.

"Joseph, please show Herr Fuhr his room. Perhaps you would like to put your things away, Herr Fuhr, and then join us for lunch."

The room was furnished with a single bed against the back wall, beside it a small desk and chair, a large floor lamp that illumined both the desk and the head of the bed, a wardrobe with shelves and a space for hanging suits. Joseph also showed him the bathroom and a place where he could leave his toiletries.

At lunch, Fuhr was persuaded to take off his suit jacket, but he preferred to retain his vest, and agreed to loosen his tie. They ate in the kitchen. Zetel sat opposite Fuhr and was for the most part quiet.

"Our Zetel is a little shy at the moment," Ettie said.

"You need not be shy with me," Fuhr said. "The one regret I have in life is not to have had a child. Therefore, I look forward to knowing you better and hope you will see me at least as an uncle."

Zetel merely nodded and the adults turned their attention to discussing the war.

With Fuhr settled in, life was busier for Ettie who now had to prepare meals for four and ensure the extra room was kept tidy and clean. However, she didn't mind and enjoyed talking with Fuhr. In fact, both Joseph and Ettie were quite taken with Fuhr. He was clearly well educated, sophisticated in matters of books and art and, of course, business. He was a classical music enthusiast and quickly identified any piece of music broadcast by the radio. As an occasional gift, he would bring home a record they could play on the windup gramophone. They also went to concerts at the Forum in downtown Montreal. In general, they felt their intellectual world had expanded, had become lively and more interesting as a result of Fuhr.

Fuhr joined in quite happily with visits to and from Joseph's family and friends and was a sought after dinner guest. Moishe reported that he'd heard from the owner of Phillips Styling for Gentlemen that Fuhr had learned quickly and was an excellent salesman.

"You have a real find there," Sylvia said when she, Hershey, Ettie and Joseph were having a Saturday lunch at Schwartz' Delicatessen close to the Landaw factory. Joseph had joined them after the factory closed for the weekend. "He's lots of fun to be with. He's somewhat cold, though. He never seems to get excited about anything."

Ettie nodded. "In Europe, you would say he's correct. I know he can't stand crooners because he squirms every time there's one on the radio, or Beatrice brings down one of her records, or she and Chaim are singing something popular. Yet he will never say anything but even hums along with the music."

"Everybody seems to like him," Joseph added ruefully, "except Zetel. Our boy is polite but hangs back. Mr. Fuhr tries very hard to be friendly with him and I believe really likes Zetel but our boy does not respond. I asked him yesterday why he isn't more friendly with Mr. Fuhr. 'I'm sure I've seen him before,' our boy says. 'But Zetel,' I say to him, 'we haven't seen him before. How could you have seen him before?' Zetel gets that stubborn look on his face, 'I've seen him before.' I pull him onto my lap. 'Zetel, even if you've seen him before, that doesn't mean he's a bad man.' And then he says something that sends chills up and down my spine. 'Papa, every time I remember seeing someone, it's someone I know from the clouds, like Gabriel and Mars.'"

"Well, I can understand why you got chills," Hershey said. "The kid really has a fixation. Maybe you should seek professional advice."

"Absolutely not," Ettie stated. "My boy is not crazy. Dr. Zabinsky says he'll grow out of it."

"Ettie," Joseph objected, "he said that three years ago and if anything Zetel seems firmer in his beliefs."

"He's not exactly grown yet. Let's give him another three years," Ettie said.

"Does it really matter if he has this illusion?" Sylvia asked. "It doesn't seem to affect his day-to-day. Most religions, including our own, have ideas about bodies and souls and where they come from and where they go. How many Hindus are there? They all believe in reincarnation. So does our little Zetel. If he's crazy, then so are all the Hindus."

"Sylvia, there's a difference," Hershey said. "Hindus don't know anything about their past lives. Zetel believes he does, plus he's personally met angels and gods."

"No, Hershey, Sylvia is right," Ettie said. "Our little boy has a wild imagination but it doesn't harm anybody. He does well in the public school and the rabbi thinks he's a wonderful scholar. Whatever Zetel's reasons were for thinking Gabriel — if that's his name — and Parme Hegimoon are bad, he was right. Perhaps it was instinct, perhaps he imagined he saw them in his view of clouds and heaven, but he was right."

"You're saying we should just live with it, Ettie?" Joseph offered.

"Yes, Yoisef. Just like you grew out of your belief that a Golem existed, he will grow out of his idea that he was once a cloud."

"Sure, just like you, Sylvia. You stopped believing in Santa Claus at some point," Hershey said, reaching out and cupping her chin. "Sylvia used to hang up her stocking when she was a kid."

"I still believe in Santa Claus," Sylvia said, laughing. "Only I believe now his name is Hershey Levitt and he better not disappoint me, or I'll hang him up instead of my stocking."

"Does that apply to me too, Ettie," Joseph asked.

"No, Yoisef, I still believe in the Golem and you're my Golem, my hero who will protect me from all evil."

"Shall we go for a walk, Zetel?" Rivka asked, after they had finished the lunch Ettie had prepared for them. "It's really quite a nice day, not too cold. The winter will soon be over."

"Do you think my mother will mind?"

"No, she said it would be alright as long as we didn't go too far and came home while it was still bright day. Beatrice and Chaim said they would come with us." Chaim was visiting Beatrice while Rivka babysat downstairs.

They walked along Bernard Avenue towards Park Avenue. "Let's go to Woolworth's soda counter," Beatrice suggested. "Do we all have money?"

They had all received their weekly allowance Friday night and Rivka said she'd treat Zetel. They turned the corner onto Park Avenue, sauntered slowly past the cinema, looking into the various store windows. The street was busy with people and traffic, streetcars stopping at the corners, Saturday afternoon shoppers alighting with heavy bags, quickly seeking the shelter of the sidewalks. Zetel became nervous and looked from side to side and behind him.

"Is something wrong, Zetel?" Rivka asked, always sensitive to him.

"Don't tell me he's spotted Gabriel," Chaim said derisively.

"Someone is following us," Zetel said, keeping his voice low.

"Here we go again," Chaim shrugged. "Let's find a policeman."

"Chaim, don't make fun. You know what happened last time," Rivka said.

The group had stopped. Beatrice, turned to face them, looked back. "I don't see anyone who seems bad," she said and then waved, "Here comes your boarder, Zetel."

"Children, what are you doing here?" Fuhr asked pleasantly. "Hello, Zetel."

Zetel nodded. "My papa said you would be at work all day."

Fuhr laughed. "Don't tell my boss. I skipped out. I had some things to do. But where are you going?"

When he heard they were going to the soda bar, he offered to be their host, that it would give him great pleasure to enjoy a soda drink with them. They quickly accepted. This would save their allowance for other things.

They managed to find five stools together at the counter. Thanks to his magnanimity, they ordered whatever tickled their fancy and relished the sweet flavours of sodas, banana splits, and milkshakes. Fuhr told them jokes which they didn't always understand but laughed anyway. The ones they did understand, they found extremely funny.

When it came time to pay, he told the counter clerk he would have to find the money. They all looked at him in surprise and began to fear they would have to give up their allowances.

"Let me see," Fuhr said and reached long, empty fingers to Zetel's ear and pulled out a 25cent piece and placed it on the counter. He reached past Zetel to Rivka's ear and again pulled out a 25cent coin. "That's 50 cents," Fuhr said. "How much more do I owe you?"

"Another 50 cents, sir," the clerk said, smiling.

Fuhr stood up and reached for Chaim's ear and then Beatrice's and produced the 50 cents. The children laughed and applauded. The clerk collected the money and was about to turn away.

"Wait, young man," Fuhr said. "You deserve something for your good service."

He held out his hands, palm up and empty. He passed his left hand over his right and handed the 25 cents that appeared to the clerk.

"You are also a magician," Beatrice said as they left the store and were slowly walking back to St. Urbain Street. "Can you teach us that trick?"

"A magician never reveals his methods," Fuhr said. "Not even to good friends."

"I know how you did the trick," Chaim scoffed. "You had the quarter pressed against your hand by your thumb and then you just pushed it out into your fingers."

"Oh ho, we have a know-it-all," Fuhr said. "Then explain this." He held out all five fingers of his right hand. "See, there is nothing in them or in my palm." He reached up and pushed his fingers under Chaim's toque, ruffled through his hair and pulled out a dollar bill.

"How did you know it was there?" Chaim asked angrily.

"A magician never reveals his methods," Fuhr said equably.

"I know where that dollar comes from," Rivka said. "You stole it from Mommy's savings cup. You better put it back or I'm going to tell her."

"Chaim, I don't want to be friends with a thief," Beatrice said, glaring at him.

"Chaim will put the money back and won't do it again. Isn't that so, Chaim?" Fuhr said.

Grumpily, Chaim agreed, and sulking, walked away. "I'm going home."

At their house, Beatrice went upstairs. Fuhr excused himself and shut himself into his backroom, while Rivka and Zetel sat in the living room.

Rivka yawned. "Oh, I can hardly stay awake. I think I need a nap."

She stretched out on the sofa and promptly fell asleep. Zetel sat quietly waiting, fear caused him to shiver, but he resisted the urge to run from the house screaming. He heard Fuhr's door open and his footsteps creaking down the hallway. Fuhr stood in the doorway.

"Hello, Zetel, has your companion fallen asleep?"

"Yes, she needed a nap," he said, his voice quavering slightly.

"You need not be afraid of me, Zetel. I mean you no harm," Fuhr said, his voice warm and solicitous. "You and I just need a little talk."

"Your magic tricks were not tricks," Zetel said. "And you have hurt Rivka." Tears filled his eyes and he began to weep.

"She is not hurt, Zetel. She is merely sleeping so we can be alone, without interruption, and come to a friendly and mutually beneficial understanding. Even if we cannot, I will not harm any of you but will merely go away. I believe you know whom I am."

"Angel Lucifer. What do you want to talk about?" Zetel said.

Lucifer chuckled. "I haven't been called an angel in a long time. Now I have many names in addition to Lucifer — The Devil, Serpent, Satan, al-Dajjal, and so on. I offer my services to protect you from Gabriel and any other agents The-One-True-God sends to bring your soul back to the Arc."

"How can you protect me? The-One-True-God is stronger than you. He sent you down below with all the other bad angels," Zetel said.

"But I'm not down below. I'm here, Zetel, despite the orders of The-One-True-God. Except to the Arc and Heaven, I can go wherever I want. The-One-True-God is indeed stronger in power than I. He is omnipotent, omniscient, et cetera, et cetera, but the ones He selects to work with Him are not as bright as He and can be fooled. You, a mere boy, thwarted Gabriel on several occasions."

Lucifer sat down on the sofa chair facing Zetel.

"Suppose Gabriel comes back when you're at work and snatches me. How will you stop him?" Zetel asked.

"Gabriel cannot simply snatch you. That's not how things work. He would talk to you, try to persuade you to give up your soul, and if you refused, he could do nothing. You must understand how heavenly directives work. They can only work through agents or agencies. That's why Gabriel came with Mars. The pagan god could take direct action — that is, kill you — but Gabriel alone could not."

Zetel puzzled over this. "All right, suppose he comes again with Mars and you're at work. How will you protect me?"

Lucifer smiled, "Because I too have agents. I do not work alone. I have many loyal subjects who watch things for me, inform me of developments, and some keep an eye on you. I will know well in advance if there is a plot against you and can intervene. You have examples of my work."

"I do?" Zetel said.

"You remember me at your bris, do you not? I was warned that Gabriel would try to disrupt it, to provide him with more time to ensnare your soul. I ensured the bris went ahead. At the café, do you believe it was coincidence that a policeman happened to be on the scene just when you needed him? And today, I was informed you would be alone with Rivka while your parents were away and decided the time had come to reach an understanding with you. So you see, I am always aware of your situation."

"Why do you want to help me?" Zetel asked, still suspicious, still unsure.

"Wait, I will show you why," Lucifer said. Zetel heard him walk down the hall to the backroom. When he returned, he was wearing his black hat pulled down rakishly so only his dark eyes could be seen, and his ragged black coat.

"The lightning bolt The-One-True-God threw at me burned off pieces of my coat that lodged in your soul. Before your soul returns to the Arc, I must recover those pieces so my coat will be whole again and I will be complete in every respect. For this, I will protect you. I will do one more thing for you. When you are of age, I will find Diana for you. Would you like that?"

For the first time since Fuhr had come to their house, Zetel smiled and looked at him entreatingly. "I would like that very much."

"Will you promise then to be my friend and release your soul to me when it becomes available. In return, I will protect you all your Zetel life from the machinations of Heaven."

Zetel wasn't sure what "machinations" meant. "Do you mean protect me from Gabriel and his helpers?"

"Precisely," said Lucifer.

Zetel suffered a momentary doubt. Both Mrs. Candlish and the rabbi had warned him that those who accepted the temptations of the Devil would suffer immense punishment and pain.

"Will The-One-True-God be angry with me if I am your friend?" he asked. "Won't he send me down to that terrible place?"

Lucifer laughed. He sat on the sofa chair again. "The-One-True-God wants you dead and your soul recovered. How much angrier can he get. Besides, my followers and I roam the Earth. We are not imprisoned in that terrible place."

Zetel needed more assurance, "What happens to my soul once you take the black parts back?"

Lucifer shrugged. "Whatever you want. You can stay with me and be part of my following or you can return to the Arc and await your next body. You will have a lifetime to decide. So — what do you say?"

"I must discuss this first with my Papa and Mama. I'm too little," he said.

Lucifer shook his head. "No, Zetel, you must not discuss this with anyone, not even with your sleeping friend here. It must be our secret. You are not too little. You are billions of years old. I am addressing you, the soul, not the little body you inhabit."

Zetel still hesitated. "And you will find Diana for me when I'm ready?"

"That is my promise to you. In addition to finding Diana, I will defend and protect you, and there are many other ways in which I can help you if you are my friend."

Zetel was still undecided and squirmed in his seat, wishing he could ask his father or Rivka what to do. He believed Lucifer could protect him and the thought was an enormous relief to him. But he understood aligning himself with the Devil could be very dangerous.

"How do I know you can find Diana?" he asked.

For the first time in their discussion, Lucifer became impatient. "Zetel, you are delaying. While I can just walk away and leave you to Gabriel and his helpers, let me show you something that will convince you."

Although it was mid-afternoon and still quite bright, the room went dark. A point of light appeared over the sofa where Rivka slept and gradually enlarged until it filled the space almost to the ceiling. Zetel saw a sunlit plaza surrounded by magnificent buildings. The plaza was alive with people, some sitting at tables sipping coffee, some just strolling about, others shopping at the kiosks lining the sidewalks. Walking towards him was a woman dressed all in white with a starched cap perched on a head of blond hair. He gasped as her alabaster face and high ridged nose, seemingly chiselled out of marble, came into view. She smiled and waved, not to him he realized, but he smiled and waved back. The picture dimmed, evaporated, and the room was light again.

"When the time comes, I will ensure you find her," said Lucifer.

"She is my best friend," Zetel said between sobs. "I will be your friend."

"Excellent," said Lucifer and reached out to shake Zetel's hand. "Now, dry your tears, and look happy. I will allow Rivka to awaken and she must find us the best of friends."

Rivka sighed, opened her eyes, slowly sat up, yawned and stretched.

"Oh, I had such a good sleep," she said, and then remembering where she was, jumped up, "Zetel, are you alright?"

She saw both Mr. Fuhr and Zetel smiling at her.

"It must have been all that chocolate you ate, young lady," Fuhr said. "It slows the blood to the point of fatigue. I have been keeping Zetel company."

"He has told me interesting stories," Zetel said. "Luc…"

A warning glance from Fuhr stopped Zetel in mid sentence. "I mean, Mr. Louis C. Fuhr and I are good friends now."

Rivka regarded Zetel suspiciously for a moment and decided he was sincere.

"Mr. Fuhr," she said, "Zetel and I had planned to play Monopoly this afternoon. Would you like to join us?"

Fuhr chuckled, "As long as I can be Banker."

When Ettie and Joseph returned home late in the afternoon, they were delighted to find the three playing together. Zetel was clearly winning with piles of Monopoly cash in front of him. Fuhr jokingly pulled out the lining of his trouser pockets to show he was finished, and an exasperated Rivka complained that Zetel's luck was extraordinary.

"Gabriel!"

The Archangel saw the massive cloud of vertical development, black and launching lightning bolts in all directions, bearing down on him and prepared for the worst.

"The soul called Zetel has formed an alliance with Satan. I sent you down with Samael to finally bring him back. What happened this time?"

Gabriel relaxed slightly. There was no doubt The-One-True-God was very angry but He seemed prepared to discuss the issue instead of simply annihilating him.

"Most holy, most sacred, most omnipotent…"

"Enough, you fool. Just tell me what happened. I don't want sycophancy. I want answers," came the stern Voice.

"Yes, Holy One. Samael and I came across the soul walking with friends on a busy street. Samael was to arrange for an auto to careen off the road and crush the soul's body. I didn't want the other children hurt and waited until the boy was closest to the road. Just as I was about to give the signal for Samael to act, Lucifer interfered and shepherded the children into a store. Afterwards, he made sure nothing could happen until he got the boy home. He then persuaded the boy to promise his soul. Now he protects him. It will be very difficult to get the soul back."

"Why is it," The-One-True-God sighed, "I threw out of Heaven the one competent angel and kept you?"

Gabriel was about to protest that his feelings of inferiority were being aggravated by the implied insult to his ability but decided to meekly bow and accept the criticism. After all, he had received nothing more than a slap on the wrist. He watched with relief as the cloud whitened and floated away.

CHAPTER 14 —
Zetel, the Bar Mitzvah boy

The summer of 1948 was not a happy time for Joseph and Ettie, Shloima and Bessie. True, the war had ended three years before and there was now a state of Israel — " a place where we can all run to at the next pogrom," Issie Goldenstein was fond of saying — but their anxious enquiries through the Red Cross, the Jewish Agency, and the Canadian Jewish Congress regarding the whereabouts of family members brought no responses. A few of Bessie's cousins turned up in Israel. As time went on, the Landaws sadly concluded that grandparents and parents, as well as many others had not survived the Holocaust.

Zetel's coming Bar Mitzvah (*confirmation rite for the Jewish 13-year old boy*) in September cheered them up considerably and provided the family with a festive focal point that required planning and organizing and pushed aside their grief.

As required of the ritual, Zetel had to read and sing selected parts of the Torah during the Saturday morning service, try to look grownup, and, at some point in the festivities, make a speech. Because of Zetel's schooling and high grades on both the secular and religious sides, his parents anticipated their son would perform well.

After three years at Edward VII Elementary school, Zetel's rabbi had persuaded Ettie and Joseph to place the boy in an orthodox parochial school in order to continue his Jewish studies. They agreed when it was clear that the full Quebec secular curriculum was also an integral part of the school.

However, at the beginning of summer, as Zetel prepared for his Bar Mitzvah, they began to doubt the wisdom of their choice. Zetel came home later than usual one day and described a meeting he had had with a dozen rabbis, some from the school's headquarters in New York.

"The rabbis got into a big argument," Zetel reported. "They yelled at each other, banged the table, jumped up and down, one even threw his hat at a rabbi who disagreed with him. I thought they were going to have a fist fight."

"What were they arguing about?" asked Joseph. "Your Mama and I are very proud of you. Your marks are excellent. Your rabbis and teachers sing your praises at all the Parent-Teacher's meetings."

"It has nothing to do with marks," Zetel said. "It has to do with clouds."

It was evening. Joseph had just returned from the Landaw factory and was pouring his shot glass of rye with which he began every evening, after he had hugged and kissed Ettie and Zetel. He drank the whisky quickly and poured himself another.

"Zetel, you didn't tell them you were once a cloud?" he said anxiously.

"Papa, they asked me all kinds of questions about my soul and what I remembered before I was born. I didn't feel I could lie to rabbis so I told them everything I remembered. All the things I've told you and Mama."

Joseph downed the second glass and was about to pour a third when Ettie placed a restraining hand on his arm. "Yoisef, you usually have only one."

He sighed. "Zetel, tell us about the argument. What did the rabbis say?"

"I don't know everything they said because they talked so loudly. It had a lot to do with what was written in books. There was a lot of talk about the Kabbalah. One quoted a famous rabbi to make his point, another showed that a second equally famous rabbi had said the opposite. And this went on and on for hours. At the end, my rabbi summarized the points — either I'm crazy and should be locked up, or I'm a boy with a wild imagination and should be punished for speaking heresy, or I'm an angel, or...

"I agree with the last part," Ettie said, smiling and ruffling his hair.

"What's the next 'or'?" Joseph said resignedly.

"Papa, Mama, I'm not making this up — or, in accordance with Kabbalah teaching, I may be a Meshiach (Messiah)."

The two were dumbfounded. Joseph shook his head in disbelief.

"Zetel, how did they reach that conclusion?" he asked.

"This is what my rabbi explained to me. The Kabbalah says that the soul of the Meshiach existed at Creation and travels from man to man as God wills. Because I'm aware of my soul and know where it came from, and no one else does, I must be a Meshiach."

"I told you he's our miracle baby," Ettie said.

"Well, Zetel," Joseph said chuckling, "first your rabbi declared you a scholar and insisted on giving you one-on-one lessons. Then he raised you to a sage. Now he believes you are the soul of a Meshiach. You are definitely making spiritual progress and I think we should all be delighted. And as soon as your Bar Mitzvah is over in September, we shall transfer you to another school."

"But, Papa, suppose I am a Meshiach. Wouldn't I be better off in that school?"

Ettie pulled him affectionately to her. "Zeesuh, I think what's bothering us is if you tell everyone you're a Meshiach, then people might believe you *are* crazy and should be locked up. At the very least, you will be laughed at and we will be laughed at too. If you leave that school, and stop telling everybody you were a cloud once, then you will have a normal life. You must learn to control your imagination. Nobody has to know except you and us."

Zetel realized his parents' view was fixed and made no further objection. He concentrated on rehearsing for his great day. Even a Meshiach — especially a Meshiach — had to do well before the congregation of Israel.

Joseph and Ettie could not afford the usual grand party that accompanied a Bar Mitzvah celebration. On the Saturday night after the synagogue ceremony in the morning, they invited a small group of family and friends to dinner and drinks at their home.

"Ettie, Yoisef, your son was terrific." "Zetel, you should be an opera star with a voice like that." "Vai is mir (*woe is me*), suddenly you're all grown up." "I can't believe you're only 13 — you're so tall and like a real adult." "I have never heard a Bar Mitzvah boy do as well as you." "Ettie, Yoisef, how proud you must be."

The adulations, the hand shaking, the pinching of his cheeks, the hugs and kisses, began to wear him down. Guests were also shoving envelopes into his jacket side pockets until they bulged. Out of curiosity, at a moment when he was alone in the hallway, he opened one envelope and found it contained a Bar Mitzvah congratulations card and a fifty dollar bill. He did a mental calculation: if all the envelopes contained similar amounts, he was a rich boy. He could afford to take all his friends out for dinner to Ruby Foo's.

"You will do no such thing," a voice said. "You will save your money for university."

He looked up. Louis C. Fuhr in black tie evening clothes was standing in front of him, smiling.

"Between what's in your pocket and what your father has received on your behalf, you have exactly $1, 250. You may spend a few dollars on your close friends and a gift for your father and mother but the rest goes into a savings account or Canada Savings Bonds."

He felt resistance emanating from Zetel and said, "It's important that you go to university. It's part of my plan for you. Remember, we made a deal — your soul belongs to me."

Before Zetel could reply, Ettie, walking by, interrupted.

"Herr Fuhr, I'm so pleased you could come," she said. "I saw you at the shul (*synagogue*) today but you were way in the back. I hope you could see and hear well enough."

"Do not worry about that, Frau Landaw," he said, bending over and kissing her hand. "Beautiful sounds from beautiful people travel far. Our Zetel's performance was outstanding. Having lived with you during the war years, I take great pleasure in how he has developed into a fine young man."

"We're so proud of him," Ettie gushed. "But Yoisef tells me you had to change apartments."

"That's correct, Frau Landaw. This time I rented a whole house in Westmount and I can play my favourite music without incurring the wrath of my neighbours. It is silly, I know, but I have become addicted to a particular piece of music — Mussorgsky's Night on Bald Mountain — which I play loudly in order to sleep."

Ettie laughed, "Herr Fuhr, I'm happy you weren't addicted to it when you lived with us. I like Mussorgsky too, but I prefer Pictures at an Exhibition." She hesitated. "You and Zetel were having a serious talk when I interrupted?"

"Frau Landaw, I was giving him a banker's lecture. Even though I am no longer a banker, I still think like one. I was urging him to save his Bar Mitzvah gift money and not to spend it frivolously. I suggested he save the money for university — I hope I wasn't being presumptuous."

"Not at all, Herr Fuhr," Ettie said, clearly delighted. "Yoisef and I plan to do exactly that — put the money away for university. But come now, and join the others. You know most of them."

He gave Zetel a knowing look, extended an arm to Ettie and accompanied her into the dining room. A chorus of welcome greeted him.

Zetel stood disconsolately in the hallway, pondering the relationship he had with Lucifer. Was he a slave now, a soul no longer independent but in thrall to the devil? In promising his soul when his body died in return for protection during its life, did that mean he had granted Lucifer full control over him? Certainly he had not understood this. He had consented only when Lucifer claimed he could find Diana and displayed the vision of her. Diana continued to remain important to him but now the urge to see her again had grown even stronger.

He had felt some vague stirrings as adolescence came upon him, but now puberty hit him like one of the thunderbolts that emanated from the cumulus cloud of The-One-True-God. Perhaps this was the Godly way of reminding mortals of a certain age that it was time to procreate. Zetel now understood the reason for the eagerness that Zeus displayed as he grasped and fell upon Hera. Yet, he knew he must wait many years before he could lie with Diana. She was a grown woman and he was still a boy.

From her position in the living room, Rivka caught sight of Zetel in the hallway, alone and looking very forlorn.

"Gosh, you seem so sad for a Bar Mitzvah," Rivka said, grasping him by the shoulders and gently shaking him. "What's the matter?"

"I was just thinking about Diana and wondering whether I will ever see her."

Despite the fact Rivka was five years older than he, now a mature young woman, already urged by her parents to find a suitable marriage prospect, Zetel still considered her a confidante. He knew she would not ridicule him when he talked about his previous existence.

"Zetel, you will find her or she will find you if she still has her goddess powers," Rivka said reassuringly. "But Zetel, don't be impatient. You still have so many years to go until you're fully grown up. Besides, you might meet someone else who might take your mind off Diana."

She saw his immediate repugnance of this idea and quickly interposed, "But only for a short time."

In the years that followed, Zetel did meet others who caused him to forget Diana from time to time but he always returned to the longing for his absent goddess friend.

PART TWO
MIDDLE YEARS

CHAPTER 1 —
Zetel has a near disaster

New Year's Day, 1962, was bright and cold. Occasional gusts of wind blew dirt encrusted snow against pedestrians and cars and the facade of the Mount Royal Hotel on Peel Street. Zetel sat in the coffee lounge of the hotel, picking away at his lunch of tuna fish salad and sipping a by now cold coffee.

"May I warm that up for you, sir?" a waiter asked, filling the cup without waiting for an answer. He noted the customer's head was bent forward even when he listlessly forked a piece of fish into his mouth. Hung over, thought the waiter and went on to the next table.

Zetel took a few more sips of coffee, another mouthful of salad, then pushed both away and sat back in his chair. He looked around glumly. He needed someone to talk to. His parents were in Florida for the Christmas-New Year's holiday although he wasn't sure he'd want to discuss matters with them. They were already somewhat disappointed with him. They never said so but he could tell. His father had hoped he would become a doctor, his mother had urged law, but he chose Commerce. He was now a Chartered Accountant intent on a career in finance and had found a job as a stockbroker intern in a dingy office not far from Place d'Armes. His parents were also concerned he still was not married and were unimpressed with his string of girlfriends some of whom he brought home. No, the problem he faced now would add to their disappointment.

Rivka, his childhood friend, had been married ten years and had three children. Very seldom now could they get together to discuss things as in the old days. Chaim and Beatrice —whose early friendship had blossomed into love and marriage — were more likely to laugh at him than give him advice. His aunt and uncle were also away in Florida.

He didn't feel comfortable confiding in Hershey and Sylvia, or Jack and Faigel. The Goldenstein's were still alive but both very old and in the Hospital of Hope at the east end of Montreal Island.

His rabbi was dead but even if he were still alive, he would have shunned Zetel. Long after Zetel transferred to another school, he and the rabbi were frequently in touch. The rabbi continued to instruct him as often as time allowed. When Zetel graduated from High School, the rabbi insisted he go to a rabbinical school in New York. Zetel refused and explained that he was going to be a businessman.

"Rabbi, even if I am a Meshiach (*Messiah*), I don't want to be. I want to make lots of money. That's what makes the difference in this world."

"But if the Almighty has destined you to be a Meshiach," the rabbi protested, "you cannot just decide otherwise. He controls your soul."

"He does not. I promised it to Soton (*Satan*)."

The rabbi shrank from Zetel in horror. "What are you saying? Then I was wrong right from the beginning. You're not a Meshiach, you're a meshuginah (*crazy person*). All these years, I've wasted my time on a lunatic."

That was the last Zetel and the rabbi met.

He sank further into his depression, aimlessly, hopelessly considering how to solve his problem.

"Happy New Year," a familiar voice said cheerfully.

Zetel gasped and sprang to his feet. Before him stood the Devil, horns sticking out of his head, a large black beard revealing only his coal-black eyes, his body encased in a long black cloak with a high collar.

"Fooled you," laughed the Devil. He pulled the mask off his head, swept aside the cloak which he deposited on the closest chair, and shook Zetel's hand jovially. Without the costume, he was Louis C. Fuhr in his usual three piece suit, carefully combed hair, and neatly trimmed beard.

"See," he said pointing to the impeccably polished shoe on a lifted foot, "no cloven hoof."

Zetel was too taken aback to appreciate the humour and sank slowly into his chair. The waiter hovered close by.

"May I get you something, sir?" the waiter asked cautiously. "You sure had me fooled. I didn't know whether to call the police or the nearest priest."

Fuhr chuckled. "We had a wild costume party New Year's Eve at my place. All my guests are still asleep or very sick. Yes, I would like a drink."

"What will it be, sir?"

"Why, something devilish, of course. I leave it up to you."

The waiter went off, shaking his head, muttering to himself, "It's time for my Famous Five."

"Well, and how are you, my friend?" Fuhr said, sitting down opposite Zetel. "You seem very disturbed."

"You call me a friend? What kind of friend am I?" Zetel grumbled. "I appealed to you weeks ago and you only come now."

"I had other matters to attend to," Fuhr said affably. "Running the nether regions is quite burdensome. Besides, you got into trouble by ignoring my advice. I thought you should just sweat for awhile. It will teach you a lesson."

"And what's the lesson?" Zetel asked sarcastically. "Have no fun and keep your nose in your books?"

Fuhr shook his head: "Despite my many years of mentoring, you still think and say stupid things. Would the Devil ever recommend against fun and encourage abject industriousness? No, no, my friend, fun, pleasure, the joys of sensuality, licentiousness — these are the essence of a happy existence. There is no other route to fulfillment in the mortal state."

"Then what is the lesson?"

"Have all the erotic adventures you can but protect yourself. Pregnancy causes unwarranted difficulties. And I warned you to stay away from married women. Adultery can be dangerous for you."

Zetel nodded sadly. "I followed your advice until I met Sandra. She looked like Diana and I fell head over heels in love with her. She was my graduate tutor and married to a professor in Archeology. He was often away on research projects. I tried to stay detached, pretending indifference and she showed no sign of interest in me. Then one day I couldn't help myself and embraced her. To my surprise, she didn't resist at all. We made love then and there right on her office floor. Later we went to my apartment and continued. It was a wonderful time for several weeks until her husband returned. We had to be more discreet and couldn't meet as often. We even decided to break it off."

Zetel paused, intimidated for a moment by the look of utter indifference on Fuhr's face. "A couple of months ago she told me she was pregnant. She planned to divorce her husband and marry me. I objected — I wasn't ready for a wife and child — and we had a terrible argument. I suggested she have an abortion and I would pay for it. She said she would have the baby and sue me for paternity even if it meant breaking up her marriage. There goes my reputation, and my job. The firm, the industry, are very strait-laced and won't keep or hire tarnished employees, especially interns who generate bad publicity. I'm at my wits' end trying to figure out what to do. That's why I called you. I'm hoping you can find a way out for me."

Fuhr laughed: "Mortal problems are so easy. I can offer several solutions. One, the husband returns home. The wife reveals her secret to him. No one else knows at this point or that you are in anyway involved. In a fit of unreasonable anger he kills her, then himself. Everyone is shocked, cannot understand why — 'they seemed like such a happy couple' — and you are free of accusations and blame."

Appalled, Zetel stared at Fuhr, "Do you have a less bloody solution?"

The waiter returned carrying a tall glass on a tray. "Here's your devilish drink, sir. It's my own concoction which I call The Famous Five. Do I have your word that no matter what happens, you won't hold the hotel liable?"

"It's that strong, is it," Fuhr said, lifting the glass and sniffing it. "What causes the red colour?"

"Blood, sir," the waiter replied very seriously, without the hint of a smile.

"Excellent!" Fuhr exclaimed. "My favourite libation. What else is in it? Why do you call it The Famous Five?"

"It is a mixture of five spirits — whisky, gin, vodka, rum and bourbon — in a punch of brandy, cherry liqueur and cranberry juice. It is very potent. I served it only a half-dozen times this holiday season. Only two finished it and had to be helped up to their rooms," the waiter said with obvious pride.

"I must try it then," said Fuhr. Raising the tall glass to his lips, he tipped his head back, swallowed the drink in one gulp, and unfazed, said. "Very good but its strength is mitigated by the punch. I will have another but leave out the cranberry juice."

The waiter, his mouth and eyes opened wide, stepped back and stammered, "Are you sure?"

"Of course he's sure," Zetel said. "He's the Devil. This is like pablum for him. You don't think that's just a costume he took off?"

Still open mouthed, the waiter retreated to the bar.

"What other solutions do you have to my problem?" Zetel asked.

"I don't believe you will like my next suggestion, but hear me out," Fuhr said. "Marry her."

Zetel began to rise from his chair, frustrated and angry. Fuhr reached out and restrained him. "Listen carefully. If she divorces her husband and you marry, there will indeed be a scandal, but there will be no paternity suit. You will demonstrate to your firm and the industry that you are a responsible individual, happy to marry the woman you love and take responsibility for the child. After awhile, your wanton behaviour will be seen as a mere peccadillo in a life of otherwise good judgement and integrity."

"I can't believe this," Zetel said, shaking his head and settling back in his chair. "The Devil is recommending a noble course of action. Here I am, eager to sin, quite willing to abandon the woman I loved and the child I fathered, and my only concern is the impact it will have on my career. And you're trying to introduce some morality into the situation. Don't you want me to keep sinning so you can have my soul?"

Fuhr sipped the drink the waiter had just brought him.

"Much better. It is stronger and more to my taste. Thank you," he said to the waiter and waved him away.

"It doesn't matter what your behaviour is. I already have your soul. All I'm trying to do is suggest ways to secure the start of your career. Since marrying her is not to your liking, I have a third solution. Her pregnancy is still unknown to her husband or, for that matter, to anyone else except you. Her husband is away next week at an international archeology convention. During this period she will have an abortion and never reveal this to her husband. Her marriage will continue and there will be no scandal."

"Fabulous. That's a great solution. But she has said she won't abort," Zetel objected.

Fuhr stood up, quickly swallowed the rest of the drink, picked up his cloak and mask, and threw a $20 bill on the table. "Since you're agreeable, that is the solution that will take place."

"How can you be so sure?"

Fuhr was in the act of leaving but turned and faced Zetel, a stern, contemptuous look on his face. "You know whom I am. I have ways."

A man in ragged clothing entered the lounge, pushed aside the protesting Maitre d'hôte, approached Fuhr and whispered something. Fuhr nodded and the man left. "I need your help. I have just been informed there is a meeting in another part of this hotel that I must pay attention to since it concerns you. Tell the waiter I'm not quite well after the second drink and just need to sit somewhere quiet for a few hours and I'll be alright."

"I knew this was going to happen," said the waiter as he and Zetel helped a tottering Fuhr into a closed function room.

"I'll keep tabs on him," Zetel said. "You don't have to worry. This is not the first time. He recovers completely after awhile."

"Lock the door and stay at the far end of this room," Fuhr instructed Zetel after the waiter left, "and be quiet. Do not approach me."

Zetel watched as Fuhr settled into a chair, stretched out his body and disappeared.

In a bedroom suite on the top floor of the hotel, Gabriel, impeccably dressed in his blue suit, seated comfortably in a sofa chair in the living room of the suite, surveyed the group that had answered his call.

In front of him, on the sofa behind the coffee table sat Michael, angel of justice and power, in his cuirass, skirt and sandals, a sword sheathed at his waist, his blond curly hair falling to his shoulders.

Next to him was Raphael, angel of God's healing force, of serious mien, draped in a red cloak. Beside him, Sandalphon, angel charged with bringing humankind together, cherubic in size and temperament, clothed in a sheepskin garment, smiled blissfully. Behind the sofa, Samael, angel of death, stood, body and face covered in a black cloak and hood, glaring hatefully at the back of Sandalphon's head. Metatron, angel and scribe of men's deeds and keeper of the Book of Life and Death, tall, wearing a long black gown offsetting his white hair which fell below his shoulders, filled the double doorway to the bedroom since he insisted on bringing his own writing table, scrolls, inkpot and pens.

Gabriel began: "I am filled with gratitude that you have come to this Angelic Council and apologize that I could give you no more than two Earth hours of notice. No one knows better than I how occupied you are with your duties and responsibilities and the demands placed on you by The-One-True-God. The continuing warfare and violence on Earth must be a constant burden for all of you. Humankind is so fractious. I wonder, Archangel Michael, how you can decide whom to strike down as all appear equally guilty of evil acts. And you, Archangel Raphael, how do you bring healing to so much ongoing pain and suffering. Samael, you must be particularly stressed shepherding all the souls from their functionless bodies back to the Arc. Sandalphon, despite your smile and benevolent appearance, you cannot but deplore the state of humankind and its tendency to split apart and wreak havoc on each other. And you, Archangel Metatron, you must be madly and endlessly scribing and adding names to the Book of Death. Therefore, I am profoundly grateful that you have given of your time to answer my call and I will try to conduct this Angelic Council with dispatch."

"You have already taken too long," snarled Samael. "Get to the point."

"Be patient, Samael," said Sandalphon. "We angels must demonstrate a kindly attitude to each other as a model for humankind to follow."

"You pint-sized lump of treacly effluvia. Keep out of my way if you know what's good for you," snapped Samael, and grasped Sandalphon by the back of his neck.

"Release me, foul oaf," cried Sandalphon, tears streaming down his dimpled cheeks. "Gabriel, is Samael necessary for this Council. If he is, then I not."

Gabriel stood , waving a warning finger, "Samael, leave him be. Sandalphon, both you and he are essential to this Council."

"Angels, this is unseemly behaviour," Metatron said in a mild but authoritative tone. "Samael, desist. Gabriel, explain the nature of this Council and why we are called."

"Thank you, Metatron," Gabriel said. "As always, your wisdom and firmness of composure..."

"Gabriel, now!" Metatron interrupted, his voice no longer mild.

Somewhat flustered, Gabriel said, "This Council is called to address an Order given me by The-One-True-God almost three Earth decades ago — namely, to return the soul known as Zalman Yaakov Zetel Ländau to the Arc. This soul escaped the Arc with the help of a pagan goddess and is considered by The-One-True-God to be too rebellious to be allowed mortal existence. Despite spirited efforts on my part to accomplish His Order, this soul has managed to evade capture. You have also declined in the past to assist me..."

"So we are to blame for your failure? Is that it? This is a finger pointing session?" interrupted Samael.

"I am merely stating the facts," an annoyed Gabriel said. "I accuse no one."

"Gabriel, just tell us the purpose of this Angelic Council. Clearly, it has something to do with the soul in question," Archangel Michael said placatingly. "How may I help?"

"Thank you, Michael, you are always understanding," Gabriel said, glaring at Samael. "Let me continue. The soul which we will call Zetel — his most common name as a mortal —has now strayed beyond the bounds of morality and has committed a most egregious sinful act which — in accordance with our sacred laws and manifested in the many holy scriptures observed by all mortals — is punishable by death. Therefore, I have called this Council together to present the evidence against the soul Zetel and to determine how best to carry out our sentence."

There was silence for a moment, the only sound the scratching of Metatron's pen as it raced across the papyrus scroll.

"That's a very serious charge," Michael observed. "What's he done to deserve such opprobrium that I and the others here must be involved? Surely the laws of humankind are sufficient."

"It is doubtful whether the laws of humankind are sufficient in this present circumstance," Gabriel said.

Michael never acted unless he knew precisely the nature of the offence and always questioned whether the sinful act was of sufficient significance for his involvement. — "With the power I have," he often said, "I must be careful to use it judiciously and prudently in order to avoid an injustice on my part." — While many of his celestial colleagues admired his thoughtfulness and rigid self-discipline, others criticized the length of time he took to come to a decision. — "By the time he makes up his mind to do something, the offender has long since multiplied his sins and in many cases is no longer a mortal," such critics were wont to say. But Michael ignored his critics and persevered in a thorough examination and detailed analysis of each event.

Michael ruffled his curly blond hair, squared his shoulders inside the cuirass that covered his upper body, smoothed his skirt and laid his sword on his lap as a sign of readiness. "We have discussed the soul Zetel before and did not find compelling reasons to induce his demise. What is the sin requiring action on our part? I am prepared to assist you but I must be sure."

Gabriel fell to his knees: "Saintly Archangel, revered Michael, The-One-True-God's defender of His Justice and Power, I bow to you in utter obeisance..."

"Gabriel, get on with it," Michael said, pretending impatience but inwardly glowing with Gabriel's adulation.

"Very well," Gabriel said, returning to his seat and looking at each of the angels in turn. "The soul, Zetel, has committed sins that transgress Commandments seven and ten."

"Terrible!' "Horrible!" "Disgusting!" "Shame!" "Those two in particular!" the angels called out. Their clamorous condemnation was meant to hide the fact that none could remember the commandments Gabriel referred to.

"And how did he do that?" asked Raphael.

"Let me explain, holy ones," Gabriel said. "As soon as Zetel reached his adolescent years, he pursued erotic adventures with many young women. In mortal terms, he is considered handsome, masculine and well formed — that, and with the help of Satan, many women found him irresistible. He attended university and his penchant for young women did not cease. In fact, it grew because there were so many more available. In one of his classes, he met a woman who acted as his tutor, and who was married to a professor at the university. He coveted her to the point where it became an obsession. At first the woman paid no attention to him apart from academic work but eventually succumbed to his advances. In other words, he has committed adultery."

A hubbub of conversation ensued as the angels conferred among themselves.

"Gabriel, we agree this is indeed a terrible sin and strikes at the very essence of morality," Michael said. "According to the Law, the punishment is very clear — death by stoning. We will simply bring their sinful act to the attention of their appropriate government officials who will carry out the sentence. I will ensure the stones reach their target accurately."

"I will make sure their souls exit quickly," said Samael.

"I will reduce the pain they feel and bring succour to their loved ones," said Raphael.

"I have noted their sins and the punishment required and will further note when the sentence is executed," said Metatron.

"I will appeal to The-One-True-God for mercy," said Sandalphon. "These are young people who do not have the judgement that comes with maturity. I will also engage with the offended husband to forgive and welcome the child as his own."

Frustrated, Gabriel tore at his carefully coiffed hair. "Angels, this is not ancient Canaan nor those parts of Earth where stoning of adulterers is carried out. Zetel lives in a country where adultery is not punishable by death. Therefore, we must decide how to take action against Zetel."

"What about the woman?" Samael asked, trying to appear indifferent but feeling his lust for blood mounting. "You keep harping on the soul, Zetel, but the woman also committed adultery. Shall we not proceed against both?"

"I object to including the woman," said Sandalphon, standing up and trying to stretch his small form. Even so, he was no taller than when seated. "The woman is with child and for the sake of the child must be spared. The child is blameless."

"I agree entirely with Sandalphon," Raphael said. "God's healing force would dictate to exempt the woman."

"That is why I identify Zetel for punishment and not the woman," Gabriel said, nodding vigorously. "Even after the child issues forth, the woman must be spared until the child is weaned, nurtured and has matured to a stage of independence. To emphasize my position, I have already infused a soul into the gestating child."

Gabriel stood and faced the angels. "Now, are we all in agreement that we must take action against Zetel? Sandalphon, we have satisfied you on the woman's account. I hope you will go along with us or at least take no action against us. The-One-True-God will not entertain your appeal because it is He who wants Zetel back on the Arc."

Sandalphon, tears streaming around the contours of his face, hung his head and slid back onto the sofa.

"Fine, we're in agreement. I wish to acknowledge the wisdom you have displayed today in coming to this painful but necessary judgement. It makes me proud to be a part of..."

"That's enough, Gabriel," Michael interrupted. "How do we proceed?"

A bell in the hallway began clanging, loudly, rapidly.

Gabriel did not like his speeches interrupted but realized the other angels were eager for action.

"We must decide how to kill him," Gabriel said. "It should be easy. At this very moment, he sits in the coffee lounge of this hotel. That's why I held our Council here, convenient to the target. But we must decide quickly. He will leave soon."

"It will be easier to kill him on the street," Samael said. "There are more opportunities."

"That's it," Michael exclaimed, standing up in his excitement and waving his sword which caused Raphael to duck. "Out on the street, I direct an automobile to drive into him. Samael withdraws the soul quickly before medical attention arrives."

Raphael shook his head. "It's a good plan but will only work if he is at the kerb in a clear space. If not, others may be hit by the automobile as well. I know Samael doesn't care, but I do."

"We all do," Gabriel insisted. "We require something to attract him to the kerb."

"Sandalphon," Michael cried excitedly. "Sandalphon disguised as a child begging alms accosts him, asks for help and draws him to the kerb."

"Me? Why me?" objected Sandalphon. "I'm against the whole thing in the first place, and you want to make me an accomplice? Besides, I have no child's disguise." He burst into sobs.

The bell in the hallway continued its incessant clanging.

Metatron left his desk and patted Sandalphon on the head. "Come, come, sweet Sandalphon. You must cooperate. It is the will of The-One-True-God. Your face and size are childlike and your garment can easily be made to look ragged. Here, I do it now, a few cuts with the blade I use to sharpen my quills and a couple of ink spots on your face and behold — a child, ragged and dirty, begging alms. I will enter into the record, Sandalphon, and bring to the attention of The-One-True-God, that without your assistance, our plan was doomed to failure."

"He needs a receptacle," growled Samael, embittered that his hated foe was getting such glowing attention.

"Why do I need a receptacle?" Sandalphon snapped back.

"For the alms, dimwitted one. When you beg, you must hold out something for the alms."

"Gabriel's hat," Michael said, pointing to the hat on the coffee table.

"Not my hat," Gabriel protested, reaching for it. "It's a Biltmore, very expensive, designed especially to complement my suit. Without it, I may not appear mortal."

Michael snatched it and tossed it to Metatron. "Carve it up a bit so it looks as ragged as the child. After today, you won't need to appear mortal, since we'll have returned the soul to the Arc."

"Very well," Gabriel said resignedly, not particularly eager to give up masquerading as a mortal but recognized it would not be up to him anyway. "The Operating Team — Michael, Samael, and Sandalphon — will follow me to the lobby of the hotel. Only Sandalphon and I will be visible. Raphael and Metatron will remain here for backup and communication. After exiting the lobby, Sandalphon will find the best spot on the street, Michael and Samael will stay close to him. I will show myself as though inadvertently to Zetel who will recognize me and come after me as I leave the hotel. I will lead him to Sandalphon. The rest is up to you. Are we all in agreement and understand our roles?"

They all nodded, silent now, tense, gripped by apprehension of the action ahead.

Raphael grumbled, "That bell is very annoying. If we can't get it to stop, I will not stay here. I am accustomed to the Elysian silence of the Arc, the music of the heavenly spheres, and the lilting themes of Heaven. Even the occasional thunder from the cloud that hides The-One-True-God is not as troublesome."

"Never mind the bell," Gabriel ordered. "Stay at your post. It's probably someone stuck in an elevator. We'll take the stairs. Let's go."

"But I smell smoke," Raphael said, sniffing the air. "It is the smoke I associate with fire and brimstone, like the smoke from the pits of Hell."

"Raphael has become our romantic poet," snickered Samael.

Gabriel opened the door to the hallway and was met by a wall of fire that blasted him and the Operations Team back into the room and filled it with smoke and flame. They tried to run out but a powerful stream of water blew them back into the room.

"That room is occupied, Captain, I believe I saw someone," shouted a fireman. He goosed the hose nozzle all around the door frame and moved into the room.

In the closed function room, Zetel had dozed off and was startled awake by Fuhr. From outside the room, he heard the clanging of the fire bell.

"Quick, my friend, we must leave the hotel immediately. We'll take a taxi to my house and you must stay with me for a short time. There, I will explain what has happened."

"What's going on?" Zetel asked.

"Never mind, just do what I say." To emphasize his instructions, Fuhr lifted him bodily and thrust him to the door.

As Zetel opened the door, the waiter pushed in, "You and your friend must evacuate the hotel. There's a fire on the top floor. Can your friend make it?"

"I'm fine," Fuhr said and left the room with Zetel. It was chaotic in the lobby as guests rushing to get out flowed around the firemen trying to get in. Fuhr and Zetel walked quickly up the street to Sherbrooke Avenue, hailed a cab and were whisked away.

Later that evening, radio and television news reported the strange circumstances of the fire in the Mount Royal Hotel. Although a fireman was certain he saw a man as he entered the suite, no body was found. The charred remains of a small sheepskin coat, probably for a child, was discovered when the Fire Marshall poked through the wreckage. The mystery deepened further when the Hotel Manager on duty insisted the top floor had not been booked at all, that there should have been no one in the suite. The cause of the fire was unknown.

"Once again Lucifer outwitted you!" shouted The-One-True-God from within His massive cumulus cloud of vertical development, now black and veined with long tracks of fiery red. The cloud burgeoned until all Heaven was filled. Lightning bolts spewed out that touched even the Earth. "What a tiresome lot you are! Look at you, bedraggled and charred with Hell fire. Metatron, I want a full report."

"Holy One, I will have to go by memory since my scrolls were all burnt," said Metatron, bowing his head in shame, his once white hair hanging in clusters of black embers, his cloak in rags.

"Where is Michael?" The-One-True-God demanded.

"Most Holy One, he must get his skirt rewoven before he can appear before You," a tremulous Gabriel replied. He, too, was almost naked, with burnt shreds of his mortal clothing barely hanging to him.

"And Sandalphon, My sweet Sandalphon, what have they done to you? Naked? Your sheepskin coat gone?" moaned The-One-True-God. "Do not cry. I shall order another one from my Andean worshippers. There. It fits you well."

Indeed, a garment appeared and covered Sandalphon's nakedness. His new sheepskin coat was better than the one he had lost. It was thicker and softer and tied with a gold belt and buckle .

"What about me?" demanded Samael, angered by the sympathy shown Sandalphon. "I lost my cloak in the fire."

"Samael, when you address Me, you will begin with the appropriate words of obeisance," said The-One-True-God. "As for your nakedness, you were created naked and so will you remain. If you must have a cloak, the next time you are in the land of the mortals, find one."

The-One-True-God's anger was clearly abating for lightning bolts no longer were emitted, and the cloud was greying and returning to its original size.

"And you, Raphael, you seem unscathed. How did you manage that?"

"Most Holy One, You who are the Lord of all Creation, I was the first to warn the others that something was wrong, and that I smelled Hell smoke. My warning was ignored. I leapt through the wall a split second before fire engulfed us."

"You didn't try to stop them from leaving the room?"

"No, Most Holy One, the danger was upon us."

"A wise angel," sighed The-One-True-God, and, almost as an afterthought, added, "and a coward."

CHAPTER 2 —
Zetel meets his bride

At the end of January, Joseph and Ettie returned home from Florida, tanned, refreshed, relaxed. Shloima had retired and Joseph was running the business which had continued to prosper. They lived now in a grand house in Outremont within walking distance of the Adath Israel Synagogue. Joseph was on the board of trustees and Ettie was a prominent member of the Sisterhood. Both were popular and very much involved in the social life of the neighbourhood.

Much to their delight, Zetel met them at Dorval Airport and drove them home.

"We were away so long," Ettie said, hugging and kissing Zetel, "that I didn't think you'd remember us."

"How's your job going and when did you get this Beetle?" Joseph asked as he helped Zetel to strap the baggage onto a roof rack.

"Papa, it's Herr Fuhr's car. He leant it to me to pick you up and sends his regards," Zetel said.

"What a kind man," Ettie exclaimed. "After all this time, he is such a good friend."

Zetel drove carefully out of the airport and mingled with the traffic heading into the city. "I'm really just getting into my job, Papa. It's very complicated but I like it very much. My boss says I'm the best intern they've ever had and he wants me on permanent staff. I'm already making good money. My boss says I've got a good eye for stocks and the customers like me."

"How can they not like you?" Ettie gushed, leaning forward from the back seat and caressing his hair.

"By the way, hope you don't mind but Faigel insisted on making dinner for you tonight and is at the house cooking. Jack is also there and the Levitts will be joining us."

Joseph groaned. "Don't get me wrong. I love these people but I was looking forward to a drink, a sandwich, and a quiet evening."

Despite his misgivings, Joseph enjoyed his friends. Imperceptibly, age had crept up on all of them. They were all in their 50's or 60's.

Joseph had stayed youthful and slim, his hair untouched by grey. Ettie was still a beautiful woman despite some rounding and wrinkles. "In Florida, every time we went to the pool, I had to beat off the lifeguards," Joseph boasted about his wife.

Both Jack and Faigel had slimmed down considerably after Jack suffered a slight heart attack. "He had to go on a diet, so I went too," Faigel said. "I think God gave us an early warning."

Hershey had lost his athletic look, as well as most of his hair while Sylvia was as voluptuous as in her youth. They had two children, an older daughter Sybil and a late arrival Jonas.

They sat around the table in the large dining room and voraciously consumed Faigel's meal of sweet and sour chicken pieces, a roast pudding of mashed parsnips and potatoes, and a ratatouille of tomatoes, garlic, onions, zucchini, eggplant, bell peppers, and a mix of green herbs.

"Yoisef and Ettie, your son is a gorgeous hunk of man," Sylvia said between bites. "Zetel, I think it's time you settled down and I have just the girl for you. She's not beautiful but attractive enough."

"And she's rich," Hershey added. "Her father owns the Lansmann Jewellery chain. He's a millionaire many times over. The girl is Jonas' teacher at Guy Drummond and we met her at one of the

Parents-Teachers Meetings. Smart girl, very caring, well-educated, and rich. Need I say more."

"I don't know if I'm ready to get serious," Zetel said.

"You don't have to get serious," Hershey said. "You just have to marry her."

"Hershey, what kind of advice are you giving my child?" demanded Ettie.

"Ettie, Hershey's just joking," Sylvia said.

Hershey shook his head. "I'm joking and I'm not joking. Or I'm joking in a not joking way. Or, to put it better, I'm not joking in a joking way," he said, looking around, immensely satisfied with his explanation.

"You lost me on the first 'joking,'" Joseph said. "Why is this girl so important that Zetel should marry her?"

"Because of Zetel's ambition in the world of finance and making lots of money," Hershey said. "He and I talked while you were away. I came to his office, to see whether he had any good tips."

They all turned to Zetel. "Tell us about your ambition, Zeesuh," Ettie said. "How come you never told us?"

"I wasn't keeping it a secret, Mama, Papa. I only came to it recently. When Hershey visited, I tried out the idea on him," Zetel said, hesitating, reluctant to broach the subject.

"So what is the idea or do you want Hershey to tell us?" Joseph said, trying to hide his annoyance.

"Papa, the idea is very simple," Zetel said, putting down his knife and fork. "I want to have my own firm.'

"Your own firm?" Joseph asked. "You mean your own stock broking firm?"

"Not only as a stockbroker," Zetel said. "I also want to manage investments, mutual funds, everything connected with finance. To do it, I will need lots of money, starting capital, private investors. But it won't happen overnight. I need to get experience first and earn a living at the same time. That's why my job is so important.

Right now, it's providing me with lots of learning, and enough money to live on but soon I'll make lots more."

"Zetel," Joseph said carefully, "it's a wonderful feeling being your own boss and having your own business. I don't want to discourage you but you will need buckets of money for such a business. Even if you start small, how much would you need just to get through the first year? Sure, your customers like working with you, but they're not your customers, they're your firm's customers. How many would follow you? It takes ages to build up such a business. And we can't help you. Everything we have was put into this house."

"The Lansmann Jewellery girl's father could get him started," Hershey said. "No, don't get excited, Ettie. All I'm saying is let Zetel meet her. If they like each other, well and good. If not, he does what he's doing now for a while longer, saves his money and finds a few investors. Like this fellow Buffet in the US or Jarislowsky here in Montreal."

"I suppose, Hershey, you'll be one of the first investors?" Joseph said sarcastically.

"Yoisef, you know my money's all tied up in my car parts business," Hershey replied. "Otherwise, yeah, I would be an investor. In fact, I'm already a client. I took a flyer on one of Zetel's tips — a mining company — and so far the stock keeps going up and up."

"Not anymore," Zetel said. "I sold your position this morning. There's news coming either late tomorrow or the next day that's very negative."

"How do you know this, Zetel?" Joseph asked.

"Papa, I have a friend in the railroad that will build the branch line to the mine. The terrain has been surveyed and the line will be cheap to build. That was the reason to buy in. Now, my friend tells me, further prospecting of the mine and analysis of the core samples does not look promising. So we sell before the news becomes public."

Joseph had a troubled look. "Zetel, is that allowable? I'm no expert in the stock market, but isn't it illegal to trade on information before the public is aware?"

Zetel reached out and put an arm around his father. "Papa, it's called research. I did some investigating and learned something about the company. Sure, it might be considered illegal by some, but everybody does it. Even the top guys in my firm, even with all their policies about ethical trading, regularly chase their contacts, find out things before they're announced and make piles of money, and not just for the firm but for their own pockets as well. It's the industry, Papa."

Hershey nodded. "Yoisef, what am I supposed to do. Your son has information, acts on it, locks my profit in, and saves me a bundle. I should tell him he shouldn't do that?"

"Yoisef, we don't know enough about it to tell Zetel he's wrong," Ettie said. "Besides, how can my boy do anything wrong?"

"Hershey, how much money did you make?" demanded Sylvia. "I need a new outfit."

"There you are, Yoisef," Hershey said, rolling his eyes. "My ill gotten gains are about to be squandered."

"Zetel, next time you have a tip, don't waste it on Hershey," Jack said.

"That's right, Zetel," Faigel said. "I need a new outfit, too."

"Zetel, do a few deals first with others," Jack said. "Get some real experience. Then when you're ready, maybe I can help you. I've got money saved for retirement."

"But Zetel, nothing with lots of risk," Faigel was quick to caution. "I have to live on Jack's retirement money as well."

Cyril Lansmann was a tall commanding figure with a large craggy face crowned with a mass of curly brown greying hair. His wife

Anna while not petite was much shorter with a pleasing figure and a pleasant face. She wore the latest fashions in dress and also served as a display case for her husband's jewellery merchandise.

"We will eat in the small dining area," Anna said to Zetel, "since we are only four tonight."

Zetel hadn't totally dismissed Hershey's advice. For many days afterward he wrestled with the idea. Certainly, a rich father-in-law — if suitably generous — would accelerate his ambitious plan. Yet Zetel was not completely convinced that this was a good thing. He needed more experience in his craft, more time to become familiar with the ins and outs of the stock market, more time to develop contacts in the right places, more time to learn from his mistakes in somebody else's employ. Besides, saddled with a wife and her family as well as his own would impact his time and focus. However, there was another reason, one he hardly dared admit even to himself. He still relished the thought of someday meeting up with Diana.

"You're a fool," Louis C. Fuhr said when Zetel consulted him on the matter. "An opportunity sits waiting to be snatched and you flounder with excuses. You don't even know whether a match would be successful so there is no point in dithering. Get yourself an introduction and discover whether there is any possibility for a marriage and whether the father would be amenable to a large investment. Then you can decide whether you want to proceed, although you would be silly at that stage not to."

Zetel did not have to plan how to meet the Lansmann daughter. A few days later, the head of his firm brought Cyril Lansmann to meet him.

"Mr. Lansmann is a new client," the CEO said. "He needs help to manage his cash flow pools and to optimize them as an asset. Mr. Landaw, please give him your priority attention and if further help is required, let me know."

"My problem is very simple," Cyril Lansmann explained. "I have oodles of cash coming in every day from my stores and supplier invoices coming in at longer intervals. So far all I do is deposit the cash and wait for the bills. I'd like to do something better than deposit interest. By the way, by chance I met your banker friend Mr. Fuhr the other day at a Jewellery Show in Toronto. We got to talking and he suggested I contact you. Spoke highly of you."

Zetel had misgivings about Cyril. He was overbearing, too sure of himself, too eager to find fault and prone to tell Zetel how to invest the cash accumulated from his jewellery stores in Montreal, Toronto, and Halifax. Cyril wanted the cash poured into stocks but Zetel insisted that was a risky strategy and invested in short term bonds and Treasuries which could be liquidated quickly as accounts payable became due.

Over the next several months, the system Zetel set up worked well and Cyril was impressed. Not only did he come to respect Zetel but began to see in him a possible match for his daughter. Accordingly, he invited Zetel to the family's Friday night dinner.

"Zetel, just remember," Joseph cautioned him, "you're going to dinner. It doesn't have to go beyond that."

"They probably want you to meet the girl," Ettie added. "So, that's fine. Meet the girl, enjoy the dinner, forget about Hershey's advice. If you like each other — great."

"Mama, Papa, I have to take up his invitation to dinner. He's a good customer and values my work. I don't know if he has anything else in mind apart from expressing his appreciation."

When Cyril announced they were having a guest for Friday night dinner, his daughter reacted immediately: "Daddy, is this another of your blind dates for me?"

"Sarah, I'm inviting this man because he has significantly improved a part of my business and I like him. What happens after that is up to the two of you. Just remember, you're getting close to thirty and no prospects in sight. Your mother and I would like grandchildren." As his daughter flared up, he added quickly, "But we're not pushing you."

"He's a very handsome man," Anna said. "I was in the office when he came to visit Daddy and met him. Let me tell you, all the girls swooned when he walked in. He's also very polite and clearly well brought up."

"I also made some discreet inquiries," Cyril said. "His parents have a nice home in Outremont and are highly regarded by their circle. His father runs a clothing factory on the upper main."

"Have you already rented the hall?" Sarah exclaimed. "Daddy, arranged marriages went out when our people left the shtetel. Do I get to choose my husband or will I meet him when we climb into bed after the ceremony?"

Cyril threw up his arms in disgust. "That's what I get for being a careful father and looking out for you." He stormed out of the room.

The meal was typical for a Friday night Jewish household: chicken liver pâté, chicken soup with matzo balls, roasted chicken and vegetables, a noodle pudding laced with raisins, and all washed down with a sweet wine; desert was an apple pie accompanied by tea with lemon. The table was elegantly set with a starched white cloth and napkins, Anna's best dinner set, cutlery carefully laid out in the correct order, and sparkling crystal wine glasses.

At first, Cyril dominated the conversation relating how Zetel had engineered his short term cash to actually make it profitable. Then, at a nudge from Anna under the table, he stopped talking. Anna sensed Sarah was interested in their guest.

"Daddy tells me you're an immigrant, Mr. Landaw," Sarah said. "Yet you speak without an accent. In what country were you born?"

"I was born in no country," Zetel said, chuckling. All three looked at him in surprise.

"I was born on a ship on the Atlantic Ocean, one day out of Halifax. I could be German because my parents were German citizens, British because the ship was British registered or Canadian because that was the first country we landed in. My parents chose Canadian for me."

Sarah laughed: "So you were one day old when you arrived in Canada. I was 0 days old when I arrived."

"Sarah is the second generation born here," Anna explained. "Cyril and I are the first."

"While I am very tolerant of immigrants," Sarah said, her eyes sparkling, "Nevertheless, because you were born outside the country, I must refer to you as a 'greener' (*pejorative term for greenhorn, new comer*)."

"Sarah," Cyril objected, "you only know Mr. Landaw ten minutes and already you're insulting him."

Zetel was laughing. "I'm sure Miss Lansmann was only joking. Besides, while I am one day behind her in arriving in Canada, I have learned a great deal about the country. For example, this is what I've learned about Montreal. Our city is not the capital of Canada nor even of Quebec, but it is the centre for everything else — finance, business, culture, education."

Sarah leapt to her feet almost knocking over her chair. "How can you put 'finance' first and 'education' last. I'm a teacher," she said, moving closer to Zetel, her hands balled into fists.

"Sarah, sit down," Anna said sharply. "You're not allowed to hit our guest."

"Not even one punch, Mommy?" Sarah said and resumed her seat. "If Mr. Landaw apologizes, there is a possibility I might forgive him."

Zetel was warming to her. He knew she wasn't angry with him, teasing him, perhaps testing him. He liked her feistiness, her outspokenness. And she wasn't unattractive. Her body was well formed, curvaceous. Her face suffered from a very prominent nose that looked like it had once been broken. Her eyes made up for it: large, brown, lit with energy. Blondish hair fell below her shoulders. Her mouth was small or seemed so in comparison to the nose.

"I know you're a teacher," Zetel said. "Friends of our family raved about you at one of our gatherings. Without you, their son hasn't a hope of making it through school."

"There, Daddy," Sarah said triumphantly, "unsolicited praise and approval. You're always knocking my profession. Even you, Mr. Landaw, put education last on your list. You're as blind and biased as all business people."

Zetel didn't reply immediately as he was chewing on a mouthful of noodle pudding.

Anna stepped in for him: "Sarah, watch your tongue. Poor Mr. Landaw, we should have warned you."

"On the contrary, let me defend your daughter," Zetel said.

Cyril laughed: "Mr. Landaw, my daughter doesn't need defending. It's us who need defending. She must like you. She hasn't called you any really bad names yet."

Zetel noticed a slight blush spread across Sarah's cheeks and realized Cyril's remark had struck home.

"But Miss Lansmann is quite right," he said. "I enjoy a profession I really like but it needed education to get me there. Therefore, I shall revise my biased opinion and put education first."

Sarah would have none of it. "You say this without conviction. Therefore, in addition to your other vices, you're also a..."

"Sarah, stop right now," Cyril shouted. He stood up and pointed a finger at her. "You are going too far."

Sarah looked at her father in mock astonishment. "Daddy, did you think I was going to call Mr. Landaw a liar? That would be terribly rude since I hardly know him. No, I just wanted to say Mr. Landaw is a tactful stretcher of the truth in order to shut me up and bring tranquillity to our family nest."

Zetel was intrigued by Sarah's forthright and passionate defence of education. Was he as passionate about his calling? He didn't think so. He saw the financial world as not inspiring in itself but as a means to make money, become rich, exert influence and power.

True, he worked hard at developing the skills and judgement required to understand and evaluate the stocks, bonds, and other financial instruments that he dealt with everyday. He relished the moments when his decisions turned out to be right and was gratified when this happened more often than not. Yes, there was excitement as he pursued his work but no deep-seated sense of existential personal value.

Some of his colleagues felt very strongly about their profession. They raved that finance was the energy behind all human endeavour. They argued loudly and vigorously that commerce was impossible without bankers and financiers and the many agents that peopled the industry. Without them, where would the money come from for businesses to invest, grow and develop?

Zetel did not allow himself such self-serving illusions. There was some truth in their assertions but there were also many exceptions. Cyril Lansmann had started his business without much cash and it was quite successful. Similarly, his uncle Shloima had begun by setting up a workshop in his basement and rented factory space as his sales grew. He boasted he never needed credit and loans until long after the business was a functioning concern and then only to buy the building housing his factory instead of paying rent.

"Why do you feel so strongly about education?" Zetel asked.

Sarah looked at him, eyes wide, startled. "Education is a foundation for each individual. What you become is what you learn. Teaching is not just a job but a vocation."

"A vacation, if you ask me," Cyril humphed. "Hours — 9 to 3:30, weekends off, holidays off, all summer off."

Tears sprang to Sarah's eyes. Before she could explode, Zetel quickly intervened. "Then you must be happy with the Quiet Revolution here in Quebec. It seems to me the government aims to take education out of the hands of the Church and make it more secular."

"It's about time," Cyril said. "The head of the CNR — what's his name, Donald something — sure put his foot in it the other day, telling young Quebecers they were too ignorant."

"That's not what he said, Daddy," Sarah objected sharply, still angry over her father's stinging rebuke of teaching. "Mr. Gordon stated that, in his view, no French Quebecer was competent to be a vice-president of CNR and he blamed the education system. It is too religious, too classical, and not enough students even graduate from High School. Just watch, Daddy, all that is going to change and for once I agree with Mr. Landaw." She gave Zetel an appreciative smile.

"It's not just education," Cyril said. "That CNR head is a Scot who came to Canada when he was fifteen years old and barely educated. But he has drive. Took a job at a bank, put himself through night school and look at him now — a top level businessman."

"True, Mr. Lansmann," Zetel said, "but he still needed education and the kind of education he required was available to him. I think what the Quiet Revolution is all about is to make that education available to everyone."

Sarah glowed. "Mr. Landaw, you are far more insightful than I had first thought. You seem to have some depth."

"Take that as a compliment, Mr. Landaw," Anna said. "Our daughter has a sour view of most business people."

"And why not, Mommy?" Sarah asked. "Most business people I've met are happy the Quiet Revolution is clearing up the rot of the Duplessis regime but are suspicious about the change the Lesage government is embarking upon. They don't see it as a fundamental restructuring of Quebec. There will be more nationalizations of industries essential to the Province. I predict there will soon be strong emphasis on French as the spoken language of business."

"But we already speak French in my stores," Cyril said.

"But not in your office," Sarah snapped.

Cyril sighed. "Let's talk about something else."

There was a long moment of silence.

"Do I have to call you Mr. Landaw?" Sarah asked. "My first name is Sarah. What's yours?"

"I have three first names — Zalman Yaakov Zetel. Everyone calls me Zetel."

"Zetel?" asked Sarah.

"Zetel?" asked Anna.

"Zetel?" asked Cyril.

"Zetel," confirmed Zetel.

"I've never heard such a name," Sarah said.

"Neither have I," said Anna. "It doesn't sound Jewish."

"Did you have a close relative called Zetel?" Cyril asked.

"No," Zetel said, amused by the reaction to his name. "I was named after a town in Germany. My parents lived there for many years. My father says it's in memory of a happy place and happy times that died after Hitler came to power."

"Well, I suppose there's a first for everything," Cyril said, frowning. "Imagine a Yid (*Jew*) named after a town — and a German town at that. Is that when they emigrated to Canada?"

"Yes, September, 1935. They didn't expect me. My mother was 7 months pregnant."

"And the next day you landed!" Anna exclaimed. "What a terrible time for your mother. How did she manage?"

"I still wonder today how she managed," Zetel said, and then added thoughtlessly, "It was very hard for her. I was too new at the time to understand the difficulties and what she was going through…"

"You remember?" Sarah interrupted.

He realized he had inadvertently strayed beyond what most people would accept as credible. "No, I'm only repeating the stories my parents have told me as I grew up," he said quickly.

"How did you get into Canada?" Cyril asked. "In the mid-'30s, the gates for Jews were closed. Did you sneak in somehow?"

"Oh, no, my father never does anything illegal. He had a special permit obtained for him by my uncle and several members of Parliament."

Sarah shook her head in wonderment. "You're quite an exceptional person, Mr. Land... Zetel. You're born in the middle of the Atlantic and prematurely. You couldn't wait?"

"I was too anxious for a body," Zetel began and then chuckled to make it appear as a joke.

As they finished dinner and lingered over tea and pie, he amused them with the story of their entrance into Canada, the experience with the Immigration and Customs officials, the long trip to Montreal and then the relief of settling in their new home.

"You tell the story as though you were actually there," Sarah marvelled.

"Well, I was," Zetel said.

"No, as though you actually remember it. My earliest memory is a birthday party when I was three."

My earliest memory goes back billions of years, Zetel thought. "I'm about the same," he said. "I'm just repeating family stories."

Sarah walked Zetel to the door as he took his leave.

"I was kind of hard on you," she said. "I apologize."

"No need. I rather enjoyed our conversation. May I see you again?"

They were married six months later.

CHAPTER 3 —
Zetel and Sarah are engaged

They gathered in the living room of the Lansmann house. Joseph and Ettie had responded quickly to the Lansmann invitation to join them to celebrate the engagement of their children.

Earlier that day, Zetel and Sarah had called upon Cyril at his office and Zetel had formally requested permission to marry Sarah.

Clearly pleased, Cyril shook Zetel's hand, embraced and kissed him on the cheek and then hugged his daughter.

"Is that 'yes,' Daddy?" Sarah asked, smiling, tears in her eyes.

"Of course, it's 'yes,'" Anna said as she pushed into the office. "Now, Cyril, call the Landaws and invite them to our house tonight."

Joseph and Ettie were overjoyed that Zetel had fixed on Sarah as a wife. They had met her on a number of occasions, liked her, and encouraged their son as he courted her. They were sure that Cyril would agree and were not surprised when he called.

Their glasses filled with wine or whisky, they toasted each other and the happy couple.

"As for the wedding," Cyril said, "it's now June. I suggest late Fall or early..."

"I want a summer wedding, Daddy," Sarah insisted, interrupting her father. "I want time for the wedding and for the honeymoon before I teach again in September. And, Daddy, I mean this summer, not next summer."

"But what's the rush?" Cyril demanded. "You know each other just a short time. Alright, you're madly in love, etc., etc. Surely, a few more months won't make a difference? Anna, do you agree with her?"

"When did it make any difference whether we agreed or disagreed with Sarah?" Anna said.

"These weddings take time to plan," Cyril objected. "I don't even know if I can find an available synagogue this summer. It's kind of late."

"Daddy, there's a cancellation on the last Sunday in August at the synagogue on the corner of Lajoie and Durocher. I've asked them to hold the date for us," Sarah said. "It's a very nice synagogue and the Cantor has a gorgeous tenor voice. Besides, it doesn't have to be a big wedding. You know I'm not partial to these enormous affairs."

"Why am I fighting her?" Cyril asked, rolling his eyes and holding up his hands above his head. "A man is willing to take this burden off my back, and I'm arguing? Zetel, where are you in all this?"

Zetel, seated next to Sarah, leaned over and kissed her. "Mr. Lansmann, I love your daughter very much. Need I say more?"

Cyril rolled his eyes again, muttered an "Oi vay,' and turned to the Landaw's. "Yoisef, Ettie, your son has totally surrendered to my daughter. Poor man faces a life of slavery. Are you in favour of a fast wedding."

Both Landaw's were silent for a moment. "I guess," Joseph said hesitantly, "speaking for Ettie and me, we don't really care. I think it's up to the bride and her family. The only concern I have is a wedding with short notice will cause speculation."

"Speculation about what?" Anna asked.

"Well, you know, speculation — why is it a hurry up wedding?" Joseph said looking very uncomfortable. "I'm not saying this should stop you from going ahead. Just be aware, there may be whispers, gossip."

"You mean," Anna said, "maybe one of us is very ill and that's why the wedding is so quick?"

"No, Anna," Cyril said, a knowing look spreading over his face. "Yoisef means some will think Sarah's pregnant."

Sarah and Zetel tried to laugh nonchalantly but it sounded more like a nervous giggle. That and the beet reddening of their cheeks was all the evidence the parents needed.

"Zetel, what happened?" Ettie asked, her voice catching. "Could you not wait?"

"Please don't blame Zetel, Mrs. Landaw," Sarah said. "We both got carried away on just one occasion."

Cyril drew himself up to his full height, balled his fists, and shouted angrily at Zetel: "You knocked my daughter up. I thought you were a decent, respectable guy who could be trusted and you couldn't even wait till after the wedding. " He turned to Sarah: "Is that why you're marrying him? Because you're pregnant?"

Joseph had stood up, wringing his hands, ready to come to Zetel's defence if Cyril started beating him but Anna intervened. "Cyril, stop this nonsense. These things happen. They're in love. Sometimes thing get out of control. Sarah, if you weren't pregnant, would you still want to marry Zetel?"

"I said 'yes' to him even before I knew I was pregnant, Mommy," Sarah said. "The only difference the pregnancy makes is to hurry up the wedding before I get round."

"It will make no difference," Cyril said, and still outraged, glared angrily at Zetel and Sarah. "Everybody will count the months."

A tense silence followed.

"But that is not a problem," Ettie said, jumping up. "Everyone knows Zetel was born prematurely. It should not be a surprise that his child is born prematurely. It's his heredity."

They looked at her dubiously.

"I think it's the mother's body that decides when the baby is ready," Anna said.

"But, Mommy, it doesn't matter. We'll tell everybody, it's a premature birth."

Cyril squinted his eyes at her and said contemptuously, "Nobody's as smart as you, Sarah, but very few are that stupid to believe such a bubbe meisseh (*fairy tale*)."

Again there was a long moment of silence. Cyril stood with his back to them, staring out the window. Ettie, her 'aha' idea shot down, sat, eyes downcast, picking fluff off her summer frock where there was no fluff. Joseph, glumly shaking his head in Zetel's direction, tried desperately to come up with a solution. Anna watched Ettie picking fluff off her skirt. Sarah, defiant, sat ramrod straight. Zetel, his brow furrowed in thought, seemed to come to a decision and stood up.

"Papa and Mama, Mr. and Mrs. Lansmann, I apologize for the problem and the embarrassment I have thrust upon you. But what's done is done. It cannot be reversed. Sarah has said she will not have an abortion and I don't want her to. Therefore, in the normal course of events, our child will be born. I think what's important is that our child — and your grandchild — is born to a married couple. So I suggest two options. One, we have a formal wedding in August as we talked about before, or two, Sarah and I find a rabbi and get married quietly. In the latter option, you can tell everybody 'these kids of today just can't wait, don't like big weddings and surprised us all.'"

Cyril was still with his back to the group as Zetel voiced his options. Now, he snapped around and levelling an accusing finger at Zetel, thundered: "Well, I have another option for both you and Sarah. I disinherit you both and kick you out of my house and my life. When the disgrace comes, let it be only yours. As for you, my daughter, I have tried to please you despite your obstinate nature and your constant arguing with me and your mother. No more! Get out."

Anna shouted at him angrily: "Cyril, she's my daughter too. You throw her out and I go with her. And you want nothing to do with our grandchild? What's the child done? A completely innocent bystander." She burst into tears and was comforted by Ettie.

"Cyril, if at the moment, you cannot forgive my son and Sarah, then I'll look after things and arrange for a small wedding," Joseph said placatingly. "I think Zetel is right and the two must be married long before the birth. Both Ettie and I like Sarah very much and are happy to have her part of our family. I hope you will someday feel the same way about Zetel. I don't want to minimize what's happened but this is the middle of the 20th century and things between young people are...(he struggled for a word)...looser."

Throughout Cyril's tirade and Joseph's attempt to quiet the waters, Sarah continued to sit absolutely straight in her chair, arms akimbo, looking directly at the nearest wall. Now she spoke quietly in a strong, firm voice: "Daddy, you don't like me, never have, but I will not get out as long as my mother is here. I have no regrets about being pregnant. Zetel and I love each other very much, and one day we lost control. So what? I want our baby born legitimate. If you don't want to do the wedding, we can arrange it ourselves. You are invited to attend. If you don't show up or make a fuss, you will never see me or our children again."

"Sarah, no!" Zetel objected. "If we start talking like that, we will never reconcile as a family. Let's not say things now that will make it impossible later on."

"But he's being so mean," Sarah said. "Why are you standing up for him?"

"Because I want a whole family for our baby. I never saw my grandparents. I want our baby to enjoy the love of two zeydes and two bubbies. Besides, we're the ones who have pitched him a curve ball. We should at least understand that and make allowances."

And without Cyril, my plan to accelerate my business will be in jeopardy, he thought.

Zetel took Sarah's hand, pulled her out of the chair and, despite her protests, drew her over to where Cyril had returned to face the window.

"Mr. Lansmann," Zetel said, wondering whether the stiff back in front of him would ever relax, "Sarah and I not only apologize but ask your forgiveness, as well as Mrs. Lansmann's and my parent's. We made a mistake but a mistake born out of love. We ask you to forgive us, not just for our sakes but also for the sake of our child. Our child needs a happy family. We need a happy family. We want all of us to enjoy family get togethers that are happy moments. No doubt there will be gossip and speculation with a swift wedding and a birth too early after the wedding. But all that will be forgotten when the baby arrives. Therefore, we beg all of you, please give us a parents' blessing for our love."

As Zetel spoke with growing emotion, Cyril slowly turned and faced them.

"You're a very convincing salesman, Zetel, but it's all coming from you. I'd like to hear it from my daughter."

"I will not..." Sarah started to say.

"Sarah, please listen to your father," Zetel interrupted her. "You feel the same way I do, don't you?"

Sarah glared at Zetel rebelliously. She saw the grim set of his mouth and the unsmiling eyes. She suddenly realized that if she defied him, it would be all over. She wanted a life with him. And he was right, punishing her father would punish the baby and deprive him of a loving grandfather. She swallowed hard.

"Daddy, I'm sorry for causing you a problem and for what I said." She hesitated, cleared her throat. "I ask your forgiveness and Mommy's and that of Mr. and Mrs. Landaw."

Cyril, eyes awash with tears, reached out an arm and Sarah embraced him. "I also apologize," he said. "I don't know why I reacted the way I did. No matter how much we argue, you will always be my daughter. Now let's talk wedding."

At the same time as the engagement celebration was taking place, Louis C. Fuhr directed his Volkswagen Beetle slowly through the night time streets of Westmount in Montreal. He stayed on the quieter side streets and finally parked on a darkened spot midway between two street lamps. A light rain was falling and soon shrouded the windows of the car in a faint mist which hid the occupant from view.

He needed some calm moments without interruption to comprehend and analyze the feeling of unease that for several days had become more and more engrossing, torturing him with a sense of impending catastrophe.

Despite much research by religious people of all faiths, no one really knows how the Devil receives and communicates information. Had anyone asked Louis C. Fuhr, he would have referred to his enormous network of contacts, spies and malcontents that extended around the world and reached into Heaven itself. However, when this network failed to inform him or warn him in a timely fashion that a plot was unfolding against him, he would become aware through a series of twitches and itches that grew in frequency and soon plagued his entire body. For several days now, he had been so afflicted. Something was brewing, he realized, but what and where?

He left the car and, standing beside it, slowly turned a complete rotation, trying to identify the direction of his unease. To his surprise, the twitches and itches that continuously harassed him increased in intensity as he faced a three storey apartment building directly across from where he had parked. While he believed that his driving had been random, intuitively he must have followed the ebb and flow of the waves of anxiety that assailed him to their source.

He studied the building closely. The windows were mostly dark or dimly lit. Here and there, he could see the blue tinge of a television set. A steep driveway led down to underground parking. There was something familiar about the building. Then slapping his head, he remembered. This was where Zetel lived. The plot involved him!

Fuhr levitated quickly to the top floor and passed through the walls into Zetel's apartment. He was not home.

Fuhr flew out to the street, circled the building and felt himself drawn to the underground garage. A line of security lights barely lit the space and the dozen cars parked there. Off to one side, occupying a no-parking space, was an ambulance, its streamlined hearse-like shape barely visible. He sensed voices inside the vehicle.

He merged with its interior walls. Four figures crowded together within the confined space of the ambulance. He recognized Gabriel immediately, fully dressed in a brown suit with shirt, tie and vest but was puzzled at first by the others. Two were wearing blue uniforms with the word 'Medic' in large white letters printed on their backs. He looked intently at their faces and identified Raphael. After awhile, he realized the other Medic was Chamuel, the angel who had expelled Adam from the Garden of Eden and was well known as the angel who punishes those who transgress against The-One-True-God. The fourth figure was diminutive and turned out to be Sandalphon dressed in a child's pyjamas and wearing a night cap. Sandalphon carried a large bulging knapsack in the form of a teddy bear.

"Now, let's make sure, we all know our parts," Gabriel was saying. "Sandalphon, you are the key player."

"The only reason I'm doing this," Sandalphon said in a child's piping voice, "is we are not killing Zetel. Do I have everyone's word that all we are doing is exchanging souls and Zetel will be alive at the end of our mission?"

"That's the intention," Gabriel said reassuringly.

Sandalphon stamped his foot and said petulantly: "I don't like the word 'intention.'"

Gabriel groaned, "Why did I ever accept this job?"

"Sandalphon, you need have no worries on that score," Chamuel said. "I punish evil doers but I don't kill them, I expel them as I did Adam. It is Zetel's soul which has transgressed, not Zetel. Therefore, I will expel his soul and Raphael and I will quickly install the soul you carry in your bear sack. Just as quickly you will stuff the expelled soul into your bear sack for delivery back to the Arc. Zetel will be dead briefly but will quickly revive. If we planned to kill him, Samael would be present."

"That's right, Sandalphon. If you are not up to the task or willing, we will have to call Samael," Raphael said menacingly.

Sandalphon burst into tears.

"Raphael, that's no way to handle Sandalphon's concerns," Gabriel said, fondling the cherubic angel. "Sandalphon, we have explained why we are using an ambulance. We will carry out the exchange inside the ambulance so that in the most dangerous moment we have life saving equipment at our disposal. Raphael also has divine healing force. We are taking every precaution."

"But something can still go wrong," Sandalphon insisted.

"Yes, Sandalphon, despite our best efforts, something can still go wrong," Chamuel said. "There are always side effects and unplanned consequences. Medicine is not an exact science yet. However, apart from aborting the mission, there is no other way."

"Angels, it is time for action," Gabriel said. "Chamuel and Raphael, drive the ambulance away and stay in readiness close by but out of sight. Zetel will soon be here."

"Neither of us can drive," Raphael said.

"Then how did you get it here?" demanded Gabriel, throwing up his hands and tearing at his hair.

"I was driving," Chamuel said. "I willed it here but we attracted attention. The engine made no sound, the wheels did not turn, but we moved just the same. People seemed to notice."

"At least, turn the engine on," Gabriel said. "And why can't you drive? Mortals drive. You are angels. Top angels. You are smarter than mere mortals. Get into the vehicle and drive it."

Chamuel looked at Raphael questioningly. Raphael had his eyes fixed on the ambulance, his brow furrowed in deep thought.

"Chamuel," Raphael said, his face lit with excitement. "You remember when I pretended illness at the place where the ambulance was kept and the medics put me into the back of one. I was looked after by one medic and you were in the forward part with the other. How did he start?"

Chamuel thought long and hard and then his face also lit with excitement. "He turned the key in the lock and pressed his right foot against a pedal. The engine started. Then he pressed his left foot against a pedal and moved a lever with his right hand and the ambulance moved forward. That's all there is to it. I can easily do it."

Chamuel jumped into the driver's seat, and started the engine. The ambulance leaped forward, scraped the garage wall, veered towards the opening, and bounced up the driveway, followed by Raphael running hard. Chamuel turned right onto the street, clipped a stone post at the head of the driveway, knocking out a headlamp, and swung from side to side up the street and disappeared around a corner with Raphael still in hot pursuit.

Even the Devil is in danger with this driver, thought Fuhr as he disengaged from the ambulance and flew back to the apartment building. He entered Zetel's flat and called the police.

To the operator who answered, he said in a triumphant tone, "The ambulance that was stolen earlier is parked on Melville near Acorn Street. There are two men inside it. If you hurry, you can catch them."

He flew back down to the garage to monitor events. The wait was long. Gabriel had fastened a beard onto his face and lay crumpled on the floor beside a car. Sandalphon sat nearby. Finally, lights lit up the driveway as an auto crept slowly down and drove carefully into the garage. It braked sharply as the lights picked up a man, face down, blocking its path.

A small child in pyjamas, holding a large teddy bear which almost eclipsed him, ran in front of the car, screaming , "Help! Help!"

Zetel sprang from the car. "What's wrong? What's happened?" He knelt beside the child.

"Mister, my father is sick. We came back from a drive because I couldn't sleep and he just fell and he won't wake up." The child's eyes were wide in fear and tears rolled down his cheeks.

Zetel ran to the prostrate body. The man still breathed but raggedly. He called out, "Sir, can you hear me?" but the only reply was a groan.

"I'll call a doctor," Zetel said.

"I called for an ambulance," the man moaned. "The wall phone. I felt the attack coming on. Heart attack."

Zetel had never seen a wall phone in the garage but there it was, a large red one with a sign over it labelled "AMBULANCE."

"Please wait until it comes and look after my boy," the man whispered and clutched his chest.

"Don't worry," Zetel reassured him. "Is there someone I can call. Someone in your apartment. Your wife?"

The man made no answer and seemed to have lost consciousness.

Zetel turned to the boy: "Don't worry. Your father will be alright. The ambulance will be here shortly. What's your name?"

"Sand..." the child started to reply, paused, then "...y. That's it — Sandy."

Fuhr slipped again to Zetel's apartment and called for an ambulance. Then he flew quickly to the corner. Eight policemen surrounded the damaged ambulance parked there, their police cars blinking red and blocking traffic. He caught sight of Raphael and Chamuel being driven away in the back of a police cruiser.

He returned to the garage. Zetel, impatient with the length of time the ambulance was taking, tried to use the emergency telephone. There was no dial tone. It was an old fashioned device with the mouth piece in the body of the apparatus, an ear piece attached by a wire, and a handle for generating a call. He tried turning the handle. The apparatus fell off the wall and crashed to the cement floor. Frustrated, he was about to go up to his apartment to make the call when he noticed an ambulance carefully backing down the driveway.

Finally, here they come, thought Gabriel. Chamuel's driving has certainly improved. Before, he could barely move forward. Now he can go backwards.

Zetel directed the two medics to the sick man. "Before he became unconscious, he believed he was having a heart attack," he explained.

A medic pushed a stethoscope against Gabriel's chest. "I'm not getting a heartbeat. Quick, bring the stretcher. We'll try resuscitating him inside the ambulance."

Gabriel, eyes shut, still feigning unconsciousness, whispered, "Not me, you idiots, him."

The two medics rolled a protesting Gabriel onto the stretcher, "Idiots, not me, him."

"Well, he is breathing but he's delirious," a medic said to Zetel. "He thinks you're the sick one."

"Quick, Chamuel, expel the soul," Gabriel shouted, as the medics lifted the stretcher into the ambulance. "Sandalphon, get ready."

"Something's wrong," Sandalphon called out. He tried to stop the medics.

"Hey, little fellow," a medic said, restraining Sandalphon, "we're taking your daddy to the hospital. He'll be ok. Not to worry. Who's looking after you?"

"His father asked me to take care of him," Zetel said, seemingly compelled to step forward and to grasp a tearful Sandalphon, still clutching his teddy bear.

"Here, let me help," Fuhr said, stepping out from behind a car. "He's quite a handful."

Zetel, surprised by Fuhr's sudden appearance, quickly realized that something extraordinary was happening. They both hauled a protesting Sandalphon into the stairwell leading from the garage. Moments later, while the medics were still struggling with a desperate and uncooperative patient, Fuhr returned and tossed the teddy bear at Gabriel.

" Please take this with you."

"You!" Gabriel exclaimed. He broke loose from the medics, grabbed the teddy bear, ran up the driveway, leaped high in the air and disappeared.

"Holy One, something went wrong," Gabriel barely whispered, hands clutching his head, steeling himself against the lightning blast that was sure to come. "Despite our well laid out plan, events interfered over which we had no control."

The three angels lay prostrate before the massive cumulus cloud of vertical development. Gabriel's clothes were dishevelled from the efforts of the medics to restrain him. Chamuel and Raphael were in yellow jump suits, a souvenir of their arrest and jailing. The large teddy bear lay close by.

"Most Holy, Archangel Gabriel is right," Chamuel said, his voice humble and pleading. "Mortal police arrived and detained us while we waited for his call and, therefore, we were unable to complete our mission."

Raphael nodded vigorously in agreement.

"Rubbish!" exclaimed The-One-True-God, His massive cumulous cloud of vertical development black with anger. "Once again, you were bested by the Devil. Why did I hurl him to the nether regions? Better I should have kept him here so I could watch him. And what do I have now to assist me? Incompetents!"

"Most Holy One, with all respect, Chamuel and I did our part as directed by Archangel Gabriel, " Raphael said, trying to distance himself from the general calumny and punishment that was to follow. "It was his plan. We did exactly as we were told. It was not a good plan."

"Shame, Rafael," The-One-True-God thundered. "You tell Me now it was not a good plan. Why did you not object at the time?"

"Not only did he not object, Most Holy, he agreed with me," an aggrieved Gabriel said.

"Yes, I am sure they both agreed," The-One-True-God said contemptuously. "The witless led by a fool. Where is My sweet Sandalphon? Has he not returned with you."

There was silence. Finally, Gabriel said haltingly, "We don't know. Satan may have captured him. But Satan did throw me the bear sack with the unused soul."

"I want Sandalphon found. You will devote yourself to this task. In the meantime, release the unused soul to return to the Arc. Look how he squirms and groans."

Gabriel quickly unzipped the bear sack. Out popped Sandalphon.

CHAPTER 4 —
Unto Zetel a wedding and a child

At the late August wedding, a discerning guest, perhaps already suspicious by the shortness of notice, could note a definite bulging in the bride's abdomen. Sarah had insisted on a tight fitting waist when she selected the gown despite Ettie's and Anna's mild objections.

"If the dress is too tight, people will see you're pregnant," Anna said.

"Besides," Ettie added, "is it good for the baby to have a tight dress?"

"I plan to get married only once and I'm going to have the dress I like," Sarah insisted. "Judging by the gossip I've heard, everybody seems to know anyway."

The other issue that arose was Zetel's choice of Herr Fuhr as Best Man. Uncle Shloima suggested his son, Chaim, but Zetel felt more comfortable with Fuhr.

"Mama, Papa, I have known Herr Fuhr since I was a child. He's been a great friend to me, always gave me solid advice, and is helping me in my career. He even made the contact that brought me into the Lansmann fold. When I eventually open my business, I will want him on my advisory board. As for Chaim, I hardly see him since we've grown up. We meet only at family events. Sure, he's a first cousin but we're not that close."

"There's no doubt Herr Fuhr is a very fine man," Ettie said. "And he's been very helpful to us as well as you. But he's not your age. And there's something strange about him. In the twenty years we know him, he looks exactly the same as when he arrived. He hasn't aged at all. I would like to know his secret."

"I asked him that at the engagement party," Joseph said. "We were sitting with Hershey and Jack. I told him, 'My face is wrinkling, yours isn't, my hair is graying, yours isn't, how come? What's the formula?' Fuhr laughed. 'I employ the infernal magic arts. You don't want to know the formula.' Zetel, for the honour of being your Best Man, ask him for the formula. We could make a fortune."

In the end, there wasn't much argument: Sarah got the dress she wanted, Zetel got his Best Man.

The wedding was talked about for months afterwards. Sarah insisted on a small wedding and fought every name on both parents' guest lists. Nevertheless, the assemblage of guests and wedding party rose to over 250.

The Wedding March was impeccably played by a quintet of string and brass culled from the Montreal Symphony Orchestra. All agreed the bride was especially beautiful in her tight fitting gown that emphasized the shapeliness of her body. The slight bulge below the waist line was forgotten about in the happiness and ostentatious display of luxury that pervaded the event.

Zetel cut an impressive figure in his white jacket summer formal wear.

"What a gorgeous man!" Sylvia whispered in Hershey's ear. "But don't be jealous. You once looked like that."

Ettie, tears dribbling down her face, said to Joseph: "Our boy is getting married. I can't believe it. He was just a little baby not so long ago."

"Not so long ago, Ettie?" Joseph said. "It was 27 years ago when he was just a little baby."

"My life will be empty, Anna," Cyril said, watching his daughter exchange rings with Zetel. "I'll have nobody to argue with."

"Thank God," Anna said. "Just think — I'll have a quiet home."

"You know who I can't get over," Faigel said to Jack. "Herr Fuhr. Look at him. He must be our age but looks closer in age to Zetel. His formal wear fits him like a glove. And he's still as good looking as the day he arrived."

Jack frowned. "There's something funny about him, Faigel. What's he live on? He doesn't have a job that he goes to regularly. Zetel says he has a pension from Germany and makes money on the stock market. Maybe. But he has a big house in Westmount — that must cost a pretty penny. When we don't see him for a long time, he says he's been travelling. Once I asked him where and he said Transylvania. 'That's part of the Soviet Union,' I said to him. 'How do you get in?' He said he has no difficulty getting in. I could see he didn't want to go into details so I let it go. I guess he's probably bribing somebody which also costs money. To my mind, he has an expensive life and no obvious income source. Suspicious."

"Oh, come on, Jack," Faigel said. "We're both retired and yet we live quite well. Are you telling me there's something suspicious about us?"

"OK," Jack said. "But we don't fly over to Transylvania. The best we could do this winter was drive down to Florida and no one would call that hotel we stayed at luxurious. So here's Fuhr. He flees the Nazis with nothing but the clothes on his back, lives in Yoisef's back room to the end of the war, and works in a men's clothing shop. Not exactly the start of great wealth."

"Will you two shut up," Hershey whispered from behind them. "I can't hear the rabbi's sermon."

At the end of the sermon, Hershey leaned towards them. "Better you should have kept talking. Can't these guys come up with something original? It's always the same twaddle — remember your obligations to each other, respect your vows, respect each other, care for each other — I swear, he lifted the sermon from our wedding."

After the ceremony, the wedding party and guests congregated in the large lobby of the synagogue where a sumptuous buffet of appetisers had been laid out. The wine was poured and the blessings made. Sarah and Zetel barely ate as guests surrounded them with congratulatory handshakes, hugs and kisses.

In the main dining hall, the guests were greeted by an eleven piece dance band and a five course dinner, an open bar and wine at each table. All took their seats and then rose and applauded as the band waltzed in the wedding party of parents, ushers, bridesmaids, Maid of Honour and the Best Man. They then played 'Bluebird of Happiness' to welcome Zetel and Sarah, both smiling broadly, and waving happily to the guests.

Joseph was stupefied by the display of Cyril's wealth. He had told Cyril he could not afford to participate in an expensive wedding. Cyril dismissed the notion. "The bride's family will look after the wedding. You get the flowers." Just purchasing the flowers eliminated the trip to Israel they had planned for the following year.

After the dinner the speeches began. Fuhr as Master of Ceremonies introduced each of the speakers. Cyril thanked everyone for coming to share the happy event with them and welcomed Zetel to the family. Joseph commented on how much they had come to love Sarah and welcomed her to the family. Zetel spoke about how lucky he felt marrying the love of his life. Sarah joked that she had tired of pushing her family around and now had a new victim whom, fortunately for him, she loved very much.

It was Fuhr's turn. He greeted the wedding party and the guests, lauded the festiveness of the event and the generosity of the hosts, complimented the chefs on their wonderful dishes, and praised the band for its fine dinner music.

"As Best Man, it is my duty," he went on, "to tell you something about the groom, something even his parents may not know, something his bride should be made aware of."

He allowed a long tense pause.

"He's a good man."

There was relieved laughter among the guests. Zetel had been holding his breath and now let it slowly out.

"I have known the groom a long time," Fuhr continued. "When the Landaw family took me in, Zetel was five years old. At first he was very suspicious of me, he accused me once of being an evil spirit, a dybbuk. I told him that in my last job in Germany I was a well-known banker and therefore, if I were going to inhabit the spirit world, an ordinary dybbuk would not do — no, I'd want the top job, the Devil. Anyway, I soon won his confidence and we have become fast friends. Even after I left the family home, we remained in close touch. Indeed it is with gratitude that I acknowledge the hospitality of Yoisef and Ettie who always make me feel like a family member.

"Earlier this evening I overheard some gossip related to how I make a living. It's very simple. No, I'm not just a lucky devil. I invested my meagre pensions with Zetel and the results are outstanding. If this sounds like bare faced advertising, it is. Put your money with Zetel. He's a married man now and needs the fees and commissions."

"I had nothing to do with this," Zetel shouted, his face reddening with embarrassment.

"But if you're going to follow Mr. Fuhr's advice, wait till we get back from our honeymoon," Sarah chimed in.

"Come, come, Zetel, do not be shy about your investing ability," Fuhr said. "In fact, let's demonstrate it. Jack, if Faigel allows you to have money, please come to the podium. Zetel, you too."

A reluctant Jack hesitantly approached Fuhr. Zetel was fearful. He knew that Fuhr liked an audience and enjoyed the admiration he invariably received. Sometimes, indulging his vanity, he did things that defied explanation unless you knew his true identity.

"Jack, give me a bill of any denomination," Fuhr said.

"Now, Ladies and Gentlemen, I could pocket the $10 bill which Jack has just given me and say that's how I make *my* money but there are too many witnesses. Instead, to demonstrate Zetel's prowess, let me place it on his open palm."

He pulled Zetel's arm straight and turned his hand so all could see the bill resting on his open palm. Fuhr carefully closed Zetel's fingers over the bill and held his hand for a few seconds.

"Jack, open Zetel's fingers."

The audience gasped. Those further away stood up to better see. Jack removed two $10 bills from Zetel's hand.

"Shall we go double or nothing, Jack?"

"No," Jack said, scurrying back to his seat as the audience applauded. "Doubling my money in 10 seconds is enough for me."

"By the way, Zetel," Fuhr said, "I hope you and Sarah are happy with my gift."

Zetel looked at him questioningly. What was he up to now? As Zetel had feared, Fuhr was reacting to the clearly warm regard of the wedding guests. *Herr Fuhr*, he thought, *don't go beyond the plausible. Don't worry*, the thought came back.

"Have you not seen it yet?" asked Fuhr. "It's in your inside coat pocket."

"There's nothing in my coat pocket," Zetel said.

"Then it must be in Sarah's purse."

"I have nothing in my purse but a handkerchief and some make up," said Sarah. She opened the purse to show everyone and a thick white envelope fell out.

"You'll find your air tickets and bookings for your honeymoon in the envelope. I sometimes forget where I put things," Fuhr said, shaking his head.

Delighted, the audience applauded.

"As you can see," Fuhr said, "I'm a bit of a magician. It's a hobby. Let me show you some of my favourite tricks. I brought with me a deck of ordinary playing cards."

He splayed the deck open to the guests and turned to show the head table.

"It's all one card, the Jack of Spades," several guests and Sarah called out.

"Oh, dear," Fuhr said. "Terribly sorry. Let me shuffle the deck."

He shuffled the deck expertly, cascading the cards from one hand to the other. He did this several times.

"Is that better?" he asked, spreading the cards in a fan and turning to show Sarah.

"It's now a normal deck," Sarah said as the guests applauded.

"Fine, Sarah. Now, take the deck of cards, pull out one card but don't tell me what it is, and show it to the audience while I turn my back, then sign the card with your first name, and put the card back."

Sarah followed his instructions. Fuhr took the cards from her and shuffled them.

"Now, Sarah, find the card you selected in the deck."

Sarah quickly ran her fingers through the cards, then started over more carefully, then with surprise growing on her face, asked Anna to help her and both carefully planted each card successively on the podium.

"It's not here," Sarah said. "You must have taken it when you shuffled the deck."

"But you watched me as I shuffled the deck. Did you see me take the card?"

"Then where is it?" Sarah demanded.

"I'm not sure, but I do have a card in my pocket. Is this it?" He held up the missing card.

"Louis, that's an easy trick," Cyril said. "You obviously palmed the card when you shuffled the deck and with Sarah's signature on it, you knew which card."

"Aha, a sceptic," said Fuhr. "Very well, Cyril, you shuffle the cards, and let the bridegroom select one."

"I don't want any part of this," Zetel said, but was pushed forward by his father.

Cyril shuffled the deck after first examining it carefully. Zetel picked a card out and displayed it to the guests, then put the card back. Cyril shuffled the cards again. Looked on by Zetel, Sarah and Anna, Cyril turned each card over.

"The card I selected — the eight of clubs — is not here," Zetel said.

Cyril looked nonplussed. "Then where is it?" he asked.

"Cyril," Fuhr said, "you did the trick and did it very well. You must know where it is. Maybe it's in your pocket."

Cyril reached into a pocket of his coat and pulled out the missing card.

This time, the guests were out of their seats and applauding madly.

"It's very clear to me," Hershey called out when the hubbub had subsided. "You're all in it together."

Zetel sighed in relief. Let them all think that, rather than start to question how Fuhr actually made it happen.

Fuhr just laughed and announced it was time to dance.

As Sarah's pregnancy neared term and birth of the baby was imminent, apprehension descended on the family. The baby's heartbeat was not solid nor rhythmic and the baby was not turning in the womb as it should. Sarah was placed in hospital at the Jewish

General and her doctors examined and tested and tried to figure out what to do.

"It's possible," one doctor confided to Zetel, "that the baby will be stillborn or not survive long after birth. We don't understand — everything tells us the baby should be normal."

Sarah began to suspect the worst and subsided into a depressive state. Zetel was frequently at her bedside as well as both the Landaws and the Lansmanns. They tried to cheer her up but they didn't feel very cheerful themselves. The time stretched past the expected date.

"Not to worry," Cyril said in a futile attempt to be reassuring. "You probably got the conception wrong. Sometimes these things take much longer."

At a late evening visit, Zetel put his ear to Sarah's swollen abdomen. "Speak to me," he whispered, propelling the thought into her womb. There was no answer.

He left the hospital and drove to Fuhr's house. The door opened and closed behind him. He followed a lit candle which moved along in mid air guiding him. He entered Fuhr's spacious library study. Fuhr was standing against a bookshelf in full devil's regalia — horns, mask, long black cape.

"Oh, for God's sake, Herr Fuhr, take off that ridiculous costume," Zetel said.

"Don't you dare refer to Him in my house," Lucifer said. He stripped off the costume. He was in formal evening wear, black tie against white frilled shirt, black jacket and trousers, and black patent leather shoes. "I was expecting you."

"I'm being punished," Zetel said. "It can't be just coincidence that our first baby is dying."

"I believe that is the case," Lucifer said, nodding. He guided Zetel to an easy chair and sat down opposite him. "I am informed by a Heavenly contact — I must say, an unexpected Heavenly contact — that Gabriel will not despatch a soul to your embryo in order to teach you a lesson."

"So the child is doomed," Zetel said. "Sarah will blame herself but it's my fault."

"You should also be aware that Samael is in the hospital," Lucifer said.

"But why?" Zetel asked. "If there's no soul, there's no soul to retrieve."

"According to my informant, Gabriel is looking for a sacrifice," Lucifer said. "You, in particular. It will be the price for your baby's survival."

Zetel, now in a deep funk, struggled with the dilemma facing him: his life or the baby's. The baby not yet born, on the threshold of life; he, still with many years ahead, surrounded by loving family and friends, his dream of owning and operating his own investment house less than a year away, all the signs pointing to a full and prosperous life. And the baby? An uncertain beginning without a father, an unknowable future, in a word, a blank slate, no more than the potential that comes with birth. But his own slate was already partly filled in, lines of progress well charted, a better bet than the unborn. One had to be pragmatic, not give way to irrational emotion. If he were making an investment decision, he would compare the upside with the downside. Surely, it would be a better bet if he chose to live. But life was not just a calculation of ups and downs. He was the baby's father, prone to defend his offspring at all costs, even the cost of his life. He thought of Sandra and his harsh and selfish treatment of her, forcing her to abort his child. Did he have the strength or the right to kill another of his children?

"They've won," Zetel said. "Help me find Samael. I will present myself to him."

Lucifer looked long and hard at him. "Are you sure? Don't expect mercy from the Angel of Death. He enjoys retrieving souls."

Zetel stood up, his head bowed, his hands shaking. "Let's go before I lose my resolve."

"Zetel," Fuhr said very quietly, "there may be another way. Go back to the hospital and sit beside Sarah. I will meet you there."

Zetel knew better than to ask Fuhr for an explanation. He drove quickly to the hospital. He greeted Sarah with a kiss. "Why did you come back?" she asked, her tone despondent. "There's nothing to come back to. I can't even make you a father. I'm a total failure."

Tears in his eyes, he gently stroked her face. "You're not the failure," he said. "I am. I'm being punished for a sin I committed."

Sarah sat up. "Zetel, what are you talking about? What sin could you have committed? You don't have venereal disease. Is it something genetic?"

Zetel was crying, great heaving sobs wracking his body. Sarah dragged herself off the bed and flung her arms around him. At that moment, Fuhr arrived.

"Mr. Fuhr, this is not a good time to visit," Sarah said. "Zetel is very upset."

"All the more reason I should be here," Fuhr said. "Let me help you into bed."

Sarah objected but Zetel, between sobs, managed to get out, "Do what he says, Sarah."

Sarah snapped up straight, crossed her arms over her bloated belly, stared defiantly at Fuhr. "My husband is suffering and I will treat him as I see fit."

"Sarah, please, Herr Fuhr is trying to be helpful."

"That's right, Sarah, I mean only the best for the two of you," Fuhr said. He reached out a hand and gently grasped Sarah's arm. She immediately acquiesced and allowed herself to be helped into the bed. "In addition to card tricks, I know some old world remedies, not practised by modern medicine."

"Zetel, don't let him give me any ..." she started to say and fell asleep.

Fuhr turned to the other patient in the room. "I hope we didn't awake you by arriving so late."

The woman shook her head, yawned, and she, too, lapsed into sleep.

Fuhr grabbed Zetel by the shoulders and shook him. "Stop that childish slobbering and compose yourself. Samael is close and we must keep him away."

Zetel noticed now that Fuhr had brought with him two large suitcases. He opened one and a naked, short, grey bearded old man with an unkempt thick patch of white hair stepped out groaning. Fuhr quickly wrapped him in a hospital gown he secured from the room closet, found an IV pole, hung a bag of IV fluid and taped the tube to the old man's left hand.

"Stop groaning, Sandalphon, you weren't in there very long and it's you who volunteered to help," Fuhr admonished him. "This sweet angel," he explained to Zetel, "is not happy with Gabriel's decision to kill either you or the baby. He is my unexpected Heavenly contact."

"On this occasion only," Sandalphon said. "And you have broken your promise not to identify me. Soul of Zetel, I'm to be called Norman."

"Norman," said Zetel bowing, "I'm extremely grateful you have decided to come to the aid of our baby and me. I don't know what Lucifer has in mind or what your role is but I thank you for the risks you are taking."

"I do what I believe is right," said Sandalphon. "Now I must go."

He left the room and pushing his pole carefully in front of him walked slowly down the long corridor to the elevator. He passed the nursing station and nodded pleasantly to a nurse who looked up from her paperwork. It took but a brief moment for the nurse to wonder what an older patient was doing in the obstetrics ward but by the time she rose to investigate, a scream from a nearby room attracted her attention.

Sandalphon plodded on, very concerned that he deliver an old man performance with conviction. Certainly, patients and late night visitors stepped aside and smiled encouragingly at him. He stopped a little ways from the elevator, partly hidden by the open door to a darkened room.

For awhile the elevator was busy with staff and visitors, leaving or arriving. Finally, the elevator door opened and a lone figure stepped out. He was tall, extremely thin, his face pale, and emaciated. He was dressed in white scrubs, his head covered by a tight fitting surgical hat, and a stethoscope hung around his neck. He studied the signage and then headed along the corridor.

He nearly collided with Sandalphon who stepped out in front of him, quietly groaning. He tried to walk around Sandalphon but was blocked by the IV pole.

"Doctor, please help me," Sandalphon moaned. "I'm in terrible pain. My chest. I think I'm dying."

"I'm in a terrible hurry," the doctor said. "I must attend to a sick patient. I see the nurses up ahead. Go to them. They will look after you."

He tried to press on but Sandalphon grasped his shirt.

"Doctor, I've been there. They just sent me back to my room. Can't you examine me?"

"You're not my patient. You must see your own doctor." Again he tried to get by but Sandalphon held him fast. "What's your name? I will ask the nurses to look after you immediately."

"My name is Norman. They won't pay any attention and I will die. I just know it. You've got to help me."

Samael was angry and frustrated. He shoved Norman roughly aside and turned away. Norman screamed, tottered a few steps and collapsed on the floor.

Two nurses came running. "What happened, Doctor?" one nurse asked.

"How would I know?" he asked irritably.

A nurse pressed the chestpiece of her stethoscope against Norman's chest. "There's no heartbeat," she said. "Doctor, shall we not try to resuscitate him?"

Samael was accustomed to receiving souls and sending them on their way to the Arc, not saving them. "How do we do that?"

The nurse looked at him in surprise. "Doctor, I will breathe into his mouth and you compress his chest rapidly. Did you not attend the demonstrations last year?"

Samael was in a quandary. Taking time to save this man would delay him in his mission but if the man were indeed dead, he would lose time anyway retrieving his soul. While he hesitated, one nurse had turned Norman on his back and was blowing air into his mouth while she pinched his nostrils. The other nurse pointed to Norman's chest. Samael dutifully began to pump the chest.

"Faster, doctor, and push down harder," the nurse said. "Doctor, don't stop now."

But Samael had paused. Norman's gown opened as he pummelled his chest and revealed an expanse of pink unmarred youthful flesh. Samael stared. This was not the skin of an old man but that of a boy, a cherub, or — he pushed the nurse at Norman's head brusquely aside and wrenched at the beard. It came off in tufts with bits of plaster and skin still clinging to it.

"Sandalphon!" Samael howled, the sound penetrating down the corridor and into the patient rooms, a wail of such intense rage and murderous hatred that screams erupted throughout the ward and the newborn babies in the nursery cried out in terror.

The nurses shrank back from the two. Samael grasped Sandalphon by the throat, lifted him off the floor and shook him. "Why?"

"Because you can't treat an innocent unborn as hostage. I won't let it happen."

Samael threw him against a wall and started running down the hallway. "He's not a real doctor," Sandalphon shouted.

"Orderly, stop that man," a nurse called out to the burly man who had appeared, attracted by the noise.

The orderly scuffled with Samael and momentarily restrained him. Samael shook him off and ran on, followed by the orderly and the nurses. He flung open the door to Sarah's room, startling the patient in the other bed. Sarah was gone. Beside her bed were two large empty suitcases.

"Where is she?" he demanded of the other woman.

"I just woke up when they took her to the birthing room. She said it was a miracle, her baby had suddenly come alive and was about to be born."

Samael looked about hopelessly. "Her husband, where is he?"

"Why, he went with her, as well as the gentleman with him. You will probably find them in the waiting room."

"Gentleman?" said Samael, the light of understanding slowly illuminating his face.

"Yes, a tall man dressed in formal wear. I hadn't seen him before."

"How could our plot fail?" Gabriel demanded.

He glanced about to make sure no one was within ear shot. He and Samael sat on an expanse of the Arc with its tethered souls. The massive cumulus cloud of vertical development was nowhere to be seen, probably on the other side of the world.

The Angel of Death pulled his black hood off his head, revealing a face even gloomier than usual.

"We were sabotaged, betrayed," Samael said. "Betrayed by one of our own. I shall accuse Sandalphon when the Almighty makes His appearance. I shall insist he be tossed into the infernal regions."

"I fear I will be the one tossed into the infernal regions," Gabriel said. "Once again, I will be chastised for failing to secure the soul of Zetel. I will be told I'm incompetent. Why doesn't He just fire me?"

"Wrong choice of words, Gabriel," said Samael, a suspicion of a smile stretching his thin lips. "You know what the word 'fire' means to the Almighty."

"Well, even Hellfire would be preferable. Satan seems to have a good time."

"I don't intend to take any blame," Samael said. "Our mission was foiled by Sandalphon's interference."

They heard a shout and looked up.

"Angels," called out Raphael as he, Michael, and Chamuel swept down on them. "We heard the good news. You are to be congratulated. Wonderful! Wonderful!"

The three angels hugged and kissed Gabriel and Samael and thumped them on their backs. Other angels appeared and all danced in a circle around the two, singing, "Hosanna" and "Hallelujah."

Attracted by the festive sounds, a mighty Host of angels, cherubs and other sacred beings gathered round, applauding and congratulating an astonished Gabriel and Samael. Not even the Angel of Death's fearsome appearance and stink of rot repelled them. The dancers pushed them together and lifted them up so all could see them,

"I believe, Gabriel," Samael said dolefully, "we have returned to the wrong Heaven. A little while ago I was assisting a retrieved soul to return to the Arc. He claimed he was an astrophysicist — whatever that is — and as a result of his life's work, he insisted there was more than one universe and therefore more than one Heaven and likely, more than one God. He called them parallel universes. At the time, I thought the shock of death had deranged him. Now, I'm not so sure. How else to explain all this euphoric approbation?"

"We shall soon know," Gabriel said. "Here comes our Holy Master and look who cradles in His cloudy mass."

Held by a puff of cloud almost like an arm, Sandalphon led the massive cumulus cloud of vertical development to the gathering on the Arc. He was snatched by angels, held high, and praised in dance and song.

"The cloud is white, not black, and no thunder and lightning," Gabriel exclaimed in surprise. "He's not angry."

"I tell you, we're in a parallel universe," Samael said.

A blast of trumpets, and all fell silent as The-One-True-God spoke: "Archangels, angels, cherubs, sacred spirits and saints, I must tell you of a great event that has occurred which has gained My deepest gratitude and admiration for Archangel Gabriel in particular and for the part played by the Angel of Death and My sweet Sandalphon. The plan created by Archangel Gabriel, in consultation with Samael and Sandalphon, was clearly ingenious and perfectly implemented by his two assistants. Sandalphon has explained the plan and how it worked and I am truly amazed. It is no secret that I have criticized Archangel Gabriel from time to time. It is clear now that I have underestimated his sagacity, his brilliance and his cunning, and for this I apologize."

Gabriel, still held on high, bowed. The others all bowed too, dropping Gabriel and Samael to the floor of the Arc. "Samael, he's apologizing to me. How can that be? What did we do?"

"I tell you we're not in the right Heaven," Samael growled.

"For some time now," The-One-True-God continued, "I have wrestled with a conundrum. At the last confrontation with Satan, a soul was captured and hidden by him. This was very worrisome to Me. I cannot countenance a soul outside My control, particularly a soul in the hands of the Devil. My constant concern has been how to recover that soul or assign it to a proper mortal. In a word, how to wrest an innocent soul from the clutches of the Devil."

The-One-True-God paused, to let the enormity of the problem sink in. Hardly a sound could be heard from the assembled Host.

"Archangel Gabriel found a way that had eluded even Me. He outsmarted the Devil and saved the soul. Archangel Gabriel set up an urgent situation where he refused to assign a soul to a baby in a pregnant womb. The Devil, under pressure from a follower, was forced to use his captured soul to save the baby. To make the pressure seem real, the Devil was told Samael would be at the hospital to retrieve the dead baby. Sandalphon pretended to stop Samael to allow the Devil time to insert the soul into the baby. What amuses Me even more — the Devil has thanked Sandalphon for interfering.

"Archangel Gabriel, Angel Of Death Samael, Angel Sandalphon, you have achieved a miraculous result with a well thought out plan and faultless execution. All hail these three angels."

The roar of approval swept around the Arc and penetrated to the skin of the world. Its reverberations caused valleys to rise and hills to crumble, rivers to overflow their banks, seas to spawn huge waves, and volcanoes to erupt. Only the urgently expressed Will of The-One-True-God calmed the Earth's sudden contortions and saved the world from rampant destruction.

The blast of a dozen trumpets silenced the throng.

"Host of Angels, Cherubs, Sacred Spirits and Saints, this shall be the sign of My high regard for Gabriel, Samael and Sandalphon. From henceforth to the End of Days, their heads will be surmounted by a golden circlet, The Sacred Halo, which shall signify to all their revered status in the Heavenly hierarchy."

As The-One-True-God uttered these words, a glowing circle of intense light appeared at the top of the three angels' heads. Gabriel blinked and covered his eyes before he could look at Samael and Sandalphon.

"We are truly blessed, Most Holy One," Sandalphon said, bowing in the direction of the cloud which was now moving away. The Host also slowly left the scene giving final huzzahs and cheers to the three decorated angels. Soon they were alone.

"Somehow, some time, Sandalphon, I will find a way to annihilate you," Samael said.

"Why would you do that, holy Angel of Death?" Sandalphon asked, looking perplexed. "Was that not the plan? Was I not simply following your orders, Archangel Gabriel? That is what I explained to my sweet and holy Master, The-One-True-God."

Gabriel hesitated a moment, loath to endanger his new status as a decorated angel. "Of course, Sandalphon, that was our plan. The Most Holy cannot be wrong. Isn't that so, Samael?"

Samael stared incredulously at both of them.

"I'm in the wrong universe," he said.

CHAPTER 5 —
Zetel in Toronto

Zetel stood at the floor to ceiling glass window on the 38th floor of the Toronto Dominion Building in downtown Toronto. He had a commanding view of the harbour, Toronto Island, and Lake Ontario beyond. A warm spring day in early May, the water showed no white caps and sparkled in the noon sun. Far out on the lake a single sail cut the blueness of the water.

"An impressive sight," Fuhr said. "Far prettier than the infernal regions to which I'm consigned. There are times when I wish I had remained an Angel."

Zetel returned to his desk to face his visitor. "You told me once, you were the inspiration for Milton's line in Paradise Lost — better to reign in Hell than serve in Heaven. I don't think you have any regrets. I haven't seen you in a while — maybe five or six years."

"Oh, I had business in other parts of my domain. Also, I took a long holiday in Transylvania. I detected no plots against you so I decided to stay out of your way. You were too busy setting up your business and then moving to Toronto. How did that go?"

Zetel let out a deep sigh. "The move was emotionally draining. Everyone was against it, my parents, my in-laws and especially Sarah."

"Then why did you move?"

"Herr Fuhr, like everyone else, I was worried about the political unrest in Quebec, particularly the bombings by the extreme separatists. But it was the 1970 October Crisis which really did it for me. When extremists kidnap a British diplomat and kill a government Minister and there are soldiers all over the place, I decided Montreal was not where I wanted to bring up my children. What clinched it was the number of businesses that left Montreal to set up shop in Toronto and took with them a lot of my clients. It was obvious that Toronto was becoming the commercial capital of Canada and the TSE the main stock exchange. This is where a financial guy has to be."

"How can we move?" Sarah had argued. "Everything we have is here. Our friends and families are here. Our kids are happy here. Elijah is in the same school where I teach so I can take him and pick him up. Marsha will be going into kindergarten close by. It seems to me the violence is over. All the bad guys are in jail or exiled. So why move now?"

He had always thought his wife was attractive despite the misshapen nose. Thanks to a plastic surgeon, the nose had been restructured into a pert appendage, rendering her face appealingly beautiful. As her anger at the thought of moving reddened her cheeks and highlighted the dark flashing eyes, he almost lost his resolve but persevered.

"Because the whole financial industry will move there, and I'm part of the industry," he told her. "I have to, at least, protect your father's investment. If I don't move, the firm will stagnate."

"I know Cyril helped to start your business. Was he very generous?" Fuhr asked.

"I think so," Zetel said. "He invested $100,000 for 35% of the shares. According to the agreement he insisted on — not that I objected — major decisions require at least a two thirds majority, so he has a controlling interest. I believe he trusts me but he's very careful. We hold regular board meetings but otherwise he leaves me alone. By the way, he wants you on the board — keeps asking for you. I told him you're in Europe."

Fuhr looked surprised, "Why does he want me on the board?"

Zetel chuckled. "You're a banker — remember?"

"Of course," Fuhr said. "My memory bedevils me at times. I appear to so many people in so many guises. It becomes difficult to remember whom I am to whom. Has your business prospered?"

"It certainly has, but it was a rough beginning. I opened eight years ago in April, 1965, hoping to take advantage of the bull market that had started three years before. By the time I got everything organized and enough people hired, 1966 was upon us, a down year for the market. Nevertheless, I managed to survive and except for the down year of 1969, we've had a bull market ever since. Right now, 1973 doesn't look good. The companies I invest in are solid but profits are down and so are their shares. Nevertheless, my clients seem happy, and new clients are signing up every month."

Zetel paused. Fuhr was deep in thought.

"Who else is on your board?" Fuhr asked.

"Just Lansmann and me, and you if you wish."

"I'll join your board," Fuhr said. "I will try to attend every meeting. What do you do at these meetings?"

"We look at results, investment ideas, issues, problems — that sort of thing."

Fuhr walked to the window, looked out at the view for awhile, then returned to his seat.

"Understand one thing, Zetel," he said. "I will not use the infernal arts to help you. My mandate with you is to safeguard your soul until it is ready to leave your mortal body. I will remain steadfast in that regard since your soul belongs to me."

Zetel nodded. "I agree but I need your advice from time to time and some things I hate discussing with Cyril. I have a problem right now. I told all my investors they could expect returns of 5% to 10%. They've taken it as a kind of guarantee. Maybe I should have been less specific but I was eager to attract clients. So far it's worked. A number of month ends produced more than the 10% so I held the surplus back and used it for the poor months."

"That seems a reasonable approach," Fuhr said. "What's the problem?"

"The past quarter has been poor so I won't even be able to meet the 5%. In addition, setting up this office, moving here, and buying Sarah the house of her dreams on Warren Street in Forest Hill — a section of Toronto that's like Westmount in Montreal, so you can guess the cost — has blown all my personal income and savings. In other words, I don't even have cash resources I can dip into to bolster the payout to my clients. My clients include my mother and father, Jack and Faigel, Hershey and Sylvia — people I just cannot disappoint. They're all in their late 60's and 70's, retired, and depend on the returns I get them."

Fuhr laughed. "I felt you had a problem. Do you think it coincidence that I showed up today? How much do you need? Shall I rob a bank for you? I could waft through the walls of a bank vault and take what's needed."

"Herr Fuhr, you said you would not use the infernal arts so I assume you're teasing me. You have solved my problems before with common sense and cunning. All I want is a good idea."

Fuhr laughed even harder. "I continue to be amazed by the simplicity of mortals' problems. While I was waiting for you in the reception area, I overheard one of your staff say that the number of new clients signing up this month was well in excess of your goals. Surely, there must be enough new money coming in to forestall your problem and meet at least your lower guarantee of 5%."

Zetel looked at Fuhr in dismay. "Well, yes, but the new investors expect their money to be invested."

"But you will only use it for a very short period, things will improve, you put the money back in and nobody will be wiser."

Zetel walked to the window but, deep in thought, did not see the view. After a long while, he turned to Fuhr. "OK, I will do it," he said. "I can arrange it in such a way that not even my office will be aware. It's really quite simple. All new money comes into my escrow account to which I have sole access. From there, I disburse it as the investments are purchased. Since the markets are faltering now, I have a good excuse for not putting this money into play but I can pay it out to current customers as returns on their investments. You're right. The markets will turn very soon and I'll be able to restore the funding I've used."

Unfortunately, as the months trickled by, Zetel realized with growing unease that the markets were continuing to slide. There were sufficient new clients joining which allowed him to maintain his payouts to current investors. It became a virtuous circle: those already on board boasted about their steady high returns which attracted others.

"I don't know how you do it, Zetel," Cyril remarked at the board meeting at the end of November. "1973 has been a lousy year for stocks, yet our investments are doing very well."

"True," said Zetel. "The stock markets are down, the economy is poor, but on the whole, we've managed. Call it good stock selection, more aggressive short selling, and some luck. I spend a lot of time on research, always looking for companies that are likely to prosper despite the year. I have lots of contacts and sometimes I hear things which are helpful."

Cyril looked at him. "Zetel, are you telling me we're helped by insider information? I really don't want to be involved with anything illegal."

"Not to worry, Mr. Lansmann," Zetel said. "It's not direct information. These are dots of information I pick up and sometimes I can connect the dots."

"Can you give us an example?" Fuhr asked who had sat quietly during the meeting.

"Certainly," said Zetel. "A month ago, I noticed the stock price of one of the companies we're invested in was edging up. Based on information available, there didn't seem to be any real reason. The company is Washington Cycle, a huge west coast US bicycle manufacturer, located just outside Seattle. I called its President. I was told he was on holiday and was not expected back until the middle of November. It struck me as strange that he would be on a long vacation at this time. They do a lot of business in the run up to Christmas and this man is a hands on type. From conversations I had had with him, I knew he usually went on vacation in January or February. Perhaps he'd changed his plans, perhaps he was ill, or perhaps he was working on a deal. I spoke to one of their financial people and during the course of our conversation, he let slip that the boss was combining business with vacation. 'I'm meeting him in a couple of days and I'll give him your number,' the financial guy said. 'If he has the time, he'll call you.'

"Now, here's where luck comes in. As the guy was hanging up, I heard a woman's voice — probably his secretary — telling him his tickets to Birmingham ... and then the phone cut off. Something in her voice said she was talking about Birmingham, England. I checked to see whether you could fly to Birmingham and there was a direct flight from New York.

"By now I was fairly certain the company was working on something. I called the commercial attaché at Britain's High Commission in Ottawa and asked about bicycle companies in and around Birmingham. After some discussion, I discovered there was Lincoln Cycles in Coventry, about 30 miles from Birmingham. 'A fabulous company,' the commercial attaché boasted. 'They distribute their cycles throughout the UK, The Netherlands, Scandinavia, and Germany. He agreed he would send me their annual report and catalogue.

"If Washington Cycle was trying to establish a European base, Lincoln Cycle would be an ideal acquisition. I called a contact in the City — that's the financial district in London — and asked him about the stock. He reported that in the last few weeks, there had been a slow but steady rise in the stock price. I immediately bought 10,000 shares of Lincoln and upped our investment in Washington. A few days ago, it was announced that the two companies were in talks. Lincoln's stock jumped immediately and Washington's also improved.

"So you see, Mr. Lansmann, Herr Fuhr, I had a hunch which turned out to be correct. The conversations I had, anyone could have had and cannot be considered illegal. No insider gave me specific information that was not available to the public. The mention of Birmingham on the telephone was entirely serendipitous and unintended. Anyway, it was only my hunch that something was up that made the mention meaningful to me."

"That was quite a story you told us at the meeting, Zetel," Cyril said. "Your husband's very clever, Sarah."

"How can anyone be considered clever who chooses Toronto over Montreal?" Sarah said.

"Now, now, Mrs. Landaw," Fuhr said. "I'm also considering moving here. I've sold my house in Westmount."

"Mr. Fuhr, my respect for you does not allow me to make rude remarks. These I reserve for my husband. According to our marriage arrangement, I'm allowed to insult him anytime I want or see the need."

"Zetel, you can't say I didn't warn you," Cyril said.

Zetel smiled. "I've looked through our marriage documents, both in English and Hebrew, and have found nothing which justifies her behaviour. As a good husband, I indulge her whims and refrain from reacting."

"Is that so!" Sarah exclaimed, stepped quickly to where Zetel sat and began pummeling her balled fists on his head.

"Sarah, stop that. You'll hurt him, "Anna said.

"Don't worry, Bubby (*grandmother*)," Elijah said. "Mummy's only fooling. If you weren't all here, Daddy would pick Mummy up, put her across his lap and spank her."

"But they only make believe," Marsha was quick to reassure them.

They were all sitting around the dining table, the children still picking away at the remnants of the lemon meringue pie, the adults sipping cups of steaming tea at the end of a sumptuous Friday night dinner. Cyril and Anna were staying with Zetel and Sarah. Fuhr had been invited to join them for dinner after the board meeting.

Cyril recounted Zetel's triumph with the bicycle companies.

"But getting the Birmingham location was strictly luck," Sarah said. "Without that, you would have missed what the Washington company was up to. You told me you did value investing and you had certain criteria before buying or selling a stock. It all sounded so cerebral."

"True," Zetel said. "Without that piece of luck, I probably would have missed the jump in Lincoln — but don't forget, value investing made me an investor in Washington Cycle long before this came up. Even without knowing about their acquisition target, we would have profited because Washington Cycle stock went up."

"Besides, Sarah," Cyril added, "Even with value investing and all the other systems that people use, there's still a great deal of luck. So many things happen that were never taken into account. The Arabs declare an oil embargo because they're mad at us for helping Israel in the Yom Kippur War. The US decides it will no longer base its currency on gold. Economic growth is down, inflation is going up. So, given all these unforeseen events, the stock market starts to slide and every one heads for the exits. If you're lucky, you got out in time."

"Ah, but our clever Zetel has bought bargains during the current downturn," Fuhr said. "The market will go back up and those who didn't panic, will do well and everyone will say they're lucky."

"Mr. Fuhr," Sarah said, "at our wedding, you showed what a great magician you are. Can you not use your magic tricks to help Zetel in selecting stocks?"

Oh my god, thought Zetel, don't get him started.

"Not a chance," Fuhr said. "I told Zetel that my magic tricks were reserved for cards only."

"We'd like to see magic card tricks," said Elijah, jumping up excitedly.

"Show Elijah the trick you did on me at the wedding," Cyril said. "I still can't figure out how that worked. Hershey insists to this day that we were all in it together."

"A magician doesn't give away his secrets," Fuhr said. "However, I will be pleased to do it again."

Please, Herr Fuhr, don't get carried away. Don't do things no one can explain, Zetel inwardly pleaded. *Don't worry*, came the return thought.

Sarah produced a deck of cards. Fuhr gave the deck to Elijah.

Fuhr stood up and put a friendly arm around Elijah's shoulder. "Now, Elijah, listen carefully and follow my instructions. Fan the deck with the cards facing your mother. Your mother will take one but not show you what it is."

Sarah took a card, looked at it carefully, showed it to the others, and put the card back.

"Now, Elijah, shuffle the deck in such a way that the card your mother took falls to the bottom of the deck."

"But Mr. Fuhr, I don't know which card Mummy took," Elijah said.

Fuhr looked nonplussed. "You don't? Here let me help you." He pulled a card from the partly shuffled deck. "Just make sure this card is always at the bottom of the deck."

"Oh, come on, Louis," Cyril said. "You'll only embarrass the boy."

"And why is that?" Fuhr asked.

"Because you couldn't possibly know which card Sarah took. You just pulled one at random."

"I was directed by Elijah," Fuhr said. "He is a fast learner. Elijah, show them the bottom card."

They all gasped, except Zetel, as the card was indeed the one Sarah had chosen.

Please, Lucifer, stop now, Zetel pleaded. *I will go no further,* came the reassuring thought. *We are about to be interrupted.*

The front doorbell rang. Fuhr looked at his watch. "If you don't mind, I'll answer the door. I'm expecting a couple of colleagues at this time. I hope you don't mind that I gave them your address. We have some important business to discuss. Thank you, Zetel and Sarah, for a very nice evening. It's always a pleasure to see you, Cyril and Anna. Elijah, next time I'll show you some real tricks. Marsha, if I may be so bold as to say, you will soon be as pretty as your mother."

He bowed, left the dining room, and walked quickly down the long corridor to the front door. Before opening the door, he stopped to look at himself in a full length mirror fronting the vestibule clothes closet. The face and figure of Zetel Landaw looked back at him. He carefully adjusted the colour of the eyes, thinned the face, and allowed a five-o'clock shadow to clothe the cheeks and jaw. Satisfied, he opened the front door, stepped out onto the spacious porch, and closed the door behind him.

He was confronted by three men in police uniforms. They each held up identification showing their pictures and badge numbers.

"Is this the home of Zalman Yaakov Zetel Ländau?" one asked, his voice authoritative, officious.

"I am Zalman Yaakov Zetel Landaw," Fuhr said.

There was a brief flurry of whispered conversation among the three.

"It's the same name," one said. "It's just pronounced differently."

"Right," said the one who seemed to be in charge. He was the same height as Fuhr, wore an ill fitting uniform and sported a large black moustache with descending points. "Mr. Landaw, we have received a criminal complaint from some of your clients who charge you with fraud. We have a warrant for your arrest and ask you to come quietly with us."

"You must read him his Miranda right," a voice said.

Fuhr looked in the direction of the voice. At the bottom of the porch steps stood a police officer in full riot gear, head covered with helmet and mask, holding a large plastic shield in front of him, and carrying a long baton. Beyond him, in the circular driveway that led off Warren Street was a police car with its dome lights flashing. Leaning against the car was a large motorcycle.

"Sir, may I point out," Fuhr said, "Miranda right is an American formulation in a decision by the US Supreme Court in 1966. It has no bearing in Ontario. Nevertheless, I waive my right to a lawyer but I insist on remaining silent until I see the warrant and understand why I am being arrested. I am not aware of having defrauded anyone. Rather, my clients enjoy better returns than most. Please show me the warrant."

There was another flurry of conversation.

"Sir, we do not have the warrant with us but will show it to you as soon as we reach the station. As to the merits of the charges against you, that is for the prosecutor and judge to decide.'

"Gentlemen, I have never heard of an arrest without a warrant," Fuhr protested. "How do I know you are really policemen and not kidnappers?"

The policeman in full riot gear, clashed his baton against his shield. "We're wasting time. Let me bash him over the head. Then he'll come quietly."

"No, no, Constable Sam," another of the policemen said. "There is no need to get impatient." He turned to Fuhr. "Sir, I am Constable Mike. Please excuse my colleague who prides himself on quick results. I can assure you, Sir, the warrant will be presented as soon as we arrive at the nick. Isn't that so, Sergeant Gaby?" he said, motioning to the one in charge.

"The 'nick?'" Fuhr said. "That's British slang for police station. Are you sure you're in the right country? Are you taking me to Britain? If so, I'll need my passport which is in my office downtown."

"Sir, Constable Mike is originally from Britain and still uses colloquial terms," Sergeant Gaby said. "You have received our assurances that the warrant will be presented to you. Now, if we may proceed, Constable Ralph will handcuff you."

"I notice Constable Mike has blond curly hair peeping out of his cap," Fuhr said. "I thought all police had to have their hair short."

"Not any more, Sir," Constable Ralph said. "Please put your arms out and the wrists close together."

Fuhr did as he was told. Constable Ralph tried to place the cuffs over his wrists but the device wasn't open. He fiddled with them for a moment without success.

"You must have a key," Fuhr suggested.

Constable Ralph searched through his pockets but could not find the key. None of the others could find one either.

"Never mind the cuffs," Constable Sam said. "I'll ride in the back with him. He won't try anything funny. Constable Ralph, you drive the Motorcycle."

"I don't know how to drive a motorcycle," Constable Ralph objected.

"You were behind me on the way here," Constable Sam said. "Surely you must have seen how to operate it."

"I was too busy hanging on. I was not terribly impressed with your driving."

"I will drive the motorcycle," Fuhr said. "I love motorcycles. I have a Harley myself. Beautiful machine. I will tell you how yours compares. The four of you can drive in the car and I'll follow you."

"I don't trust that he'll follow us," Constable Sam objected. "I will ride on the seat behind him."

"As you wish, Constable Sam," Fuhr said. "The sooner we get to the police station, the sooner I can end this nonsense."

The convoy took off down the street. Fuhr, following the police car, its siren wailing, quickly saw what he needed. He drove onto the lawn of a house, flattened himself between the handlebars, and swept under a hanging "For Sale" sign which knocked Constable Sam off the cycle. He regained the road, passed the police car and turned left on St. Clair Avenue.

"Samael is missing and the soul Zetel is getting away," Michael shouted. "Gabriel, get after him."

"I knew we shouldn't have let him on the motorcycle," Raphael said.

"But he seemed so complacent," Gabriel said, driving as fast as he could to overtake their fleeing prisoner.

Fuhr twisted and turned through the busy streets, always allowing the pursuing car to keep on his trail. He turned down Yonge Street, left on Carlton and down Jarvis. Soon he saw his destination and drove precipitously into a small parking area fronting a building, followed moments later by the police car, its siren still in full blast.

Fuhr leapt off the motorcycle and shouted at the police officers who erupted from the building: "I'm being chased by kidnappers dressed as policemen."

One policeman grasped Fuhr by the arm, the others turned their attention to the car.

"Hey, that's Hagerty's car, the one stolen earlier today," a policeman called out. They surrounded the car, pistols in hand. The three occupants slowly, reluctantly emerged.

"I can explain everything. It was just a joke we were playing on our good friend," Gabriel said. "Isn't that so, soul of Zetel?"

He looked hopefully in Zetel's direction and found himself staring into the smiling face of Louis C. Fuhr.

"You!" all three exclaimed in unison.

"Well, yes," Fuhr said. "Who else? Your intention was to take me to the police station, so here we are. Just tell the police why you arrested me."

"We didn't arrest you," Michael said. "We arrested the man known as Zetel."

"We're going to be in big trouble," Gabriel said. " Once again, you fooled us and made a mockery of our mission."

"I knew this was not going to work," Raphael said.

"You went over the plan with me and said it was ingenious and how proud you were to be included," Gabriel rounded on him angrily.

"Gentlemen," a police officer with gold braid epaulettes spoke up, "Can one of you explain what is going on?"

The three angels stood against the car as though it were a refuge. In all the excitement, no one noticed the massive cumulus cloud of vertical development that had spread across the sky. Thick and black, it rumbled as though in anger as it moved overhead. A sudden bolt of intense lightning accompanied by a deafening roar of thunder enveloped the car and flung the policemen off their feet. The car burst into flames.

"Take cover," the lead policeman shouted. "She's going to blow."

The policemen ran from the blazing car. The car exploded and burned with a ferocity that arriving firemen claimed they had never witnessed before.

News reports told of the bizarre events at the central police station. Strangest of all was the complete absence of any sign of the three men who had stolen the police car. "They could not have escaped and must have been completely incinerated." Furthermore, the man who claimed the three were trying to abduct him could not be found. To add to the mystery, a policeman in full riot gear lay on a lawn near where the stolen police car was first seen and was presumed either badly hurt or dead. However, upon investigation, there was nothing inside the uniform except for a long black hooded robe which exuded a foul sickening stench of rotting flesh. On the Arc, three figures stood, bowed and stooped, their skin blackened, stubs of charred hair barely supporting the haloes encircling their heads. A fourth, naked, pale, clutched his arms tightly around his chest as though seeking warmth.

"Here He comes," one of them said.

"We're in for it now," said another.

"I shall protest if He removes my halo," a third said. "Once again, we followed your plan, Gabriel, and once again it failed."

One of the blackened figures objected, "And once again, you are pretending, Raphael, that you weren't party to the plan and took no part in its preparation and did not proclaim it a good plan."

"Oh, stop this foolish bickering," said the pale figure. "What more can He do to us?"

"It's fine for you to talk bravely, Samael," Gabriel said, rubbing away at his face until the black diminished to smudges to reveal his features. "You escaped the lightning. Besides, no angel will ever take your job so you are safe. He cannot dismiss you from His Service."

The massive cumulus cloud of vertical development drew closer. Strange sounds emanated from deep inside the cloud, sounds they had never heard before.

"He cannot be angry," Gabriel said. "The cloud is white."

"But the cloud throws its burgeoning masses high in the heavens and rocks sideways and forwards and, now, look — backwards," said Michael combing his fingers through his hair in a vain attempt to restore his blond curly locks.

Raphael, the third blackened figure, exclaimed: "Listen to the sound He makes. First a low rumble as though in anger, yet too light to be true anger, then it rises to a shriek and changes to a cascading din of screams and cries until it rumbles again."

The cloud was close now. Fearfully, they awaited the inevitable punishment for failing in their mission. Would there be more lightning or, like Lucifer before them, would they be tossed into the infernal regions to be eternally roasted with penal fire?

They shrank from the terrible noise emanating from the cloud. Great heaving rumbles, screams, cries, ear splitting shrieks battered them prostrate. They clung to the Arc, shaking as the sounds reverberated and tossed their bodies up and down, awakening the souls on which they lay. Frightened, the souls called out in terror adding to the cacophony. Slowly, the cloud moved off, the horrible noise diminished until, after a short time, perhaps an eon, silence prevailed.

The three blackened figures raised their heads cautiously.

"What was that all about?" Gabriel asked.

"I don't know. It was most strange," Raphael said, his teeth still chattering in fright.

"Perhaps it's a new form of punishment, but we are unscathed," said Michael.

Samael, head slumped forward, pushed himself to his knees. Tears fell from his eyeless eye sockets and groans convulsed his body. His usual arrogant posture and threatening demeanour had become one of shame and humility.

"He laughs at us."

CHAPTER 6 —
Zetel at 50

For both Sarah and Zetel, reaching the age of 50 was unsettling. In mid-July, 1985, Sarah, a few months older than Zetel, was first to turn 50.

Zetel returned home early on her birthday, carrying a large bouquet of pink roses, a bottle of Veuve Cliquot Champagne, and a heart-shaped box of Godiva chocolates. He shouted "Happy Birthday!" when he found Sarah in the living room staring out the window. She didn't move or acknowledge his presence. He put down the gifts and embraced her.

"It's just a number," Sarah said. "Men still look at me. I still have my periods, even if they're uneven. Nothing's changed from yesterday."

Zetel knew she was hurting despite her attempt at nonchalance and held her close. "Nothing's changed," he said. "I still look at you. You're still as beautiful as when we married — even more beautiful. In a few months, I'll be in the same boat and we can row into old age together."

She pushed away and looked at him. "Where does a narrow minded financial guy get such poetry? Women no longer row. You will row and I will steer."

"Can't we at least take turns?"

"When you become decrepit, from time to time, I will row," she said, easing back into his embrace. "How do you plan to celebrate my fiftieth birthday?"

He turned her around to see the gifts. "In addition, I've reserved a window table at Scaramouche for tonight at 8. You have lots of time to get ready."

"They're rather pricey," she said. "I know I deserve it, but can we afford it?"

"Bull market, these days."

He was pleased to see heads turn as they entered the dining room at the restaurant and were led to their table. Sarah, in a low cut gown that amply displayed her décolleté and clung tightly to her narrow waist and trim buttocks, exuded sensual warmth and sexuality. Her face with its mostly unblemished skin and pert upturned nose, large brown eyes, and curls that graced her shoulders completed the vision of the ultimate in femininity.

"Everyone's looking at you," he whispered.

"And so they should," she said with her characteristic acerbic tongue.

He watched in amusement as the Maitre d' eagerly assisted Sarah to be seated, then surreptitiously leaned over slightly for a better view of the rounded treasures nestling in her gown.

They were barely seated when a short stocky man in formal wear with thin, carefully combed grey-black hair came over.

"Zetel, what a pleasure to see you," he said.

Zetel stood up. "Saul, what a nice surprise."

"Now I know why your fees are so high," Saul said chuckling. "I have to mortgage my house to eat here." He beamed inquiringly at Sarah.

"Saul, this is my wife Sarah. Sarah, this is Saul Rubinoff who's head of the General Hospital Foundation and is an important client."

"That means you have to be nice to me," Saul said gaily, grasping Sarah's hand and holding it a little too long.

"The only man I've ever been nice to is my husband," said Sarah. "And even he complains."

Zetel laughed. "I complain to her father and all he says is 'I warned you.' Saul, you're in black tie. Is there an occasion?"

"Yes," Saul said and a look of complete satisfaction came over him. "My boy is finally getting married and we're celebrating the engagement. We're the big table over in the corner."

"Well, Mazel Tov, Saul, I'll come over later and say hello."

"You should talk to him, Zetel, not now, not tonight, give me a call tomorrow. He can't figure out how you achieve your results. He's emulated your stock picks and he never gets the same returns. I've told him, I don't care how you get your results, as long as you keep getting them."

"I'll be happy to talk to him, Saul," Zetel said. "But bear in mind, I do have a system. It's proprietary and I won't reveal my methods. It's my competitive edge and I don't intend to give it away."

They shook hands and Saul returned to his table.

"What was that all about?" Sarah asked. "You started to sound a little testy."

"I've discovered that success breeds envy. Several times this past year, I've had analysts challenge my results. It's become annoying. I don't want to waste my time answering stupid questions from people who think they know all there is to know about the market."

"Zetel, even daddy wonders how you do it."

"Yes, I know, he's asked me about it at some of our board meetings. Look, in order to keep my method secret, I've even hived off the fund management side from the brokerage. I'm CEO of both companies but I run the funds company alone and divulge nothing to the brokerage except to process some of my buys and sells. So you see, not even my broker employees know my method. Now, let's stop discussing business and concentrate on your birthday."

She laughed. "Sounds like a female put down but on this occasion I accept it. The waiter is coming with champagne. You may toast my health and wish me all the best over the next 50."

They picked up their champagne flutes, interlocked arms, and drank from each other's glass. "To the next 50," Zetel said.

"For both of us," Sarah responded. "Don't forget your big day is coming up. In a couple of months you'll be an old man."

Zetel grimaced. "Don't remind me. Will you still love me when I'm 64?"

"You're only turning 50. I'll reserve judgement when you're 64," she said, smiling. "It's bothering you too, isn't it?"

Zetel nodded. "I have to admit it is — one of those cataclysmic dates in life. I suppose it brings into focus one's inevitable vulnerability. Everyone I love and feel close to are either dead or slowly dying off. My uncle Shloima is gone. My aunt Bessie is in The Hospital of Hope. Jack Greenberg is gone. We attended Hershey's funeral last month. My father is ill and the prognosis is not good. My mother is still in good shape for an 80-year old. So is Faigel. Thank God, your parents are both well. Sure, I know it's stupid but I thought all these people would continue on forever. Then, too, I wonder whether I've achieved all that I could or wanted to, whether I am where I should be at the age of 50."

Sarah looked at him wonderingly, tears glazing her eyes.

"Sweetheart, you're an amazingly successful man, not only in business but also in your selection of a wonderful loving wife and two beautiful children. I guess I'm smitten with the same anxiety. We are about to supplant the older generation. Our turn is coming up. Yet we're both still young and in good health. I'm still happy teaching — well, at the elementary level — where the children still think I'm wise and with it. Maybe, we're working too hard. Maybe we should jump out of our standard routine. How about a nice vacation somewhere, just the two of us. Somewhere I've always wanted to go. In 1957, Daddy took Mommy and me all over Italy except one place — Venice. He said the city was slowly sinking into the lagoon in which it is built and he didn't want to be there if a big storm came up and washed it all away. Venice would make a nice romantic spot for us. You could hire a gondola and sing me Italian love songs as we slowly sail down a canal."

Zetel smiled. "I like everything except the singing part. Venice it is. I've never been there either. Come to think of it, my forays to Europe are always for business and tend to be to the City in London or conferences. When shall we go?"

"How about two weeks in September with the 16th in the middle. You turn 50 on the 16th, so we can commiserate with each other."

"It's pretty short notice," Zetel said. "Besides, you start teaching again in September."

" I will request the time off. You can easily get away — you're the boss. We have enough time to give everybody notice and to arrange our trip. You don't have to do a thing. I will organize everything. You just have to supply the money."

Supply the money, he thought. For a moment, the delight of their evening outing and the pleasurable prospect of an excursion to Venice tottered on the edge of a deep abyss. Despite his best efforts and the rise in the stock market, he still needed the investments and fees of incoming members to his equity funds in order to meet his promise of exceptional gains to his current clients. True, he had whittled away at the growing debt but it was still too large. The trip to Venice would make things worse. All he needed was a half year of no exceptional expenses, a cut on those that had become normal, an outstanding bull market and he might get control of the debt situation. Yet, the cost of the trip to Venice was a mere piddle in the pool, so why worry about it.

"Is something wrong, Zetel? We do have the money, don't we?"

"Yes, yes, of course. I was just wondering whether there was anything I had to do in September. Everything's fine."

Is it? a voice asked.

Zetel twisted around sharply. Two men were sitting at a table not far from them. One, in a natty blue suit, his handsome youngish face framed by golden curls cascading to his shoulders, was staring at him. His companion was examining the menu.

"What do you want?" Zetel asked out loud.

"I beg your pardon," Sarah said. "What do I want?"

"Not you," he said. "Them. Those two men over there."

Sarah turned. "But, Zetel, they haven't talked to us. Do you know them?"

"Archangel Michael is the one looking this way. Gabriel is the other one," he said. "They mean me harm."

"Archangel Michael? Gabriel?" Sarah said, startled. "No, Zetel, these are just two guys having dinner." She reached out a hand across the table. "Please, Zetel, calm yourself. You're just having a bad moment. You've been working too hard. It's a good thing we're planning a vacation."

We mean you no harm, the voice continued. *This is an opportune moment to give up your reckless endeavours and return to the Arc with us. It can be easily arranged at a time and place convenient to you but it must be very soon.*

I will not go with you. My soul does not belong to you. It belongs to the Devil, Zetel said.

That's right, another voice, a familiar voice, said.

"Zetel, look who just walked in — Herr Fuhr, and in evening dress," Sarah said. "He knows those two. He's going to their table."

It was clear the two men were not pleased with Fuhr's arrival. They barely spoke but Zetel detected a long and bitter argument between Fuhr and the two Archangels. Finally, the angels left the table and the restaurant. Gabriel gave Zetel a hard look as he walked past.

Until next time, he said. Zetel merely nodded.

Fuhr pretended to notice Zetel and Sarah for the first time.

"Hello, you two. I didn't expect to find you here," he said, bowing and gently bringing Sarah's hand to his lips. Zetel stood up and they shook hands.

"We're celebrating my birthday," Sarah gushed, savouring his courtly greeting and aware of the impact it was having on the tables around them. "But, Herr Fuhr, who were those two men? Zetel was very upset. He says they're Archangels."

Fuhr laughed. "And so they are, sweet lady. It's an investment industry term. They are called angel investors. They finance early entrepreneurial businesses. These two in particular are very devious and are quite prominent in the industry. Hence their nicknames. I came to ruin their evening because they were about to treat one of my clients very badly. Zetel knows them quite well. They would upset anybody's dinner."

Sarah chuckled. "I honestly thought Zetel was having a nervous breakdown when he said they were Archangels. I told him he needs a vacation."

"I'm sure he does," Fuhr said. "Go somewhere far away. Italy is a wonderful place to visit. I strongly recommend Venice, so completely unusual."

Astonished, Sarah said, "That's what we were talking about. A trip to Venice in September. How do you know?"

"I'm a magician," Fuhr said. "But sometimes I get lucky. Enjoy your dinner tonight and your vacation in September."

They landed in Milan, took the Milan–Venice train and arrived at Santa Lucia Railway Station on Monday, September 9, in the early afternoon.

"This gives us a week before your birthday and a week after," Sarah explained. "We just missed the 42nd Venice International

Film Festival so it shouldn't be too busy. Besides, all the kids have gone back to school."

"So, we'll be the only ones in Venice?"

"There are, of course, the Venetians," she countered. "And there may be a few tourists like us."

He chuckled, "I didn't hear much Italian spoken on the train, at least not on the car we were in. I heard lots of English, German and some others but no Italian. I don't think we'll be alone."

"Zetel, please control your cynicism until after we are safely home," she said. "The lady across the aisle from me insisted September is a good month to visit. It's still quite warm and it rarely floods at this time of year. She also said most of the tourists have gone home. Only the interesting ones are left."

"Like us," Zetel said.

They each had a large suitcase on rollers and a small backpack. They exited the station and walked slowly to the water bus stop, enthralled by their first glimpse of Venice. A seemingly endless array of old and antique buildings crowded to the edge of the Canal and swept back into the distance with steeples and domes rising above the roof lines.

"The church with the green dome in front of us is the church of St. Simeon," Sarah said, consulting her guidebook. "The figure on top is the saint himself waving hello to everyone arriving."

They pulled their luggage onto the vaporetto (the water bus) and found seats close to the exit.

The sights and sounds of the Grand Canal enveloped them as they pulled away from the dock. Astounded, they watched in awe the helter-skelter of traffic on the waterway. Vaporettos, water taxis, barges loaded with goods, gondolas carrying people or freight, private motor craft, the occasional police boat, garbage scows, all swept back and forth with no discernible traffic pattern and yet without mishap.

Zetel smiled at Sarah's intense scrutiny of her guidebook. "Put the book away, Sarah, and just enjoy the sights. The city is magnificent. Look at the mansions and palaces all along the canal. This is one place where you wouldn't want to walk out of your house dead drunk."

"Zetel, I am a teacher and I shall report back to my students everything I saw. This is an absolutely historical place. Every building is antique and has been left in place. Not like in Toronto where you see the occasional plaque describing what once stood there. Look, we're passing an intersecting canal called the Cannaregio. You see those tall buildings far down? That's part of the Jewish Ghetto. It's where our people lived starting in 1516. Now, if I hadn't told you that, you'd never know."

Completely engrossed in the sunlit blue water of the Grand and Cannaregio Canals, the endless variety of canal traffic, and the spectacular sight of the colourful buildings lining the canals, he said without thinking, "Oh, I did know. I met someone who had lived there. Mind you, it didn't mean anything at the time." He remembered a soul who had taken an empty space beside him on the Arc and recounted his adventures in what he said was the ghetto of Venice.

Sarah turned to him in alarm. "Zetel, what are you saying? Someone who lived there in 1516?"

Horrified, Zetel realized he had strayed into dangerous territory. "N-no," he stammered, "s-someone I met — at a conference — yes, an Italian — he had a flat near the Ghetto and told me all about its history."

Sarah continued to regard him nervously, "What else did he tell you about the history?"

"I can't remember," he said. "I wasn't much interested." At least that is true, he thought.

"You're all upset," Sarah said, wiping the sweat off his forehead with a handkerchief. She took his hand. "Sweetheart, this is going to be a real vacation for you, for us. All we have to do is enjoy the city." She stuffed the guidebook into her backpack.

He put an arm around her and pulled her close. "As long as you include lots of outdoor cafes and nice eating places in our tours and walks, I shall be very happy here," he said.

They sat in silence for a while.

"There's the Rialto bridge," Sarah said, as the vaporetto made its way around a bend.

The single span stone bridge with its arched portico came into view. Scores of people stood at the balustrade of the bridge watching the unceasing activity below. The cries of hawkers selling everything from tourist gifts to apartment rentals, the shouts of gondoliers, the din of the fish and vegetable markets close by filled the air.

The vaporetto slowly inched its way through the bustle of gondola and water craft around the bridge or navigating the narrowed passage. It passed under the bridge to reveal quayside restaurants on either side of the canal. Gondolas awaiting customers lined one bank and undulated at their moorings in harmony with the gently rolling current and wakes of the boats.

The vaporetto continued down the canal. Spellbound, Zetel and Sarah stared in awe at the baroque and gothic palaces, stately mansions, warehouses topped with merchant quarters, the occasional church, all edged along the canal, the buildings worn, paint peeling, bottom floors flooded, masonry crumbling but still magnificent.

"What a glorious city this must have been in its heyday!" Sarah exclaimed.

"Yes," Zetel agreed, "in the 1600's, it was the richest place on earth."

She looked at him worriedly. "I suppose your Italian friend told you that too?"

I better pay attention to what I'm saying, Zetel thought. "Common historical knowledge," he said.

She grabbed him by the lapels of his travel jacket. "I'm a teacher and I studied history and in our school system which we both went through, I don't remember anything about Venice. So it's definitely not 'common historical knowledge' for us. What you know about Italy could only have come from your Italian friend."

Suspicious, she narrowed her eyes. "Was this friend a man or a woman?"

He laughed. "Jealousy is flattering. I see I shall have to tell you the truth. My informant whom I met long before I knew you was neither man nor woman. We were souls awaiting reincarnation and in our discussions, he — or rather, it — recommended Venice as the ideal place for life. Fortunately, I was posted to Canada where I met this beautiful, charming, dynamic woman who allowed me to marry her."

She pulled him towards her and kissed him on the lips.

The vaporetto virtually emptied at the Piazza San Marco stop. They followed or rather were dragged along by the crowd heading for St. Mark's Square. They passed between the columns of St. Theodore and St. Mark and headed up the Piazetta, the narrow square leading to the Basilica and the main Piazza.

"This is unbelievable," Sarah said. "Absolutely breathtaking!"

Like two automatons, they revolved slowly, taking in the large Square, the arcaded buildings surrounding it, the bell tower and finally the magnificent opulence of the Basilica. The Square was busy but not crowded. Flocks of pigeons surrounded one group of tourists. Other groups clustered around their tour guides listening intently and turning as the guides pointed out the sights. A few kiosks dispensed wares to memento seeking visitors.

"There's my idea of outdoor sport," Zetel said, pointing to tables and chairs set out in front of a restaurant. "Coffee on the Piazza watching people go by."

"I have in mind a more energetic holiday but I will allow some time for leisure," Sarah said. "But first, let's find our hotel. It's supposed to be no more than fifty metres from the Piazza."

Zetel looked serious. "Can we walk there or do we have to swim?"

She raised a fist and bonked him gently on the nose. "Very funny. Make yourself useful. Look for a street called Sotoportega del Cavalletto. According to my map, it's through the Arcade."

They made their way slowly through the Piazza, stopping frequently to admire the buildings surrounding it and the vastness of the square itself. A late afternoon sun, its warmth mitigated by a fresh breeze wafting in from the Adriatic, sent long shadows over the square and emblazoned the portico of the Basilica.

Sarah sighed. "After the Garden of Eden, God created Venice and St. Mark's Square. I've seen paintings of St. Mark's by Canaletto and it hasn't changed much. Just the clothing of the people. All very casual now. Do you see the street yet?"

Zetel asked directions of several passersby and led Sarah to a portal that opened up on a laneway. They stood for a moment on a small bridge over a narrow canal. They watched a gondolier bend down as he propelled his craft under the bridge. They proceeded along until they came to a small square with shops and a café along its sides and a church at the end. Several tables and chairs graced the square near the church.

"This is it," Sarah said. "This is Campo San Gallo. The hotel is right here."

A sign over a doorway indicated Hotel San Gallo. They entered and faced a long stairway leading up to the hotel.

"Sarah, sweetheart," Zetel said, smiling. "You're absolutely right. This is going to be an energetic vacation."

They dragged their suitcases up the stair and arrived panting in the lobby. A cheerful member of the staff greeted them warmly and after registration helped them to their room, up two more flights of narrow steps. The room was small but quaintly decorated, with a view of part of St. Mark's Square and the Adriatic beyond.

"You unpack," Sarah ordered, "while I take a bath."

He opened the window, breathed in the sea air, and stared enraptured at the scene. To his right, he could just make out a cruise ship edging slowly towards the city, accompanied by tug boats and lighters. To his left, he could see the domes of the Basilica and everywhere a vast assemblage of red tile roofs. For a fleeting moment, he wondered whether he could establish an office and conduct some of his business from Venice. It's a ravishingly beautiful place, he thought.

He was still staring out the window a half hour later when Sarah emerged from the bathroom, a towel draped over her shoulders.

"You haven't done anything yet," she accused him. "The bags are still unpacked."

He gently pulled the towel from her shoulders. "I was saving my energy," he said, as he pushed her onto the bed and quickly stripped.

Afterwards, they slept for a half hour, dressed and headed back to St. Mark's. They ate at one of the restaurants on the Square, then wandered down to the canal, took a vaporetto towards the Rialto and saw the night come alive with myriads of lights glinting off the water and dimly illuminating the buildings and quayside cafés.

For the next week, they explored the canals and back streets of the city, visited the museums and churches, hired a gondola for a day to explore at a leisurely pace the Grand Canal, the Cannaregio Canal, and some of the smaller canals. They ate breakfast in the hotel, went for coffee to St. Mark's Square, lunched and dined wherever their forays took them, and returned at night for a drink in the hotel.

On the 16th, Sarah insisted on a special routine. They started off with breakfast at Café Florian on the Square.

"This is considered the oldest still running cafe in the world," Sarah said. "We must order their macchiatone. These are considered the best combination of milk and espresso."

"Today I am fifty," Zetel said. "Do I get to make my own decisions?"

"Discretion is always bad for a man," Sarah said. "For a man of fifty, it can be dangerous. However, since it is your birthday, you may choose your coffee."

The breakfast was delicious with delicate pastries and quarter sandwiches and, of course, macchiatone, several cups of the special coffee. They lingered long, watching the crowds slowly filtering into the Square, many led by the ubiquitous guide.

After breakfast, they wandered into the Basilica to once again admire the thousands of mosaics filling the walls and domes of the massive church, with its warm golden background. The domes floated like bubbles over them, some dark, some partly lit by the morning sun poking through the upper windows and intensifying the gold on the mosaics.

They took a vaporetto to Murano, walked along the quayside on the main canal, bought apples from a floating kiosk, ate lunch under a tent in a small piazza, visited several of the glass blowers, and bought a few figurines and glasses.

Back in St. Mark's, Zetel was eager to settle down in the Square and have a beer but Sarah announced she had a special duty to perform on behalf of her parents. "We must go to the Mercerie," she said.

The Mercerie was a series of streets that comprised the shopping district of Venice. It led from the clock tower on the Square and eventually joined other streets to the Rialto Bridge.

"My father insists as a birthday gift you must have some Italian silk shirts and a couple of nice silk ties. He says your suits are fine but he doesn't like your shirts and your ties are too sombre. He has given me the money and I'm to help you make the selection."

Zetel rolled his eyes but did not protest. They spent the rest of the afternoon fulfilling Cecil's gift to him.

They returned to the hotel, carrying their purchases, and, fairly exhausted, slowly climbed the stairs to the hotel and their room.

"It's bath and lie down for me," Sarah said. "The reservation at Quadri is at eight. We have a couple of hours. Since it's your birthday, you may do as you please so long as you're washed, sweet smelling and properly dressed when we leave for the restaurant."

Zetel sighed. "The extent of my discretion is overpowering. Given all I have to do, I have about ten minutes to do as I please."

"I saw you pick up the Herald Tribune in the lobby," she said. "You can read it except for the financial pages since you're on vacation."

He heard her filling the bath, stripped off his clothes, carefully folded them away and joined her.

"To save time, let's bathe together," he said and stepped into the bathtub.

"I'm not sharing my bath with some dirty old man," she protested, laughing and sponging his face with a soaped wash cloth. He splashed her back and they sloshed around in the tub, splashing water onto the bathroom floor. Soon the lust for each other took over and drove them out of the tub. Zetel threw a towel on the floor and they made love.

"Not bad for a fifty year old but you could have picked somewhere dry," Sarah said, dreamily stroking his face.

"I didn't want to get the bed wet," Zetel said. He stood up and edged towards the door. "Consider yourself lucky. I gave up the Herald Tribune so you could have sex."

He bolted out the bathroom door as a slipper came flying at him.

Sarah had made a reservation at Quadri Restaurant to be seated on the second floor with a view of the Square. They made an impressive couple as they followed the Maitre d' to their table. Zetel was in beige slacks and a tan linen jacket which emphasized the pale blue thin striped silk shirt and natty floral silk tie. Sarah wore the Scaramouche gown with its generous display of bosom and tight fitting waist and hips. Here, too, Zetel suppressed a smile as he noted the Maitre d' lean surreptitiously forward as he helped Sarah to be seated.

"What an elegant place," Sarah said. "Starched white tablecloths, porcelain dishes, silver cutlery, and those chandeliers. They must be from Murano."

They ordered the tasting menu with wine for each of the many courses. They enjoyed the view of the Square, dark now except for the lights of the outdoor cafes. They could see small bands playing, the music wafting into the restaurant through an open window. Tourists, now shadowy figures, meandered slowly around the Square, stopping for coffee, or looking into the shops in the arcaded buildings. Where they sat, they could just make out the dark mass of the Basilica and the Doge's Palace beside it.

It was after eleven when they left the restaurant and, full with wine and food, walked unsteadily back to their hotel.

"Thank you," Zetel said, hugging and kissing Sarah, as they climbed into bed. "This was the best birthday any one could hope for. Everything was perfect. You organized it all beautifully — I even forgot I had turned fifty. You know, Sarah, this is such a marvellous city. Wouldn't it be wonderful to live here?"

Sarah, who was beginning to doze, sat up, wide awake. "No, Zetel, we can't live here. How would you make a living here? I don't know whether I can teach here. We can come back every year if you'd like, but we can't move here permanently. Sure it's a beautiful city but we're well-to-do tourists and we can skim off the best. And what about our families and our kids? Please, sweetheart, put it out of your mind. It's just the wine and food talking. I know running a finance company can be very stressful. But if we lived here, the novelty of Venice would wear off after a while. Then you'd want to return to where the action is."

Maybe so, he thought, but at least for a time I would escape worrying about the mess I can't seem to clear up in Toronto. Sooner or later it'll be discovered that I'm running a Ponzi scheme. But if I left Toronto and didn't manage the funds, it would be discovered right away. No, there's no easy way out. I've got to hang in and clear things up.

"You're right, Sarah. We couldn't live here long term. Let's just enjoy the rest of our vacation. It was just a momentary thought."

CHAPTER 7 —
Zetel meets an old friend

The next morning they slept in, missing the hotel breakfast. Zetel dressed but Sarah declared she would spend the rest of the morning in bed.

"OK," Zetel said, "but I'm going to the Square for coffee and something to eat. I'll be back in a couple of hours."

He made his way to Florian's and sat at a table at the edge of the Square. He sipped his coffee and munched away at a plateful of pastry. The air was crisp but a hazy sun tried its best to warm him. The Square was busy with tourists either following their guides or milling about the kiosks. He leaned back in his chair.

Abruptly, he sat straight up, dropped his coffee cup clattering to its saucer, and stared into the crowd. Zetel remembered a vision that Fuhr had presented to him. Like the vision, he was in a sunlit plaza surrounded by magnificent buildings. The plaza was alive with people, some sitting at tables sipping coffee, some just strolling about, others shopping at the kiosks lining the sidewalks. Walking toward him was a woman dressed all in white with a starched cap perched on a head of blond hair. He gasped as her alabaster face and high ridged nose, seemingly chiselled out of marble, came into view. She smiled and waved, not to him he realized, but he smiled and waved back. She looked at him quizzically but continued walking.

"Diana!" he called out and stood up so quickly that he knocked his chair over.

She turned and said something in Italian. "Diana," he repeated the name and stepped towards her. She shrank back. "Diana," he said, and then very softly, "Diana, the Huntress, we meet once more." She looked wildly about, turned and walked quickly away. He made to follow her but the waiter, to whom she had waved, intervened.

"Sir, the lady does not know you and clearly does not wish to know you."

The waiter restored the fallen chair and held it for Zetel to be seated. Zetel waited until the waiter went to serve other tables. Trying to effect a casual nonchalance, he sauntered in the direction the woman had taken, caught sight of her passing the Basilica, and quickened his pace. He followed, keeping her barely in view. Her white uniform was a good marker and allowed him to stay back. They crossed a couple of canals and then entered the square of the Santa Maria Formosa church.

She entered the church. Cautiously, he walked up to the entrance, peered inside but could not see her. He went in. The interior was fairly bright. There were two banks of pews down the centre facing the altar. Stone arches on either side contained the chapels. There were only a small number of visitors but Diana did not seem to be among them. Bitterly disappointed, he sat on a pew close to one of the pillars, mulling over what to do. Her appearance had awakened all the many years of his longing for her. He was certain it was Diana. She looked exactly as he remembered her and as Fuhr's vision had predicted. Of course, he thought, apart from her clothing, she hasn't changed but I have. Her last view of me was a small cloud.

He became aware of her presence behind him.

"Who are you?" she asked. "Why do you call me Diana the Huntress?"

Elation flowed through him as he stood and reached out a hand to touch her. She moved back and started to turn away.

"Don't go," he said, keeping his voice low. He noticed a church guide watching them. "You were my friend on the Arc. You helped me escape."

Clearly startled, she looked hard at him. "It cannot be. You cannot remember. Souls do not remember the Arc."

"But I do," Zetel said. "I remember the many talks we had, the long years of our friendship, your golden hair, your two hunting dogs, the attack by Mars and how we rid the Arc of him, and how you cut me free. Lucifer promised I would see you again and here you are."

She joined him on the pew bench and they sat beside each other. He tried to hold her hands in his but she pulled hers away.

"It cannot be," she said shaking her head. "Souls do not remember. Yet what you described did happen. Are you indeed a mortal? What are you called? Where do you live? You are not Italian."

"I am a mortal. My name is Zalman Yaakov Zetel Landaw. Everyone calls me Zetel. I live in Canada. I am visiting Venice. I often sit in the Piazza for coffee. I never expected to see you there."

They were both silent for a moment. "Is your existence a happy one?" she asked.

He related the events of his life, his early years, the attempts by Archangel Gabriel to return him to the Arc, his ties to Lucifer, his marriage to Sarah, his children, his business and its difficulties, and the need for a period of rest which brought him and Sarah to Venice. Diana listened intently, smiling at the humorous events, indignant at the machinations of Gabriel, distressed by some of the sadder moments in Zetel's life.

"What happened to you after you cut me loose?" he asked.

"It is a rather sad story," she said, dolefully. "The-One-True-God was very angry but he spared me a fiery damnation. I was exiled to the country of Italy, since I am a Roman goddess, and confined to

Venice. However, I have yet to suffer more. As those who worship me decline in numbers, so does my immortality diminish. Soon I will be as mortal as you. I, too, will age and die, but I will not return to the Arc. A goddess *is* a spiritual entity — as such, she has no soul. Therefore, when a goddess dies, her spirituality dies with her and she simply ceases."

Zetel took her hands in his and held them despite her feeble attempt to withdraw. "I am truly sorry. I am the cause of your punishment."

"No, it is not your fault. My end is inevitable, no matter where. In fact, in many respects, I find life in Venice more interesting than had I remained on the Arc."

"Then what do you do here?" he asked. "How do you live? That white uniform you wear — are you a nurse?"

She laughed. "I am a nun, a nursing sister, I belong to the Order of the Sisters of Mercy. When I fell to Earth and was confined to Venice, I quickly realized that I would need a place of refuge as my immortality and my powers as a goddess declined. What better situation than a convent, in which I could also protect my oath of virginity. Through the Order, I became a nurse. I serve at Ospedale SS. Giovanni e Paolo in the natal department helping mothers deliver and making sure their babies survive. Remember, as goddess of the Hunt I'm also the goddess of Fertility. I have become quite renowned for my skills and healing abilities.

"Diana, that's wonderful," Zetel said, leaning forward to kiss her but she drew back.

"You must refrain from calling me Diana. My name is Sister Angela della Caccia. I live in the convent just the other side of Piazza San Marco. Sometimes, I walk through the Piazza on my way to the hospital. By coincidence, we have met again."

She asked many questions about Sarah. "I am jealous of her," she admitted, "but I can't offer you what she can. I asked for and was granted in perpetuity the gift of virginity."

" Diana," he began, but at a warning glance from her, said, "Sister Angela, as you become mortal, does your oath persist? Surely, your oath was part of being a goddess. If you leave the Order, you are also not bound by its oath."

She stood up precipitously and backed away from him.

"What are you suggesting?" she asked. "I become your mistress? And what about your love for your wife?"

He faced her, his hands outstretched. "Diana ... sorry... Sister Angela, I loved you long before I knew Sarah. Even as a little boy, I voiced my love for you. I hunted in books for pictures of you. I sold my soul to Lucifer because he promised I would see you again. I desire you more than anything in the world. I will give up everything for you. You are alive — you are here — that's all that matters."

She backed further away. "I loved you on the Arc," she said, "but that was more of a love for a child or the love between two friends. I said once that if you were a god, I might be tempted to disclaim my oath. Indeed, you resemble a god. Both in face and figure, you are desirable in every sense. Truly, I am sorely tempted but I must refrain. You will go back to Canada and I will stay here. We will share a common memory but that's all we will share. Goodbye and enjoy the rest of your life. I leave now or I shall be late."

She turned and walked rapidly away.

"Wait! We can't just part forever," he said, following close behind her. "We have only just met again. We are different from all others. We were together for billions of years. How can we just walk away?"

At the church exit, she faced him. "Because we must. You do not grasp what becoming mortal means to me. I am still beautiful, much like I was on the Arc. But if you look closely, you will see lines forming on my temples and my slimness thickening. As immortality deserts me, I will age very quickly, far more quickly than your Sarah and far more quickly than you. How long, how many years? I do not know. It will be soon and you will lose your desire for me. We must never see each other again. Don't try to find me at the hospital or at the convent. I will call the security guards, and if you persist, the police. Goodbye."

He tried to retain her but she signalled to the church guide who had stayed close by. The guide blocked him.

What to do? he thought as he made his way back to the Piazza. He still shook from the lust and desire that had engulfed him in his meeting with Diana. He did not doubt she would make a scene if he attempted to seek her out. There was no point in asking for her at the convent. He would not be let in and she would not allow a meeting. He also didn't relish waiting for her at the hospital, hoping to catch a glimpse, to be ousted by security guards in a very public place.

Profoundly troubled, deep in thought, he arrived at the Piazza and heard his name called. Sarah! He'd forgotten all about her.

"Where have you been," she said. "I've waited over an hour. I've looked in the Basilica and all over the Square. You said you'd be here."

Besotted by the chance meeting with Diana, hardly aware of Sarah, he joined her at a table in front of Florian's. Absentmindedly, he nodded at her, mumbled "sorry," and stared vacantly at the Campanile.

"Zetel, what's wrong? What happened?" Sarah asked. "Are you angry with me because I slept in?"

"Angry? You slept in?" he said. "No, not angry. Forgot."

She leaned forward and banged the table with her balled fists. "Zetel Landaw, I am not a woman who accepts being forgotten, specially by her husband. Something happened. Now, come out of your fog and tell me what happened."

Still faraway, he said, "I met someone I knew a long time ago."

"Was this someone a woman?" Sarah asked, sharply.

"Yes. A nun. A nursing Sister. Works at the hospital. Was a huntress when I knew her," he said and continued to gaze into space.

Bewildered, Sarah stared hard at him. "A huntress? You mean she hunted animals?"

Without a thought, he answered, "No, she blessed the hunters and the hunt and fertility."

A worried frown on her face, Sarah came around the table, grasped Zetel by the ears and twisted his face to confront hers. A memory had flashed through her mind. She remembered Joseph and Ettie telling her about a fixation Zetel had even as a young boy on Diana the Huntress, how he had claimed that they were friends and he would someday marry her.

"Zetel, you did not see Diana the Huntress. You saw someone who looked like pictures of her. The woman you saw awakened childhood obsessions in you. Come, let's go back to the hotel and do nothing today. You definitely need more rest."

At the hotel, he lay down on the bed and fell fast asleep. Sarah unlaced and pulled off his shoes and covered him with a blanket. Concern traced furrows on her brow, as she sat on the edge of the bed and looked at him. She was convinced he was having a nervous breakdown despite a full week of vacation. She smiled at the thought that she was competing for his love with a nun who looked like a mythological goddess. Just a deeply buried obsession that had somehow flared up again. If it persisted over the next day, she would insist they cut short their stay and go home.

The next morning they awoke early, stayed lazily in bed, listened to the bells of the many churches, and ordered breakfast to the room. Sarah was relieved to find Zetel refreshed, relaxed, much the same as she knew him.

Over the next two days, they wandered aimlessly through the narrow lanes and streets, climbed occasionally onto a vaporetto for a ride along the Grand Canal, did more shopping on the Mercerie, and continued to enjoy meals at cafes and restaurants that they came across. Short blustery squalls late in the afternoon of the second day sent them scrambling dripping wet back to their hotel.

They got out of their wet clothes, towelled themselves down, chilled, held each other close, fell on the bed and made love.

"I need a hot bath," Sarah said. "Why don't you read the paper and then we'll have supper in the hotel."

"I'll take the paper with me and wait for you in the dining room," Zetel said, pulling on dry clothing. "I need a drink. Don't take too long. I'm also hungry."

"You're not allowed to tell me what to do," she snapped back playfully. "Your role is to cater to my every whim."

He slapped her lightly on the buttocks. "You're right. I almost forgot."

She hurried through the bath, and dressed, and went to the dining room. The room, lit dimly with Murano chandeliers, was cosy and elegant, not large, with tables set closely to each other, served by waiters in black trousers and white shirts. All the tables were taken by guests but Zetel was not among them.

She asked at the concierge desk. "There was a message for Mr. Landaw," the concierge said, "that was just called in about a half hour ago urging his immediate attendance at the Convent of the Sisters of Mercy. Did he not inform you?"

She shook her head, increasing dread causing her stomach to constrict. "Do you know who sent the message?"

"Yes, it was Sister Angela, a well known healer and nurse in our city," the concierge said, and then, chuckling, "You must not worry, madam, your husband is meeting a nun in a convent."

"Give me the address and directions," Sarah said.

She turned right onto Sotoportega, left at the Calle San Gallo, crossed the Ponte Tron, found the Fondamenta Orsoleo and soon located the convent. It was a rather unprepossessing building, more decayed than its neighbours. Several broken stone steps led to a small door with a ring pull bell. A window in the entrance door opened and a barely visible shadow shrouded face peered out. Sarah asked for Sister Angela. The window closed abruptly. Sarah pulled the ring bell again and knocked loudly at the door. This time the door opened. A tall slim older woman in white habit and wimple stood smiling in the doorway.

"You are English speaking, I believe, and you are asking for Sister Angela. Are you a family member or a friend?"

For a moment, Sarah hesitated. "Sister Angela is a friend of my husband and I have come to talk to her about him. Is she in?"

The nun sighed. "I am the Mother Superior here. Sister Angela left the Order earlier today. She took with her all her belongings. You may call on her at the Ospedale since she is still a nurse and this is the time for her usual tour of duty."

"My husband had a note to meet her at the convent. Was he not here?"

The nun sighed again. "No, madam, he was not here. You are the first to call today."

The dread building up in Sarah now burst as tears ran down her cheeks. "My husband can't be running off with a nun," she said and grasped the Mother Superior's arms.

The Mother Superior embraced her and held her tightly. "My child, I do not know but we mustn't judge too quickly. Come inside and I will call the hospital and talk to Sister Angela. There must be a logical explanation."

She seated Sarah in a sparsely furnished, shabby reception room and stepped into an adjoining office. Sarah could hear the phone conversation and, without understanding the Italian, knew something was wrong.

The Mother Superior frowned as she returned to Sarah. "I'm afraid my information is disappointing. Sister Angela has not appeared at the Ospedale today and has left no message as to her intentions. However, one of the staff on his way to the hospital saw Sister Angela in her white nurse's habit and a man at dinner in one of the quayside restaurants at the Ponte Rialto. If you hurry, you may find them and discuss the situation. May God be with you, my child."

Sarah raced as fast as she could through the narrow laneways clogged with people, along the Mercerie and the connecting streets that led to the Rialto Bridge. She no longer saw Venice as a city of picturesque antiquities. It was now just a labyrinth of walkways impeding her goal to stop her husband from an infatuation caused by a mental aberration and save their marriage. She advanced onto the quayside of the Rialto Bridge and marched through the open air restaurants on either side of the Canal. There was no sign of Zetel or of a woman in a nurse's white uniform. She inquired of several waiters to no avail. Finally, the Maitre d' in one remembered seeing Sister Angela and a man having dinner in his restaurant.

"We are always happy to see Sister Angela," said the Maitre d'. "Her work and healing is well known among Venetians. The man with her is either a patient or a donor."

"The man with her is my husband," Sarah said impatiently. "Did you see where they went?"

The Maitre d' laughed, "Madam need not worry. Sister Angela is a nun. I know they took a gondola because I waved to them as they passed by heading up the Canal Grande."

She boarded an idling water taxi near the gondola rental area and gave the driver precise instructions as to what she was looking for — a gondola with two people on board, one dressed all in white.

Zetel, Herald Tribune in hand, was comfortably self-satisfied as he descended the steps to the Hotel San Gallo dining room. He felt released from his sudden infatuation with Diana, cured by the two easy days he and Sarah had enjoyed, as well as their lovemaking which bound him even closer to her. His moment of madness for Diana was completely irrational, he had concluded. What had happened on the Arc was eons in the past, a relationship between a trapped soul and an unattainable goddess. True, he owed her a debt of gratitude for helping him escape. Perhaps he could keep her as a friend and provide her with some financial security as her powers declined. He was sorry that her future seemed so bleak but, in terms of mortality, his own future was just as bleak. He would end up back on the Arc and likely never get reassigned — an eternity in a prison without possibility of parole. In her case, even had she remained on the Arc, as her votaries on Earth diminished, she would have deteriorated and eventually disappeared.

He selected a table and was about to sit down when the headwaiter presented a folded note to him.

"Sir, this was just telephoned a moment ago."

He glanced at the note, in excitement dropped his newspaper, and reread it: *Mr. Landaw, please call upon me at my convent. Urgent. Directions are below. Sister Angela della Caccia.* Something must have happened was his immediate reaction. Perhaps the deterioration has already set in.

He ran down the Hotel stairway and burst into the Campo startling two tourists who jumped back precipitously. He turned towards the Sotoportega but was stopped by a woman in a white nurse's uniform.

"Diana!" he said. "What's happened? What's urgent?"

"Sir, my name is not Diana but Sister Angela. Please refer to me by my rightful name," Diana said, her firmness belied by a smile. "We can't talk here."

She led the way through the narrow, darkened Calle San Gallo and into the maze of equally narrow lanes which brought them to the Rialto Bridge and the quayside restaurants. She chose one that was not well patronized and selected a table well back from the few that were occupied.

Zetel, conflicted, confused, pounded by a tumult of rising desire and guilt, followed her blindly. He thought he had put all feelings for her aside but here he was, eagerly watching her every movement, the lithe movement of her waist and buttocks, the seductive heave of her bosom and the sculptured marble profile of her face as she turned towards him. What did this meeting mean? She had made it clear — there would be no more contact. Had she changed her mind about him? And if so, what about Sarah? He loved Sarah very much. Could he leave her? What about their children? Three days ago, in the exultation of his finding Diana, he was ready to chuck everything and fly away with her. Did he still feel the same way? He had left no message for Sarah. What must she think of his disappearance?

"Let us talk while we have dinner," Diana said, beckoning the waiter.

"I have to let Sarah know where I am," Zetel said, hesitantly. "Perhaps she can join us."

Diana rattled off menu selections to the waiter. "Soon you will have to decide between me and Sarah," she said. "Joining us now or even knowing where you are is not a good idea."

"But you said there was no possibility of a love between us. You are a goddess and a nun sworn to virginity," he said.

"I am no longer a nun. I left the order early today along with my oath. My goddess days are numbered and I no longer feel bound by that oath. I am a normal woman, in love with a man, and I desire him like any mortal woman. Tonight I will surrender my virgin state to this man. What comes after that I do not know. You may choose Sarah or me. If you select me, I will dedicate the rest of my existence to you."

He pondered the situation while they ate the dinner that arrived quickly along with a bottle of Amarone. He drank a glass of the red wine hoping it would settle his confused state but he found himself light headed and less able to think clearly.

"I don't know what to do," he said. "This conversion of yours has caught me totally by surprise. I had put away all thoughts of you after our talk at that church. I resolved to focus entirely on my wife, my family and my work. Now I'm completely mixed up."

The restaurant was beginning to fill up. Tables around them were taken. Zetel noticed several of the guests were looking at them curiously.

"We must go," she said. "Let us continue our discussion where we cannot be interrupted."

He paid the bill and they walked out onto the quayside. Diana hailed a gondola from the gondola rank. "We can best talk in the gondola," she said. "We will be alone and in the middle of a noisy Canal Grande. The gondolier will be too busy working to overhear us."

He started to object but she climbed into the gondola and beckoned him. A seductive smile lit up her face and added to her beauty. He found himself compelled to join her. They sat in the prow facing the gondolier who pushed the boat free of its mooring and slowly paddled into the traffic of the canal.

The gondolier was in the usual costume of striped shirt, black pants and shoes and a white topper with black band and ribbon. He was heavily bearded. The white topper barely sat on a head full of black hair. He began to sing "Arrivaderci, Italia" off key and in an accent that did not sound Italian even to Zetel. Diana shushed him.

He must be just learning, thought Zetel. The gondolier leaned heavily on the oar but failed to propel the gondola in a straight line. They swerved precariously through the water traffic. A vaporetto issued a warning blast on the horn and reversed engines. Zetel watched the bow of the water bus slide past him. Diana shouted at the gondolier and seemed to be giving him instructions on how to operate a gondola. He appeared to settle down into a more rhythmic handling of the oar. Slowly, laboriously, weaving dangerously, they headed under the Rialto Bridge, past the crowded traffic at the fish and vegetable markets, and into the quieter reaches of the canal. With more open stretches of water around them, the gondolier's lack of competency exposed them to less chance of collision.

The air had cooled and the breeze strengthened to a steady wind. Diana pulled a blanket folded on a thwart over her and Zetel. "I am chilled," she said and leaned closely into him. He put his arms around her and they embraced and kissed. Lust engulfed him as he ran his hands over her body.

She laughed softly, "Not here. Not now."

"Where are we going?" he asked.

"When I left the convent this morning, I secured a lodging in one of the palaces along the canal. The bottom floor is empty because of flooding but the upper floors are rented out. It is not far."

Night had fallen when they reached a dimly lit part of the canal. The Gondolier clumsily manoeuvred them over to a darkened stretch of buildings. In one, a light shone through an upper window. They moored alongside the quay and Zetel and Diana disembarked. A liveried servant in red buttoned tunic and breeches and wearing a white formal wig stepped out from the doorway, a lit candle in hand which immediately blew out. Apologizing, he stepped back into the building, tripped on the raised sill, and fell heavily. They rushed to the doorway. The servant scrambled to his feet, adjusted his wig, brushed off his tunic, picked up the candle and lit it quickly.

"May I show you to your room?" he said.

They followed him up a grand staircase to the second floor. Zetel noticed the servant was obviously not used to wearing formal traditional wear for he had put the wig on backwards with the neck part extending out in front of him. Clearly, Diana was trying to insert some ceremony into the historic occasion of giving up her virginity. He smiled. She should have picked better actors.

He was still very much conflicted. On the gondola, next to her, under the blanket, he wanted nothing more than to make love to her, no decision necessary, a rapturous moment of impulse. Now, he was no longer so eager. He needed to think it through.

The servant led them down a long hallway, opened the door to Diana's room, bowed deeply, caught his wig as it fell off his head, and turned quickly away.

The room was large, lit by a dozen candles in stands and wall brackets. A canopied bed, its curtains open, blankets pulled back, stood against a wall with serving tables on either side. A bottle of wine and two glasses embellished one of tables. On the other, was a bowl filled with chocolate and sweetmeats. On an opposite wall was a small divan and coffee table. Next to the window was a wash stand and basin with two jugs of water, a dish of soap, and towels neatly folded on a rack below the wash stand. A picture of Diana the goddess of the Hunt hung on the wall over the divan. Next to it, an ornamental hook held her bow and a quiver of arrows.

She swept into his arms and grasped him tightly to her. She felt the lust rise in him but also recognized the resistance. "Wait," she said. "You must see me as I once was."

She took off her white cap and dropped it to the floor. She released her golden hair so that it fell loosely past her shoulders. "You remember how often you caressed my hair with your fingers of cloud."

She slipped off her white hose to reveal slim well formed legs. She unbuttoned the white nurse's uniform. Underneath, she wore the short tunic and blouse. She retrieved her quiver of arrows and slung it on her back and held the bow in one hand. Her hunting knife — the one that had cut Zetel loose from the Arc — was belted to her side.

"I am Diana the Huntress," she said proudly, "goddess of the hunt."

There was a knock at the door. Diana humphed impatiently and opened it. He heard a whispered angry conversation in Italian. He wandered over to the window and stared out into the darkness and lighted spaces of the canal. What to do? Dressed as the goddess, she didn't seem inclined to give up her virginity. His own ardour had cooled, replaced by a haunting guilt regarding Sarah.

He looked down at the quay. Surprisingly, the gondolier was still there. He had taken off his hat and was wiping his face with a rag of some kind which Zetel realized was his mass of black hair and the beard. The Gondoliers own hair fell in golden ringlets to his shoulder. The liveried servant was also on the quay, talking to the gondolier. He, too, had taken off his wig. I've seen those two before, Zetel thought, racking his memory. Then, a stroke of sudden recognition and terror flashed up his spine and raised the hair on his neck and head. He heard the door slam and Diana return to the bed. He whirled around, his throat constricted, and managed to squeak out, "What's going on?"

He threw himself sideways and the arrow Diana had shot narrowly missed him and smashed through the window. She quickly pulled another arrow from her quiver and fixed it to the bow. He grabbed a jug from the wash stand and hurled it at her. It hit her hard on the cheek and knocked the bow out of her hand. Momentarily stunned, she fell back on the bed.

"Why?" he screamed at her.

"Why?" she repeated dully, still dazed. "They promised me immortality if I would tempt you here and kill you. Immortality. Do you know what that means to me. I would remain Diana the Huntress forever, free to roam the universe as I wished, free from debilitating decay, free to enjoy youth and beauty forever. Is that not something to fight for. All I had to do was kill you, a mortal who would someday die anyway."

"What about our friendship, our love?" he objected. "Does that not count for something?"

" I befriended you when you were a cloud, a soul. That's all I know or care about you. You were your own undoing. You professed such love for me that the agents of The-One-True-God saw a way to entrap you through me."

"I don't believe you," he said. "I know I meant something to you. You admitted it yourself in the church. I know now that love between us is impossible but surely we can still be friends."

She laughed. "Some friendship. I am the one who must sacrifice for our friendship. No, my friend, you must make the sacrifice." Raising her voice, she shouted, "You escaped my arrows but you will not escape my knife."

She drew her hunting knife but still sat on the bed, her head lowered. "Run, you fool," she whispered. "You can still escape. Otherwise, I must kill you."

For a moment, he didn't move. She left the bed and advanced towards him. He raced to the door, threw it open, bowled over a cloaked figure standing there, ran down the hall way and the grand stair case, and out the door onto the quay.

"Stop him," he heard Diana shout. "He's getting away."

He shouldered his way past the two men, ran down the quay until it ended and dove into the canal. He swam under water until breathless, surfaced, gasping for air. He looked back. The gondolier was trying desperately to move the gondola into the mainstream while the liveried servant standing in the prow searched the water. A vaporetto sideswiped them, dumping them both into the water. The last he saw of them, they were clinging to the hull of the capsized gondola. He dove again and stayed underwater as long as he could. Surfacing and diving, he made it to the other side of the canal and climbed onto a narrow landing lit by a hanging lamp. Exhausted, chilled, soaking wet, he sat on the landing, hoping his pursuers would not see him. A water taxi passed by, did a sudden u-turn, and came alongside the landing.

A woman leaned out, "Zetel, for God's sake, what's happened to you? Come on board."

It took both the water taxi driver and Sarah to get him onto the boat. At St. Mark's, Zetel had recovered sufficiently that, leaning heavily on Sarah, he could walk to the hotel, drag himself up the long staircase, and into the hotel and their room. He was shivering uncontrollably and exuded the stench of the canal. Sarah stripped his clothes off, helped him into a hot bath, then towelled him dry, and got him into bed.

"Sarah, I didn't betray you," he mumbled. He had stopped shivering but could barely speak.

"I'm glad to hear it. I'm anxious to know what happened. But right now, just sleep," she said solicitously.

"Sarah, don't let anyone in. Tell the desk," he muttered and fell asleep.

He slept long into the next morning. Sarah dared not leave him and ordered breakfast into the room. He finally arose and, fortified with coffee, felt well enough to talk.

"The Grand Canal may be picturesque but it's not fun to swim in," he said.

"Why were you swimming in it?" Sarah asked. "It's clear to me you were running from something. Was it your girlfriend? I want to know what happened last night."

"The short and the long of it was a simple abduction and ransom attempt. I was a damn fool to be so easily tempted into a trap. Sister Angela was the bait. I was so completely hung up on her as Diana the Huntress and that she needed my help, that I just went along. When I got her message, I started for the convent but she was waiting for me at the hotel door and insisted we find some place to talk. We had a bite to eat at one of the Rialto Bridge canal side restaurants and then she insisted we continue our talk on a gondola."

"But what was there to talk about?" Sarah said.

Zetel blushed. "She had left the Order, was in love with me, and wanted to marry me. She said she was Diana the Huntress but she no longer had magical powers and was just an ordinary woman. Sarah, please believe me — sure, I fell completely for the story but I couldn't see giving you up. We continued to debate the issue until we reached one of those partly flooded palaces. We were led by a servant in a white wig and tightly buttoned tunic — just like in olden times — up to a candle lit room. I told her I couldn't do it and started to leave. She came after me with a knife. I ran out the door and knocked over some guy waiting there and then took on the gondolier and the servant, dove into the canal, made my escape, and managed to get to the other side where you found me."

Sarah recounted her own adventures to track him down. "I was close to giving up when I spotted you sitting on the landing. You looked more like a beached whale."

They were silent for a few minutes. "Will you forgive me for being so stupid?" he asked. "Nothing happened between me and Angela. Also, my obsession with Diana the Huntress is gone. It should have ended when my days as a young boy ended."

"Well, I agree with that," Sarah said. "Quite apart from forgiving you, are you or we in any danger? After all, your ex-goddess and probably the others know where you live. Shall we go to the police?"

He winced at the thought. His ex-goddess had allowed him to escape. He knew the gondolier was Archangel Michael, the servant was probably Archangel Gabriel, and the man at the door was likely Samael, waiting for his soul. "I don't think the police will believe me. Sister Angela is well known in Venice and venerated. The police will believe that I enticed her and tried to rape her. The case will go on forever. The others in the plot will most likely never be found. My word against hers. I won't have a chance. We're leaving in a few days. Let's just enjoy the rest of our stay."

"No," she said firmly. "This incident has unnerved me and you don't look all that easy. If we stay here, we'll always be looking over our shoulders. Apart from last night, we've had an enjoyable vacation. It's time to go home."

CHAPTER 8 —
Zetel and a death in the family

"Zetel, I can't go on like this much longer."

Zetel listened intently to the voice on the telephone. Fred Peterson always spoke softly. He ran a small accounting firm with Zetel as his main client. His wife, Sally Peterson, was the bookkeeper in Zetel's funds management office.

"Fred, you better speak more loudly. I'm calling from the lobby of the Jewish General in Montreal and it's not exactly quiet here. Did I understand you correctly? You can't go on? How do you mean, Fred? Are you not well?" Zetel asked. "Do you need some time off?"

Fred was in his early fifties, fit-looking and tanned from the golf courses he frequented, still sporting a mass of thick black hair with an occasional streak of silver.

"You can't be thinking of retirement," Zetel said.

Fred raised his voice slightly. "I'm well, Zetel, I have enough time off, and I'm nowhere near retiring. Look, Zetel, I know this is not a good time for you, what with your dad so sick. We can put our conversation off for a while. I'm just getting awfully worried. What we're doing is illegal. If we get caught — well, you know what I mean. And Sally, too, is involved, maybe even more involved. She prepares all the documents and I pretend to audit them and make all the proper reports. So far it's worked, but it can't last. I want out and I want Sally out too."

"Look, Fred, this cannot be a five minute discussion. I don't have the mind for it right now. I'm calling you because Sally said you wanted to see me on an important matter. I agree. This is an important matter, but we have to work something out carefully. And definitely not on the telephone. Can we put it off for now?"

"Sure, Zetel," Fred said. "I didn't realize I was dragging you away from your dad's bedside."

He and Sarah had barely arrived home from Venice when his mother called and announced tearfully that his father was very sick. "Zetel, the leukemia has come back and it doesn't look good."

He flew to Montreal and sat beside his dying father in the palliative care unit of the Jewish General. Whenever Joseph was awake, they talked of the old days. Ettie was often there and she and Joseph would regale Zetel with stories of his youth.

"Remember your interest in Diana the Huntress," Ettie said in one of their conversations. "I'm so glad you left that behind when you grew up."

Zetel winced. "I don't want to remember. I'm happy with the goddess I have."

Early one Saturday evening, Fuhr entered the hospital room. Sarah and the children had flown in for the weekend and joined Ettie and Zetel around the hospital bed. They all rose to greet him.

"Herr Fuhr," Ettie said, "How nice of you to come. But you are in evening dress. Surely you must be attending an important event."

Fuhr bowed, kissed Ettie's and Sarah's hands, greeted the children and grasped the raised hand that Joseph offered. "No, my sweet lady, not an important event. Just some foreign dignitaries that I must entertain tonight, here in Montreal."

"Are you going to show them magic tricks?" Elijah and Marsha asked almost in unison.

"Of course," Fuhr replied. "We are a gathering of magicians. My, how you children have grown. You are now young adults, and if you are like your parents, very clever."

"Complimenting them just goes to their heads, Herr Fuhr," Zetel said.

"Actually, he complimented us," Sarah said.

Fuhr embraced Zetel. "This is a trying time for all of us, my dear Zetel. I meet with our famous archangels later on, but no more of that now."

"Not the ones we saw at Scaramouche," Sarah said. "The angel investors that so disturbed Zetel?"

"The very same," Fur nodded. "They continually misbehave."

He turned to Joseph. "Herr Landaw, how goes it?"

Joseph looked up at him sorrowfully. "Not very well, Herr Fuhr. It is clear to me that my end is near. I regret leaving the people I love." He gasped for breath and motioned Fuhr to come closer. "Herr Fuhr, you have been a good friend to me and my family. Hopefully, my Ettie and Zetel can have your wise counsel and strength in the days ahead."

To Zetel's surprise, tears glazed Fuhr's eyes. "Have no concerns, Herr Landaw, I shall be at their beck and call."

Fuhr amused them during the rest of his visit with card tricks. Even Joseph perked up and seemed to enjoy the demonstration.

"Herr Fuhr," Sarah said as he left, "thanks for allowing us a few moments of pleasure."

Zetel and Fuhr met in the hallway. "What's your meeting all about?" Zetel asked.

"I am delivering a message to Gabriel and Michael. I became aware too late that you were in danger in Venice and I congratulate you on escaping their trap. I am informed that The-One-True-God knows nothing about their attempt and its failure. Also, He abjures his angels from having any contact with pagan gods and goddesses, let alone offering Diana perpetual immortality. My message is if they don't leave you alone, The-One-True-God will discover what happened because I will set them up as a laughing stock among the angels. The-One-True-God will have no choice but to punish them severely. If he casts them out of heaven, I become their liege lord. They will do anything to avoid such an outcome. You are safe for a long time to come."

Joseph slowly sank deeper. The comas became longer, the periods of lucidity less frequent and shorter. Shortly before the end, he awakened late at night and nudged Zetel who was dozing beside the bed.

"Zetel," he gasped, "look after your mother when I'm gone. Make sure she's happy. Bring her to Toronto."

"Don't worry, papa, she will not be left alone."

Joseph was quiet for a moment and Zetel thought he had fallen asleep. Then he reached out and took Zetel's hand.

"There is one more thing," Joseph said, so weakly that Zetel had to put an ear close to Joseph's mouth. "For all our sakes and for your beautiful wife and lovely children, do something with your business. I don't know much about stocks but I know something is wrong. Remember, it's a father's love for his only child that tells you this."

Zetel started to protest but realized his father had lapsed into a coma again.

It was his last for Joseph died in the early hours of the morning. Zetel, still beside the bed, was holding his father's hand. He heard the heart monitor start to beep and felt the warmth slowly seep out of his father's fingers. He watched a nurse turn off the monitor and a doctor make a quick examination and write notes into the file stashed at the foot of the bed. He saw the doctor signal to the nurse and they both left the room.

He continued to sit beside the bed, his head bowed, crying unashamedly. Do something with my business, he thought. I'm trying so hard, papa. It's always one step forward and two steps back. If I'm exposed, at least you won't witness my shame.

It took the better part of three months to clear up all the details of the estate, to sell the Outremont house, and to move Ettie to Toronto. She refused to live with them — "It will only cause trouble" — and settled for a small suite in The Broadview, an assisted living establishment that catered to Jewish residents, and a ten minute drive from Zetel's home.

With that all settled, he met with the Petersons. It required several long sessions to persuade them not to desert him. He set up an offshore company in the Cayman Islands to which he flowed all the documents. The offshore company hired Fred to do the accounting and to submit the files back to the company. Fred was thus separated from direct involvement. Several times each year, Fred would travel to the company to do the necessary Board reviews and, coincidentally, indulge in his love of golf. As a final measure, Zetel ended Sally's employment with the firm, and set her up as an independent consultant working off site, and contracted her to do the bookkeeping.

"I plan to get us back into the straight and narrow," he reassured them. "I just need more time."

PART THREE
LATER YEARS

CHAPTER 1 —
Zetel faces more challenges

Zetel celebrated his 52nd birthday at dinner at home with his family. Ettie arrived shortly after lunch and insisted on preparing the meal. Sarah said she would be home by four and would help. Cyril and Anna arrived early as well. They had moved to Toronto and lived only a short distance away. Elijah and Marsha showed up late afternoon and resignedly answered all the questions their grandparents put to them. Herr Fuhr joined them around six and apologized for being late.

"The traffic was so bad," he offered as an excuse.

You mean the air traffic from Transylvania, Zetel thought and smiled.

Tut, tut, my boy, the thought came back,

"Well, Zetel, you seem very hale and hearty tonight," Fuhr said, when they were all settled in the living room having a pre-dinner drink.

"Who can be unhappy in this bull market," Zetel said laughing. "It's settled down now for a bit but the Dow Jones is up 44% since January. It's an investor's dream."

"Well, if it's up so high, how come my returns are only ten percent?" Cyril asked. "Are you holding money back?"

"I don't hold money back," Zetel said, rather sharply. "I'm increasing the cash portion of the portfolio because the market is high at the moment and I fear there will soon be a correction. I stopped buying a couple of months ago and I've done some selective selling. I'll start buying again when better opportunities for equity purchases emerge."

"And when will that be? You know, I'm on the board of our condo and the other board members are getting more than ten percent. One man saw his portfolio jump by thirty percent."

"Daddy," Sarah interrupted, "this is a birthday gathering, not a board meeting. Leave my Zetel alone. You can attack him in his office tomorrow. I'm sure he's doing what's right and smart. Mr. Fuhr, are you happy with your returns?"

Fuhr nodded. "Yes, sehr geehrte frau, the funds are doing very well. Of course, there are many risks to investing, but Zetel seems to have found the right balance. Besides, he has delivered better than average results no matter what the market is doing. Herr Lansmann, ask your condominium board colleague who earned thirty percent, how well he has done in previous years."

"I know," Cyril said. "There were times when he complained loudly about his losses and he's changed money managers several times. He thinks the whole financial industry is peopled with crooks. Zetel, at one of our meetings, he even named you as a fraud but stopped his rant when I told him you're my son-in-law. And by the way, Mr. Fuhr, I'm happy to hear you extol Zetel's abilities but you don't have any money invested in his funds. You have no skin in the game but I have my entire body in it. If something bad happens, you can wash your hands and walk away but I will take a bath."

Sarah clapped her hands, threw back her head and laughed, "Daddy, what a beautiful metaphor. But that's enough now. Off business or I will talk about my revolting school experience today where one of the children became terribly sick and evacuated at both ends of his little body and I had to clean him up and then the mess because the school nurse and the janitor were at a union meeting."

"Well, Sarah, you have now talked about it," Zetel said. "What more can you add? I think I prefer hearing Cyril lambaste me."

"Let's change the subject," Ettie said, holding up an empty glass which Zetel quickly filled with wine. "Herr Fuhr, we are all getting older except you. How do you stay so young looking?"

Fuhr stood up and bowed, "Sehr geehrte Frau Ländau, you flatter me. Appearances can be deceiving. There are days when I feel billions of years old, as old as the universe. When I was a banker in Frankfurt, business life was less harried. There was time for lunches in fine restaurants, invitations to fashionable salons, vacations to beautiful and interesting places and all without business interruptions. Now, I must travel a great deal, fly about the world to keep an eye on my many business dealings, and be constantly available to help colleagues and associates with problems. It is rare that I get a full night's sleep, so frequent are the telephone calls. In my car now, I must carry one of those new portable telephones. The only truly leisure and pleasurable moments I have is when I join a Ländau gathering, for which I am eternally grateful."

"Perhaps that's what keeps you young, Mr. Fuhr," Anna said. "You have no time to grow old."

"I don't care if I grow and look old," Cyril said. "I'm happy to be out of the rat race. Retirement is a wonderful occupation. I strongly recommend it. But that's why I need to see the money coming." He looked significantly at Zetel.

"But Herr Lansmann," Fuhr said, "ten percent return on your funds invested, year in, year out, should look after your needs very well. That's why investors are clamouring to put their money with Zetel."

"Yes, Mr. Fuhr, so far everything has worked out," Cyril said. "But this is a worrisome world. Things happen over which we have no control. Take the Iraq-Iran war. It's been going on for six years now. If the US gets more involved, who knows what will happen to the stock market."

"But, Daddy," Sarah said, "The US is involved, has taken attacks on its ships in the Gulf and still the market goes up as my happy husband is quick to inform me every day."

"They're not directly involved," Cyril said. "So far the US just provides supplies and intelligence to Iraq. By getting involved, I mean putting troops into the fray."

Zetel shook his head. "Cyril, I can't see the US ever putting troops on the ground in the Middle East unless it's to rescue Israel. Right now you have two enemies of Israel fighting each other. There's an effect on oil but even that hasn't stopped the market from climbing. Besides, things are getting better between the USSR and the West. Gorbachev with his glasnost and perestroika is trying to reform. Reagan has met with him and reports are that diplomacy is winning. All this is bound to have a good effect on the world economy. So, Cyril, stop worrying. Sure there will be a correction because that's how the market works. People will start taking profits and the market will adjust. But I'm prepared."

"And we're prepared too," Sarah said. "Come, let's all go to dinner. We owe it all to Ettie and mommy tonight, with a bit of help from me, of course, and table setting by Marsha and Elijah."

Exactly a month later, the smile left Zetel's face and was replaced by ashen cheeks. The optimism with which he had greeted every session of the stock markets in New York and Toronto during 1987— an optimism buoyed by the rise in values of the various funds and portfolios that he managed as the markets climbed ever higher — an optimism bolstered by his diminishing need to use new clients' money to pay off established clients — an optimism that collapsed entirely, along with stock markets all over the world, on October 19, the day that became known as Black Monday.

He had not been worried the previous week even as the New York Stock Exchange daily results faltered. An urgent telephone call from Cyril on Friday morning demanding to know what was happening did not faze him.

"Nothing to worry about, Cyril," he explained. "As I said at my birthday dinner, I was expecting a correction. I've kept more cash, I have significant hedges in place, and I'm watching the market in order to buy in at the right moment. I'll let you know on Monday if there's any action I'll be taking."

Cyril grumbled an "Alright," and hung up.

Rule number one in successful investing, Zetel thought. Never get involved with a family member's money. Then he mentally kicked himself. Without his father-in-law's money, he would never have started his own business, at least, not that quickly.

Friday morning, many of his investors called and to each he offered the same advice "Don't worry, just a correction." What he feared most was a sudden rise in redemptions if his investors panicked. There was enough cash for a small number but not enough for a run on his funds. His house of cards would collapse and in the resulting bankruptcy, his scheme of using new money to bolster the accounts of established clients, and to claim better than actual results so as to attract new money would be exposed.

The markets had barely closed when Fred Peterson called. "Zetel, the market's going crazy. Over 300 million shares were traded today. That's some kind of record —largest volume ever. There were more sellers than buyers, more losers than winners. Zetel, what are we going to do?"

"Take it easy, Fred. There's nothing to panic about. It's just a correction as I've been predicting. Maybe faster and deeper than I thought but still just a correction. You'll see, on Monday it will level off or even start to climb again as people buy the lows. Even this afternoon, I signed up more investors. If they're not worried, why should you?"

There was a long sigh on the telephone. "Because I know and they don't," Fred said.

"Fred, don't go negative on me," Zetel said. "Look, the brokerage side of the business has done very well this year, today as well, from commissions and fees. If worse comes to worse, I can borrow money from the brokerage side. Besides, as a hedge, I sold a number of shares short and they're already in the money. So we have enough cash to stave off a modest redemption. Let's see how Monday shapes up. We'll meet in my office late morning, size things up and decide what if anything we have to do."

Several journalists called him, and he appeared briefly on TV. To all, he gave the same reassuring message. "It's just a correction. There's nothing happening that will send the market down a la '29. Every bull market has a moment of pause and turns down. Enough investors feel the market's too high and are taking profits. Soon investors will start buying again, probably as early as Monday."

Despite his show of confidence and unwavering assurance, he was worried. He stifled the growing tension within him so as not to alarm Sarah, or Cyril with whom he and the family were dining Friday night. The weekend went agonizingly slowly as he strove to maintain his outward demeanour of calm despite his increasing uneasiness. In an automaton like daze, he went about his weekend duties, chores, and social arrangements: grocery shopping with Sarah, lunch with his mother, raking and bagging leaves from the oak trees that graced his property, Saturday evening dinner with some friends, a lacklustre appetite for his favourite Sunday morning breakfast of lox (*smoked salmon*) and cream cheese on a bagel, a movie on Sunday, television Sunday evening.

In bed, he tossed and turned for a couple of hours. Around one am, he arose and, without waking Sarah, dressed quickly and left for the office. The Asian markets will be well into their day, he thought, and that will give some indication of what will happen when New York and Toronto open.

With trembling fingers, he switched on the Bloomberg terminal and immediately realized that what he had feared most was happening. "This is not a correction," he said out loud to the empty office. "This is a rout."

All the key Asian markets were showing severe downturns: Japan, Hong Kong, Singapore, Australia, New Zealand. Horrified, he watched the news clips come in with their message of stock market collapse. To steady his nerves, he brewed a pot of coffee in the office's small kitchen. Cup in hand and munching on a stale cookie, he returned to the Bloomberg screen. He could see that panic had set in. The markets were in free fall.

He switched off the terminal, moved to the window overlooking the lake, and stared out moodily at the lights below stretching to the dark smudge of the water. There was no doubt in his mind that the stock market carnage would infect New York and Toronto. If his own fund investors panicked and demanded redemptions, could he withstand the onslaught? It wasn't just a matter of bankruptcy that he feared. With bankruptcy would come disclosure of his Ponzi scheme, criminal charges and, most likely, jail. His shame would break up his marriage and hurt his children very badly, and possibly affect the income of his mother and the Lansmann's. He poured himself another cup of coffee and sat at the small conference table. Desperately, he tried to find a solution, a course of action, any idea that would save him from catastrophe. Then, as fright took hold of him, and he felt himself sinking in the quagmire of what he had wrought, an answer began to form in his beleaguered brain, an idea so simple that he wondered why he had never thought of it before. It might just save him.

He dozed off and was awakened when the lights in his adjoining brokerage office came on. A wall clock showed five am. He wandered into the office and was greeted by one of the brokers.

"I know the news in Asia is bad," he said. "Despite the storm that hit Britain on Thursday and Friday and closed the Exchange, the UK is open now and we'll see what happens there. I expect my clients who invest in the UK will be calling."

It was quickly apparent that the UK was faring no better than its Asian counterparts. Early trading indicated a deep downturn with the drop in value more apparent as the minutes ticked by.

Others of his brokers showed up. The office began to bustle as the television sets and terminals were turned on, precipitating groans and shouts of disbelief. Although it was only a little after six am, the telephones started ringing. Still, the office was relatively quiet. Several clients called about their stock positions on the London Exchange, most wanting out. Some investors, surmising that what had happened in the Asia markets and was happening in London, would affect New York and Toronto, gave the brokers Sale orders to be exercised when the markets opened.

At 9:30 am, the office erupted in a cacophony of intense telephone calls, shouts from brokers trying to place orders, near hysterical screaming of clients on speaker phones, shrieks of profanity as calls to the stock exchanges remained unanswered or delayed, the constant clacking of the ticker tape machine as it spat out volley after volley of transactions.

Zetel returned to his office. The telephone rang. "Zetel, are you ok?" came the worried voice of Sarah. "You weren't in bed this morning. What's happening? Daddy called, looking for you."

He explained that what he thought was a correction was a severe downturn. "I've been here all night, following the Asian markets and the UK. It's bad news everywhere."

"Zetel, are we going bankrupt?" she asked. He marvelled at the steadiness of her tone, like someone asking, "Is it going to rain."

"No, I don't think so. We'll see how bad it is by the end of the day."

He heard a school bell ring. "Recess is over," she said. "I'll call you later."

The next call was from Cyril. It wasn't so much a conversation as a rant. Cyril was not interested in answers but in venting his frustration and anger. "You said it was just a correction — the market would start upwards again on Monday. When on Monday? It's now 11 o'clock — do you see a turnaround? Or are you thinking, maybe at three this afternoon. What about my funds with you? Have they reached zero yet? If they do, get your spare bedroom ready. We'll be moving in. Why I trusted you, I don't know."

"Cyril, you've had good results all these years," Zetel replied weakly. "I never promised no setbacks. Let's see how the markets go today. Not all stocks are affected. My short selling is way in the money. I just have to wait for the dust to settle, the markets to bottom and then start buying. Just hang in."

Cyril grumbled some more and then hung up. Zetel wiped the sweat off his forehead. Cyril hadn't threatened to redeem.

The Peterson's arrived shortly after. While Sally was neatly and impeccably dressed, Fred was disheveled, unshaven, dark rings around his eyes. I probably look like him, Zetel thought, remembering he hadn't even washed.

Sally chuckled, "I know what Fred looks like in the morning, Zetel. Now I know what you look like."

He smiled. "It's been a tough night, Sally, watching the world collapse."

"I'm not worried about the world collapsing," Fred said. "I'm worried about you collapsing and taking us with you."

They sat at the conference table. "I think I have a partial solution and I've tested it up to a fall of thirty percent. For the first time in our funds history, we will show zero gain instead of the usual ten percent. That means about fifty million we don't need to worry about. Depending on how much the markets tank, we can even show a modest drop in our funds value. I think our investors will accept some bad news as long as we're well above the markets. Our results will be far better than anyone else's, so that should discourage redemptions. I will also take or borrow from the brokerage side about twenty five million so I can buy the stock sold short as soon as the markets bottom. I'm sure that will be a few days yet. Nobody's going to jump into buying tomorrow — not after such a crash."

"Looks good, Zetel," Fred said. "It's funny. I was going to suggest we reduce our results this month but I thought you'd never agree."

"There was no other way, Fred," Zetel said. "Showing positive results in a market like this would have raised suspicions and led to questions being asked. Let's meet again at five. By then we'll know how badly things are."

At five, they stood in the brokerage office and listened to the brokers reporting on their day's activities. New York was down over twenty percent, Toronto eleven. The two stock markets hadn't been able to keep up with the transactions and the ticker tape was an hour behind instead of the usual fifteen minutes.

Zetel congratulated the brokerage staff for their hard work in a very difficult situation. He met briefly with the Petersons who seemed confident that the worst was over and they would survive. Zetel invited them for lunch the next day to assess the morning's results.

At home, Cyril awaited him and began to harangue him even before he could take off his coat. Sarah intervened, "Daddy, you will stop right now. He's been up all night. He will clean up first, then we will all have a drink, and then we will have supper, and after supper, if Zetel is still awake, you can talk to him about your investments."

Cyril knew better than to argue with his daughter and grudgingly backed off but still glowered at Zetel.

"Cyril," Zetel said, "every market analyst, every fund manager has been swamped by what happened today. There's not a stock market anywhere that hasn't shown a severe drop in value. It's too early to say definitively, but it looks like my funds will break even or suffer a small loss which will be easy to make up. We'll know better as the week progresses. But if you feel you'll be better off somewhere else, by all means, redeem your fund units. Now, I must obey my wife."

Zetel met the Petersons for lunch the next day at a posh restaurant in The Royal York.

"Why this largesse when we might even be bankrupt?" Fred asked. "Don't get me wrong. I'm not complaining."

"You saw the morning's results," Zetel said. "The crash is over. New York recovered slightly and the other exchanges will come around shortly. Oh. It will be volatile for awhile, but I believe we're safe."

"The UK is still going down," Sally said. "Their stock market dropped eleven percent yesterday and another twelve percent today."

Zetel nodded. "True, but the storm that hit them last Thursday and Friday slowed them down. They were closed on Friday, very few City types could get to work. So they fell behind the selling parade."

They talked of the storm that had paralyzed Britain.

"It was a hurricane," Zetel said. "Completely unexpected. In fact, a woman reported to a BBC weatherman that a hurricane was on its way, and he just laughed at her."

"Let's not laugh at the weatherman. Who predicted this crash?" Fred said.

Zetel chuckled, "Well, I did say a correction was coming. Let's talk about something else. You're both back from Cayman. How was the holiday."

The rest of the lunch was spent discussing the beauties of the Cayman Islands.

He returned to his office, caught up on the latest reports, stretched his legs onto his desk, and sipped a cup of coffee. He was satisfied he would not be exposed this time.

"Two rabbis are asking to see you," his secretary informed him. "At least, I think they are rabbis. Big fedoras, bearded, long coats — you know, the really orthodox kind. They wouldn't give their names or organization. They want to talk to you about investing."

He rose as his secretary ushered the two in. Their appearance puzzled Zetel. Their hats were wide brimmed and brown, coats long to the knee, belted at the waist and also brown, their trousers blue jeans, their feet encased in sturdy polished work boots. They were heavily bearded so that with their hats pulled low, all Zetel could see of their faces was a nose and eyes.

"Good day, gentlemen," Zetel said. "Given the current market crash, I didn't expect to find investors still willing to invest." Then he went into full sales mode. "Of course, for the discerning investor, this is indeed a good time to invest. The markets will soon bottom and for those willing to risk it, the return to previous levels will mean great profits. I'm sure you have examined our annual reports and agree our returns are extremely good compared to our competitors and to the Indexes. Please sit down and tell me what we can do for you."

They continued to stand. They looked at him quizzically. "Are you Jewish?" one asked.

"Yes," Zetel replied. "Why do you ask?"

"Your head is not covered."

Zetel began to doubt whether he wanted their investment. "Rabbis, I belong to a Reform Synagogue where head covering is voluntary. I hope we can still do business together."

The one who had started the conversation smiled: "We are not rabbis. We are Brothers of the First Church. My name is Mathew Binder and this is my good friend—" he paused — "what's your name again?"

The other one laughed. "My friend Jeremiah sometimes has lapses of memory. My name is Mathew Plough. We are farmers from the St. Jacobs area. We live a very plain simple Christian life. Coming to Toronto to see you is more excitement than we are accustomed to which perhaps accounts for my friends lapse of memory. Isn't that so, Jeremiah?"

"Yes, too stressful for me. All those people and cars. And the tall buildings. And the noise." He looked blankly at Mathew and said in a lower voice, "Am I Jeremiah? I thought I was Mathew."

Mathew laughed even harder, "Pay no attention to him, sir. Jeremiah, your middle name is Mathew — Jeremiah Mathew Binder but we all call you Jeremiah."

Jeremiah shook his head. "I never liked the name Jeremiah. Jeremiah is from the Old Scripture. Mathew is from the New Scripture. I prefer Mathew."

"But we both can't be called Mathew," Mathew objected, exasperation beginning to colour his voice. "It's too confusing."

"Gentlemen," Zetel intervened, "To avoid any confusion, I will refer to you by your last names — Mr. Binder and Mr. Plough. By the way, given your simple lifestyle, how did you get here? Did you drive?"

"No," Binder replied, "We flew."

"You flew? How do you fly from St. Jacobs? You have your own plane?"

"No, no," Plough cut in. "Jeremiah is being funny. We came by train which he found too fast compared to the horse and buggy that usually gets us around. Isn't that so, Jeremiah."

"I thought we agreed my name is Mathew."

Zetel had to turn away in order to stifle an imminent paroxysm of laughter. He breathed deeply, recovered his composure and said: "Gentlemen, please sit down. Let's talk business."

This is some kind of Candid Camera program, Zetel decided. It can't be a scam — they're too poorly prepared. I shall play along.

"How can I help you?" Zetel asked. "What are your investment needs?"

The two looked at each other and said in unison: "We have an important amount of money that we wish to invest safely."

Wow, thought Zetel, they must belong to the St. Jacob's Choral Society.

"It would be better if only one of you spoke at a time," he suggested.

"I will speak first," Binder said. "We collect a regular tithe from our community members. Over the last two decades, we began to save part. This part has accumulated to a very sizeable amount. We keep it in safety deposit boxes in a bank vault."

"In securities?" Zetel asked.

"No, in money."

"You mean cash? You keep it in cash?" Zetel said. "How much are we talking about?"

"About a 100 pounds."

"But we only want to consider investing 50 pounds at this time," Plough added quickly.

"Gentlemen, that's a very small fraction of what we expect from our investors. Fifty pounds sterling is a little over $100. Our investors usually start off with $10,000. I think you're better off with Canada Savings Bonds."

"Sir, you mistake us." Plough said. "We are talking about 50 pounds of money in weight."

Shaking his head, Zetel stood up. "Is it all in one dollar bills or quarters? Gentlemen, I believe this charade has gone far enough."

"Sir," Plough said, "we are serious. The money is in gold bars — about 50 pounds of gold bullion available for investment. Here — I've brought a sample."

He took from his briefcase a small parcel and carefully unwrapped the heavy butcher's paper enclosing it. "This is a kilobar," he said and handed it over to Zetel.

Despite its small rectangular shape, the bar felt heavy in his hand. He relished its gold colour glinting in the light from the windows. It was stamped with the words 'Brothers of the First Church' surmounting the image of a cloud-like platform.

"I'm not a gold expert," he said, "so we'll need an assay done. Assuming the kilobar is authentic, you have slightly over two pounds of gold here. Are you telling me you have another 98 pounds in your safety deposit boxes?"

"Yes," said Plough, "we have another 49 kilobars like this one and we want to invest 25."

Zetel did some rapid calculating. "The current price for gold is $447 per troy ounce. Your 25 kilobars are worth approximately $360,000. That would make a very sizeable investment."

"Too sizeable," said Binder. "I didn't realize we had so much. The Elder of our community said gold was only $35 an ounce. Mind you, he's often wrong, isn't he, Mathew?"

Plough rolled his eyes. "This is not the moment to criticize our Elder, Jeremiah —"

"Mathew — we agreed to call me Mathew."

Plough was clearly exasperated. "Jeremiah Mathew Binder, are you forgetting our purpose in coming here? Our community demands we invest the money properly and safely and insists it has to be with Mr. Landaw. All other considerations fall by the wayside in view of our primary goal. Do I make myself clear?"

"Well, I was against the idea," Binder spluttered. "I see no reason to slavishly follow a plan just because the Elder sets a goal based on wrong information."

The two glowered at each other.

"Gentlemen," Zetel said, "your Elder quoted a price that has long since changed. On the positive side, your savings are now worth far more than you thought. Shall we not discuss the mechanics of getting your investment funds here? Do you plan to sell the gold and transfer the funds to me? Or do you want me to sell it?"

The two Brothers looked at each other blankly.

"We can't sell the gold," Plough said. "Our Elder did not give us permission. Our community is against parting with the gold. You know what the value of 25 kilobars is. Just invest that value. It can be done very quickly."

"And where do I get the cash to make the investment?" Zetel asked, and stood up. "Look, I'm sure your bank will lend you the money against the gold if you can't part with it. Of course, loan interest will lessen your investment results. Please come back when you've made suitable arrangements."

He opened the office door. "Call before you return and I'll make sure I'm available. Good day, Gentlemen."

Binder walked toward the door, shaking his head. "I knew this wouldn't work. I said so but who listens to me?"

"Wait," Plough said. "The kilobar. How much is it worth? Can you invest that amount?"

Zetel consulted one of his reference books and punched away on a desktop calculator. "Assuming the bar is authentic, its value is $14,371.05. Yes, I can invest that. It's above the minimum $10,000 that's acceptable in my shop. I can double it on margin. Do you want me to go ahead?"

"Yes, yes," Plough said and sighed with relief. "It's important to get things underway. We will let you know as soon as possible about the rest. Come, Binder, we had best go in order to catch our return train."

Plough took his briefcase, grasped Binder by the arm and propelled him out of the office.

Zetel returned to his desk and was about to lock the kilobar in his office safe when he remembered he hadn't given the two a receipt for the gold. He walked quickly through the outer office and ran to the elevators. They weren't there.

"Did you see two men waiting for the elevator?" he asked a couple of people in the hallway.

"I saw two strangely dressed men a moment ago take the stairs," one said.

Of course, Zetel thought, they live the simple life. They won't take the elevator even if we're on the 38th floor.

The elevator arrived at that moment. Zetel took it to the ground and waited at the stair exit. After a few minutes, he entered the stairway but could hear no sounds of the two. He ran up a couple of floors but still could hear nothing. Puzzled he returned to his office and asked an assistant to find out when the train stopping at St. Jacobs was leaving. Perhaps he could still get the receipt to them. There was no train to St. Jacobs, the assistant reported, but there was one to Kitchener leaving in about an hour.

With document in hand, he raced to the station. The train had still not boarded. He searched in vain through the waiting line up and stayed until the train left. No Brothers of the First Church showed up.

The next morning, he took the kilobar to a gold dealer and converted it into cash. He placed the total in Cecil's account and then made out the necessary paperwork to hide the transaction.

Returning to his office after lunch, he found the two Brothers waiting for him. Binder was pacing up and down the reception area, hands held firmly behind his back, his head lowered. Plough sat rigidly upright in his chair, staring straight ahead. Neither greeted Zetel.

"Gentlemen," Zetel said, after ushering them into his office and closing the door, "I am happy to see you again. Have you made a decision regarding the rest of the gold?"

"I knew it was all a waste of time," Binder expostulated. "Gabriel gets it wrong all the time."

"Gabriel?" Zetel asked, a cold sweat beginning to seep down his spine.

"He's our Elder," Plough said quickly. "Gabriel Thresher. He's decided it is not a good idea to give up our gold. Therefore, we came for the kilobar. Our Elder insists we return it to the safety of our community."

"But you told me to invest it," Zetel said. "I sold the bar this morning and have already invested it."

"Mr. Landaw," Binder said, "uninvest it, buy us a kilobar so we can return to our quiet community as quickly as possible. Jeremiah, this is the last time I go on any more missions for Gab…our Elder. He can go next time."

"You're Jeremiah, I'm Mathew," Plough said resignedly. "Please, Mr. Landaw, can you not return the kilobar?"

"No, I cannot," Zetel said. "It cost money to sell the kilobar — assay and dealer fees — and then commissions to invest it. It will take more commissions to sell the security and more fees to buy a kilobar. If you could wait, the investment would grow in value and enable me to buy a kilobar without requiring additional expense."

"We cannot wait," Binder said. "Our Elder is adamant and we have to catch our train."

"Like the one you caught last night?" Zetel asked.

Plough ignored the question. "Mr. Landaw, calculate the total costs incurred by you in the matter of our investment and deduct it from the value of the kilobar. We will take the result in cash. I'm sure our Elder will understand."

"I will get my staff to do a proper calculation. I suspect the amount will be around $13,000. I will send you a cheque by the end of next week. You will need to give me an address."

"That's not possible, Mr. Landaw. We want to conclude the transaction now. Just give us $13,000 in cash," Plough insisted. He moved menacingly close to Zetel. "Give us the cash now!"

Zetel retreated behind his desk. "You can threaten me all you want, Mr. Plough. The fact is, I do not have $13,000 in cash just lying around. I doubt any investment house right now has any cash lying around. In case you forgot, there's been a stock market crash which has dried everything up. All our cash has gone into shoring up our positions. Even if I sell your investment, it takes three days for the settlement which means next Monday. Now go away and come back next Monday."

"Nonsense," Binder said. "Gabriel told us you have money from new clients. Just give us $13,000 from that money. Then we can leave."

"Mr. Binder, Mr. Plough, are you suggesting I do something illegal?" Zetel asked. "Perhaps Elder Gabriel should come himself and make his request."

"An excellent suggestion," said Binder. "Gabriel might learn something. Don't you think so, Jeremiah?"

Plough rolled his eyes. "You are Jeremiah, I am Mathew," he whispered.

"Mr. Landaw, we don't want to cause any trouble. We just want our money back," Plough said. "Even $10,000 will do right now, the rest at some later time."

"It's entrapment, isn't it?" Zetel said. "To get rid of you, I finally give in and use new money. Then you threaten to inform the authorities unless I give extra to your community. Blackmail is the game, isn't it? Well, if it's hardball you want, then hardball it is. Why should I give you any money at all?"

"Mr. Landaw, you invested money we gave you. We are simply redeeming our investment. You do not have the cash to redeem because you have placed it elsewhere. We could inform the authorities now," Plough said, his voice harsh.

"What investment are you talking about, Mr. Plough?"

"You know very well what investment we're talking about," said Binder. "Don't try any tricks with us. We gave you a gold kilobar which you sold and invested.?"

"What's your point, Mr. Landaw," Plough said.

"I received nothing from you. We discussed your store of gold bullion but you were supposed to talk to your Elder about how much to invest. So far, all I've heard from you is your demand for redemption of an investment of a kilobar that you showed me but never gave me."

"We certainly did give it to you," Binder insisted and angrily thumped Zetel's desk with a fist.

"You have proof?" Zetel asked. "Let me see the receipt. Surely you wouldn't leave a kilobar with me without a receipt. We always give receipts when receiving an investor's assets."

Binder looked aghast at Plough. "Did we get a receipt?"

Plough sighed, "No, we did not. Landaw will simply deny we left the kilobar with him. We cannot pursue this."

"But he did sell a kilobar," Binder objected. "The dealer will confirm this."

"That kilobar was my own property," Zetel said. "I had to sell it in order to have some liquidity in a difficult market."

"But the bar was inscribed with our community signature," Binder persisted.

Zetel laughed. "Your community? My assistant checked the entire St. Jacobs area, spoke to a number of religious organizations, and discovered the Brothers of the First Church doesn't exist. I intend to call the police now and have them remove you from the premises. You can explain to them why you are here under false pretences."

"I knew this wasn't going to work," Binder said. "I told Gabriel so."

"You did not. You thoroughly agreed with him. I was the one with doubts," said Plough. "Mr. Landaw, you know whom we really are?"

"I can make an educated guess," Zetel said, his hand still on the telephone.

"As you suspected, the goal of our mission was to entrap you — but not for money," Plough said in a solemn voice. "Once entrapped, we would offer you a satisfactory way out from your fraudulent practices, a way to make things right for all your investors and family, to show true regret and remorse, and therefore to escape from the Devil and to restore your soul to the heavenly Arc. It is still possible."

"I'm not ready to die," Zetel said. "I believe I can fix the problem. I need more time and a long bull market."

"Quite rightly so," said Louis C. Fuhr as he pushed open the office door. "I heard some former colleagues of mine were visiting you. As Chairman of the Board, I must insist they depart."

"No need to insist," Plough said. "We have no desire to prolong the supreme displeasure of your presence, Satan. As for you Mr. Landaw, should you reconsider, pray for Michael and I shall appear. Come, Raphael, let us go."

The two wafted through the ceiling.

CHAPTER 2 —
Zetel in transition

On Sunday, two weeks after Black Monday, Zetel, Sarah and Ettie drove to Montreal for the funeral the next day of Bessie Landaw. Long mired in the dense fog of Alzheimer's, Bessie Landaw had died. Although in essence she had left life many years before, the finality of death made for a sad and mournful funeral. After the cemetery, the family came together in Chaim's Westmount home for the Shiva, the mourning period of seven days.

Over the years, Zetel had visited Chaim and Beatrice and Rivka and her husband intermittently when business took him to Montreal or to see his parents and in-laws when they still lived there.

Chaim had grown quite stocky as he aged. He had done extremely well with his accounting business and was in the process of selling it so he could retire early. "Then Beatrice and I can spend a year travelling the world. The kids are old enough to look after themselves," he told Zetel.

Rivka had aged gracefully and still retained the attractiveness that had marked her younger years. Her marriage of thirty years had slowly deteriorated over financial issues and the spendthrift ways of her husband. The divorce had been largely amicable. She received no alimony because as a voice therapist at Montreal General Hospital she earned a regular income, while her husband depended on commissions from infrequent and unpredictable sales. The children were grown up and helped out as best they could.

On the day after the funeral, during a gap in the stream of visitors, Zetel sat beside Rivka. He still had a strong affection for her. She had been his boyhood confidante, somehow aware of the magical forces that haunted him, yet never ridiculing him as her brother had. He regretted that their special relationship had disappeared as she grew older and developed her own friendships and family, and he pursued his studies and business.

"As a child, you had many strange ideas," Rivka said. "You even had me convinced that I saw what you saw. You had a thing about Diana, goddess of the Hunt and — and, oh yes — Mars, god of War. Remember, I told you that man you were afraid of just suddenly disappeared. I guess my imagination was as wild as yours. How do you feel now? Still looking for Diana?"

Zetel was silent for a long moment. Perhaps his affection for Rivka and the nostalgia he felt about their childhood relationship lessened his usual guarded reticence about his origins.

"No, I've given up on Diana. I did see her again but she tried to kill me."

Rivka chuckled. "Well, it's nice to see you've developed a sense of humour. Mind you, those early visions I had still seem so real that I sometimes wonder whether in fact they were just visions. Although I was only five years old, I vaguely remember your bris (*circumcision*) and those strange men who came through walls. Maybe I was asleep and dreaming."

"Yes, I member it too," Zetel said very quietly. "You were not dreaming and these were not merely visions. This is not something we want to talk about where others may hear us."

She looked at him, her eyes widened. "You really believe in a magic world, don't you? You really believe all those strange things happened. Tell me something nice will happen to my mother since you're in touch with the spirit world."

Again, Zetel was silent. Finally: "I will tell you provided the information stays with us. You cannot divulge it to anyone. Promise?"

She nodded.

"A large band of souls — a huge Arc — encircles the world, invisible to us. Your mother's soul will rejoin this band and stay there until she is reassigned."

Rivka stood up excitedly. "But that's reincarnation. You believe in reincarnation? Why didn't you say so? I've read quite a bit about Buddhism and I lean towards reincarnation. It all depends on your morality and spirituality during your lifetime. My mother was very moral, very good, very generous with charity and the poor. I believe she'll be reborn as a great woman. That's much more satisfying to think about than your idea of a band of souls." She sat down. "What do you want to be reborn as?"

"It's not up to me," Zetel said. "When I die, I will join the Devil. I will have much more fun with him than lying forever on the Arc of Souls."

"My, you have a devilish outlook," Rivka said laughing. "Did the Devil help you survive Black Monday?"

"No, that one I did all by myself," Zetel said. "It was a close call — in many ways." He wasn't sure which was worse — the threat of bankruptcy and disclosure or the attempt on him by the two archangels.

He told her about the two frauds dressed as Mennonites who showed up at his office. "They were so clumsy and ill-prepared, I thought I was on Candid Camera. One couldn't even remember what his name was supposed to be. They tried to convince me they had 50 kilos of gold to invest. Fortunately I was able to get rid of them."

"It sounds like the financial business is far more colourful than I thought," Rivka said. "How did you get rid of them? Did you call the police?"

Zetel chuckled. "No, I didn't have to. They saw they were going nowhere with their scam, so they just drifted away."

Rivka looked at him suspiciously. "Drifted away? Through the walls? Like the men at your bris."

"Actually, through the ceiling," Zetel said, smiling. "Come to think about it, they may have been the same men. That's the problem with these immortals, you can never get rid of them."

Rivka laughed. "I presume you're just joking but you seem so serious. Besides, you can't possibly remember what happened at your bris. You were only eight days old."

"I was very precocious," Zetel said.

Their conversation was interrupted when Sarah, who was helping Ettie in the kitchen, brought Rivka coffee and cookies. She saw the distant look on her husband's face.

"Everything ok, Zetel?"

"We've been discussing our childhood, Sarah," Rivka said. "Zetel hasn't forgotten the wild and weird things he imagined as a child. In fact, he still believes they're true. He thinks we're all souls from some Arc that surrounds the Earth and my mother will go there until she's reborn. That's not a bad idea since I also believe in reincarnation. Some of his early hang-ups he's gotten over — Diana the Huntress tried to kill him so she's off his best friends' list. Two men dressed as Mennonites tried to scam him but he thwarted their plot and they escaped through the ceiling. Sarah, I think Zetel should have been a writer — and, oh yes — he's sold his soul to the Devil."

You're saying far too much, a thought came to him unbidden.

Somewhat alarmed, Sarah stroked Zetel's hair. "He's just worn out from Black Monday, Rivka. It was a very trying time. He didn't get much sleep for several days and he spent endless hours reassuring clients. Maybe we need a holiday, Zetel."

Not Venice, the thought was peremptory. *She still lives there.*

There was a knock at the door and Ettie went to open it.

"Herr Fuhr," they heard her say.

Speak of the Devil, Zetel thought.

Tut, tut, my boy, the thought came back. *As a good old friend, I'm here to offer my condolences.*

Fuhr shook Chaim's hand and kissed Beatrice's, offered his sympathies, then kissed Rivka's hand and repeated his message of condolence. He greeted Zetel and kissed Sarah on both cheeks.

Fuhr looked older. His hair had greyed considerably and wrinkle lines were very visible on his forehead, around his eyes and mouth. He was dressed in normal business attire, dark suit, blue shirt, striped tie.

Who's your makeup artist? Zetel thought.

Simply a matter of will, Fuhr shot back. *One must look the part, my boy, otherwise people may think I have some special secret.*

Now, how would anyone ever get that idea?

"Do you still do magic tricks, Mr. Fuhr?" Rivka asked.

"Of course, geehrte Frau, but this is not an occasion for levity," Fuhr said.

"I agree," Zetel said quickly, apprehensively.

"Just one trick, Mr. Fuhr, to cheer us up," Chaim said as he joined them.

"My dear friends, I will perform one trick," Fuhr agreed. "However, given that you are in mourning for a very worthy woman, I cannot promise to cheer you up." He turned to Ettie. "Frau Landaw, would you please bring me a serving tray and a tea towel."

Ettie held the tray. Fuhr leaned over the tray, lifted the tea towel and waved it vigorously in the air as high as he could reach, then brought it sharply down to cover the tray as he straightened up.

"Please lift the tea towel," he said to Rivka.

They all gasped as Rivka removed the towel to reveal two small framed pictures. Fuhr handed one to Rivka and the other to Chaim.

"It's a picture of mommy and daddy," Rivka exclaimed, eyes filling with tears. "Taken some time ago. I've never seen this picture,

Mr. Fuhr. And it's not a photograph. It's a painting. Who painted it? How did you get it?"

Fuhr bowed and chuckled. "A magician never reveals his tricks. I thought you would like to remember them this way." Rivka hugged him, Chaim grasped his hand tightly, both thanked him profusely.

"Will you stay for dinner, Herr Fuhr?" Ettie asked. "Family and friends have overloaded us with food. Help us eat it."

"It will be my pleasure," Fuhr replied. "But first, I need to speak with Zetel about some important business events. May we withdraw to a private room?"

Chaim ushered them to his home office. "No one will bother you here."

"I met with your father-in-law yesterday," Fuhr began. "He insisted we act as board members without you present. At first I objected to meeting without you. However, I could tell there was something bothering him, so I finally agreed. He announced he would be redeeming his entire portfolio under your care and looking to place it elsewhere. He said there were too many people casting doubt on your wealth management and he, too, felt there was something wrong. 'For my peace of mind, I've got to get out,' he insisted. I know that his portfolio is real and that you could return it without endangering your business. But if your earliest investor and supporter and father-in-law to boot deserted you, it might cause a stampede of redemptions on the part of your other investors and ruin you. I explained this to him but he was adamant. 'Besides,' he said, 'Zetel still has the brokerage side of the business and it's doing very well.'"

Fuhr paused, noting the ashen colour that slowly swept over Zetel's face.

"You're absolutely right," Zetel said. "If he goes, the others will too. No new money will come in. Not only will I be bankrupt but exposed. He doesn't realize it but he's sending his son-in-law to jail. What am I going to do?"

"Right now, you should be safe. I persuaded him to put off his decision until much later," Fuhr said.

"How did you manage that? Did you use your magic?"

"I didn't have to," Fuhr said, allowing himself a smile of smug satisfaction. "I explained to Mr. Lansmann that in order to expand your business, you are embarking on a campaign of interviews for print and TV. I told him you are also a candidate for president of the Society of Wealth Managers. If he pulled out now, he would scuttle your campaign and hurt your candidacy. Of course, he was surprised by my news and said he wished you had talked about it. After more discussion, he agreed to hold off redeeming."

"Wonderful," said Zetel. "I take it you're recommending I embark on such a campaign."

"Indeed, I knew you'd see the wisdom of the idea. I've lined you up for your first interview on Friday with Ian McRae."

"McRae? He's the top business columnist at the Globe? How did you arrange that?"

Fuhr's smile of smug satisfaction broadened: "Yours is not the only soul I own."

Ian McRae was in his early sixties, tall, slim, grey hair neatly combed, a pleasant face belying the steely analysis and skepticism of his journalism. He had thirty years experience in the industry. He had started his career in local community newspapers but soon graduated to the Star, the Post, and now the Globe. They met in Zetel's office.

"I've called your chairman Fuhr several times over the past year, including just after Black Monday, asking to interview you," McRae began after setting up his recording device at the conference table, "but he always refused. What changed?"

Zetel had carefully considered with Fuhr the questions McRae might ask and had rehearsed answers.

"The success of my wealth management system has caused a lot of jealous sniping in the investor community. I've even been called a fraud. For a long time, Fuhr and I thought interviews would just add to the controversy and turn potential investors off. Now we realize by not allowing interviews, we are adding to the suspicion. You have a reputation as a tough, independent-minded experienced journalist. After an interview with you, no one can say I'm hiding."

McRae shrugged. "Mr. Landaw, I don't do public relations. You might not like what I say about you in my column. I might confirm what your worst detractors believe."

"I doubt it. If you look at who my detractors are, they're all at the lower end of portfolio returns. The guys who perform at my level have never criticized me," Zetel said.

"Fine, so let's get at it. According to your investors, they receive returns that are consistently well above the New York and Toronto stock exchange indices. Other portfolio managers — including some of those who perform at your level — say they can't replicate your returns. They accuse you of doing something underhanded. So, how and why does your system seem to work so well?"

"My system works for a number of reasons. First of all, I'm a value investor. I go through an exhaustive series of tests and checks using all the usual value investing ratios and concepts — you know, things like Price/Earnings, Free Cash Flow, Dividends, Earnings Growth, etc. I also spend a lot of time checking out the industry, competitive situation, ease of entry. I visit and talk to management of the companies I'm interested in. I never jump at so called opportunities or rumours. When I buy, I hold. I don't trade a lot."

"But, Mr. Landaw, everybody says they do what you just described. Most of the portfolio managers claim they are value investors and they all insist they are following the same concepts. So what's your specific secret?" McRae demanded.

"That I can't tell you," Zetel said. "I've developed a proprietary system that I reveal to no one. Not even anyone in the brokerage side of my business knows my system. All the securities I buy and sell are managed within my Landaw Secure Opportunity Fund. Over the years, my Fund has grown, returning earnings that are very attractive. We've had some reverses — Black Monday, for example. So my system is not foolproof, just better than most."

McRae was annoyed. "If we can't discuss your secret system, what's the point of this interview. It's no wonder you have critics."

"I'm sorry," Zetel said. "But if I disclose my proprietary system, I lose my competitive edge. I absolutely will not and cannot reveal the system I've developed through hard work and which has benefitted my clients."

"And you too, I suppose," said McRae. "Mind you, I've checked around. You don't seem to live high on the hog. Do you have a yacht, a place in Florida, numerous high-priced cars, first class cruises, etc., etc.?"

Zetel shook his head. "It's not our style. We have a comfortable home in Forest Hill, a couple of cars — one's a minivan, the other a hybrid, a cleaning company comes in once a week. My wife is a teacher, so holidays in warm places during the winter are limited to school breaks. During the summer we sometimes travel overseas. We like concerts, museums, movies. Besides, putting two children through university doesn't leave much cash for non-essentials."

McRae steered the interview into more personal subjects. Zetel related the circumstances of his birth, the arrival in Halifax, and his time in Montreal. He talked about his parents, his family, extolled his wife and children. By the time, the interview ended, McRae seemed suitably charmed.

His column the next day was a mixture of acerbic criticism of Zetel's unwillingness to reveal his system and thus clarify his investment success and a rather positive view of his character and life history. There were quotes from Zetel's clients complimenting his investing prowess and their resulting returns. "Even Black Monday didn't hurt us as badly as others — we just didn't get our usual returns," said one investor. Cyril was quoted, "I got Zetel going with his business and he's never let me or the other investors down. I don't know how he does it, but he does it." The quotes from other portfolio managers were more critical, claiming Zetel couldn't possibly have such high returns on an ongoing basis without doing creative bookkeeping. The final quote put the criticism to bed. A finance professor at the U of T pointed out, "The long term average annual increase in stock market value is 9%. Careful portfolio management should do better than this. So Zetel Landaw is both astute and careful. Good stock selection, riding the long term bull market, and insightful timing and you have his system."

"Why do I have to learn how your system works from a column in the Globe," an exasperated Cyril demanded. "I've been asking you for years."

The family was gathered at the weekly Friday night dinner.

Unperturbed, Zetel replied: "Thanks for your nice quote. As for my system, that professor just scratched the surface. I will never reveal what's below the surface. I haven't told anyone, not even Sarah."

"Well, I guess I will have to live with that," Cyril grumbled. "What's next on your PR campaign?"

"Zetel has TV interviews coming up," Sarah said. "Including a couple in New York."

"After you become so famous, will you still talk to me?" Ettie asked.

"And to me too?" Anna said.

Zetel put up a hand in protest but Sarah jumped in: "Of course, he will. We'll all just have to make appointments."

The round of television interviews went extremely well. Each interviewer tried to tweak out elements of Zetel's system but gave up after his calm and thoughtful reasoning about his competitive edge. They then focussed on his personal life. They marvelled over his family's narrow escape from Germany, his birth in mid-Atlantic, his early years in Montreal, and his quick climb to business success. He talked about Black Monday and how even his system couldn't offset the world wide crash of stock markets.

"I lost a lot of sleep those few nights but all I could do was hang tight, persuade my clients not to panic, and not follow the herd over the cliff. What was gratifying to me was during the storm, my client base actually grew, a real vote of confidence."

"But you must have lost scads of money," one interviewer insisted.

"A lot less than you think," Zetel said. "I anticipated a correction was coming and held back investing in the few months before the crash. I also did some short selling. Of course, a crash is much more than a correction so my portfolio did suffer but it recovered rather quickly."

He looked attractive on television, reasonable, trustworthy, modest — how could anyone think him dishonest, a fraud.

"My PR campaign seems to be working," he told Sarah one evening at dinner. "I signed up five more clients this week alone. There are also more requests for interviews. Plus I meet with the board of trustees of the Society of Wealth Managers next Tuesday to discuss my candidacy for president. Mind you, they made it clear there are other candidates."

"How could they choose anyone else?" Sarah said. "But seriously, Zetel, you're likely to be appointed and your business is growing exponentially. Can you handle all this extra burden? At the Shiva for Bessie, you looked very tired and according to Rivka said some strange things. I know you were totally strung out after Black Monday and that was before all this additional responsibility that's coming your way. Should you hire a couple more people?"

"Can't, Sarah," Zetel said after some thought and while he sipped his tea. "My secret would be out in no time at all. Besides, there's not much extra work from the business. My formula applies to all and it's just one big fund. Once I decide on an action, I put the orders through and Sally simply adjusts the holdings of each investor. I think being president of the Society will be the real extra workload. It's not just a ceremonial position."

"The Christmas school break is coming up. That will give us two weeks for a nice vacation in which you will promise not to do any work but spend all your time making sure I'm happy," Sarah suggested in a tone of voice that meant "no" was not an answer.

Zetel laughed. "I heartily agree. What do you have in mind?"

Sarah thought for a moment. "No idea. I will surprise you. Probably one of those resorts where all we do is eat, drink, and rekindle our love."

CHAPTER 3 —
Zetel on vacation

"OK," said Zetel, bouncing against his arm rest and nearly falling into the corridor separating the two rows of seats, as the safari vehicle drove down a small embankment and sloshed through a shallow creek. "Thanks to the Arusha Lodge last night, we did eat and drink, but where's the water and the swimming?"

"I never said anything about water and swimming," Sarah reminded him. "As for water, we're going through some right now. I'm sure the driver will stop if you feel like swimming."

"What about rekindling our love? When do we do that?" he persisted.

"You didn't seem to need any rekindling last night," she said.

The vacation she had selected was a safari tour to the Serengeti. Arusha in the north of Tanzania was the starting point for the tour. The safari vehicle, rectangular shaped with a pop up roof for ease of viewing and photography, was furnished with four single seats on each side of a narrow corridor, and held eight passengers..

They'd arrived in Arusha the previous afternoon after stopovers in London, Nairobi, and Kilimanjaro, and from there a long bus ride. Despite their travel fatigue, they were too excited to sleep, explored the city briefly, and then enjoyed a sumptuous dinner with dishes of West Kili lamb, Wellington game bird, and a fine bottle of South African wine.

They slept in the next morning and began the tour shortly after lunch. Both were outfitted with safari clothing, safari hats, walking boots, cameras and binoculars. They joined the other tourists at the assembly point.

"You two look like you've done this before," one of their fellow passengers said. "This is my first. I'm just wearing my usual fishing clothes."

He was a tall, fleshy man in ill fitting jeans, a white t-shirt, and a canvas jacket. A baseball cap sat on a mass of white curly hair that descended down his cheeks into a full beard. His open canvas jacket revealed a sheathed long knife strapped around his waist. Rubber Wellington boots squished as he walked.

"My name's Mike," he said and grasped Zetel's hand. "This is my wife Lily."

Lily was much younger. She was graced with a voluptuous figure and a rather attractive face. She was dressed in a tan shirt tucked into a beige canvas skirt. Its hem fell just below her knees and revealed a short length of shapely legs that ended in moccasin-like boots.

"Zetel?" Mike said after the introductions. "Strange name. Never heard it before. Where you two from? We're from the US."

'We're from Canada," Sarah said. "Toronto. And this is also our first safari. This is what the outfitter at home told us we had to wear."

"There you are, Mike," Lily said. "Some men know how to look after their women." She gave Zetel an appreciative look.

They drove for several hours to reach Lake Manyara National Park. The safari truck meandered slowly through the park. Zetel photographed hippos, bands of monkeys, and a tree climbing lion that sought refuge as the truck came into sight.

They had dinner and stayed overnight at one of the tented campsites.

"I don't like the way she looks at you," Sarah said. "She's a bit too friendly. Every time you stood up to take a picture, she was right beside you, pretending to point out things you should photograph."

They were lying in twin cots in their so-called luxury tent.

"How do you know she was pretending?" Zetel asked.

"You'd have to be blind not to notice what she pointed out. Besides, she kept leaning into you. I think Mike was upset because they had a long talk after we left the truck and they stayed behind. I'm sure that's why they didn't join us for dinner."

"Well, don't let her bother you," Zetel said. "I want this to be a vacation just for us. No one else is welcome."

The tour left early the next morning through a cool, gently falling rain. After a few hours along fairly decent roads, sometimes paved, mostly hard packed, they entered the Serengeti. Broad endless plains dotted with spindly flat topped umbrella acacia trees greeted them. They had to stop briefly while a herd of elephants crossed the road. "They're hurrying to a water hole," the driver explained.

In the far distance, they could see a large herd of buffalo grazing on high grass. Gazing through her binoculars, Sarah exclaimed, "Look, Zetel, there are lions creeping up on the buffalo."

Zetel quickly jumped up and stood beside her. He could see several lions, quite a distance yet from the herd, making their way stealthily through the grass.

"May I borrow your glasses?" Lily said as she joined them, grasping Zetel by the shoulder to steady herself.

"Here, take mine," Sarah said and shoved her binoculars past Zetel to Lily. "These are specially designed for women."

"Oh dear," said Lily. "Should we not alert the herd? I see lots of baby buffalo."

"We're not allowed to intervene," said the driver. "Besides, the lions won't attack yet. They're too young. They'll wait for the big guys. You know, the grown up ones, the big mothers. These buffalo are too strong and big for the kiddies by themselves."

They drove on, stopping frequently to view herds of gazelles, zebras, wildebeest, several cheetahs, more buffalo and a pride of lions lounging in the shelter of a clump of acacia trees. The rain had stopped, the clouds had cleared by the time they arrived at a lodge for lunch.

"How beautiful everything is," Sarah said, grasping Zetel by an arm and dragging him away from the truck. "The rain has caused the Serengeti to bloom — look, the plains are covered with flowers and even the grass is greener."

They stood for a few minutes, arm in arm, admiring the view.

"Zetel, sweetheart, that woman is after you. She's always there when we stand up to take pictures. I see Mike trying to restrain her, but that only slows her down. I think you've got to make it clear to her that you're not interested. Or are you?"

He pulled her close and kissed her. "So much for my interest in Lily. Now stop worrying and just enjoy. The country is fascinating, the weather warm, the animals are everywhere, the accommodations are comfortable, and the food excellent. Apart from the backbreaking experience on the safari truck, even it is just right. I don't even think of work and I feel greatly refreshed and revitalized. You've picked the ideal vacation. Don't let concerns about Lily get in the way. And just look at the sky — totally blue, not a cloud."

"There is a cloud," Sarah said. "There, close to the horizon, fluffy white but quite large."

He followed her pointing finger. The cloud appeared to be touching the ground, obscuring a range of hills. "As long as it stays there, it won't bother us," Zetel said.

"As long as Lily, the cloud in my life at the moment, stays far away, it won't bother me either."

Archangel Gabriel, in a flowing white gown, his head lit by the reflected light of his golden halo, sat on a wicker chair, facing a group of angels. The angels, also on wicker chairs, were clustered around a large table.

"Angelic Colleagues, Rafael, Metatron, Samael, Sandalphon, and Chamuel, I greet you as always with respect and love and express my sincere and profound gratitude that you were able to separate yourselves from your many onerous responsibilities to attend this hastily called Council. Full well, I know from our millennia of collaboration on behalf of The-One-True-God to pursue His vision..."

"Get on with it," Samael snarled, "so I can get back to collecting souls from the corpses that are piling up."

"We know this is an important meeting," Metatron said in his usual mild, thoughtful voice. "Therefore, Archangel Gabriel, please get to the point quickly."

"Can we not move this cloud higher," Raphael asked." Right now, we're stationed on a swamp."

"Yes," Samael snapped, "the stench is terrible."

"How would you know?" Sandalphon quipped.

Samael turned on the diminutive angel, grasped him by the nape of his furred gown, and was about to hurl him beyond the cloud. Chamuel, a burly figure, intervened.

"Stop, Samael. I, Chamuel, punish those who transgress against The-One-True-God," he proclaimed. "I do not quarrel with my own kind nor tolerate it. Samael, restore Sandalphon to his rightful place among us. Gabriel, I urge you to relate the reason for our attendance."

"Well put, Chamuel. I shall record your statement in the Record for this meeting," said Metatron, as he dipped his quill into the ink and turned to the parchment scroll before him. "Gabriel, take heed. We are not in the mood for circumlocution."

"Great Metatron and angels, I do not mean to be long-winded," Gabriel said. "I had merely wished to extol your virtues for the difficult task that lies ahead of us. Why have I called you if not because of your superior strength and divine skills. Surely...

"Gabriel! Now!" Metatron screamed.

Gabriel, startled by Metatron's departure from his usual calm and even voice, gulped, wiped an arm across his forehead (forgetting that angels don't perspire) and blurted out: "It concerns the soul of Zetel Landaw."

"Don't tell me that old ember has been relit," Raphael groaned. "He must be getting on in age. Can't we just let him expire in his own time?"

"Why do we have to tamper with this man's life," whimpered Sandalphon. "We always fail anyway."

"Besides," Samael added, "the Devil owns his soul and always finds a way to stop us."

"But that's just it," Gabriel said. "The Devil is nowhere near but Zetel is. He is on a Safari, something humans do to view the beautiful lands and animals that The-One-True-God has created. We have a chance to finally collect his soul and return it to the sanctity of the Arc. Otherwise, he will be possessed by The Devil."

"It would serve him right," Samael said. "Instead of the ethereal tranquillity of the Arc, where he could bask in sublime contemplation of the heavens and observe the constant beauty of the sun and the stars, he will join Satan in an eternity of penal fire and the total enmity of the Almighty. I say we do nothing."

"I cannot abide doing nothing," Chamuel declared. "The-One-True-God has judged that the soul of Zetel be returned to the Arc. The Creator's wish is my command to zealously carry out His Will. When I was ordered to expel Adam from the Garden of Paradise, I admit I had some misgivings. I felt the punishment was not proportional to the sin but who was I to question the Master's wish. Fellow angels, we must act."

"What do you propose?" Raphael asked.

"I? I propose nothing," Chamuel said. "I will do whatever the plan is."

They all turned to Gabriel.

"I have a plan but it will need your concurrence. The plan is as follows," Gabriel said. "According to the tour booklet which I have here"— he held up a brightly coloured pamphlet — "and which I have studied, the Safari will soon approach a herd of buffalo. Samael will cause the herd to panic into a stampede and overrun the Safari. In the process Zetel will be killed, his soul released and captured by us for return to the Arc. Are there any questions?"

"I object," Sandalphon said, showing his indignation by leaping into the air above them. "Your plan will kill all the innocent people travelling with him, including his wife. I will appeal to the One to have this plan quashed."

"You snivelling lump of saccharine rot, I have said many times I cannot help it if collateral damage occurs in an operation," Samael said contemptuously.

"Wait, I side with Sandalphon," said Raphael. "There is no need to have a massacre just to get one soul. Surely, in this land of many animals, there must be dangerous ones that can be incited to attack only Zetel."

The angels fell silent, each trying to envision how to manage one limited attack and which animal to use.

"I have an idea," Gabriel said, excitedly, lifting from his chair. "A lion — it has to be a lion. A lion is ferociously deadly and kills quickly. Here's how the plan will work. Zetel steps away from the others and is attacked by a lion. Death is quick, no one else is harmed, we snatch his soul and race to the Arc, all before Satan is even aware." He settled back on his chair, a triumphant look on his face.

After some reflection, all the angels agreed it was a good plan.

"However, Gabriel," Metatron said in his grave, calm voice, "your plan is excellent but it requires some development of the details. For example, how do we persuade Zetel to leave some distance between himself and the others so that the lion attacks only him? How do we ensure that the lion is close enough to attack and desires to attack? What if the Safari leader sees the danger in time and quickly dispatches the lion?"

"Yes, Gabriel, your plan is excellent strategy but lacks the requisite tactical detail," Raphael said. "For this reason, it is likely to fail."

"Before we all eagerly criticize," Samael said, "let us at least consider how best to resolve the problems that Metatron raises. The answer to Metatron's last question is simple. Arrange for two lions. The first lion attacks, the second lion may also join in but if it sees the Safari leader about to intervene, it charges the leader and kills him."

"No!" cried Sandalphon as loud as his squeaky voice allowed. "We agreed to one death only."

"Yes," Chamuel said. "One death is sufficient. If the first lion attacks and fails, the second lion finishes the task."

"Wonderful. Two lions is the right solution. What about the other questions Metatron raises?" Raphael asked still unconvinced Gabriel's plan was a good one.

After a long moment of intense thought, Gabriel again leapt from his chair.

"For the lions to do our bidding, two angels must inhabit their bodies." he exclaimed.

The angels looked uneasily at each other. "Which angels are you thinking of, Gabriel?" they asked almost in unison.

"Will you be one of the angels, Gabriel?" Rafael asked.

"No, Rafael, of course not," Gabriel was quick to reply. "I am the general in charge of the operation. I must be in a position to gauge its success and take alternative actions as the situation warrants. Generals always stay back from the action."

"David always led his troops into battle," Chamuel objected. "Nevertheless, which of us do you have in mind?"

"Why, it is obvious," Gabriel said. "Samael is the Angel of Death. Therefore, he must inhabit the body of the first lion. And who is the strongest and most zealous in his pursuit of those who transgress against The-One-True-God? Why, of course, it is Chamuel, and he must inhabit the body of the second lion."

Before the two angels could object, Metatron announced authoritatively, "It shall be so and I shall so write it in the Divine Record of this Council. I shall add that the two angels are to be commended for their ready acceptance of a difficult challenge."

Samael merely glowered but Chamuel glowed with pride.

Raphael, relieved he was not selected, but still doubtful about the plan, asked: "How do we entice Zetel away from the others so only he dies?"

"I have an idea," Gabriel said. "I was not sure we could develop a plan in our Council, so I planted a spy in the Safari to ensure we had a backup. I will inform this spy about our plan and I am sure he can separate Zetel from the others. Let us begin our operation. There is a pride of lions not far from here. There we will find two adult lions."

The cloud moved imperceptibly away from the swamp and the range of hills. It drifted slowly, slightly above the ground, and soon approached an acacia tree standing alone in the sundrenched plain. The cloud converged on the tree. Curled up and snoozing in the tall grass were several females, a dozen cubs, and barely visible under the tree, a male adorned with a thick luxurious mane. One of the females stretched, yawned, stood up and stretched again, revealing a powerful body, larger than the others.

"Quick, Samael, that's the one. Go!" Gabriel ordered.

Samael leaped and disappeared into the body of the lion.

"Fah!" Samael's voice rang out loud and clear. "Disgusting! Nothing but bones, muscles blood. Anger, hunger. This lion is terribly hungry, ready for the hunt, eager for the hunt. It smells the herds and drools at the thought of prey."

"You are right, Samael," Gabriel said. "It is awakening the others and you will soon set off."

"Wait," Samael shouted. "This lion is a female. You put me in a female body. I want a change of body."

"It's too late. They are all up and moving. Quick, Chamuel, occupy the one with the mane," ordered Gabriel.

Chamuel leaped and disappeared. "Not pleasant here either," he said almost instantly. "This one is also hungry and very irritable but something else seems to be bothering him."

The pride was now on the move. The young lions ran ahead, the several females trod the high grass methodically and carefully, saving their energy for the hunt. The head of the pride, a superb, full maned model of the ultimate African male lion, walked majestically a few paces behind. A small cub tried to keep up but the male growled and cuffed it aside.

"Sandalphon, occupy the cub and follow the pride as best you can. Let us know if things do not go as planned," Gabriel said.

By the time Zetel and Sarah joined the group for lunch, most of the tables were occupied. Lily waved from one table where there were two seats available. Sarah looked around but there were no other seats.

"I guess we can't be rude," Sarah said. "But it's not a coincidence that those are the only seats available."

"Quick, you too," Lily called out, "I saved these seats."

The two empty chairs were between Mike and Lily. "Why don't you sit beside me, Sarah," Mike suggested. "Otherwise you two women will only talk about hair care and fashions. In my earlier days, I was a teacher, too."

With much misgiving, Sarah watched Zetel take his seat beside Lily.

"Don't worry about Lily," Mike said quietly. "She loves to flirt. If she becomes bothersome, just tell me and I'll talk to her."

Sarah wasn't sure Lily was just flirting but she thanked Mike anyway for his reassurance.

"You know, Mike, with your hair and beard, you would make a good Santa Claus. Tonight's Christmas Eve. You could make your debut tonight," she teased him.

"Santa Claus?" he asked. "I'm not familiar with that name. Is this something Canadian?"

Sarah laughed, "You're putting me on, Mike. I guess I can't blame you. You must be teased quite often about Santa Claus. I apologize."

"No need to apologize," Mike said, sounding somewhat relieved. "Yes, I'm asked all the time. Let's discuss your teaching."

Always a delightful subject for Sarah, she excitedly told Mike all about her students and the challenges she and they confronted. She quite lost track of the time, talked while she ate her lunch, and prattled on. She stopped when a buzzing noise came from his knapsack. Mike pulled out a bulky telephone device and put it to his ear.

"Excuse me," he said. "I better take the call outside. Lily, there's a call."

Lily was giving Zetel her full attention as he described his financial world. She merely nodded and turned again to Zetel.

"Mike has one of those new cellular phones," Zetel observed. "I left mine at home. I was told they don't work overseas."

"Never mind the phone," Lily said. "Tell me more about your world. Should Mike and I invest in your business? That would allow for more contact. We could become close friends."

A sudden misgiving clouded the pleasure Zetel had enjoyed talking to Lily. He was flattered by Lily's interest in him but there was something too calculating in her attention. Besides, the fact that Mike could receive cell phone calls on a device that should not work an ocean and a continent away from the US was also troubling. He was still puzzled by Mike's remark to Sarah about not knowing who Santa Claus was. Despite Mike's off putting explanation, he seemed genuinely ignorant of Santa Claus. These are not Americans, he thought. Then what are they, and what are they up to?

"Oh, I never have contact with my investors," he said quickly. "I handle their money, the results are almost always good, and I communicate through a monthly newsletter. Face-to-face contact would become an impossible burden and take me away from market analysis and stock picking. Besides, I have no American clients nor, because of different tax laws and regulations, do I want any."

He watched the rapturous look on her face slowly dissipate into a grim-mouthed mask.

"I better see what Mike's call is all about," she said and left the table.

"What a put down," said Sarah. "You could have been less cold. But thank you."

The lion pride hid in the grass downwind from the herd of buffalo.

"Chamuel, you still there?" Samael asked.

"Yes, Samael, but there's something wrong, something's really troubling this lion. At times, it seems like he's not even interested in being fed. I don't know whether I can control him when the moment arrives."

"Concentration, Chamuel, concentration is what does it. Assert your will. These are but beasts."

"I am asserting my will, Samael. These creatures are all instinct with little reflection. The forces they feel drive them. These are powerful forces, not easily manipulated. I shall do my best. Here comes the Safari."

Zetel and the others had seen the lions hiding in the grass. The driver stopped the truck just short of cutting off the lions' view of the herd. The lions moved forward, paused in front of the truck, then edged closer to the herd which was grazing contentedly and oblivious to the danger close by.

When a sufficient space lay between the advancing lions and the truck, the driver announced it was safe to leave the vehicle to take pictures. If he honked the horn, they were to return immediately. Except for Lily and Sarah, the remaining six left the truck.

"I know it's nature and the lions have to eat, but I don't want to see it," she told Zetel. Lily said nothing but sat in sullen silence.

The tourists fanned out in front of the truck and began photographing. Zetel took a couple of pictures but waited for the real action.

Mike set up his video on a tripod next to Zetel.

"Mike, can we talk?" Zetel said quietly.

Mike nodded. "Is it about Lily?" he asked.

"It's about Lily and, also, about you," Zetel said. "What's going on, Mike? I know you're not what you say you are."

Mike was silent for a moment. "Zetel, let's talk but not here," Mike said. "Let's get away from the others — the far side of the truck, where the acacia tree is."

"Is that a good idea?" Zetel asked. "We'll be closer to the herd and the lions."

"Zetel, not to worry. We're still close enough to the truck."

They walked away from the safari vehicle to the tree.

"The target is being led away by the spy," Samael shouted jubilantly. "It's now or never."

Samael managed to turn the lioness in the direction of the acacia tree, closely followed by Chamuel in the male.

"Samael, my charge has livened up but it does not seem to be the hunt. I can barely control it. Its whole attention is focussed on the lioness."

Unaware of the advancing lions, Zetel focussed closely on Mike. "Look, you're not Americans. You have no idea who Santa Claus is. You receive cell phone calls where such calls cannot be received. At first, I was flattered by Lily's attention, but I realized at lunch, there was some agenda going on. So, what are..."

At that moment, the two lions burst on the scene. "Zetel, your time has come," Samael screamed. The lioness snarled and prepared to leap on the two men. Mike ran madly to the truck but his feet seemed to cross with Zetel's. Zetel tripped and fell flat on his face. The male lion bellowed and launched himself on the lioness.

"What are you doing, you fool? You're attacking me," shouted Samael as his lioness turned to ward off the lion.

"I can't help it. It's got nothing to do with food or hunting. It's not angry. I don't know what is happening," said Chamuel desperately.

The lioness snarled and tried to throw off the male. He gave a full throated bellow and once again threw himself on the lioness.

"I can't believe this," Samael shouted. "Chamuel, your lion is mating. I'm being mated. I, the Angel of Death, will be giving birth. How can you do this to me? Gabriel, where are you? Your plans never work but this is too much."

By now, the truck was honking, the tourists shouting as they fled into the vehicle, followed by Mike.

"Where's Zetel?" Sarah screamed terror stricken. She tried to leave the truck but the driver restrained her. The driver pulled a carbine out of its holster above his head and left the truck. He walked warily toward the tree, his finger on the trigger of the gun. As he came level with the tree, he saw a lioness running away with a lion in full pursuit, still within gunshot range but of no danger to his tourists. Walking towards him was the man he expected to find terribly mauled and perhaps dead. Apparently unharmed, he held a small lion cub which he stroked absentmindedly.

"That was close," Zetel said, his voice shaking. "Too close. I need a drink."

Astounded, the driver walked around Zetel. "You're not scratched, your clothes are not torn, you haven't even been touched. Do you know how lucky you are? Did they not attack you? I've never seen anything like this."

Back in the truck, after calming a hysterical Sarah, Zetel explained he had been saved by love and sex. "The lions were more interested in mating than eating," he said ruefully. "After they ran off, I was still lying flat on the grass, this little fellow jumped on me. So, you see, ladies and gentlemen, the lions mated but I got the baby."

His fellow passengers laughed but Sarah was still shaken. "It's not funny," she exclaimed and grabbed him by the shoulders. "What made you leave the truck area? Just to get a better picture? You are totally irresponsible."

Zetel still held the lion cub. It reached out its forepaws and touched Sarah's shoulders. Immediately, she felt her agitation dissipate. She took the lion cub and cradled it. "OK, I forgive you," she said to Zetel.

"The noise the two lions made has spooked the herd and it's moved on," the driver said as he started up the truck. "We'll go on. By the way, you can't keep the cub. We'll have to leave it at the nearest refuge. It must have wandered off from its pride."

They stopped for the night at a lodge. They had drinks before dinner in the rustic bar area with its stuffed animal heads decorating the walls. Zetel waited until he saw Mike and Lily walking away and followed them. He caught up with them as they were exiting the bar.

"Mike, I'd like to know why you tried to kill me," he said. "Was this another archangel plot?"

"Zetel," Mike objected, "what are you talking about? It was just an accident. I didn't realize I had tripped you."

"Rubbish. Over and above the noise of the lions, I could make out voices coming from them. Those lions were being directed.

Just another archangel attempt to get me back to the Arc. Which archangel are you, Mike? Probably Michael, I bet. Was your job to get me away from the truck? Well, the plot almost succeeded. Your colleagues couldn't control instinct."

"Zetel, this incident has completely deranged you. Sure, my full name is Michael, so what? What's all this talk about archangels? We were both attacked by the lions. I managed to get away — I hope this is not causing you to resent me. It wasn't until I reached the truck that I realized you were not behind me. Look, maybe you should see a doctor."

"Oh, I will be consulting with one," Zetel said smiling. "I've requested his presence. This is the doctor who recommended I take a vacation. He's world famous. Perhaps you've heard of him — Lucifer."

Mike lost his look of offended innocence and became grim.

"You are a damned fool," he said. "You put your faith in hell. We offer you salvation."

"Yes, some salvation! An eternity glued to the Arc of Souls."

"You could be reassigned. You could return to life," Michael said persuasively.

"You know that will not happen. I will never be reassigned. Therefore, the Devil is my better option."

"Salvation is always the better option," Michael said. "I will carry out the sentence myself."

He pulled the long knife out but before he could plunge it into Zetel, Lily slipped in between them.

"Put your knife away, Michael," she said. "I will not let him die."

"Lily, I order you out of the way," Mike hissed.

"I am Lillith. My orders come from elsewhere. You promised me an exceptionally desirable, adulterous man, but he is loyal to his wife. Therefore, I am no longer with you. Your knife will not kill me but I will put on a convincing act. Go. Your plot has failed."

"Exactly so," a familiar voice said. Near them in the doorway stood Louis C. Fuhr, dressed in full safari regalia. "Little did I realize when I decided to go on Safari, that I would meet such an illustrious personage as you Michael, and my sweet Lillith — in your company, no less! — and my investment colleague Mr. Landaw. What a marvellous coincidence! The world is indeed small."

"How did you get here?" Michael demanded. "Gabriel said you were far away."

"It is a good thing I did get here," Fuhr replied smiling. "Who were you about to kill? My sweet Lillith or my friend Mr. Landaw. I suggest you depart. Tell the safari leader you must return immediately to your country. Lillith, you must go with him to ensure he leaves. Michael, I will replace you on the tour."

"I will not leave," Michael said. "You cannot force me."

Fuhr laughed. "I will not force you, Michael. I will persuade you. Consider the following scene. Lillith will scream that she is attacked by you, that you have a knife, that you are going to kill her. There are many safari leaders and guides here who will immediately respond. Is that the attention you desire? Leave us, Michael and tell your colleagues to go away as well. It's important that the Landaws have a traumatic free vacation. I will ensure their safety by staying close to them."

Chastened, Michael said, "I cannot endure your presence for very long. Therefore, I will go but I want the lion cub."

Puzzled, Fuhr turned to Zetel."Lion cub?"

"After the lions ran off, a little cub jumped onto me. Sarah has it now. We must leave it at an animal refuge."

Fuhr looked keenly at Michael. "No, I think we will keep it for a while. I bet it's sweet and likes to cuddle and exudes a sense of peace, is that not so?" Zetel nodded.

"What's going on here?" Sarah asked, joining the group. "Oh, Mr. Fuhr, what a surprise! Are you also on Safari? Is this a coincidence or did you and Zetel arrange this? He promised he would not even think of work on our vacation."

Fuhr bowed and kissed Sarah's hand. The cub in her other arm yowled and snapped at him. He put a restraining hand on the cub's head. "There, there. You need have no fear of me. We will soon return you to where you belong." The cub growled but retreated further in Sarah's arm.

"Well," Sarah insisted, "did you or did you not arrange your showing up?"

Fuhr smiled, "Madam Landaw, I can assure you I had no intention whatsoever of joining you on vacation. I had no idea you were on Safari. Independently, I registered for an African tour but all the immediate tours were filled. Then I was informed that two people were leaving this tour and there was a place for me. And here I am, wholly by coincidence."

"Mike and Lily just told me they were leaving the tour. The lion attack has quite unnerved them and they're returning to the States," said Zetel.

"I quite understand it, Mike and Lily," Sarah said solicitously, trying hard not to show her delight that Lily was leaving. "Nearly losing a husband is very upsetting. Both you guys were pretty lucky. I was ready to call it quits, too, but this little cub seems to need me. When do you two actually leave?"

"As soon as they pack, they will leave on the safari car that brought me here," said Fuhr. "It is returning to Arusha tonight."

Sarah was startled. Fuhr's statement and his tone sounded more like a command than a simple statement of fact. Before she could wish them well, the cub leaped from her arm and was caught deftly by Mike. Both he and Lily turned and walked quickly away.

"Good riddance," said Zetel.

"What's going on, Zetel, Mr. Fuhr," Sarah demanded. "This was not a friendly parting."

"Lily admitted there was a plot against me," Zetel said. "She was supposed to seduce me and then they would blackmail me. In return for keeping my adultery from you, they would demand the secret of my investing success. However, when her efforts to seduce me failed, she wanted out. So good riddance to both of them."

"Their misfortune is my good fortune," said Fuhr. "This way, I get a seat on the bus. And with them gone, there is nothing to mar the rest of your vacation."

CHAPTER 4 —
Zetel at the Millennium

The decade leading up to the year 2000 was both tragic and triumphant for Zetel.

His mother Ettie died at the age of 87 after several months of increasing illness brought on by a bout of pneumonia. In her final days in hospital, Zetel sat by her bedside, holding her hand, reminiscing about old times. They talked about Joseph, the escape from Europe, early times in Montreal, the family's growing prosperity, and their many friends. She had difficulty talking and frequently dozed. The beauty that had so characterized her had shrivelled and left behind a sallow corpse-like gauntness.

Sarah came as often as she could, the grandchildren visited on the weekend. During one of these visits, Ettie roused herself.

"You have been a good son and daughter to me," she said, barely above a whisper. "After the hard times, you have helped me have a good life. And you" — she beckoned Elijah and Marsha to come close — "you are good children. Be as nice to your parents as they have been to me."

She was too frail to hug but they all leaned over the bed and kissed her, tears in their eyes. She fell into a deep sleep. Zetel stayed behind after the others left. A few hours later, weeping, he went to the nursing station. "I think she's gone," he said.

Ettie had asked to be buried next to Joseph. Accordingly, her body was moved to Montreal. The internment took place on Sunday, May 10, 1992 at the cemetery on de la Savane Avenue where Joseph was buried in a double plot. Scattered clouds and moderate winds kept the temperature cool. All the family and many friends who had known Ettie in Montreal were there. The rabbi conducted the brief service and made a few remarks. Zetel spoke briefly and reminded everybody that today was Mother's Day, "a day in which we celebrate all our great mothers and mine was among the best."

Rivka invited everyone to her house for coffee and cake before the out-of-towners headed back to Toronto.

"Chaim and Beatrice can't be here but send their condolences," she told them. "As you know, Chaim sold his business and now they're travelling in Europe — Paris, at the moment — and then they're off on a Volga river cruise through Russia. Poor people like me can't afford it."

"How's your ex making out?" Sarah asked. "Does he contribute at all? To the kids?"

"Oh, he contributes alright," Rivka replied. "Last month he contributed an urgent appeal to help him out. His car had broken down, he didn't have enough money to repair it, and he needed it for his sales business. I bailed him out — $1500. A couple of weeks later, I discover he used the money to lease a BMW. 'I need to show my clients I'm successful,' he explained. 'But don't worry, it will all be paid back with interest.'"

"Will he pay it back?" Zetel asked.

"No," Rivka said. "That's why I'm not worried. What I am worried about is whether I can retire in a couple of years."

"Surely, Zetel, you can help her," Sarah said. "While you're in Toronto, Rivka, find some time with him. My father has all the Lansmann money invested with Zetel and he's done very well. So have all his other investors."

Zetel wasn't anxious to have more family investors. His fund was still not fully invested, he still needed new money to satisfy his performance promise in the ten percent range. As a new investor, Rivka would be most vulnerable should he become incapacitated or exposed. To get around this, he would not treat her as new money but would fully invest her.

During the seven day mourning period which was held at the Landaw home, Rivka flew from Montreal and stayed with them. After a few days, the flow of visitors had slowed and allowed Zetel time to talk to her.

He kept an office in his basement and they met there. It turned out her savings were much larger than he had anticipated. She had managed to keep most of her inheritance from her father, and her share of the net proceeds from the sale of her house during the divorce. In all, she had a little more than $300,000 invested in long term Government bonds.

"Relatively safe but earning very modest returns," was Zetel's conclusion. "I can do better," he assured her. He also recommended she delay her retirement for several years after age 65. "Between your additional income and the returns on your investments, we'll try to get your portfolio up to $500,000. Then, with your hospital pension, government pensions and withdrawals from your portfolio, you should be able to retire very decently."

"I don't mind working longer," Rivka said. "I like my job very much, I like my colleagues, and I enjoy the occasional conferences that I go to. You've reassured me I won't live in poverty. You're so clever and successful. I should have married you. In my teenage years, I thought of it quite often, despite the five year difference in our ages. I would have waited until my mid-twenties if you were agreeable."

"I had the same thought," Zetel said. "Unfortunately, we are first cousins, not a good idea."

"I thought better of it for the same reason. That's why I married so early — just to get you out of my system. After my divorce, I considered going after you but you were already married to Sarah and seemed very happy. Life is unforgiving. You married well. I didn't."

"Don't be too hard on your ex," Zetel said. "In business life, there is a fine line that divides the hero from the heel. During Black Monday, I came close to being pushed across the line. Then I would have been bankrupt and you would have congratulated yourself on not marrying me."

"But you didn't end up on the other side of the line, and Dave never made it to the hero side."

Zetel walked over to her, kissed her on the lips, "Let's stay just friends. Let's talk about something else."

"Too bad. I was just getting warmed up," she laughed. "I shall treasure the kiss. What shall we talk about?"

"How about my mother?" he said after a long moment of silence.

"Do you still believe in reincarnation?" Rivka asked him. "I do. It takes about forty days before Auntie Ettie will be reincarnated. Or does your band of souls work faster?"

Zetel was startled. In all his grief, he had simply mourned. He had never thought about his mother's future. Now, he realized, his mother was likely secured in the Arc of Souls awaiting reassignment. What did it matter? She was gone from him forever. How long would it take? Where would she go? Fervently, he hoped it would be a nice, easy life for her.

"It's unpredictable," he said. "Archangel Gabriel makes the decision and no one knows how he decides."

"You're smiling," Rivka said, "but you really believe it, don't you? Sometimes I think about our early days and those strange visions I had. The men who floated through the walls, the man who disappeared. Then I think, maybe they weren't visions. What if they were real. That would mean you have strange powers or divine knowledge. Sarah told me about your adventures in Venice. She put it down to a morbid infantile fantasy with Diana the Huntress that nearly got you killed. But if you have these powers, maybe it really was Diana. Now I'm thinking about it, when Uncle Yoisef died, I remember Auntie Ettie telling us the story of how your public school teacher called them because you believed in reincarnation — and you only six years old — and your rabbi believed you were the Meshiach because you could remember when you were a soul. We all laughed but maybe we laughed too soon. And Sarah told some of us yesterday about your safari and how you were attacked by two lions and walked away unscathed. Too many strange coincidences, Zetel, I could be easily persuaded there's something more."

Zetel said nothing. He toyed with the thought of reviving the warmth of their childhood trading of confidences. It would be nice to have a believing mortal to talk with. Rivka would accept or would come to accept his description of his origins and the forces trying to extract his soul. He could never convince Sarah. She believed his reference to mysterious happenings were evidence of a need for vacation or less stress at work.

A thought came to him unbidden. *You are making a mistake if you divulge your secrets to her. She is not discreet and will gossip. People will come to believe you are mentally disturbed. Not a good reputation for a financial advisor and portfolio manager.*

They heard the front doorbell ring. "I will be back in a moment," Rivka said. "It's probably someone with more food."

Zetel sighed. "It's Mr. Fuhr, come to console us."

Sarah emerged from the kitchen and got to the door first.

"Hello, Mr. Fuhr," they heard her say, "how nice of you to come."

Rivka looked at Zetel, "I guess you also have telepathic powers."

Zetel laughed, "We were expecting him."

It seemed to Zetel that his mother's death precipitated the deaths of the remaining people who had been part of his growing up and marriage.

A few months later, Sylvia Levitt succumbed to breast cancer. She had refused treatment and ended her days peacefully in a palliative care hospice. She and Hershey had had no children and had no living family members. Zetel and Sarah arranged the funeral. The internment took place in the same cemetery where Ettie and Joseph lay. A small group gathered at the grave site. Sylvia had been popular with her small circle of friends. Everybody said nice things about her.

What will they say about me? thought Zetel. Fraudster? A destroyer of people's savings? So prominent, so respected and at bottom a crook? What would Sarah think? The children? Cyril would shout to the world — "I knew it. I never trusted him." Ironically, Cyril's portfolio and therefore Sarah's inheritance was secure. I have to fix this problem so every one of my investors will be secure. I'm so close now. Just a good bull market will do it. "I must do it," he muttered.

Sarah saw his lips moving but couldn't make out what he said. He seemed stressed and worried. She concluded he was working too hard again.

If there were exposure and shame to come to Zetel, Cyril would never witness it. He died of a heart attack in the Fall of that year. At the funeral service, a mournful Sarah, sobbing uncontrollably at times, barely able to talk, admitted she had not always been a good daughter, had caused her father much anguish at times, yet he continued to love her, was devoted to the grandchildren and very supportive of her husband.

In his remarks, Zetel acknowledged the help he had received from Cyril. "In fact, I wouldn't be where I am today without his believing in me, investing in my business, and, best of all, entrusting me with his daughter." He noted Cyril was a fine example of a 'rags to riches' story, starting off his working life with nothing, and after working several years for others in the jewellery business, opening up his own store which soon became a chain.

At the grave site, Anna was completely overtaken with grief. Theirs had been a long and occasionally stormy marriage, aggravated by frequent arguments between Cyril and Sarah. Yet, they had loved and that's what she remembered now.

Her grief was her undoing. As she turned from the gravesite, eyes clogged with tears, she tripped and fell. There was a flurry of activity as Zetel and others helped her up. She insisted she was just bruised, nothing serious but was taken to hospital. X-rays showed a hairline crack in the hip. Two months later, she was given a new hip. She did not respond well and was kept in hospital. She never recovered and gradually slipped away.

Faigel Shuster was the last of the older group to go. She hung onto life until she was ninety-three. During her last days, Zetel visited her in hospital. She paused often for breath but related again all the circumstances of his birth and the trip through immigration and customs.

"Your father was so funny, trying to be nice and respectful to these officials who couldn't care at all and just wanted to get on with a job they clearly didn't like. And when you peed on the immigration man, how we all laughed."

She laughed now or tried to, coughing and gasping for breath. "How tough those early days were," she said. "Everything changed for me when I met Jack, thanks to you. How many girls can say they met their love at a bris?" Again she tried to laugh but was racked by a paroxysm of coughing. "He left me too early, that sweet man."

She paused for a moment until she felt well enough to proceed. "I've never told anyone this but I'd like to tell you. A few years after Jack passed away, I was still grieving, feeling particularly lonely and missing him terribly. One night I was lying in bed, trying to sleep and crying like a baby. I must have fallen asleep because I had a strange dream — at least I think it was a dream — it seemed so real. I dreamt that I was paid a visit by Mr. Fuhr which in itself is surprising since I didn't see him very often, usually only at your family gatherings."

She paused to catch her breath. Zetel, apprehensive, asked, "What was the dream about?"

"I dream I'm in my living room, bawling my eyes out. There's a knock at the door and Fuhr walks into the room. 'Sweet lady," he says, "I hate to see you suffer so. All bodies must end, but life is not over. He is gone from you but he lives now elsewhere. Come with me and I will show you.'" He takes my hand and suddenly we're on a large lawn in front of one of those British mansions — you know, very large, turrets, lots of chimneys. A bunch of children are playing in front of some men and women having tea. Mr. Fuhr leads me over to one child. He's a toddler, maybe three years old. He looks at me and smiles. 'This is your Jack,' Mr. Fuhr says. 'This is his new life. See, he recognizes you, because he sees you. No one else does. I don't think he will be unhappy here.' We stay there a while and I watch him. There is a resemblance to the Jack I knew. 'Come, it is time to go,' Mr Fuhr says. I wave goodbye and the little fellow waves back. I hear one of the women say, 'To whom are you waving, Johnnie?' And my little Jack says, 'That nice nana.' The next I know I wake up in bed, still missing Jack but feeling much better."

"Wow," said Zetel. "That's quite a dream. So your Jack is now a little English boy living in a castle."

"I know it seems crazy," Faigel said. "But, Zetel, I was really there. Please don't make fun."

"Make fun?" Zetel chuckled. "Faigel, I strongly believe in reincarnation so what you saw is quite possible."

"I keep wondering though — why Mr. Fuhr?"

"It doesn't surprise me at all," Zetel reassured her. "You probably remember him as a magician and you were looking for something magic to happen."

"But it wasn't just magic," Faigel insisted. "I think it was an angel disguised as Mr. Fuhr and sent by God."

He was about to reply but she had drifted off. She never regained consciousness and died a few days later.

"Thanks to you she went with a sweet thought," Zetel said to Fuhr at the funeral. "But imagine, she believes you're an angel."

"I *am* an angel," Fuhr reminded him. "Just a fallen one."

"Oh, there's something else I should tell you," Fuhr said. "In a little while, you will receive a letter edged in black — that's the German system when announcing a death — that I have died and my ashes scattered in Transylvania. I'm too old by your mortal chronology to maintain my existence as Louis C. Fuhr. So show some grief when the letter arrives."

On the eve of the third millennium, Zetel and family gathered for the usual Friday evening dinner. Zetel raised his glass of wine: "I propose a toast — first to the older generation that has passed from our presence but not from our memories, and to remind you all how much they meant to us, did for us, sacrificed for us — second to the love of my life, Sarah, who has made a home and a life for all of us — and third to the young generation, our son Elijah and daughter-in-law Sheila and our first grandchild Joseph and our daughter Marsha and son-in-law Mort. May we all enjoy good health and prosperity in 2000 and the years following."

Zetel had much to be thankful for. He had profited immensely from the stock markets' meteoric rise in the previous five years. To his great relief, his investment business was now fully legitimate. As a result of his fund's exceptional results, he had cleared up any unfunded investors. He invested all new money instead of using it to pay off previous investors. He could no longer be exposed as a fraud. He had learned his lesson. If the markets fell again, he would do nothing illicit but simply record the losses or lesser returns.

Fred and Sally Peterson had retired the day the portfolio became solidly and fully invested. Fred had wound up the Cayman Islands company. He and Sally had moved to the west coast of British Columbia and were living in a small town — Halfmoon Bay — on the Sunshine Coast.

Sarah had retired from teaching but had opened a training and tutorial service for young people. Elijah was running the brokerage, and Sheila worked from home as a translator of French scientific essays and looked after three year old Joseph. Marsha was a medical researcher and Mort was an associate professor of biology, both at McGill University.

At the stroke of midnight, they all clinked glasses, hugged and kissed, wished each other well, and revelled in the sense of contentment and happiness that pervaded their little group.

CHAPTER 5 —
Zetel faces another plot

Sandalphon was not happy. The most beloved of all The-One-True-God's angels, Sandalphon was usually optimistic, often ebullient, eager to fulfill his mandate to bring humanity together, to work collaboratively with his colleagues (except Samael, of course, whom he challenged at every opportunity), and to respond quickly and devotedly to any wish, suggestion, command of the Almighty.

But now he was clearly despondent. He had concluded that his mandate had failed and was not likely to succeed. It was now ten years after the Millennium, a time of renewed hope and expectation that things would change. Yet humanity was still terribly divided, locked in endless fractious threats and wars, murdering each other in the name of some ideology or led by egomaniacs in their thirst for power. He had infused some mortals with a desire for peace, and an ability to speak up to try to persuade the combatants to put away their arms and negotiate. They were invariably scorned, arrested, or killed. Underlining his sense of failure was a recent aside by The-One-True-God that perhaps it was time for another Flood.

All that was bad enough. Recently, however, the Almighty had convened a special meeting to discuss Zetel. If Zetel were allowed to live out his normal life, the Devil would automatically receive his soul, the Almighty declared. If Zetel were made to part with his soul, then he could be saved.

"Get his soul," The-One-True-God thundered. "No more failures."

Sandalphon rather liked Zetel and did not relish the thought of killing him. It would be one more violent death to add to the world's misery, one more violent death to deprive a family of a husband, father and grandfather. He could lie low or pretend to pursue the goal or pursue it half-heartedly. However, his love of, and devotion to, the Almighty meant he would feel compelled to cooperate and participate to his fullest extent to retrieve Zetel's soul.

He sought a deserted spot as a haven where he could think without interruption and for as long as needed. He first chose a pinnacle in the Himalayas. There, clothed in his Andean llama coat, he curled up his four foot cherubic body into a small round ball and snuggled under the snow. Unfortunately, the mountain he had sought refuge in was Everest. It was summertime and the peak was soon inundated with climbers. Since the top of the world was too crowded, he chose the bottom and housed himself in a wreck in the north Atlantic. This too proved temporary as submarines and then divers investigated the wreck. He tried the Sahara but camel trains passed over him. In the jungle, the animals were too noisy. Finally, he chose the centre of Antarctica. A howling blizzard soon covered him up completely and allowed him the peace he needed to thoughtfully reflect on his unhappiness and decide what to do about it.

He contemplated the state of the world and quickly realized there would be no short term solution to settling humanity's many antagonisms. He would just have to keep working at it and not get impatient or disenchanted.

He turned next to the Zetel problem. He rephrased the problem from how to capture Zetel's soul to how to capture Zetel's soul without killing him. After many hours, unable to resolve the conundrum, frustrated, he slept through the Antarctic winter. He awoke refreshed. He pushed through the snow covering him and relaxed in the pale sunshine.

He considered the problem anew, and, slowly, a possible plan began to emerge. With careful execution, and the right team, it could work. Who was the right team? Gabriel had proved his incompetency on a number of occasions. Raphael looked after himself first but was the Divine Healing Force. Certainly, he must be involved. Michael? Uriel? Metatron? He needed to discuss the plan and the team with someone he trusted. Chamuel? Chamuel was always quick to defend him and to support him in his confrontations with Samael. Chamuel it must be.

He stretched to his full four feet, ruffled snow from his curly locks, pulled his coat more snugly around him and streaked from the land of ice and snow to the heavens above.

On September 16, 2010, Zetel reached his 75th birthday and decided to retire. Sarah had already packed it in the year before. His wealth management fund had remained fully and legally invested. Its returns were no longer routinely spectacular, but still strong enough to attract new money. There was no temptation on his part to inflate the returns with the funds of new clients and return to his Ponzi scheme days. The 2008 global financial collapse had hurt him badly. However, he had suffered no guilty loss of sleep during the crisis and the business had since recovered.

He restructured the ownership of the entire business into thirds. He kept one third and ceded the other two thirds to Elijah and Marsha with his son as CEO. Zetel set up a small board of directors with himself as chairman. He agreed to stay active until Elijah became familiar with the wealth management side.

Zetel hired one of the banks to formalize the arrangement. One afternoon, the investment bankers and lawyers spent hours drawing up the required documents. To while away the time, Zetel and Elijah talked about his son Joseph's upcoming bar mitzvah.

"Dad, it's not going to be a gala. Just the service and then a lunch afterwards with close family and some friends. Is that ok with you?"

Zetel nodded his assent. "I'd like to invite the new board member."

Fuhr had returned in the form of Abel Satansky, a young man with a background in finance from Wall Street — or so he claimed. Zetel had insisted he join the board although Elijah was uneasy.

"Dad," Elijah had objected, "I've checked his background — no one seems to know him."

Zetel had chided Abel, "Picking a name like Satansky is hardly creative, and you could have set up some background references in New York."

"Tut, tut, my boy," Abel replied. "The important thing is that I'm close enough to look after you when I must."

Sarah liked Abel immediately. "You know, Zetel, this is crazy but he reminds me of Mr. Fuhr. He has the same caring attitude, speaks a little like him, and there's even a faint resemblance."

Zetel laughed: "Maybe he's an outcome of some sexual adventure. Fuhr was a good looking man."

It was well into the winter before Zetel considered Elijah ready to operate by himself. More-or-less free of daily business requirements, Zetel and Sarah set out on a long holiday in the south of Spain.

"This is a holiday for both of us. No organized tours," Sarah insisted. "We're going to have an unrushed trip. We'll stop at all the sights but maybe only one per day. We will stop for coffee and meals regularly and at outdoor restaurants if the weather allows. This includes when we're on the road. You will get some sun because you're awfully pale. We will sleep in whenever we want. You will avoid all stressful situations. Is that clear?"

Zetel shook his head in awe. "With all those commands, I'm already stressed."

They arrived in Madrid and planned to stay a few days in the capital city before travelling on. Ensconced in a luxury hotel, bedroom with an adjoining sitting area, full bathroom with Jacuzzi, they were loath to leave the room. They slept the rest of the first day, had a quick dinner, and slept into the next morning. They were awakened by a waiter who served them coffee and pastries.

"Today we will visit the Prado," Sarah announced. "That will take quite a few hours but we can have lunch in the museum. Then we will explore the main square and find a nice restaurant for dinner. So let's get going."

"I thought this was going to be an unorganized, non-rush trip," Zetel said. He pulled her, protesting, from the sitting area back to bed. A little after noon, they showed up for lunch in the hotel's coffee shop, an informal restaurant for snacks and sandwiches. They sipped their coffees waiting for their order to be served. A man and a little boy came in and took the table next to them.

"Well, we're way off our schedule," Sarah said. "By now we should have been at the Prado having lunch."

"You don't want to have lunch there," said the man at the next table. "It's expensive and not very good at times."

The man was quite tall and fleshy, with a bluff square face, deep set eyes, unkempt brown hair, a large nose and thick lips. He was dressed in casual beige slacks, a loose fitting yellow shirt that barely enclosed his bulk and a leather jacket which hung loosely from his shoulders. The boy was in jeans and a tee shirt and wore a leather jacket that fit snugly. It was difficult to make out his face because a baseball cap covered his head with its visor pushed low over the thick glass spectacles that covered his eyes.

"I notice the boy's cap sports the Blue Jays moniker. Are you from Toronto?" Zetel asked.

"Indeed we are," the man replied. "And you?"

"What a coincidence," Sarah said. "So are we. Are you also touring through Spain?"

"I suppose you could call it touring. I like to think of it as travelling through Europe. We began our travels about three months ago. Probably go another three months or earlier if we get fed up. It's not entirely a happy trip. It's more a trip to settle our grief. My wife — his mother — died six months ago. We just couldn't handle it, so I took him out of school, sold our house in Rosedale with all its memories, and we've been on the road ever since."

"That's a very sad story," Sarah said and reached out to touch the boy's shoulder. "You must have loved your mother very much."

The boy nodded.

"He doesn't say much," his father said. "It's been really traumatic. By the way, my name is Shmuel Lipzig and my boy is Sydney."

"I'm Zetel Landaw and this is my wife Sarah." They shook hands with Shmuel and Sydney. "Where are you off to next or are you planning to stay here?"

"Another day or two, then I thought we'd go south. Toledo, Cordoba, Granada, Malaga. From your name, I take it you're Jewish, like us. Toledo had a large Jewish population before 1492. Cordoba too. Maimonides was born in Cordoba. Granada has the Alhambra and Malaga the Mediterranean. From there I have a hankering to visit Gibraltar. By the way, your name is very familiar. Are you the famous portfolio manager who defied all the skeptics?"

"I don't know whether I was famous or infamous but I did manage to do well for my investors. I'm retired now. My son has taken over, and I know he'll be successful. It's nice being free of clients and away from the action. What do you do, Mr Lipzig? You look too young to be retired."

"Call me Shmuel," Lipzig said. "No, I'm not retired. I'm in the shmatte business. Clothing stores — L-CHIC for Professional Women. My brother's running them while I'm gone. You heard of us?"

Sarah laughed. "If your business isn't listed on the stock market, Zetel will not have heard of you. I haven't heard of your stores either. But then, I don't do much shopping anymore. By the way, it's quite a coincidence. Here we are in a hotel coffee shop in Spain, both from Toronto, and we're also planning to see the same places as you. How do you get around? Do you go on any organized tours?"

"No, we travel independently between places, sometimes by train, sometimes by taxi. In the more celebrated spots, we take sightseeing tours. Often we just walk around. It's good exercise for both of us."

Their orders arrived and interrupted the conversation. Sydney picked away at a scrambled egg slathered with cheese.

"Sydney's not a good eater," Shmuel explained. "Give him French fries on a bed of pasta and it's like he inhales the food. Once in a while I give in but not too often. I want to keep him healthy. You folks are having quiches, I see. Remember, this is Europe. Nothing is low fat."

"We're on holidays," Sarah said. "We can eat unhealthy for a while." She pointed to his sandwich. "A Reuben is hardly a model for good eating."

Shmuel laughed. "I'm a proper model. Don't do what I do."

They parted after lunch. "Might see you before we leave," Shmuel said, "or maybe on the road."

They saw them again that evening. They spent all afternoon at the Prado Museum, enthralled by the visual richness of the finest art of Europe clothing the walls of its palatial corridors and halls. At eight pm when the museum closed, the last daylight fading, they took a taxi over to the Plaza Mayor, a large open square in Madrid's centre surrounded by arcaded buildings. Despite the spring coolness, they selected an outside table and ordered wine and several tapas dishes. They nibbled on the food and sipped the wine in silence, tired from the long session in the Museum.

"Hi, there," a voice called. "We're just on our way back to the hotel. How did it go? Did you enjoy the Prado?"

"It was wonderful," Sarah said, motioning to Shmuel and Sydney to join them. "The collection on display is truly magnificent. The El Greco's, Velasquez, the Goya's — particularly The Executions which I found shattering — Tintoretto's Christ Washing the Disciples Feet, Van der Weyden's Descent From the Cross, Rembrandt, Titian, Veronese — the Prado has everyone. Gorgeous, awe-inspiring. I'm totally exhilarated. Unfortunately, it was too much for Zetel. He is exhausted and I'm trying to revive him."

"Seven hours looking at art would exhaust anyone," Zetel said. "Would you like a drink or something to eat?"

"Well, we can stop for a little while," Shmuel said. "I don't like keeping Sydney out too late."

Zetel ordered more wine and a selection of tapas dishes.

"Don't worry. We won't be staying out too late either. I could fall asleep right here," Zetel said, stifling a deep yawn.

"These financial types can't handle art," Sarah said. "It wasn't a straight seven hours. We stopped several times for a rest and a cup of coffee."

"Well," Zetel said, "appearances to the contrary, I did enjoy the museum. The picture that gave me angst was a side panel on the one by Fra Angelico where an angel announces to Mary that she will soon be with child. The side panel shows Adam and Eve getting kicked out of Eden. What struck me was the resignation on their faces as they calmly accepted their fate. If they'd only behaved and stayed away from the apple tree, we'd all be living in Paradise."

Shmuel laughed. "I guess Paradise for you would be an eternal bull market."

"You're absolutely right, Shmuel," Sarah said. "You know, what struck me most about that painting is the angel hovering over them in a cloud encouraging them on. In all the Banishment paintings

I've seen, the angel enforcing the expulsion is big and fearsome. But in this one, the angel is small and cherubic looking."

"That's because the painter never saw the real angel," Sydney said. "The real angel was tall and tough."

Shmuel chuckled. "Now, Sydney, let's not get carried away with the stuff you learn at school. The painter was just using his imagination so he painted the angel small. Other painters also using their imaginations paint him brawny and tough. Nobody has seen the actual banishment. These are painters just imagining what it must have been like. It's all imagination."

Sydney started to protest but Shmuel reached out and playfully tweaked an ear. Sydney fell silent.

They walked back together to the hotel, in good humour, and planning the next day.

"Zetel, I think you should take it easier tomorrow," Shmuel said solicitously. "You look worn out."

"Shmuel, we're on holidays," Sarah said sharply. "Don't talk him into feeling sick."

"I do feel rather peaked," Zetel said. " I think a good night's sleep will fix that."

The next day, Zetel complained of fatigue and stayed in bed most of the morning. Sarah went sightseeing with Shmuel and Sydney and returned for lunch at the hotel. Zetel was sound asleep. She woke him and was startled by his haggard appearance, face white, breathing ragged. He managed to get out of bed and seemed to recover slightly.

"Pain in chest," he mumbled. "Must be bad case of indigestion. Something I ate last night. Some of that jamon. Didn't agree with me." He settled into one of the sofa chairs and massaged his chest gently with the fingers of one hand.

"Zetel, it sounds more like angina, like daddy had." Frightened, she kept her voice calm and steady and telephoned the reception desk. "My husband is ill. Do you have a doctor available?"

There was no doctor but a nurse came to the room. She spoke some English and motioned Zetel to remove his pyjama top. She inserted a thermometer in his ear, then attached a blood pressure cuff to his left upper arm, and pressed the chest piece of the stethoscope against his chest in several places and on his back, asked him to breathe deeply a few times and listened intently. She examined the thermometer and the blood pressure reading.

"Small fever," she announced. "Pressure sanguinea high. Heart no good. I call ambulance. Need hospital. Hospital Universitario La Paz very good. Very good doctors."

Zetel shook his head. "No hospital," he said. "I go home."

"For God's sake, Zetel, just do what she says," Sarah implored, her voice shaking, her tears starting to flow. His sudden fragility completely unnerved her. He had never been seriously ill before, pneumonia once, the usual colds and flu. The nurse was clearly concerned. The thought that he could suddenly leave her became an overpowering realization that almost shattered her ability to act.

"No go home now. See doctor first. Then go home," the nurse offered trying to keep Zetel calm.

Sarah exerted all her willpower and clamped down on the terror sweeping through her. "The nurse is giving us good advice," she said. "We have to make sure you're healthy enough to get on an airplane for an eight hour flight. So let's do what she says."

She didn't wait for an answer from Zetel but said to the nurse, "Call ambulance."

A few doors down the corridor, Shmuel sat at the desk in his hotel room and drummed his fingers impatiently. Sydney, sitting cross-legged on a sofa chair, had removed his ball cap and glasses, allowing his curly hair to fall to his shoulders. Intense lines of worry etched his forehead.

A third person paced slowly up and down the room. Tall, slimly built, his long hair tied tightly in a ponytail, his even features youthful and handsome, he wore a white medical coat over a blue shirt and trousers. A stethoscope bulged out of a pocket in his coat.

"The best laid plans collapse when Gabriel gets involved," Shmuel said. "Everything was working beautifully. I had narrowed the arteries leading to his heart to cause the target some stress but I can't leave it too long or there will be permanent damage."

"Rafael, could you not persuade him?" Sydney asked.

"Like we agreed, Sandalphon, I requested Gabriel to release a soul to me so that, as part of my mandate to bring Divine Healing Force, I can revive an individual who is about to succumb to cardiac arrest. I emphasized the urgency of the need. It was hopeless. He demanded to know the circumstances, who the individual was, why was Samael not involved, and on and on. I refused to give him any details. Finally, he consented but insists on bringing the soul himself. Chamuel, Sandalphon, he promised to be here 30 Earth minutes ago. I just hope it's not too late."

"Sarah has just asked the nurse to call an ambulance," Sandalphon said.

"If the ambulance gets here before Gabriel, we'll have lost an opportunity," Chamuel said. "Then we'll have to move our operation to the hospital which will make it more difficult to intervene. Come with me, Rafael, we shall try to delay things. Sandalphon, you wait here for Gabriel."

He knocked on the Landaw door and was let in by a surprised Sarah.

"The concierge told me you were asking for medical help. This is Dr. Angelo who is visiting from New York. He's attending a medical research conference in the hotel and responded when I asked for urgent assistance. Hope you don't mind."

"Mind?" Sarah exclaimed. "Shmuel, you're a godsend. Zetel's really sick."

Rafael pushed past Sarah, nodded to the nurse, attached his stethoscope to his ear, told a startled Zetel to be calm, and listened carefully to his chest.

"Now be very still, sir, I need absolute quiet to hear your heart and lungs properly. Quiet please," he said to Sarah who was talking excitedly to Shmuel and to the nurse who was about to telephone for the ambulance.

He listened to Zetel's chest again and at length. "Your heartbeats all over the place," he said. "I have to pinpoint the source of the disturbance in order to recommend what to do. Your problem might be serious or simply a reaction to something you ate. It's somewhat common to mistake indigestion for a heart problem."

He clutched Zetel's midriff. "Any pain here — or here — or here?"

Zetel gasped. "If you grab me like that, what do you expect?"

"Let me check your reflexes. Sometimes the problem is neurological. Put one knee over the other."

He tapped Zetel's knee joint and elicited a slight response. "Well, there seems to be true nerve connections although the reflex was weak. Let me listen to your heart and lungs through your back. Turn around."

He applied the chest piece of the stethoscope to various locations on Zetel's back, at times asking him to breathe deeply or not at all.

"There's definitely a problem with your heart," Dr. Angelo concluded. "Let's take your blood pressure again to see whether there is any change. We never rely on one reading."

He motioned to the nurse who applied the cuff once again to Zetel's arm. The results were a steep drop in blood pressure. Before

Dr. Angelo could react, the nurse raced to the telephone and spoke excitedly in Spanish to the operator.

"Ambulance coming," she announced.

"What's going on?" the angry voice of Gabriel demanded as he slowly materialized. "There had better be a good reason for this exceptional soul request."

Sandalphon spied the small white cloud folded over Gabriel's arm. "You have the soul," he said with relief. "Give it to me and I'll bring it next door. You're just in time. We can complete the procedure before the paramedics get here."

"What paramedics? What are you talking about?" Gabriel insisted. "I will not release the soul until I know what you are all up to."

"It's a trick you once tried, Archangel Gabriel. We are substituting the soul you brought for the soul of Zetel. That way, Zetel does not die and cause his family grief. Just wait here and we'll bring you Zetel's soul promptly," Sandalphon said, employing his most ingratiating tone.

"Zetel!" Gabriel exclaimed. "You are about to achieve the task of capturing his soul, a task that I have spent untold angelic energy trying to achieve and you planned to do it without even advising me. How dare you? I will participate in the final action and I will be given credit for the triumph or all action ends right now."

"Let's go," cried Sandalphon, as he detected the paramedics arriving at the hotel. "There's not a moment to lose."

They raced next door and floated into the room. Sarah was crying hysterically, clutching Zetel, the nurse was trying to calm Sarah down. Chamuel and Rafael were aware of Gabriel's entrance and were shouting orders, urging Gabriel to move quickly.

"You know my conditions," Gabriel said. "This is my plot and I will be given full credit. I shall summon Metatron to validate my conditions and to act as witness. Archangel Michael and Samael should also be here."

"Gabriel," Rafael said. "There is no time for a meeting. If you don't stop talking and get over here with the soul, this plot will end like all your other plots."

Chamuel gently pulled Sarah and the nurse away and Sandalphon in his guise as Sydney took over the task of calming Sarah.

"Sydney, what are you doing here? My Zetel is dying. Who is that man in the long white gown?" Sarah said, holding Sydney tightly.

"He's another one of those doctors," Sandalphon said. "Don't worry, Sarah, Zetel will not die. The doctors will save him."

For a split second, Zetel saw Gabriel in the room and at the same time recognized Rafael. Total fear gripped him as he lost consciousness and felt himself grasped by one of the doctors. He hovered by his side and watched the cloud go into his body, saw his body seemingly revitalized as it moved and sat up in the bed. At that moment the paramedics burst in and converged on the recovering body. They worked feverishly to stabilize and prepare him for transport to the hospital. After ten minutes, the paramedics turned to the nurse and began questioning her. Finally, one who spoke English said to Sarah, "We will take him to hospital to be certain but we can find nothing wrong at the moment. His blood pressure is normal, his pulse good, we hear no anomalies of the heart or lungs, his oxygen level is where it should be. Ask him some questions. We want to be certain he is lucid."

Greatly relieved, Sarah asked, "What's your name?"

"Zetel Zalman Yacob Landaw, born September 16, 1935 on a ship in the North Atlantic. And you're my beautiful wife Sarah. We're having a holiday in Spain. And as soon as the hospital releases me, we'll continue with our holiday."

"He's lucid," she said to the paramedic.

"Sarah, if you don't mind, I will go with you and Zetel to the hospital, just to make sure," Shmuel said. "Sydney, please stay in our room until I return."

When they were all gone, Zetel the soul said, "How come a new soul knew so much about me?"

"The new soul taps immediately into your whole brain and body system, including your memory structure," Rafael said. "As far as Sarah and Zetel the body are concerned, there is no change."

"I'm giving my wife to a total stranger," Zetel the soul said ruefully.

"Not so. He is you in every respect," Sandalphon said reassuringly. "And remember, we have retrieved your soul without causing Sarah or your family any grief."

"That's great. But what about my grief? What happens now — to me?"

"I have fulfilled the Almighty's command to capture you," Gabriel said triumphantly. "What happens to you is of no interest to me. I will take you before The-One-True-God. It will be up to Him to decide. No doubt, He will consign you back to the Arc of Souls."

"Where I will languish forever. I suppose I should console myself that I had a nice run while it lasted, but I don't feel very comforted."

CHAPTER 6 —
Zetel and the Divine Conclave

Escorted by Gabriel and Rafael, followed by Sandalphon, the soul Zetel left the Earth and found himself in the shade of the Trees of Knowledge and Life in the sublime sun-lit Garden of Paradise. Aided by a light breeze, the air was redolent with the scent of fruit and blossoming flowers. Orchards and vineyards stretched away to border vast plains of wheat, corn, oats, and barley, and endless carefully cultivated rows of vegetables.

In the far distance, he could see the massive cumulus cloud of vertical development slowly moving towards them. A sense of foreboding filled Zetel's soul. He knew exactly what was in store for him: banishment to the Arc with the unlikely prospect of ever being reassigned. The-One-True-God did not take challenge to His Authority lightly.

"Most Holy," shouted Gabriel to the advancing massive cumulus cloud of vertical development, "it is with inexpressible delight that I have the honour to announce that I have recaptured the soul of Zetel as per Your most recent request and submit him to Your Court for Judgement."

"My most recent request?" mused The-One-True-God. "It seems to Me, Archangel, that My request for the return of the soul of Zetel goes back decades to when he was falsely released from the Arc. Nevertheless, let Me not be peevish, you have finally succeeded for which I am grateful. I summon Metatron to record the events of the capture."

Immediately, Metatron appeared, seated at his desk, scrolls and quills ready.

"Who else was involved?" Metatron asked, looking rather sceptically at Gabriel.

"I alone," Gabriel began and then responding to a quick elbow, added, "and Archangel Rafael."

"Metatron, I too was part of the rescue team," Sandalphon piped up, "And so was Archangel Chamuel."

"Sandalphon, My sweet Sandalphon, I did not see you. Come here and tell Me what happened," gushed The-One-True-God.

Sandalphon was careful in his description of the plan. He gave Gabriel as much credit as he could. He noted the quick urgency with which Gabriel had appeared with the substitute soul. He complimented Rafael and Chamuel on narrowing the arteries of the body Zetel so that cardiac arrest would take place to release the soul of Zetel and provide entry for the substitute soul. Also, he praised Chamuel for tracking Zetel on vacation and managing the operation. He made no mention that he had conceived the plan.

"Where is Archangel Chamuel?" asked Metatron, who had carefully recorded Sandalphon's report.

"He is staying close to the body Zetel and his wife to make sure all goes well with them," Sandalphon said.

"The body Zetel still lives?" The-One-True-God said. "That sounds like a Sandalphon arrangement. Well done, My sweet Sandalphon. Metatron, please note the plan was carried out without a death. I congratulate all of you on a plan well formulated and implemented."

Metatron completed his report and carefully sanded the ink to dry it.

"Most Holy, how shall we dispose of the soul Zetel?" he asked.

"Soul Zetel, step forward to receive your Judgement," Gabriel ordered.

The soul Zetel was about to remind him that since he no longer inhabited a body, he could not step at all but decided it was not an appropriate time for witticism.

Before he could move, a sudden explosion, a blast of fire, and clouds of soot erupted close by. A clear sharp voice shouted: "STOP!"

The angels, illumined in red and choking on the soot, shrank back. Satan emerged from the black sulphurous fog and leapt between Zetel and The-One-True-God.

"Mighty Ruler of Heaven and Earth, this soul is mine," Satan said. "He sold himself to me at the age of five. I have protected him since then. I have reiterated my claim many times. Heaven cannot have him. He is mine and mine alone. He is part of me. Part of my clothing was ripped from me when You blew me from Heaven through the soul Zetel. See — the soul is not pristine white. Remnants of my clothing causes a graying of his soul."

Satan was dressed in black ragged clothing.

"Therefore, with all due respect, the soul Zetel is inextricably bound to me and must return with me to the Nether Regions."

A slight breeze ruffled the outer fringes of the massive cumulus cloud and soon turned into a strengthening wind of gale force proportions. It blew through the soul Zetel, whipped out the black bits of fabric from his soul and flung them at Satan.

"Your coat is complete again, Serpent, begone now," thundered The-One-True-God.

But Satan was not to be so quickly dismissed.

"Almighty One," he said, bowing, "He Who is Supreme, He Who reigns over Heaven and Earth, He Who is eternally mindful of the frailty of the creatures of Creation, He Who judges with fairness and compassion and mercy, I, a fallen angel, of no worth whatsoever, humbly beg You, in accordance with the laws and conventions regarding souls that have completed their assignments, that a formal trial take place of the soul Zetel to determine whether his behaviour was such as to merit a return to the Arc of Souls or, that my claim be honoured and the soul Zetel return to my possession."

An ominous rumble issued from the massive cumulus cloud of vertical development. Clearly irritated, The-One-True-God spoke: "The laws and conventions I have established to guide the angelic powers apply to Satan as well. Therefore, Satan has a right to request a trial and I so ordain that a trial be held."

There was a long pause. The rumble subsided. The Almighty continued: "Archangel Gabriel, you will be the Judge and you will convene a Divine Conclave which will hear the case. Metatron shall record the proceedings. The Jurors will be chosen from the Heavenly Host which will be called upon to assemble. Chamuel will be the Litigant on Heaven's side and Satan, the Litigant for the Nether Regions. The Litigants may call witnesses. The Judgement rendered by the Divine Conclave shall be final. I leave you now but I shall not be far away."

Having made and announced His decision, The-One-True-God moved slowly away.

Gabriel glowed with self-importance. "You have all heard the Divine Decree. I expect full cooperation from all those called upon to assist me in this grave and just enterprise. Litigants, conduct your investigations, research your positions and develop your lines of questioning. The Litigants will select the Jurors and ensure that those selected cleanse their minds and divest themselves of all prejudices and biases. Are there any questions?"

"There are no questions," Satan said. "Shall we get on with the Divine Conclave?"

Gabriel hesitated, paused, as though to make sure there were no questions.

"Yes," Michael said and clashed his sword against his shield. "Get on with it. Right now! No more wasting time."

"Truly, truly, Michael is right. Convene the Divine Conclave," shouted the others.

Still Gabriel hesitated. He looked around, his brow furrowed in thought. The massive cumulus cloud of vertical development was nowhere to be seen. Finally, he turned to the assembled angels, "How does one convene a Divine Conclave?"

There were cries of derision and impatient anger. "The Judge appointed to head the Conclave doesn't know how to do it. Let us consult The-One-True-God."

"No," said Satan. "Then we'll be here for millennia. Metatron, consult your records. When was the last Divine Conclave held and how was it convened?"

A cloud appeared over Metatron's desk. He reached into the cloud and began pulling out huge scrolls and laying them on his desk. Laboriously he skimmed through the scrolls.

"Since everything is in the cloud, why not scan and digitize your records," Satan suggested. "That's what I've done for the Nether Regions."

Metatron paid no attention but continued to study the scrolls. Finally, after many Earth hours, he announced triumphantly, "The last Divine Conclave was held when The-One-True-God was unhappy with Creation. The Conclave, after many years, decided to destroy life with the Flood. Noah and his family were dispatched to build an Ark and salvage as many pairs of animals as could crowd into their boat."

"Excellent," said Satan. "Soul of Zetel, you are clearly as important as a hearing to destroy life. Does the record tell how the Divine Conclave is called?"

Metatron once again devoted himself to the scrolls. "Yes," he called out, "I have found a letter of instructions, *Protocol for Convening a Divine Conclave*."

"What is the procedure?" a relieved Gabriel asked.

"Yes, yes," Satan said impatiently. "Tell Gabriel what the procedure is so we can move ahead."

"The procedure consists of seven Steps," Metatron said, reading carefully from the scroll. "Step One — Summon the Seven Trumpeters."

"Are there seven?" Gabriel asked.

"Never mind how many there are," Satan said. "Just call them. Put your undoubted leadership qualities to use and call them. Say ' I, Archangel Gabriel, ...'"

"Thank you, but your advice is not needed," Gabriel said. He turned to the vast plains of the Garden of Paradise, held his head high to emphasize the halo that topped it, and, in what he believed was a regal voice, called out: "Hear O denizens of Heaven, Archangels, angels, cherubim, seraphim, spirits, saints. I, Archangel Gabriel, acting under the orders of The-One-True-God — blessed be He — to convene a Divine Conclave, a terrible responsibility granted me for which I am humbly grateful, do hereby call upon the Seven Trumpeters to come immediately to my side."

His call echoed around the world and throughout the Garden and Heaven. No one came forward. They waited in the pervasive silence. Finally, two figures could be seen running from the tropical pool network of Paradise, a series of connected pools of pristine water, some cold, some hot, shaded by overarching palm trees and surrounded by bushes of bougainvillea in full bloom. The two were naked but pulled on their gowns as they came. Each carried a bright golden trumpet with a long lead pipe and large bell. They arrived gasping for breath.

"Why are we called? Is it the End of Days?" one asked.

"Or some other disaster?" said the other. "We expect to be called in perilous times only. There was no forewarning, that's why we were in the tropical pools."

"Where are the other five?" Gabriel demanded.

"We've alerted them. They are looking for their trumpets and will be here shortly."

From the Arc of Souls high overhead, two figures floated down and landed in a heap on the first two. "What's going on?" one of the newcomers asked. "We haven't been disturbed for centuries. This better be important otherwise I shall address my concerns to the Almighty."

From the far distance, a barely visible edge of the massive cumulus cloud turned black and emitted a bolt of lightning that snapped over the head of the Trumpeter.

Shaken and quivering with fear, the Trumpeter said quickly, "The Almighty has made it clear this is an important situation and I am proud to be part of it."

The final three showed up immediately afterwards, hastily polishing their trumpets with the hems of their gowns.

"Step Two," intoned Metatron, "the Trumpeters will form line abreast with their backs to the Tree of Life and The Tree of Knowledge and face toward the vast lands of the Garden and Heaven stretching as far as one can see."

With some help from the assembled angels, the seven Trumpeters were lined up as the Step required. Two, claiming they were enervated by long immersion in a hot pool, tried to lean against the two Trees but a lightning bolt snapping just above their heads quickly reminded them of their duty.

"Step Three," said Metatron, his face buried in the scroll. "The Seven Trumpeters will sound their Trumpets seven times, not once, not twice, not thrice, not four times, not five, not six, but seven times, seven times shall the Trumpets sound to all of Heaven, seven times shall the holiest of fanfares sound."

The Trumpeters raised their Trumpets but did not hold them to their lips.

"I am the Head Trumpeter," one of them said. "Remind me. How does that fanfare go?"

"How should I know?" snapped Gabriel. "I'm not a Trumpeter. What did you play to convene the last Conclave?"

"That was three thousand five hundred Earth years ago," the Head Trumpeter objected. "How are we supposed to remember?"

"Earth years are but minutes to angels," Michael said, pulling his sword out of its scabbard. "Remember and remember quickly."

"We will not be intimidated," the Head Trumpeter said, angry and resolute. "We are not merely angels but artists — artists who insist on a high standard of quality performance."

"Exactly so." "Right on." "Musicians first." "We need a performers' union like they have on Earth," muttered the other Trumpeters.

"We do not wish to intimidate you, sweet Trumpeters," Uriel said. "Just seek the Light of the Almighty, allow yourselves to bathe in the Light, and the memory will return."

The Trumpeters fell silent. Finally, the Head Trumpeter said: "Uriel is right. Blessed be Uriel. The fanfare is coming back. Remember, it went something like this — dah di di dah — pause — repeat — dah di di dah—then, dah dah dah di di dah dah dah — then, the usual flourish, and end with a long dah."

"I disagree," a Trumpeter said. "As I remember, after the flourish, there is no dah."

"That's not all," another said. "You have too many di di's."

"I am the Head Trumpeter, and what I say goes. Does Archangel Gabriel agree?"

"Sounds good to me," Gabriel said, eager to get the fanfare going. "Are you ready?"

"We must rehearse first," insisted the Head Trumpeter.

They each went through the fanfare several times, keeping the sound as low as possible.

"All together now," directed the Head Trumpeter.

A cacophonous blast of sound smote the ears of the assembled archangels, Satan and the soul of Zetel and sent them reeling back into the shrubbery behind the two Trees. Gabriel crawled out from under a bush, screaming, "This will never do!"

"We just need more practice," the Head Trumpeter said. "We haven't played together for centuries."

"If you don't improve quickly, you won't play for more centuries," snarled Gabriel. "You fool, you startled the Almighty. His Cloud is coming toward us. Quickly, into Limbo and practise there."

The Trumpeters disappeared. After some hours, they reappeared.

"We are ready," the Head Trumpeter announced. (Much later, it was discovered that their rehearsal had caused many of the souls in Limbo to flee to Purgatory.)

"May I remind you," Metatron said. "Sound the Trumpets seven times, not once, not twice…"

"They know how many times," Satan interrupted. "Just line them up and let them blast away."

And blast away they did. The first fanfare was somewhat ragged, the second and third were greatly improved, the fourth was near perfect, the fifth and sixth superb, the seventh was heavenly.

"Let's do it again," the Head Trumpeter ordered.

The Trumpeters needed no encouragement. The next seven fanfares were outstanding. Even Satan said, "These guys are good."

Gabriel objected to their playing more than one set but Metatron noted that Step Four required the seven fanfares to be repeated seven times.

As the fanfares continued, the vast plains before them began to fill with thousands of angels, seraphim, cherubim, saints, and other holy spirits. The din of voices, many in constant prayer, and in praise of the Almighty, as well as from those questioning the reason for the unexpected gathering, was deafening.

The fanfares also brought forth the followers of Satan: Satyrs, Goblins, Gargoyles, as well as many souls, garbed in human form, that owed loyalty to the Devil. They gathered on either side of him in an unruly mob. Their threats and obscenities against the Heavenly Host added a raucous note to the general uproar.

Gabriel walked to a small hillock a short distance away, stretched himself as tall as he could and raised his arms. No one seemed to notice and there was no abatement in the all encompassing noise.

Metatron left his desk and shouted into Gabriel's ear, "Step Five. The Head Trumpeter shall sound one final fanfare and the Host shall fall silent."

The Head Trumpeter marched to the hillock, pushed Gabriel aside, smoothed his long hair to fall behind his shoulders, lifted his trumpet to his lips, and blew one long uninterrupted rising note, ending in a pitch that pierced even the ears of the angels. The din abruptly subsided. Satan's followers continued their barrage of insults, but a command from their leader stifled them as well.

Gabriel regained his spot on the hillock and addressed the throng: "Exalted members of the Heavenly Host, Archangels, angels, cherubim, seraphim, saints, and other holy spirits, I, Archangel Gabriel, have the honour to address you and, in accordance with the command of The-One-True-God, to welcome you to this Divine Conclave. Today..."

"Gabriel," Metatron interrupted, "It is too early to address them and definitely not from a simple hillock. Step Six states you must mount the Judge's Throne first before you can address the Host."

"Today," Gabriel continued, "I will first mount the Judge's Throne and then inform you of the enormous responsibility we have before us."

"Where's the Throne?" he whispered to Metatron.

Before Metatron could answer, Gabriel felt himself borne upward as the Throne appeared to sprout from the hillock under him. He looked around. He was the same height as the two Trees, and could see the entire Heavenly Host as far as its furthest member. (It has been suspected for some time, by both religious scholars and secular thinkers, that unlike the Earth, the Moon, the Sun, planets and stars, and space itself, Heaven does not curve and is a flat plane to infinity. Thus, Gabriel could see all.)

"Step Seven," Metatron said, "Address the Divine Conclave."

At this moment, Chamuel arrived. He seemed oblivious of the huge audience and smiling broadly, declared, "You will all be pleased to hear that Zetel the body was released from hospital with a clean bill of health. He and his wife are pursuing their travels in Spain."

"Why am I pleased to hear that?" said the soul Zetel. "My former body lives and sleeps with my wife."

"Why am I pleased to hear that?" said Samael. "If exchanging souls becomes the norm, I will be out of a job. Besides, I prefer a clean decisive break — the body dies, the soul is captured and returned to the Arc. World population is growing and will require more souls. Thanks to Sandalphon, we just lost one."

"Why am I pleased to hear that?" said Gabriel. "The substitution cost me much wasted effort and nearly ruined my plan to extract Zetel's soul."

"The rest of us are pleased, Chamuel," Uriel said. "Now, in case you haven't noticed, we are in the midst of a Divine Conclave, and you are one of the officials."

For the first time, Chamuel looked around, saw the enormous Heavenly Host as well as the gathering of the Devil and his followers. "What is happening?" he said in open mouthed astonishment. "And to think, I could have stayed in Spain."

"Step Seven," Metatron repeated very loudly, "Archangel Gabriel will address the Divine Conclave."

Gabriel stood on the Throne, raised his arms, adjusted his halo, and in a commanding voice spoke:

"Once again, I, Archangel Gabriel, ask for your complete attention that I may explain the importance of, and reason for, this Divine Conclave. It is a Trial. The soul which once inhabited the body of Zetel Zalman Yacob Landaw — hereinafter called Zetel

— is on trial. The Almighty wishes Zetel be returned to the Arc of Souls. Satan claims that Zetel belongs to him. The Almighty has decreed that Jurors will be selected from the Heavenly Host and will hear the arguments and decide. Satan will act as Litigant for the Nether Regions. Archangel Chamuel will act as Litigant for Heaven."

"How many Jurors?" asked Chamuel.

Gabriel looked nonplussed. Metatron reached into his cloud again.

"It's very simple," said Satan. "The number of Jurors must equal the number of seats in the jury box."

"That's what I was about to say," Gabriel said. He stood up and looked down. "There are six seats."

Satan and Chamuel selected six angels at random. Each one objected strenuously. "I am not qualified," one said. "I know nothing of trials." The others insisted they, too, were not qualified. They had never received proper training in such an important responsibility. Besides, the jury was supposed to be made up of the defendant's peers. None of them had ever been a soul. They objected loudly and firmly to their selection until a bolt of lightning crackled ominously over their heads. They quickly scrambled into the jury box. Gabriel admonished them to hear the evidence, weigh it carefully, and decide whether the soul Zetel returns to the Arc or joins Satan.

Satan took up a position on one side of the stairs leading up to the Throne and Chamuel was directed to stand on the other side. Zetel was locked in a glass enclosure in front of the Throne.

"What is a Litigant?" Chamuel called softly up to Gabriel. "What am I supposed to do?"

"A Litigant," said Gabriel grandly, "argues on behalf of the side he represents in order to achieve the goals of the side he represents."

"I thought everyone knew that," Michael said disdainfully, still smarting over his exclusion from the plot that snared Zetel.

Chamuel merely shrugged. "Judge Gabriel, I need time to assemble my arguments and to get the necessary information. Therefore, I ask for an adjournment."

"I object," said Satan. "We are simply wasting time. Surely, all the facts related to Zetel are well known. I and you and your angelic colleagues have battled for decades over his soul. I can represent both sides if that is more convenient."

"What effrontery," Chamuel said indignantly. "The Devil wants to represent Heaven? I am not asking for a lengthy adjournment. Just enough time to consult with my colleagues. A proper Litigant needs to be prepared and I have been away until moments ago."

"Metatron, what does the Holy Record show?" Gabriel asked.

Once again, Metatron reached up into the cloud that appeared over his head, pulled out several scrolls and read through them carefully. Finally, he put them away with a satisfied air and announced: "There is a Protocol for Litigants. They are allowed time to forge their arguments. The Judge, as convener and leader of the Divine Conclave, has full authority to decide how much time to allot."

"Very well then, I, Archangel Gabriel, appointed by the Almighty to be Judge of this Divine Conclave, do hereby decide there will be no adjournment. The Conclave will stay in place, but there will be a brief recess in which the Litigants can do their investigation and preparation."

While Satan wondered how brief was a "brief recess," Chamuel immediately turned to Michael, Raphael, Samael, Sandalphon and Uriel to get facts of Zetel's life that he wasn't aware of.

Zetel whiled away the recess, glancing idly around the vast expanse of the Garden and the myriads of celestial beings tightly crowded together. He watched the followers of Satan and was disturbed by the abject sycophancy they displayed to their leader. Was this his future if Satan won the trial? And if Heaven won, would he be eternally incarcerated in the Arc and controlled by Gabriel? Neither alternative struck him as desirable. His life as a mortal had

had its difficulties and challenges but at least it was a life, filled with excitement, successes and ultimately, fulfillment. They call it a trial, he thought, but I am already convicted. All that's left is to determine the sentence.

Not far away, he noticed a large lake with a white sandy shore all around it. No one was in the lake or even lying on the beach. The water was very black, not terribly inviting. Perhaps, he reasoned, that's why no one is there. Then through the black, he caught a glimpse of the Earth below and realized it wasn't a lake at all but a large open space cut into the fabric of the Garden.

"That space is a hole through Heaven," he said out loud. "Why is it there?"

"Why indeed?" said Gabriel from the top of the Throne. "You, having been a mortal, should know the answer. It's all because the mortals became prideful and arrogant and cast their powerful spears at Heaven. Much was our Garden pierced before The-One-True-God willed that a space be opened to let the spears through. Look there! Even as we speak, a spear approaches."

Zetel saw a sudden blaze of light, and a cylindrical tower with what looked like an airplane strapped to it shot through the hole and mounted high into the sky.

"That's not a spear," Zetel said. "That's a rocket carrying the space shuttle to the space station. We must be over Cape Kennedy."

"It matters not what it is." Said Gabriel angrily. "It is another example of mortal arrogance. Through the Creation, the Almighty gave mortals a beautiful place to live, to survive and to thrive. But that was not enough for mortals. Besotted with hubris, they chose to encroach upon Heaven, first with their flying machines, and now with their spears. Before the space was opened, the Garden became riddled with gaps which had to be closed and the damage repaired. If it were up to me, I would raise the ocean levels and flood mortals to extinction."

"You tried that once but it didn't seem to help," Zetel objected. "Mortals were given intelligence and are using it. You cannot condemn their success because of a few holes in Heaven."

"Enough," Gabriel said. "Archangel Chamuel approaches."

Chamuel announced he had completed his preparations.

"Satan, are you ready," Gabriel asked.

"I have been ready for the soul of Zetel from time immemorial," Satan replied.

"Good, then let us begin," Gabriel said.

CHAPTER 7 —
Zetel on Trial

Gabrielle faced the Heavenly Host. In his most majestic voice and manner said, "Let the Trial begin. Litigant of Heaven, present your case."

There was an audible sound of gowns rustling as myriads of holy and saintly beings shifted their positions to see and hear better the drama that was about to unfold before them.

Chamuel stepped away from the stairs and placed himself closer to Zetel. He cleared his throat: "Archangel Gabriel, honourable Judge of this Divine Conclave, and members of the Jury, it is with heartfelt humility that I address you and plead on behalf of Heaven."

He paused and noted with satisfaction that the Jury hung on his every word.

"Get on with it," muttered Samael.

"Heaven's case is very simple," Chamuel continued. "Like many souls who inhabit a human body for a period of time, Zetel has sinned but he has also done much good. It is Heaven's contention that the good has far outweighed the bad and, therefore, it would be an injustice, and contrary to precedent in this matter, to allow Satan's spurious claim to succeed. Clearly, the claim of the Almighty pursued over many Earth decades to return Zetel to the

Arc of Souls must prevail. We will prove our contention over the course of this trial."

There was a general hubbub of approval from the assembled Host and cries of ridicule and derision from Satan's supporters.

"Silence," shouted Gabriel. "Silence or I will clear the Court."

Metatron called softly to Gabriel, "You can't clear the Court. If you do, the Divine Conclave is aborted, contrary to the will of The-One-True-God."

"They don't know that," Gabriel said and was relieved to hear the noise subside.

"Litigant of the Nether Regions, present your case."

There was a roar of raucous support from his followers as Satan stepped forward. He held up a hand and silence ensued.

"Judge Gabriel, my case is even simpler. I have a contract with the soul Zetel which he agreed to as a young boy and has since maintained with me. In return for protecting him from you and your angelic colleagues' machinations to strip him of his life and return his soul to the Arc — an outcome he did not want — he agreed to be my loyal servant and to give his soul to me once it was available. Therefore, heaven has no choice. A contract is a contract."

"Objection," Chamuel said. "The Devil did not protect Zetel in the last instance. In fact, he was nowhere present or even close. Thus, he failed to fulfill the contract. Therefore, as a consequence, the contract is null and void."

"The objection is sustained," Gabriel said. "At this moment, there is no valid contract between Zetel and Satan. The Litigant for the Nether Regions, in accordance with the laws and conventions of Heaven, must demonstrate that the soul Zetel is sufficiently evil if the Litigant is to prove his claim."

"I appeal the Judge's decision," said Satan, face flushed in anger. "There was no penalty clause in the contract. It cannot be arbitrarily annulled. Therefore, I appeal."

Metatron did not wait for instructions but delved quickly into the cloud over his head. Scroll after scroll appeared, was scrupulously examined and returned to the cloud. Hours went by. Satan stood ramrod straight, arms akimbo, glowering. Chamuel paced up and down before the Throne, clearly irritated and impatient. All waited, silent, anxious. The only sound to penetrate the intense quiet was the roar of a rocket which flashed through the open area and mounted into the black of space.

Finally, Metatron gave a cry of triumph and held up a clay tablet.

"Metatron, please state your finding," Gabriel said.

"This ancient tablet — which predates all the scrolls — states clearly that decisions made by the Judge of the Divine Conclave are infallible. Thus, there is no appeal."

A rising tide of approval swept through the Host accompanied by a bedlam of hoots and snarls and shouts of "Shame!" from Satan's followers.

"Wait," Satan said. "Who was the Judge when that rule was carved into the tablet?"

Metatron consulted the tablet. "It was the Almighty."

"Of course His Word is infallible. To whom could I appeal if He were the Judge of this Conclave? Clearly, that rule cannot apply to an angel, even an archangel. Surely, I can appeal to the Supreme Judge."

"You cannot," Metatron said. "The Almighty gave Archangel Gabriel full authority to proceed. Further, the tablet makes no mention of exceptions."

"I insist that we move on," Gabriel said. "The question of whether a contract exists or not will be left with the Jury as part of the evidence. Now, Litigant of Heaven, proceed."

"Judge Gabriel, I, the Litigant of Heaven, call my first witness, Angel Esther."

Close by, an angel arose and walked to the witness box. Of medium height, with long black hair framing an attractive face, she was the epitome of an angelic angel. She bowed to the Judge, bowed to the Jurors, smiled at Chamuel, and at the cloud in the glass cage,. She stood in the witness box and raised her hand, prepared to take the oath.

"Angel, there is no need for an oath in Heaven," Gabriel said sternly. "As holy creatures, we are obliged to tell the truth."

The angel blushed and dropped her hand.

Chamuel smiled encouragingly, "Angel Esther, please tell the Court your name in life before you became an angel."

"My name was Mrs. Ettie Landaw."

Zetel inadvertently cried out, "Ma!" He thought she looked familiar as she approached.

Chamuel continued, "And what was your relationship with Zetel Zalman Yacob Landaw?"

"He is my son," Angel Esther replied.

"*Was*, angel," Chamuel corrected her gently. "He *was* your son."

"No, no, Mr. Chamuel," Ettie said. "For a mother, her child is always her child."

"Fine, fine," Chamuel said impatiently. "Is, was, it makes no difference. Tell the Court what sort of child was he? Was he considered a good son? Was he respectful of his parents? Did he help you as you became older?"

Angel Esther glowed with pride. "Mr. Chamuel, he was a sweet boy as a child. Listened to us. Was very good in school, always did his homework without needing to be told. All his life, he worried about us, did what he could to make life good for us, and was there when we grew old. He was a comfort to Yoisef in his last days and also to me. He insisted and helped me move to Toronto so we could be close. I can say nothing bad about my Zetel. All mothers should have a boy like Zetel."

Chamuel looked directly at the Jury. "So, Angel Esther, is it fair to say that Zetel was exemplary in every respect as a dutiful son who recognized his responsibilities to his parents and willingly fulfilled them?"

"Kin ain ahora, (*without a hex*) Mr. Chamuel, Zetel was everything a mother and father could ask for."

"Thank you, Angel Esther."

"Litigant for the Nether Regions, you may cross-examine the witness," Gabriel said.

Satan stood before Angel Esther and smiled encouragingly. Sudden recognition widened her eyes. "Herr Fuhr! Is it you?"

"Yes, sehr geehrte Frau Landaw, that was my name when I was a happy member of your family," Satan said as he lifted her hand and kissed it. "It does not surprise me that you are an angel."

"But you are Satan," she said. "You are evil, a devil, you live in Gehenna. But you were so kind and helpful to us and you were a real friend of Zetel. I don't understand."

"Ma, he meant well for us," Zetel called out.

Angel Esther looked in Zetel's direction. "I hear my boy but I do not see him. All I see is a cloud in the glass cage."

"That is your Zetel," Satan said. "Or, to be technical, it is your son's soul released from his body."

"I object," Chamuel declared. "This is a trial, a Divine Conclave, not a family reunion. Satan is simply currying favour with the witness."

"Objection sustained," Gabriel said, angrily. "Angel Esther, you will answer any questions put to you. Satan, either cross-examine or dismiss the witness."

Satan bowed. "Angel Esther, we must put aside our remembrances until later. I will now begin examining the witness. In your memory of Zetel's childhood years, did he ever seem to have unusual ideas?"

Angel Esther fell deep in thought. Then her face lit up. "Yes," she said, chuckling. "He would tell us that when he grew up he would marry Diana the Huntress. He would speak out against Mars, the god of war who was his enemy. We didn't know where these ideas came from. He showed us a book from the library which had pictures of Diana and Mars. He said Diana was much more beautiful and Mars was bigger and uglier. We, of course, did not take these childhood fantasies seriously."

"I ask the Jury to remember these fantasies," Satan declared solemnly. "Were there any other ideas that he expressed that struck you as strange?"

After another moment of deep thought, Angel Esther responded: "Yes, yes. It's all coming back now. Oi vai, it was so long ago and so much has happened. I'm sorry, Herr Fuhr, for being so slow."

"Angel Esther, just answer the question," Gabriel said very sternly. "Do not waste time on extraneous conversation. One more caution. The Litigant for the Nether Regions is Satan, not Herr Fuhr."

"But that's how I know him," Angel Esther protested. "He was such a good man to us."

Gabriel threw up his hands in disgust. "How does a woman who thinks Satan is good become an angel?"

"Because in life, she was an angel," Satan said. "But let me repeat the question, Angel Esther, were there any other strange ideas?"

"I remember he got into trouble on the same day with his two schools. In his Protestant public school, he told his teacher that souls sleep in a large band across the sky and are sent to occupy bodies. When the person dies, the soul goes back to its sleeping place and then is sent to another body. The teacher was very upset. She telephoned us that night and said Zetel was talking heresy, believed in reincarnation, and had to stop."

"Please note, members of the Jury, in expressing his belief in reincarnation, Zetel was speaking against the profound beliefs of both Judaism and Christianity and therefore was behaving sinfully." Satan paused to allow his statement to sink in. "You mentioned another school, Angel Esther?"

"Yes, Herr Fuhr. Oi, I beg your pardon — Herr Satan. After the public school, Zetel went each day to a Jewish school for boys. The rabbi told them the story of Beraishis."

"You mean the Creation, do you not, Angel Esther," Satan interrupted.

Angel Esther nodded vehemently, "Yes, yes, he told the story of how the world got created. The rabbi told them that Adam was made in the image of God. Zetel upset the rabbi by insisting that no one could say Adam was the image of God because God never came out of his big cloud and no one knew what he looked like. The rabbi threatened to throw him out of the school for believing such nonsense, clearly against the Torah. Yoisef calmed both teachers. It's funny, after a while, the rabbi came to believe that Zetel was the messiah. Years later, the rabbi called us and said that Zetel was crazy because he believed he had sold his soul to the devil. Even when he was an adult, he still had these ideas."

"Please note, members of the Jury, once again, Zetel's expressed beliefs were considered sinful by the Jewish authorities," Satan directed.

"Objection!" Chamuel snapped. "Judge Gabriel, everything Zetel said about the soul and the cloud of The-One-True-God was correct. How can that be sinful?"

"Judge Gabriel, I disagree," Satan said. "In the context of his life and time, Zetel's beliefs were blasphemous and therefore his behaviour was sinful."

Gabriel had a hurried conversation with Metatron. "After careful thought," Gabriel announced, "the question of whether Zetel's beliefs and therefore his behaviour should be considered sinful or not must be left to the Jury."

Both Satan and Chamuel bowed to the Judge.

"I have a further question to put to the witness," Chamuel said. "Angel Esther, quite apart from Zetel's beliefs and statements, do you agree that his behaviour throughout his life and his treatment of you and Joseph was exemplary?"

"Yes, I do?" Angel Esther said and left the witness stand. She walked to the glass cage and pressed her hands against it. Tendrils of Zetel's cloud body reached out and covered the spots where her hands were.

"Hi, Ma," he said. "Nice to see you again. Are you happy here?"

"My Zetel, my Zetel, how can I not be happy? I'm living in Paradise. I hope you will be alright. I'm so surprised about Herr Fuhr. Did you know he was the Devil?"

"Yes, Ma. Even as a young boy, he protected me. I may stay with him. He will treat me well."

"Angel Esther, you must not converse with the Defendant," Gabriel shouted. "The Jurors will take your conversation into account. Return to your seat. Now!"

A wave of her hand to Zetel, head lowered, she retreated to her place in the Heavenly Host.

"I, Chamuel, Litigant of Heaven, call my next witness, Angel Tsippor."

Somewhat further away, Angel Tsippor rose above the Host. Somewhat plump, arms held out, head high, dressed in a long white gown with gold trimming at the neck and hem, she floated slowly and majestically to the witness stand. As she descended to the stand, she smiled coquettishly at Chamuel and modestly lowered her eyes.

"Angel Tsippor, when you are called as a witness to a trial, you must move with alacrity," chided Chamuel.

"Please forgive me, Archangel," she said. "I was awestruck by the honour and excitement of being called by you."

Chamuel rolled his eyes and scowled at his snickering colleagues.

"Angel Tsippor, what was your name in life?" he asked, softening his voice to hide his annoyance.

"My name in life was first Faigel Shuster and then Faigel Greenberg," she replied, "after I married my beloved husband Jack. He was an excellent husband and I praise and thank Archangel Gabriel for finding him a nice spot."

"Angel Tsippor, I acknowledge your gratitude," Gabriel said in a stern voice. "However, you must confine your statements to simple answers to the questions put to you."

She nodded meekly. "You are quite right, Archangel Gabriel. Please forgive me. I am so accustomed to freely speak my mind I find it difficult to restrain myself in the presence of so many great angels."

"Your witness, Litigant," Gabriel said desperately.

"Angel Tsippor, what was your relationship with the soul Zetel?"

Angel Tsippor bristled. "Oh, Archangel Chamuel, I never had a relationship with him, only with Jack my husband."

"Angel Tsippor," Chamuel shouted, "let me rephrase the question. How did you know him?"

Angel Tsippor looked crestfallen. "I'm so sorry," she said. "I didn't mean to offend you."

"That's fine, Angel Tsippor. Just answer the question."

Angel Tsippor became rhapsodic. "I was a great friend of his mother and father, lovely people, and was present on the ship when he was born. I helped the family when we arrived in Canada. We remained lifelong friends. I watched the boy grow up, become a man, and be a success. We were all so proud of him. He was such a good boy, not only to his parents but to me and Jack as well. We were at his wedding. He married such a fine girl. Sure, the first child came a little early but so what? Such naches (*pleasure*) he brought to his family. Am I going on too long?"

"No, not at all," Chamuel said smiling. "So, in your view, he was a good man?"

"Yes, very good," she said.

"Some people claimed his business dealings were suspicious. Do you know anything about that?"

"Lies," she said. "It was all sour grapes. He did well where others didn't. His investing for Jack and me was perfect. Without him, we would have been in the poor house. He's a very good and honest man."

"Thank you, Angel Tsippor. Your witness, Satan."

"We see each other again, Angel, although in different guises," Satan said, smiling engagingly.

The angel shrank back. "When you were Mr. Fuhr, I thought you were a good man. You were always so helpful to the family, to me. But you are Satan, evil. It's a wonder that Zetel turned out to be so good and honest."

"Did he, Angel Tsippor? Were you with him all the time or only during family gatherings, dinners and holiday celebrations?"

"I couldn't be with him all the time," the angel replied. "However, when we were together, and also based on things Ettie told me, I saw him only as a good and honest man."

Satan laughed. "Like you saw me as only a good and honest man. Would you not agree with me, Angel Tsippor, that your exposure to Zetel was sporadic, that you had no direct knowledge about his personal life, and apart from your investment reports knew nothing about his business life."

"Well, of course, I wasn't with him 24 hours a day. But..."

"That's all, Angel Tsippor, thank you very much," Satan said and turned away. Angel Tsippor grimaced at Satan, smiled engagingly at Chamuel and slowly wafted her way back to her place in the Heavenly Host.

Chamuel called Archangel Michael as his next witness. Michael stepped forward, carefully removed his sword and scabbard and laid them on the ground, adjusted his halo so as to be perfectly visible to the entire Host, stroked his curly locks so they fell below his shoulders, and, head held high, walked slowly and majestically to the witness box. He did not notice Chamuel roll his eyes.

"Please recount the events that occurred between you and the Defendant shortly after the event called Black Monday," Chamuel said.

"Archangel Rafael and I, disguised as members of the Amish church, offered the defendant a large amount of money to invest on behalf of our community. We had heard rumours that his business practices were questionable. Our idea in offering him the money to invest was to see what he would do with the money, and if his business was indeed fraudulent, to thus entrap him."

"And what happened?"

"He felt we were not qualified to offer the amount we were talking about and sent us back to our community to consult with our Elders. In other words, he refused to do business with us thus confirming his basic honesty and innocence."

"Thank you, Archangel. Your witness, Satan."

Satan scowled as he approached Michael and stared deep into his eyes. Michael returned his gaze unflinchingly.

"Archangel Michael, since I was also involved in the events you describe, I fear not all the story has been told. I could accuse you of lying. However, that would be a most ungenerous charge to make to an archangel and not in keeping with your exalted position. Nevertheless, I believe only a part of the truth has been recounted. For example, what kind of money and its value did you offer?"

Michael hesitated, looked appealingly at Chamuel.

"What difference does the value make or the manner of the investment?" Chamuel objected. "The fact of the matter is the Defendant's reputation remained unsullied."

"Judge Gabriel, Jurors, if Michael answers my question truthfully, his testimony will cast real light on the Defendant's lack of honesty and highlight his sinfulness," said Satan.

Gabriel conferred with Metatron. "The witness must answer the question," Gabriel declared grandly.

"I repeat the question," Satan said. "What was the nature of the money offered the Defendant and what was its value?"

Michael had lost some of his proud bearing. "To entice the Defendant, we offered gold and deposited with him a one kilobar brick. He said it was worth $14,000."

"And what happened?"

"He said he would need to have it assayed to make sure it was gold."

"And what happened?"

"The next day, we came back. He said it was authentic and had sold it in order to have cash for our investment. We said we had changed our mind and did not want to go through with the project."

"And what happened?" Satan looked and sounded bored.

"Nothing. We left."

"Nothing?" Satan sounded incredulous. "Well, did you get the kilobar back or its cash value?"

Michael appeared thoroughly deflated. "No," he said.

"And why not? Why did you not call the police?"

Michael's face was flushed. "We had no proof we had given him the kilobar. He had not given us a receipt."

"So, Archangel Michael, the Defendant accepts your kilobar of gold, cashes it, and keeps the money. Would you not agree with me that an act of clear theft and dishonesty has taken place? Can you still claim that the Defendant has an unsullied character devoid of sin? And supposing you had remembered to ask for a receipt, he could still not have returned the money because he had already used it to cover another investor which was the basis of your plot. Would you not agree, Archangel Michael, all this is further evidence the soul Zetel is not the honest and innocent soul the Litigant of Heaven professes."

Michael didn't answer. He looked mournfully at Chamuel. He gazed longingly to the far ends of the Garden.

"That is all, Archangel Michael," Satan said dismissively.

Michael slinked off, away from the Throne, away from his colleagues, deep into the pomegranate bushes behind the two Trees and disappeared from sight. As he went, Chamuel growled, "You idiot. Why didn't you tell me the whole story?"

Chamuel next called a series of witnesses, all of whom had known Zetel for long periods during his youth and adult years. Shloima and Bessie Landaw came from the Arc, as did Hershey Levitt and Cyril Lansmann. Each spoke highly of Zetel and commended his probity and honesty. Cyril admitted he had had reservations about Zetel's business practices but could never find anything incriminating and was generally agreeably satisfied with the results. After the debacle with Michael, Chamuel was confident the Jurors would rule in his favour.

He turned to the Jury. "Jurors, I believe all the witnesses I have summoned demonstrate that the soul Zetel was good, helpful to and respectful of his parents and parents-in-law, kind to his other relatives and friends, honest in his extensive business operations, a very decent and faithful husband and a responsible and loving father to his children. Yes, I am sure the Litigant of the Nether Regions will find some minor areas where he has sinned. However, I believe the soul Zetel has passed the test where his good deeds far surpasses the bad. Therefore, I strongly recommend that you find the soul Zetel sufficiently innocent to return to the Arc of Souls, there to await his next assignment."

There was a groundswell of approval from the Heavenly Host and hoots of derision from Satan's followers.

"Silence!" shouted Judge Gabriel. "The Litigant of the Nether Regions will now present his case."

Satan faced the Jury, bowed, and smiled engagingly.

"The Litigant for Heaven has presented witnesses who have all attested to Zetel's innocence and honesty. However, as I showed during my cross-examination, they could not be with him all the time and, thus, knew nothing of his amorous adventures and the real nature of his business practices. I admit the soul Zetel has some good sides. However, I will prove conclusively that the preponderance of his lifetime activities were sinful and therefore his soul belongs to me."

Satan paused to allow his words to sink in.

"Jurors," he continued, "I could cite my own experience with the soul and mortal Zetel but my testimony would be seen as self serving and unacceptable as evidence. Therefore, I will rely on my witnesses to convince you. I call my first witness Sandra Wisk."

It took some time to find her. Metatron looked through the Angel Listings but could find no appointment record. Satan scanned his Smartphone and could not find her. Gabriel dispatched messengers to search the Arc. Finally, she was found on the Arc under another name since she had since served in another body which had also ceased to function.

"Tell the Jury what was your relationship with Zetel when you were Sandra Wisk," Satan directed her.

"As Sandra Wisk, I was Zetel's graduate mentor at university. We met weekly to discuss his work and to review his MBA thesis. He was a brilliant student."

"That was not the extent of your relationship, was it?" Satan prodded.

"No. I fell madly in love with him, and we had a very intense love affair."

"There was a problem with that, wasn't there?" Satan had the same bored expression as he had when Zetel told him about the problem.

Sandra paused. "Yes, there was. I was married. My husband was away for several weeks but even after he returned, our love affair continued, just more secretly and less often."

"Did Zetel know you were married?"

"Yes, of course. My husband was an archeologist at the same university."

"Then Zetel committed adultery," Satan said triumphantly turning to the Jurors. "Clearly sinful and clearly against the commandments in the Bible."

He addressed the witness again. "Were there any other developments in your relationship?"

"Yes, I became pregnant. I wanted to divorce my husband and marry Zetel but he refused, insisted I have an abortion, and left me in the lurch. He said he was not ready for fatherhood and husband. So much for his grand professions of love."

"Jurors, please note," Satan said. "Not only was the Defendant guilty of sin but displayed egregious and wilful immorality."

After cross-examining Sandra, Chamuel pointed out to the Jurors that Zetel was a very young man at the time, Sandra, a little older and wiser, could have stopped him cold but consented and drew him on. Granted, Zetel did not handle the situation very well, but a youthful incident should not compromise him for the rest of his mortal life.

"For my next witness, I call Diana the Huntress, goddess of the hunt."

Wielding a cane, an old woman staggered in from behind the Trees and carefully approached the witness box. Her once attractive features of face and form had become heavy and sagged lugubriously. She no longer wore her huntress uniform but a long gown tied at the waist with a thin leather strap. She was devoid of weapons and dogs.

"Diana, I'm so sorry," Zetel said.

"Don't 'Diana' me," she said. "All I had to do was kill you, all you had to do was let me kill you, and I would be immortal and beautiful. Now, you're dead anyway, and I will soon be."

"The witness will not talk to the Defendant," called out Gabriel.

"Diana, how do you know Zetel?" Satan asked.

"We became friends when he was still a soul on the Arc. We had an affectionate regard for each other. He was very restive and desired to escape. I helped him by slashing away at the restraints which tied him to the Arc."

"Tell us about the time you met again."

"It was in Venice. Our meeting was completely coincidental. I was a nun and a nurse and he was a tourist. He saw me, recognized me, and made himself known to me. We had a brief discussion and that was that. Later that same day, delegates from Heaven persuaded me to exert my charms on him, kill him, and I would be rewarded with immortality. I had no difficulty with tempting him. He responded and made it clear he would run away with me, leave his wife and family. I invited him to my room and he eagerly accepted. In the end, the plot failed."

"Nevertheless, he was prepared to commit adultery, and leave his family?" Satan asked.

"Oh, yes, he was completely enraptured with me."

Satan faced the Jurors. "So, not only as a young man, but even in his later adult years, the Defendant had adulterous intentions. Clearly, sinfulness was not just youthful mischief."

"Diana," Chamuel said, "did you and Zetel have sexual relations?"

"Not the full extent," Diana replied choosing her words, "but under the blanket in the gondola, there was much petting and fondling."

"But it never resulted in full sexual relations?" Chamuel persisted.

"No."

"Therefore, while he may have been tempted to commit adultery, in actual fact, he never did. Is that not correct?"

"Yes," Diana said. "For some reason, he became suspicious, and fled."

"Jurors, please note, despite the fact the Defendant was entrapped, despite the temptation confronting him, he did not commit adultery then, nor ever has, during his married life. I don't think Satan will deny that."

"Jurors," Satan said. "Zetel may not have committed adultery in this instance but he knew he was doing wrong by responding to Diana as the plot unfolded. Therefore, he sinned."

Chamuel and Satan argued at length over the exact nature of sinning. Finally, Gabriel insisted the trial continue.

Satan turned gravely to the Jury. "To examine the Defendant's business practises, I call upon Fred Peterson."

Sally Peterson looked out the kitchen window and watched a bear eating the offal from the knocked over garbage bin. She would have to remind Fred once again to secure the bear lock on the top of the bin. Thinking about Fred reminded her that he was not yet up and it was already nine o'clock.

Life had turned out well for them. They enjoyed their Redroofs Road bungalow and small village life in Halfmoon Bay. They had enough money to live comfortably and enjoy occasional travel. They had formed a circle of friends and frequently exchanged social and dinner invitations. For extra cash and professional interest, they ran a small accounting and bookkeeping service for small businesses from Gibson to Sechelt.

She made the morning coffee, set the breakfast table and turned on the radio. She had sipped her first coffee when Fred appeared. She was startled by his appearance. He was shaking uncontrollably, wild eyed, and talking incoherently.

"My God, Fred, what's happening to you?" Sally leapt to his side and dragged him to a chair. She flung her arms around him and held him fast until the trembling stilled and his body relaxed. She poured him coffee and insisted he drink it slowly. After he had calmed sufficiently, she asked him carefully, "What's wrong, Fred? You seem very upset."

He didn't answer immediately but continued to drink the coffee. Sally poured him another cup and waited patiently.

"I've had a dream like I've never had before," he said. "It was so real I could swear it wasn't a dream, like I was actually there. What a terrible experience."

"Can you remember the dream, Fred? Can you talk about it?" Sally asked. She took the coffee cup from him because his hands had started to shake again. "If it's too painful, we can talk about it another time."

"No," Fred said. "I need to talk about it now. This really makes me wonder about my sanity. "

He took the coffee cup back, and drained it. "I was fast asleep when a man appeared beside my bed. My first thought was to defend myself, to attack him. He wore a long brown cloak or gown, carried a book, and had the sweetest youthful face I've ever seen. He looked so peaceful, I knew he was not out to rob and kill us. He smiled and said, 'My name is Uriel. You will not be harmed. Please come with me.'

"He took me by the hand and suddenly we were somewhere else. A huge open space with flowers everywhere and crowds of people all wearing white or golden gowns. I mean crowds, thousands upon thousands, all looking at me. I was led to a space in front of stairs with a guy sitting on a throne at the top. 'Uriel, explain to Fred Peterson why he is here,' the guy at the top shouts. Uriel tells me I'm a witness in a trial to determine whether a soul is predominantly sinful or predominantly good. If sinful, the soul goes to Satan. If good, the soul stays in Heaven. Uriel says I knew the soul as Zetel and points to a glass cage. But I don't see Zetel, just what looks like a little cloud. Before I can get my mind around what is happening, the guy at the top shouts, 'Satan, your witness.'

"A man dressed all in black comes up to me and says, 'Mr. Peterson, tell the Jurors how long you know Zetel and what was your association with him.' Sally, I nearly faint then and there. The man they call Satan is Fuhr, Louis Fuhr, Chairman of our board, long time friend of the Landaws. I'm open mouthed, I cannot talk.

" 'Mr. Peterson,' Fuhr or Satan, or whoever he is, says, 'No doubt I look like someone you knew. Please ignore the coincidence and carry on with your testimony.' Well, somehow I get control of myself and manage to look at the Jurors and start talking.

"My name is Fred Peterson. Until my retirement in 2000, I was Zetel's accountant and had worked with him for about thirty years.

"The guy they call Satan says, 'You were very much involved in his business on the wealth management side. Tell the Jurors exactly how Zetel managed his investments and your role. Mr. Peterson, it is very important that you tell the truth. You are not on trial, Zetel is.'

"Sally, I had no option. I told them everything. The whole Ponzi scheme, the false reports, the false audits, the Caymans' off shore company to evade detection, in a word, everything.

"Then Satan, the one who looks like Fuhr, says, 'Explain to the court how a Ponzi scheme actually works and what Zetel did.'

"Sure," I say. "The investment manager receives money from investors to buy stocks, bonds, funds. The investment manager instead of investing the money keeps it and issues false certificates. As more money comes in from new investors, he distributes this money to the earlier investors and again gives false certificates to the new investors. He also uses this money for his own living expenses. As new money continues to come in, the investment manager must show better rates of return in order to continue to attract new money. These rates of return are usually false, but investors don't know this and think the investment manager is just superb.

"Zetel started off clean and for a while did have excellent rates of return because he's a clever guy and is good at the trade. But at one bad market period, his rates faltered and rather than admit it, he used new money to keep the older investors happy. It was so easy, that he continued to build up more clients on false pretences.

" 'Is what he did legal?' Satan asks.

"No," I say. "Ponzi schemers go to jail when discovered.

" 'Can ordinary people get hurt as a result of a Ponzi scheme?' Satan says.

"Well, yes, most of the newer investors lose their money, their pensions, their lifelong savings and end up ruined."

" 'Thank you, Mr. Peterson, you have been very helpful,' Satan says. Then he turns to the Jury, 'Members of the Jury, clearly, Zetel is guilty of illegal behaviour in his long business career, and immoral behaviour that would have hurt vulnerable people. This is not only sinful behaviour in itself, but sin carried out over a long business career. In other words, sin is a predominant characteristic of his life.'

"Imagine the nerve of this guy, Sally. Zetel once told me the idea for using new money to bolster his results came from Fuhr, and this Satan is Fuhr — he looks like him, he sounds like him, and he's smooth like him. All these years, the chairman of our board was the Devil himself. Well, at least as far as this dream goes — if it is a dream.

"Next, Satan steps away and this big, burly guy dressed in a white gown trimmed in gold, a gold halo on his head, and a threatening mean face comes up to me. 'My name is Chamuel,' he says in a belligerent way, 'and I will cross-examine you. Based on your testimony, you are an unsavoury person yourself since you were a participant. It is in your best interest to tell the whole truth in this

Supreme Court. Hold nothing back. Remember, I drove Adam and Eve out of Paradise because of their gross misbehaviour.'

" 'Objection!' Satan calls out. 'The Litigant for Heaven is intimidating the witness.'

"The guy on the Throne says rather mildly, 'Chamuel, we all recognize and applaud your fervour for righteousness. However, just examine the witness.'

"The big mean guy looks at me. Sally, I was scared. By now, I believe I am somehow in Heaven. Maybe I'm dead. Maybe after Zetel, I'm on trial.

"Chamuel asks, 'Did the Ponzi scheme collapse?'

"No."

" 'Did any investors lose their money? Were any left in poverty?'

"No," I say rather proudly. "Most made money. At first just the initial investors but as time went on, most did very well and are still doing well."

" 'Is it still possible for the Ponzi scheme to collapse, and Zetel be exposed as a fraud?' Chamuel asks.

"No," I answer.

" 'And why not?'

"Because Zetel cleaned up the scheme. It always bothered him, and he made every effort to end it. Over the years, he took advantage of market upswings and gradually converted the false investments into real investments until there was no more Ponzi effect. He's running a clean investment business now and has been for over ten years. New money is invested properly."

" 'So, in effect, despite becoming involved in a fraudulent business — which we would all condemn as sinful — he turned his efforts to rectifying the situation so that no one suffered and many profited — clearly the action of a good and honest man. Is that not so, Mr Peterson?'

"Well, yes, I guess so. He definitely felt bad about the situation and worked hard to fix it.

"Chamuel turns to the Jury: 'Jurors, once again, we see Zetel as a man who makes a mistake and then pursues a course of remediation. Why? Because he is essentially a righteous man and therefore predominantly good and not to be punished with Satan and Hell.'

"Then, a loud argument breaks out between Satan Fuhr and the big bruiser Chamuel and they debate the good and the bad of Zetel. This goes on for some time. They keep pointing to the little cloud in the glass box and referring to it as Zetel. For all I know, the argument may still be going on. I'll never know, because Uriel takes me by the hand and the next thing I know I'm back in bed. Sally, it was either a terrible dream or a terrible experience, it was so real."

"Fred, just calm down. You had a nightmare, nothing more," Sally said. "My guess is your time with Zetel has built up feelings of guilt and by means of this dream, you got it off your chest. It's like a form of therapy. Now, let's have some breakfast."

"What about Zetel?" Fred said. "In the dream it almost sounded like he died."

"I can settle that concern very quickly," Sally said and picked up the telephone. Fred poured himself more coffee and walked out onto the patio. The bear looked up, sniffed suspiciously, decided Fred was not an aggressor and went back to munching on the garbage. Sally joined him twenty minutes later.

"They're all fine, Fred. I spoke to Zetel. He's very much alive. Let's have breakfast."

CHAPTER 8 —
The judgement of Zetel

For weeks the argument went on. Zetel, bored, moved restlessly around the glass cage and wondered anxiously what the judgement would be. In truth, he relished neither an eternity with Satan nor endlessly strapped in the Arc of Souls. Freedom, independence, adventure or, at least, some excitement was what he wanted. He might get some of that with Satan, or he might be pardoned by The-One-True-God after a millennium or two and be reassigned, but he would always be under their thrall.

"Even as a soul tethered to the Arc, Zetel was rebellious, angered the Almighty, and managed to escape," Satan was saying. "What more proof of sin do we need?"

"Many prominent souls had sinful or dubious beginnings and then led a righteous life," Chamuel responded. "Consider Moses. Brought up in the Egyptian court, he doubtless engaged in all the vices of the privileged class, but became a leader of the Jewish people, and a follower of the Almighty. St. Francis also began life as a privileged and indulgent rich man, but rejected it all for purity and devoted his life to the Almighty. The same can be said of Buddha. Therefore, how you start your life is not the issue, how you live it is."

The points and counterpoints were always the same. Satan would cite an example of Zetel's sinfulness and Chamuel would show it was short-lived. A witness would declare how good a man Zetel had been and Satan would show the witness was not present when bad behaviour occurred. Neither Satan nor Chamuel were prepared to rest their cases and the interminable trial continued.

Zetel fidgeted restlessly, helplessly. Neither outcome of this Conclave is good for me. I need to get away, he thought. I need to escape. But how? Diana helped me escape the Arc, but we were alone until the Almighty spotted us. Here I'm surrounded by thousands and The-One-True-God is not far way. How can I escape?

He focussed his attention on the problem, and shut out the Trial from his thinking. After hours of deliberating, an idea began to form. For the idea to work, he needed help. Who could help him?

I will try, a thought came to him. *I like your idea.*

The thought seemed to come from the seated archangels. He noticed Sandalphon smiling at him and slowly walking away. Zetel was elated. Sandalphon had helped him out before. True, Sandalphon had successfully recaptured him. Yet he had done it in a way that saved his former family from grief. Of course, Sandalphon's intervention, if not successful, could make things worse. All Zetel could do was hope for the best and expect nothing.

"T minus 10, 9, 8, 7, 6, 5, 4, 3, 2, 1 —ignition and liftoff of the Atlas 5 rocket with Juno on its trek to Jupiter."

The calm, detached voice of the desk controller reported the progress of the rocket as it climbed at first laboriously and then rapidly into the cloudless blue sky above Kennedy. A slight leak from an outside pressure tank caused a brief moment of concern but was quickly fixed. No one noticed the resulting almost imperceptible course alteration as Juno separated from the booster and continued on its way.

The control room operators erupted in applause, handshakes and bear hugs to celebrate the successful launch.

"Juno will take five years to get to Jupiter," a NASA spokeswoman said to several reporters, "and will orbit Jupiter for two years before finally dropping into the planet in February, 2018. We'll be manoeuvring it in space and sending it around Earth to get a gravity assist to build up enough speed to get to Jupiter."

"I was here very early this morning," a reporter said, "and there was a security alert. What was that all about?"

The spokeswoman laughed, "A kid was seen near the launch pad climbing the scaffolding around the rocket. The guards went after him but he managed to elude them. Although they searched the area thoroughly, they could not find him. No doubt, he'll grow up to be one of our astronauts someday."

Satan and Chamuel were in the middle of a shouting match, and Gabriel was banging his gavel trying to restore order when the rocket smashed through their location in the Garden of Paradise. The impact blew Chamuel far over the Heavenly Host, blasted Satan back into Hell, destroyed the Throne and sent Gabriel head over heels onto the branches of the Tree of Life where he fell to the ground in a heap of apples. The rocket scattered the Jurors and the archangels, reduced the glass cage to smithereens, and pulled Zetel clinging desperately to it through the massive cloud of vertical development and out into space.

I saw no one in the cloud, he thought, maybe the cloud is Him.

He wafted into the rocket and shrank into a small cavity between the equipment.

"I bet this is the first rocket with a soul," he said out loud, chuckling.

You're on your way to Jupiter, the thought came to him. *You'll have seven years before Juno destructs. You can stay forever on Jupiter or find other satellites you can catch if you wish to travel elsewhere. It will be a long time before anybody notices you're gone. Enjoy an eternity of freedom.*

Thank you, Sandalphon, thank you for helping me to escape. Explore space is what I wanted to do back in the early days on the Arc. Thank you for making it possible. Perhaps we shall meet again, Sandalphon, sometime in the infinite future. Stay as you are, loving and eager to assist humanity and the occasional wayward soul. Farewell, sweet friend, farewell, Sandalphon.

There was no answering thought. Perhaps they were too far apart, perhaps the other angels had recovered and were too close.

He stuck part of his cloud body out the top of Juno. He marvelled at the sight of the blue Earth, the white brightness of the Sun, the yellowish Moon, and the endless array of myriads of stars blanketing the black of space.

He was extremely happy. He was free; free of servitude to Satan, free of confinement to the Arc of Souls, free of the clash between Heaven and Hell. He, a liberated soul, would fly among stars and planets, chase meteors and comets, and some day leave the confines of the universe for distant galaxies at the extremities of space. A new horizon every moment — forever. What more can a soul ask for?

END

ACKNOWLEDGEMENTS

As always, I am grateful to Rachael Preston (Sheridan College) and Richard Scrimger (Humber School of Writers) for teaching me the essential basics of creative writing. Whatever craft I have, I owe to them.

This is my third book with Friesen Press. As for the first two books, the help and support of the publisher was indispensable to completing the project.

CPSIA information can be obtained
at www.ICGtesting.com
Printed in the USA
LVOW12*1019091217
559109LV00003BA/87/P